ALL ROADS LEAD TO ROME

BAEN BOOKS edited by HANK DAVIS

BAEN BOOKS edited by DAVID AFSHARIRAD

To purchase these titles in e-book form, please go to www.baen.com.

ALL ROADS LEAD TO ROME

EDITED BY
HANK DAVIS &
DAVID AFSHARIRAD

ALL ROADS LEAD TO ROME

This is a work of fiction. All the characters and events portrayed in this book are fictional, and any resemblance to real people or incidents is purely coincidental.

Copyright © 2025 by Hank Davis and David Afsharirad

A Baen Books Original

Baen Publishing Enterprises
P.O. Box 1403
Riverdale, NY 10471
www.baen.com

ISBN: 978-1-6680-7269-1

Cover art by Kurt Miller
Interior illustration: Randall Garrett

First printing, June 2025

Distributed by Simon & Schuster
1230 Avenue of the Americas
New York, NY 10020

Library of Congress Control Number: 2025934498

Printed in the United States of America

10 9 8 7 6 5 4 3 2 1

ACKNOWLEDGMENTS

Our thanks to those authors who permitted the use of their stories, and to the estates and their representatives who intervened for those authors unreachable without time travel (we raise a glass to absent friends). Our specific thanks to Joshua Bilmes of the JABberwocky Literary Agency; to Joanne Drake, who gave us permission to reprint the late David Drake's story; and to Lucille Flint, who gave us permission to reprint the late Eric Flint's story. Special thanks to Michael Gants, who had the idea for the book's theme, proposed the title, and proposed a list of possible stories for inclusion, six of which were selected. And thanks to the Internet Speculative Fiction Database (ISFDB.org) for existing and being a handy source of raw data, and to the devoted volunteers who maintain that very useful site.

Road Map

There's No Place Like Rome

An Introduction, with Unpardonable Digressions

Hank Davis

◇◇◇◇◇◇

Of course, Rome is known as the Eternal City. I'm sure the long-suffering reader was expecting me to mention that, so I thought I'd get it out of the way right off the bat. It's true that a city is unlikely to endure longer than the planet it's sitting on, and current astronomical thinking about the Earth and its sun is that the latter will engulf the former in four to seven billion years. Yes, and engulf Rome, too. However, this is a science fiction anthology, so my immediate thought is that, if humans, or the highly evolved descendants of humans are still around then, they might slap a dome over Rome or surround it with a spindizzy-type force field (pardon my borrowing, please, James Blish) and lift the still-eternal city to a younger star that's good for a few more billion years yet. Might make an interesting story, but that idea is not in this book. (I should add that James Blish did end, not just the sun, but his entire spindizzy universe in *The Triumph of Time/A Clash of Cymbals*, but that was accomplished by nothing so trivial as a main sequence star bloating into a red giant.)

But I'm getting off the subject, and having too much fun doing it, too, and must reluctantly steer away from subjects about which I know a great deal, such as science fiction, and back to Rome, *Roma* in Latin, about which I know... well, I have seen movies such as *Quo Vadis, Ben-Hur, Spartacus, The Fall of the Roman Empire, Gladiator,* and *A Funny Thing Happened on the Way to the Forum* (plus the 1996 Broadway revival), etc., and that's about it.

Even so, Rome is in the background white noise, and bits of it have snuck in. When Cole Porter wrote "You're the Top," and praised that "You're the Coliseum," he wasn't talking about a mere football stadium. From Rome, we get the word *senate* and the occupation of senators (I'll let you decide how grateful we should be). Our calendar, with some tweaks, is a mostly Roman creation, and if you're in the northern hemisphere, like me, the two hottest months are named after Roman emperors (regarding gratitude, repeat previous parenthetical remark). When I was in grade school, we had to learn Roman numerals, though nowadays, I'm not sure that students even have to learn the English alphabet.

As for science fiction, if an author wants to have an interstellar empire, or even a galactic empire, will she or he make it up, or turn to history for a model to base it on? Yes, *that* model. (Dr. Asimov, I'm looking at you.) But before an interstellar empire can be founded, the would-be founders have to take account of, and possibly even fight wars over, the planets in the Solar System, all of whom are named after Roman gods. Of course all these Roman gods used to be Greek gods, albeit with different names and sometimes different characteristics, so there's a question of originality here. But then, the Greeks were big on originality, what with Hero inventing jet-propulsion, Aristotle arguing that the world was round, Euclid and Pythagoras founding geometry, and Socrates and his sidekick Plato inventing the talk show millennia before TV, even if Socrates still got killed in the ratings. But I need to get back to the later Romans, and after all, they did conquer most of the known world and built big, impressive buildings which have defied time, decay, and urban renewal, and influenced architecture down through the centuries, as in buildings with big domes and towering rows of columns, as in Washington, D.C. And their legions could really do a forced march, tromping along on those superbly engineered roads of theirs (and, since you've seen the title already, you know where those roads led).

Once again, ancient Rome lingers on in the air and in the background noise, so it's not surprising that science fiction writers have invoked Rome in many ways, either directly, as in an episode early in Doc Smith's Lensman series set in the period, or surviving into the modern world, as in Edgar Rice Burroughs's *Tarzan and the Lost Empire*, in which Lord Greystoke, in his ape-man aspect, is searching for a missing explorer when he stumbles across a surviving lost outpost of Rome, surviving unchanged to the present (that is, the 1930s), complete with a coliseum and bread and circuses. Of course, the bad guys really shouldn't have thrown Tarzan into the coliseum. And then they compounded their error by turning a gang of apes loose on him. *Big* mistake, toga-boys!

But I'm digressing again, even if I have brought up the picture of the Coliseum, filled with bored, but bloodthirsty mobs cheering on gladiators fighting to the death, an image that has been repeated in many SF stories, including one which was suggested for this book, but which I vetoed for other reasons. It also appeared early in the Flash Gordon comic strip. When the first Flash Gordon serial was filmed, a version of the episode was repeated, perhaps not wisely, since the budget required that the action be moved from a huge coliseum to the throne room of Ming the Merciless, and Buster Crabbe only had to battle a guy in a gorilla suit with a horn added to its forehead. The episode was also parodied in the early days of *Mad*, when it was still a comic book, in Harvey Kurtzman and Wally Wood's brilliant satire "Flesh Garden." A lesser example of satire was the second season episode of *Star Trek* when the *Enterprise* discovers a planet duplicating ancient Rome, with the added wrinkle that the gladiators have at each other on TV while a commentator describes the action for the sports fans in a very familiar manner. Unfortunately, the cleverness in the script ran out at that point.

And I've already mentioned the influence of the example of the Roman Empire on many of SF's interstellar empires, such as Isaac Asimov's celebrated Foundation series, Poul Anderson's Sir Dominic Flandry epic, and others.

Heading back into the past, rather than the future, L. Sprague de Camp, a writer possessing considerable historical knowledge, wrote a classic of science fiction, *Lest Darkness Fall*, telling of Martin Padway, a young student in 1930s Rome, who is struck by a lightning bolt which snaps him back in time to 535 A.D., in the declining years of the Roman Empire. He has no hope of returning to his own time, and he knows that after the empire finishes its collapse, the dark ages wait in the wings. With his modern knowledge, can he keep the dark times from coming? But first, can he even manage to survive?

The story first appeared as a short novel in the December 1939 issue of the now-legendary fantasy magazy, *Unknown* (later retitled *Unknown Worlds*). De Camp preceded the novella with an author's note which, I think, is worth reproducing in part here:

> This story represents the realization of two ideas that have been bothering—in a nice sense of the word—me for some time. One is that of writing a story on the Connecticut Yankee theme. The other is that of writing a story about the period that Toynbee calls the Western Interregnum—a period that has not, I think, had as much attention from writers of historical fiction as its melodramatic history entitles it to.
>
> The present story is laid shortly after the time of King Arthur—assuming that Arthur actually lived. Fortunately we know a lot more about Gothic Italy than we do about post-Roman Britain. (About the latter, in fact, our knowledge is practically nil.) So I did not have to draw too heavily on my imagination for the setting of my story. Just about half the characters mentioned by name were real people, including Thiudahad and his family, Mathaswentha, Wittigis, Urias, Cassiodorus, Honorius, Belisarius and his generals, Bloody John, Antiochus—Thomasus the Syrian's cousin—and a lot of others. As far as possible, I have tried to make their actions consistent with what is known of their real characters—often precious little.

All that might lead the long-suffering reader to expect to find de Camp's novel in the pages which follow, but there wasn't room for a novella of over a hundred pages (in the case of the *shorter* magazine version), but we have included a bit of comic verse recapitulating the novel's events by Randall Garrett, once called the "Clown Prince of Science Fiction," and followed that up with a sequel by David Weber, best-selling author of the Honor Harrington novels. Also, Mr. de Camp's author's note might be a handy thing to show to the next dingbat who complains that science fiction writers "just make up all that stuff."

The Roman Empire has also been figuring in online mentions in the last couple of years or so (though it may have taken a while for me to notice it, since the topic first popped up on TikTok, with which I have no diplomatic relations), that is, that people may think of the Roman Empire, and even do it several times a day. And supposedly, men do it more often than women. In fact, women reportedly find the whole thing baffling, not that there's anything new about the sexes baffling each other, but while I'm not one of those Rome-thinking males (I'm much more likely to think of Diana Rigg, though she is now as gone as the Roman Empire, alas), that is another example of how ancient Rome still influences our allegedly modern world.

One male who must have been thinking of Rome is Michael Gants, who not only suggested to publisher Toni Weisskopf the theme of this anthology, but also provided the title and a list of possible stories, six of which are included between the covers of the book in your hand. While his name isn't on the cover, it really belongs there more than mine, and any gratitude you have after finishing these pages should be directed largely his way, though not exclusively. To quote another aphorism about the subject matter, "Rome wasn't built in a day," but sometimes, it seems like this anthology had to be put together nearly that quickly, so my thanks to coeditor David Afsharirad and production wizard Joy Freeman, who should have their photos in the dictionary next to the definition for the word "indispensable."

We all hope you enjoy the book. And now, I will try thinking about other things than Rome. There's always bourbon. . . .

—Hank Davis
March 2025

RANKS OF BRONZE
DAVID DRAKE

Roman soldiers were the finest fighting men the Earth had ever seen—and now the rest of the galaxy was going to have that fact demonstrated in battle.

◇◇◇◇◇

The rising sun is a dagger point casting long shadows toward Vibulenus and his cohort from the native breastworks. The legion had formed ranks an hour before; the enemy is not yet stirring. A playful breeze with a bitter edge skitters out of the south, and the Tribune swings his shield to his right side against it.

"When do we advance, sir?" his First Centurion asks. Gnaeus Clodius Calvus, promoted to his present position after a boulder had pulped his predecessor during the assault on a granite fortress far away. Vibulenus only vaguely recalls his first days with the cohort, a boy of eighteen in titular command of four hundred and eighty men whose names he had despaired of learning. Well, he knows them now. Of course, there are only two hundred and ninety-odd left to remember.

Calvus' bearded, silent patience snaps Vibulenus back to the present. "When the cavalry comes up, they told me. Some kinglet or other is supposed to bring up a couple thousand men to close our flanks. Otherwise, we're hanging...."

The Tribune's voice trails off. He stares across the flat expanse of gravel toward the other camp, remembering another battle plain of long ago.

"Damn Parthians," Calvus mutters, his thought the same.

Vibulenus nods. "Damn Crassus, you mean. He put us *there*, and that put us *here*. The stupid bastard. But he got his, too."

The legionaries squat in their ranks, talking and chewing bits of bread or dried fruit. They display no bravado, very little

1

concern. They have been here too often before. Sunlight turns their shield-facings green: not the crumbly fungus of verdigris but the shimmering sea-color of the harbor of Brundisium on a foggy morning.

"Oh, Mother Vesta," Vibulenus breathes to himself. He is five foot two, about average for the legion. His hair is black where it curls under the rim of his helmet and he has no trace of a beard. Only his eyes make him appear more than a teenager; they would suit a tired man of fifty.

A trumpet from the command group in the rear sings three quick bars. "Fall in!" the Tribune orders, but his centurions are already barking their own commands. These too are lost in the clash of hobnails on gravel. The Tenth Cohort could form ranks in its sleep.

Halfway down the front, a legionary's cloak hooks on a notch in his shield rim. He tugs at it, curses in Oscan as Calvus snarls down the line at him. Vibulenus makes a mental note to check with the centurion after the battle. That fellow should have been issued a replacement shield before disembarking. He glances at his own. How many shields has he carried? Not that it matters. Armor is replaceable. He is wearing his fourth cuirass, now, though none of them have fit like the one his father had bought him the day Crassus granted him a tribune's slot. Vesta...

A galloper from the command group skids his beast to a halt with a needlessly brutal jerk on its reins. Vibulenus recognizes him—Pompilius Falco. A little swine when he joined the legion, an accomplished swine now. Not bad with animals, though. "We'll be advancing without the cavalry," he shouts, leaning over in his saddle. "Get your line dressed."

"Osiris' bloody dick we will!" the Tribune snaps. "Where's our support?"

"Have to support yourself, I guess," shrugs Falco. He wheels his mount. Vibulenus steps forward and catches the reins.

"Falco," he says with no attempt to lower his voice, "you tell our deified Commander to get somebody on our left flank if he expects the Tenth to advance. There's too many natives—they'll hit us from three sides at once."

"You afraid to die?" the galloper sneers. He tugs at the reins.

Vibulenus holds them. A gust of wind whips at his cloak. "Afraid to get my skull split?" he asks. "I don't know. Are you,

Falco?" Falco glances at where the Tribune's right hand rests. He says nothing. "Tell him we'll fight for him," Vibulenus goes on. "We won't let him throw us away. We've gone that route once." He looses the reins and watches the galloper scatter gravel on his way back.

The replacement gear is solid enough, shields that do not split when dropped and helmets forged without thin spots. But there is no craftsmanship in them. They are heavy, lifeless. Vibulenus still carries a bone-hilted sword from Toledo that required frequent sharpening but was tempered and balanced—poised to slash a life out, as it has a hundred times already. His hand continues to caress the palm-smoothed bone, and it calms him somewhat.

"Thanks, sir."

The thin-featured tribune glances back at his men. Several of the nearer ranks give him a spontaneous salute. Calvus is the one who spoke. He is blank-faced now, a statue of mahogany and strap-bronze. His stocky form radiates pride in his leader. Leader—no one in the group around the standards can lead a line soldier, though they may give commands that will be obeyed. Vibulenus grins and slaps Calvus' burly shoulder. "Maybe this is the last one and we'll be going home," he says.

Movement throws a haze over the enemy camp. At this distance it is impossible to distinguish forms, but metal flashes in the viridian sunlight. The shadow of bodies spreads slowly to right and left of the breastworks as the natives order themselves. There are thousands of them, many thousands.

"Hey-*yip!*" Twenty riders of the general's bodyguard pass behind the cohort at an earthshaking trot. They rein up on the left flank, shrouding the exposed depth of the infantry. Pennons hang from the lances socketed behind their right thighs, gay yellows and greens to keep the lance heads from being driven too deep to be jerked out. The riders' faces are sullen under their mesh face guards. Vibulenus knows how angry they must be at being shifted under pressure—under his pressure—and he grins again. The bodyguards are insulted at being required to fight instead of remaining nobly aloof from the battle. The experience may do them some good.

At least it may get a few of the snotty bastards killed.

"Not exactly a regiment of cavalry," Calvus grumbles.

"He gave us half of what was available," Vibulenus replies
with a shrug. "They'll do to keep the natives off our back. Likely
nobody'll come near, they look so mean."

The centurion taps his thigh with his knobby swagger stick.
"Mean? We'll give 'em mean."

All the horns in the command group sound together, a cacopho-
nous bray. The jokes and scufflings freeze, and only the south wind
whispers. Vibulenus takes a last look down his ranks—each of them
fifty men abreast and no more sway to it than a light-stretched cord
would leave. Five feet from shield boss to shield boss, room to swing
a sword. Five feet from nose guard to the nose guards of the next
rank, men ready to step forward individually to replace the fallen
or by ranks to lock shields with the front line in an impenetrable
wall of bronze. The legion is a restive dragon, and its teeth glitter
in its spears; one vertical behind each legionary's shield, one slanted
from each right hand to stab or throw.

The horns blare again, the eagle standard slants forward, and
Vibulenus' throat joins three thousand others in a death-rich
bellow as the legion steps off on its left foot. The centurions are
counting cadence and the ranks blast it back to them in the
crash-jingle of boots and gear.

Striding quickly between the legionaries, Vibulenus checks
the dress of his cohort. He should have a horse, but there are
no horses in the legion now. The command group rides rough
equivalents which are...very rough. Vibulenus is not sure he
could accept one if his parsimonious employers offered it.

His men are a smooth bronze chain that advances in lock
step. Very nice. The nine cohorts to the right are in equally
good order, but Hercules! there are so few of them compared to
the horde swarming from the native camp. Somebody has gotten overconfident. The enemy raises its own cheer, scattered and
thin at first. But it goes on and on, building, ordering itself to a
blood-pulse rhythm that moans across the intervening distance,
the gap the legion is closing at two steps a second. Hercules!
there is a crush of them.

The natives are close enough to be individuals now: lanky,
long-armed in relation to a height that averages greater than that
of the legionaries. Ill-equipped, though. Their heads are covered
either by leather helmets or beehives of their own hair. Their
shields appear to be hide and wicker affairs. What could live on

this gravel waste and provide that much leather? But of course Vibulenus has been told none of the background, not even the immediate geography. There is some place around that raises swarms of warriors, that much is certain.

And they have iron. The black glitter of their spearheads tightens the Tribune's wounded chest as he remembers.

"Smile, boys," one of the centurions calls cheerfully, "here's company." With his words, a javelin hums down at a steep angle to spark on the ground. From a spear-thrower, must have been. The distance is too long for any arm Vibulenus has seen, and he has seen his share.

"'Ware!" he calls as another score of missiles arc from the native ranks. Legionaries judge them, raise their shields or ignore the plunging weapons as they choose. One strikes in front of Vibulenus and shatters into a dozen iron splinters and a knobby shaft that looks like rattan. One or two of the men have spears clinging to their shield faces. Their clatter syncopates the thud of boot heels. No one is down.

Vibulenus runs two paces ahead of his cohort, his sword raised at an angle. It makes him an obvious target: a dozen javelins spit toward him. The skin over his ribs crawls, the lumpy breadth of scar tissue scratching like a rope over the bones. But he can be seen by every man in his cohort, and somebody has to give the signal. . . .

"Now!" he shouts vainly in the mingling cries. His arm and sword cut down abruptly. Three hundred throats give a collective grunt as the cohort heaves its own massive spears with the full weight of its rush behind them. Another light javelin glances from the shoulder of Vibulenus' cuirass, staggering him. Calvus' broad right palm catches the Tribune, holds him upright for the instant he needs to get his balance.

The front of the native line explodes as the Roman spears crash into it.

Fifty feet ahead there are orange warriors shrieking as they stumble over the bodies of comrades whose armor has shredded under the impact of the heavy spears. "At 'em!" a front-rank file-closer cries, ignoring his remaining spear as he drags out his short sword. The trumpets are calling something but it no longer matters what: tactics go hang, the Tenth is culling its way into another native army.

In a brief spate of fury, Vibulenus holds his forward position between a pair of legionaries. A native, orange-skinned with bright carmine eyes, tries to drag himself out of the Tribune's path. A Roman spear has gouged through his shield and arm, locking all three together. Vibulenus' sword takes the warrior alongside the jaw. The blood is paler than a man's.

The backward shock of meeting has bunched the natives. The press of undisciplined reserves from behind adds to their confusion. Vibulenus jumps a still-writhing body and throws himself into the wall of shields and terrified orange faces. An iron-headed spear thrusts at him, misses as another warrior jostles the wielder. Vibulenus slashes downward at his assailant. The warrior throws his shield up to catch the sword, then collapses when a second-rank legionary darts his spear through the orange abdomen.

Breathing hard with his sword still dripping in his hand, Vibulenus lets the pressing ranks flow around him. Slaughter is not a tribune's work, but increasingly Vibulenus finds that he needs the swift violence of the battle line to release the fury building within him. The cohort is advancing with the jerky sureness of an ox-drawn plow in dry soil.

A windrow of native bodies lies among the line of first contact, now well within the Roman formation. Vibulenus wipes his blade on a fallen warrior, leaving two sluggish runnels filling on the flesh. He sheathes the sword. Three bodies are sprawled together to form a hillock. Without hesitation the Tribune steps onto it to survey the battle.

The legion is a broad awl punching through a bell of orange leather. The cavalry on the left stand free in a scatter of bodies, neither threatened by the natives nor making any active attempt to drive them back. One of the mounts, a hairless brute combining the shape of a wolf-hound with the bulk of an ox, is feeding on a corpse his rider has lanced. Vibulenus was correct in expecting the natives to give them a wide berth; thousands of flanking warriors tremble in indecision rather than sweep forward to surround the legion. It would take more discipline than this orange rabble has shown to attack the toadlike riders on their terrible beasts.

Behind the lines, a hundred paces distant from the legionaries whose armor stands in hammering contrast to the naked autochthones, is the Commander and his remaining score of guards. He alone of the three thousand who have landed from the starship knows why the battle is being fought, but he seems to stand above it. And if the silly bastard still has half his body-guard with him—Mars and all the gods, what must be happening on the right flank?

The inhuman shout of triumph that rises half a mile away gives Vibulenus an immediate answer.

"Prepare to disengage!" he orders the nearest centurion. The swarthy non-com, son of a North African colonist, speaks briefly into the ears of two legionaries before sending them to the ranks forward and back of his. The legion is tight for men, always has been. Tribunes have no runners, but the cohort makes do.

Trumpets blat in terror. The native warriors boil whooping around the Roman right flank. Legionaries in the rear are fac-ing about with ragged suddenness, obeying instinct rather than the orders bawled by their startled officers. The command group suddenly realizes the situation. Three of the bodyguard charge toward the oncoming orange mob. The rest of the guards and staff scatter into the infantry.

The iron-bronze clatter has ceased on the left flank. When the cohort halts its advance, the natives gain enough room to break and flee for their encampment. Even the warriors who have not engaged are cowed by the panic of those who have; by the panic, and the sprawls of bodies left behind them.

"About face!" Vibulenus calls through the indecisive hush, "and pivot on your left flank. There's some more barbs want to fight the Tenth!"

The murderous cheer from his legionaries overlies the noise of the cohort executing his order.

As it swings Vibulenus runs across the new front of his troops, what had been the rear rank. The cavalry, squat-bodied and grim in their full armor, shows sense enough to guide their mounts toward the flank of the Ninth Cohort as Vibulenus rotates his men away from it. Only a random javelin from the native lines appears to hinder them. Their comrades who remained with the Commander have been less fortunate.

A storm of javelins has disintegrated the half-hearted charge. Two of the mounts have gone down despite their heavy armor. Behind them, the Commander lies flat on the hard soil while his beast screams horribly above him. The shaft of a stray missile projects from its withers. Stabbing up from below, the orange warriors fell the remaining lancer and gut his companions as they try to rise. Half a dozen of the bodyguards canter nervously back from their safe bolthole among the infantry to try to rescue their employer. The wounded mount leaps at one of the lancers. The two beasts tangle with the guard between them. A clawed hind leg flicks his head. Helmet and head rip skyward in a spout of green ichor.

"Charge!" Vibulenus roars. The legionaries who cannot hear him follow his running form. The knot of cavalry and natives is a quarter mile away. The cohorts of the right flank are too heavily engaged to do more than defend themselves against the new thrust. Half the legion has become a bronze worm, bristling front and back with spearpoints against the surging orange flood. Without immediate support, the whole right flank will be squeezed until it collapses into a tangle of blood and scrap metal. The Tenth Cohort is their support, all the support there is.

"Rome!" the fresh veterans leading the charge shout as their shields rise against the new flight of javelins. There are gaps in the back ranks, those just disengaged. Behind the charge, men hold palms clamped over torn calves or lie crumpled around a shaft of alien wood. There will be time enough for them if the recovery teams land—which they will not do in the event of a total disaster on the ground.

The warriors snap and howl at the sudden threat. Their own success has fragmented them. What had been a flail slashing into massed bronze kernels is now a thousand leaderless handfuls in sparkling contact with the Roman line. Only the leaders bunched around the command group have held their unity.

One mount is still on its feet and snarling. Four massively equipped guards try to ring the Commander with their maces. The Commander, his suit a splash of blue against the gravel, tries to rise. There is a flurry of mace strokes and quickly riposting spears, ending in a clash of falling armor and an agile orange body with a knife leaping the crumpled guard. Vibulenus' sword, flung overarm, takes the native in the throat. The inertia of its spin cracks the hill against the warrior's forehead.

The Tenth Cohort is on the startled natives. A moment before the warriors were bounding forward in the flush or victory. Now they face the cohort's meat-axe suddenness—and turn. At sword point and shield edge, as inexorable as the rising sun, the Tenth grinds the native retreat into panic while the cohorts on the right flank open order and advance. The ground behind them is slimy with blood.

Vibulenus rests on one knee, panting. He has retrieved his sword. Its stickiness bonds it to his hand. Already the air keens with landing motors. In minutes the recovery teams will be at work on the fallen legionaries, building life back into all but the brain-hacked or spine-severed. Vibulenus rubs his own scarred ribs in aching memory.

A hand falls on the Tribune's shoulder. It is gloved in a skintight blue material; not armor, at least not armor against weapons. The Commander's voice comes from the small plate beneath his clear, round helmet. Speaking in Latin, his accents precisely flawed, he says, "You are splendid, you warriors."

Vibulenus sneers though he does not correct the alien. Warriors are capering heroes, good only for dying when they meet trained troops; when they meet the Tenth Cohort.

"I thought the Federation Council had gone mad," the flat voice continues, "when it ruled that we must not land weapons beyond the native level in exploiting inhabited worlds. All very well to talk of the dangers of introducing barbarians to modern weaponry, but how else could my business crush local armies and not be bled white by transportation costs?"

The Commander shakes his head in wonder at the carnage about him. Vibulenus silently wipes his blade. In front of him, Falco gapes toward the green sun. A javelin points from his right eye socket. "When we purchased you from your Parthian captors it was only an experiment. Some of us even doubted it was worth the cost of the longevity treatments. In a way you are more effective than a Guard Regiment with lasers; outnumbered, you beat them with their own weapons. They can't even claim 'magic' as a salve to their pride. And at a score of other job sites you have done as well. And so cheaply!"

"Since we have been satisfactory," the Tribune says, trying to keep the hope out of his face, "will we be returned home now?"

"Oh, goodness, no," the alien laughs, "you're far too valuable for that. But I have a surprise for you, one just as pleasant I'm sure—females."

"You found us real women?" Vibulenus whispers.

"You really won't be able to tell the difference," the Commander says with paternal confidence.

A million suns away on a farm in the Sabine hills, a poet takes the stylus from the fingers of a nude slave girl and writes, very quickly, *And Crassus's wretched soldier takes a barbarian wife from his captors and grows old waging war for them.*

The poet looks at the line with a pleased expression. "It needs polish, of course," he mutters. Then, more directly to the slave, he says, "You know, Leuconoe, there's more than inspiration to poetry, a thousand times more; but this came to me out of the air."

Horace gestures with his stylus toward the glittering night sky. The girl smiles back at him.

L. SPRAGUE DE CAMP'S
LEST DARKNESS FALL:
A REVIEW IN VERSE

RANDALL GARRETT

L. Sprague de Camp's novel Lest Darkness Fall *is both a landmark classic of time travel and a vivid picture of the declining Roman Empire. But adding a novel to an anthology would strain the seams, even if the shorter version as it originally appeared in* Unknown *were used. Fortunately, the late Randall Garrett once did a series of recapitulations of classic SF stories in rhyme, and the one for the de Camp classic is below.*

◇◇◇◇◇

The reader's tossed into this tale with great impetuosity.
The hero, struck by lightning, sees a burst of luminosity!
His vision clears, and he is overcome with curiosity—
    The lightning's tossed him back in Time to ancient Gothic Rome!
At first, poor Martin Padway thinks he's stricken with insanity,
To find himself immersed in early Roman Christianity,
But finally he buckles down to face it with urbanity;
    He knows that he's forever stuck and never will get home.

Now, Europe's just about to start the Age of Faith and Piety,
And such an awful future fills our hero with anxiety,
So he begins to bolster up this barbarous society
    With modernistic gadgets that the Romans haven't got.
A moneylending Syrian of singular sagacity
Succumbs, in time, to Mr. P's remarkable tenacity,
And, though he makes remarks decrying Martin's vast audacity,
    Proceeds to lend him quite a lot of money on the spot.

11

Now, in return, our hero starts, in manner most emphatical,
To show the banker how to solve his problems mathematical.
And one clerk gets so sore he ups and takes a leave sabbatical;
     "I can't take Arab numerals," he says; "I've had my fill!"
But Mr. Padway takes the resignation with passivity.
The other men have shown a mathematical proclivity,
So, confident the system will increase their productivity,
     He takes his borrowed money and goes out and buys a still.

Then, trading in on what he knows about historiography,
Our Martin Padway next invents the art of mass typography.
He hires a bunch of Roman scribes (He's fond of their chirography),
     And makes them all reporters for his paper: *Roman Times*.
Because of a Sicilian he fired without apology,
He gets in lots of trouble on a charge of demonology.
But, using all the very best of Freudian psychology,
     He gets himself released from prosecution for the crimes.

The Roman city governor, a certain Count Honorius
(A man who is notorious for actions amatorious),
Is then convinced by Padway, in a very long, laborious,
     And detailed explanation of how corporations work,
That he (the Count), in order to insure his own prosperity,
Should use his cash to back, with all expedient celerity,
A telegraphic system Paddy's building for posterity.
     The Count proceeds to do so, with an avaricious smirk.

But while our hero is engaged in projects multifarious,
An army of Imperialists under Belisarius
Invades the Goths, who find that their position is precarious,
     So Padway has to help the Gothic army win the fight.
He saves the King from being killed, to win his royal gratitude,
And though our hero's hampered by the King's fogheaded attitude,
He gets appointed Quaestor, which affords him lots of latitude.
     He whips the Greek invaders in the middle of the night.

The King becomes so useless that he's almost parasitical,
And Padway finds himself up to his neck in things political;
He has to learn to tread with care, and not be hypercritical
     Of how affairs are run in the Italo-Gothic state.

The Byzantines send in another army with rapidity,
And Bloody John, the general, attacks with great avidity.
Because the Gothic nation lacks political solidity,
  The Byzantines march northward at a very rapid rate.

The Greeks go up through Italy with thundering and plundering;
The Gothic troops, as always, just continue with their blundering,
While Martin Padway, at their head, is worrying and wondering
  Just what the Hell he's gonna do and where he's gonna go!
At last he comes in contact with Joannas Sanguinarius!
(The battle's very bloody, but de Camp makes it hilarious.)
And just as he's about to lose, the turncoat Belisarius
  Comes charging in with cavalry and quickly routs the foe!

Now, though all through the novel we've been jollied with jocundity,
The story's ended on a note of very great profundity:
The Roman Goth society's been saved from moribundity!
  For two years, Padway's been in Rome—and things have sure
    changed since!
The greatest fighting man in Rome since Emperor Aurelian,
The sneaky little tricks he pulls are quite Mephistophelian;
Though modest and retiring once,
    he's changed like a chameleon
  To something like a character
    from Machiavelli's "Prince"!

TEMPORAL DISCONTINUITY

DAVID WEBER

And now that you've been introduced to Martin Padway's situation, flash forward a few years to when his activities have attracted the attention of a time cop who doesn't approve at all—and the penalty is death.

◇◇◇◇◇◇

"*That's* 'Mysterious Martinus'?" Captain Yawen Clasen-Hematti demanded.

"It is," Thvarstar, her AI partner, replied over her cochlear implant.

"He doesn't look like much." Yawen's tone was doubtful.

"Looks can be deceiving, Yawen," Thvarstar said dryly. "Judging books by covers, anyone?"

"You know what I mean!"

"I might point out that *I* don't 'look like much' by the standards of you flesh-and-blood types."

"No, you don't, and those standards don't *apply* to you, because you *aren't* flesh and blood," Yawen shot back. "Just a few tiny clusters of molycircs tucked away in an unused corner of my brain."

"Picky, picky, picky."

Yawen chuckled. Her partnership with Thvarstar went far deeper than their professional relationship, and she especially treasured the AI's sense of humor.

But her amusement faded as she put her eye back to the eyepiece, gazing down and across into the villa's courtyard from her vantage point on the hillside above it.

Martinus Paduei, she thought. *Why did you do it? Surely you knew the penalty!*

He wasn't a very tall man. At least a centimeter shorter than

15

she was, in fact. And that nose of his dominated a bony face that might have been almost handsome without it. The gray which had crept into his hair surprised her a bit. According to their records, he'd been here in the sixth century for little more than ten years, and he couldn't possibly be much over fifty.

"Have you completed your analysis?" she asked Thvarstar without looking away from the courtyard.

"I have," the AI replied. "Unfortunately, it doesn't look good."

"I was afraid of that when we saw how wide he's cast his net," Yawen said sourly.

"The probability of a clean reabsorption is no more than eight percent, assuming an immediate termination of any future extra-temporal influences."

"That bad?" Yawen frowned unhappily.

"No, that *good*," Thvarstar said. "He's kicked too many things into the timestream, and he's got too many people on his team. In fact, that eight percent is the high end of my estimate. There are more imponderables than usual this time, and the low end is only about *three* percent."

"*Fèihuà*," Yawen muttered.

"We could improve the percentages by eliminating the indigenes he's involved. For example, King Urias. We gain a good four percentage points if he's removed from the equation. Belisarius would give us five, in his own right. If we eliminated Urias *and* Belisarius, we'd gain ten points, and adding the Syrian banker to the mix raises it to almost twelve. Nobody else we added would move the numbers significantly, I'm afraid."

"No," Yawen said firmly.

"I don't much like the thought, either," the AI acknowledged. "But for a discontinuity this severe, it would clearly be in policy."

And if we don't *do it, at least some of our esteemed superiors are going to argue that we should have,* Yawen completed Thvarstar's point to herself. *And it's not as if any of these people should have existed as the people they are, anyway.*

"No," she said once more. "He's the one who broke the law, not them."

"That is *so* hopelessly moral of you," Thvarstar sighed, and Yawen's lips twitched a smile. But then the smile faded.

Despite his teasing tone, and the fact that she knew he actually agreed with her, there was a certain point to his observation.

Her attitude *was* moralistic—although she preferred "principled," herself—and the vast majority of Temporal Restoration Corps' personnel would have called it naive, as well. Or, more likely, stupid. The TRC's job was to prevent things like this from happening, and the integrity of the timestream was far more important than any abstract principle of justice.

Well, that's just too bad, she thought. *There's a right way and a wrong way to do this job, and I'll be damned if Thvarstar and I are going to start doing it the wrong way just because it's expedient!*

"Still no sign of his chronoport?" she said out loud.

"No." Thvarstar's tone was the equivalent of an unhappy frown. "No, there isn't."

"Not even a trace resonance?"

"None. The only explanation I've been able to come up with is that he must have traveled a lot farther than D&R projected after he made timefall."

"Could be, I suppose," Yawen acknowledged, although her tone was as doubtful as the AI's.

Detection and Research didn't make mistakes like that. But even if this "Martinus" had brought back something capable of actually destroying a chronoport, which would have been a nontrivial challenge even with modern technology, their own instrumentation should pick up at least a trace temporal resonance from its destruction if they were anywhere within seven hundred kilometers of the site.

"Do you think it's possible he found a way to destroy it without any traces?" she asked.

"Doubtful. If he did, it's got to be something really new."

"But it's not outright impossible."

"Of course it's not 'impossible,'" Thvarstar said a bit testily. "It's just impossible as far as anything *we* could do. And I might point out that TRC is supposed to have better temporal technology than any of these lunatics can cobble up from the black market."

"Then I suppose it might be a good idea to find out how he did it...assuming he did, instead of just hiking seven hundred-plus kilometers down sixth-century roads."

"And just how do you propose to do that?" Thvarstar asked suspiciously. "I'm glad you asked that," Yawen said, and smiled.

✧   ✧   ✧

Martin Padway took another sip from the brandy snifter, set it on the small table beside his chair, and closed the leather-bound book and laid it in his lap as evening slid over into night.

The applied mechanics section of the Schola Iunxit Nevittam had finally designed a practical electrical generator, but trying to mine and smelt enough copper for power cables—even with the more efficient mining techniques made possible by decent explosives—would be one of the harder bottlenecks he'd had to overcome. And until he managed it, electrical lights were nothing but a fond memory from a world he sometimes had trouble believing in himself these days. In the meantime, he tended to stop reading—during the summer, at least—with the sunset. Even the best reflectors he'd managed to produce were incapable of turning the light of an oil lamp into anything a man could read by without serious eyestrain.

He smiled a bit sadly as that thought reminded him of King Thiudahad. He didn't think about the nearsighted, ineffectual, befuddled old would be scholar very often these days. And when he did, it was usually to reflect upon how much more satisfactory young King Urias had proven. Of course, Urias was no longer all that young himself, was he? Which was fair enough. Padway wasn't either, after ten years in the sixth century. But their original friendship had grown into something much deeper. In fact, Urias—and Belisarius—were the only two men to whom Padway had confided the true circumstances of his arrival here.

He'd been more than a little nervous about letting even them into the secret. He doubted that Pope Efraim would be prepared to sign off on the notion of time travel, although he might be doing Efraim a disservice. He was a lot more... mentally inflexible than Pope Silverius, his immediate predecessor. Urias had been forced to spend a lot of political capital cajoling Silverius out of anathematizing some of Padway's "bizarre" concepts. Like the germ theory of disease, for example. Although, to be fair, the reason that particular theory had made so little ground outside the Schola here in Florence was to be found less in the Church's opposition than in the obstinate resistance of the established physicians.

Which was especially tragic at this moment in history.

He sighed with a frown and ran his fingers through hair which had become thinner than he liked. It was 545 A.D., and the Plague of Justinian was finally dwindling in ferocity, thank God.

He'd warned Justinian what was coming, but of course the Emperor had ignored him. He ignored anything Padway had to say, on the theory that if it wasn't dangerously heretical, it had to be some kind of subtle trap instead. A ploy to maneuver him into doing something Padway and Urias wanted him to do.

Because that was the only reason *Justinian* would ever offer else "good advice." The Emperor was just as suspicious, smart, and arrogant as all Padway's readings had suggested. In fact, he was more suspicious and arrogant than Padway had really believed was possible before he confronted the reality in person.

Justinian was perfectly happy to adopt any handy tool Padway and his Gothic allies might introduce, like crossbows, although that seemed to be because he'd "stolen" the concepts rather than having them freely offered. Padway was confident that he'd be ready to steal the plans for the expansion steam engines about to be installed in King Urias's steadily expanding navy, too. For that matter, Urias's spies reported that Justinian had already broken ground on his first cannon foundry, which was going to make life even more interesting and bloody. But anything—*anything*—Padway offered him no-strings-attached was automatically tainted in his eyes.

Including the germ theory of disease. He'd been even more resistant than the physicians' guild here in Italy. And right along with it, he had rejected Padway's warning about what history would come to call the Plague of Justinian.

Padway closed his eyes and shook his head slowly.

His memory of where and when the plague first manifested had been a lot less precise than he could have wished. But he'd known that it was in 541, barely six years after his own arrival in Rome, and he'd known that it started in the docks of Constantinople, probably from one of the grain ships arriving to feed the imperial capital.

He'd warned Justinian about all of that and told him that the disease would be spread by fleas carried by infected rats. There was nothing Justinian could have done to simply stop those ships from arriving, rats or no rats, of course, because Constantinople's population was *enormous* by sixth-century standards. Rome's population had declined to no more than thirty thousand, but Constantinople's was over *six hundred* thousand. No one could have fed that many hungry mouths without massive food imports, and in a preindustrial age, there was no possible way to transport that food overland. It *had* to come by ship. Padway understood that, just as he knew there was no magic treatment for bubonic plague. There hadn't been one even in his own native time. He *knew* that, but there were still so *many* things Justinian might have done to mitigate the worst consequences.

And he hadn't.

Urias, on the other hand, had listened to everything Padway could tell him. But even with the King's fervent support, there'd been limits to what Padway could accomplish, particularly given the physicians' near-universal opposition to the entire notion of tiny, invisible creatures called "germs" spreading disease when everyone knew that ill humors and "miasmic airs"—and, of course, curses—were what caused sickness. And why worry about hygiene, or boiling water to kill the germs, when a good bleeding or the relic of a deceased Saint would be so much more useful?

Pope Silverius's attitude hadn't helped, either, although the Gothic notion of religious toleration had blunted the worst of the established church's opposition. And Silverius's death—from the plague, which seemed ironically just, somehow—had cleared the path for Efraim, who held quite a different attitude towards disease prevention and treatment.

During the Middle Ages, at the height of the Black Death, the peasantry of Europe had made matters even worse by exterminating the cats which otherwise might have helped hold down the rat population, because cats were believed to be favored familiars for witches and evil sorcerers. Personally, Padway doubted that rats truly had been the primary disease vector. Oh, they'd certainly been *a* vector, but it seemed more likely to him that once the disease was loose in the human population, fleas biting infected humans would be just as capable of spreading it as fleas biting infected rats. He was still willing to plead the cats' case, although his own reputation as a sorcerer would have made that somewhat... suspect. That was why he'd floated it through Vultuulf, a distant cousin of his own longtime bodyguard Fritharik, and one of the better generals in Urias and Belisarius's "New Model Army."

For his own part, he'd concentrated relentlessly on the need for public hygiene, reestablishing the Roman bath as a central social meeting place, having the sewers covered, and insisting on fumigation as a way to drive out fleas and lice. It was a hard sell, and the number of people who'd taken him seriously had been tragically small. But when the plague swept through the Italian peninsula, it had touched the new imperial capital at Florence only lightly, and people had observed that those who *had* taken his warnings seriously had experienced far fewer cases.

He still wouldn't have trusted anyone else's blankets or sheets, but Florence had become a remarkably better-smelling city than Ravenna or Rome. And, wonder of wonders, more than a few patricians had begun discovering the effete pleasure of cleanliness and lack of body odor.

It wasn't a magic shield, and he knew this bout of the plague still had three or four years to run here in the West, but he could hope he'd at least ameliorated it, a bit. And even without him, this pandemic had hit the West historically without the devastating power with which it had hit the Eastern Mediterranean. Constantinople, for example, had lost at least twenty percent of its total pre-plague population. Even Justinian had been infected, although he was one of the lucky ones who'd survived.

There were times Padway was tempted to conclude that there truly was no justice in the world.

Still, even if the West got off relatively lightly this time, there were so many threats floating out there in the years ahead. So many...

He leaned back in his chair, eyes closed, massaging the bridge of his nose. Sometimes he thought about all those future dangers and felt powerless in the face of them. Like the Plague of Justinian. He knew about it, he knew what caused it, he knew measures that could have hugely reduced the death toll, and he could see them applied only sporadically, in small enclaves.

But then, he lowered his hand without opening his eyes, and thought about all the changes he *had* made. Changes which should survive, no matter what, because they were spread too broadly, had proven themselves too useful, to be discarded or suppressed.

Until the Black Death, at least. Not this outbreak, but the one coming in 1347. The one that would kill between a third and a half of the entire population of Europe. That was his great fear. Technology depended on enough people who understood how to make it work, and if enough of those people died...

"Excuse me," a voice said, and he twitched, because he didn't recognize it. That was a bad sign in a society that still settled scores with discreet—and sometimes not so discreet—assassinations.

That was his first thought. His second was that the voice was female, which didn't mean that it didn't belong to an assassin, of course. And his third was that its Latin had an odd accent, much more like that of classic Latin than the debased version of the language current in sixth-century Italy. But not quite that, either.

His eyes popped open, then widened.

The woman standing before him was attractive and clearly Asian, which was peculiar enough here in Florence, but she was also young. Absurdly young. He'd never been good at estimating Asians' ages, but she couldn't be more than perhaps in her early twenties.

Both of those observations were interesting, but nothing compared to the fact that she wore what was obviously a uniform, with tailored green trousers and a cherry-red tunic.

Or compared to the fact that, despite her serene expression, her oval eyes were very hard...and she was pointing what was obviously a gun at him in an ominously steady two-handed grip. Not one of the clumsy matchlocks he'd originally introduced, or the better flintlocks which had become available to supplement the New Model Army's armored pikemen in the last year or so. Not even one of the cap-and-ball revolvers with which the artificers down at the Regio Apparatu were beginning to tinker.

In fact, as numb shock gave way to cogitation, he realized it was not like any handgun he'd ever heard of even in the twentieth century. It was sleek and slim, with a tiny bore and some sort of complicated sighting apparatus. One that projected a thin beam of red light that created a tiny pinprick of brilliance, squarely in the center of Martin Padway's chest.

Silence stretched out, uncomfortably, humming with an inner vibration as his pulse fluttered. It was odd. He didn't remember being this frightened even during his first desperate fight with Optias to prevent Thiudahad's assassination. Maybe it was the nature of the threat, especially the fact that this...person was clearly from the future. And not *just* the future. Judging by the bizarre weapon in her hand, she had to be from well beyond even his own home time.

Finally, he cleared his throat.

"I don't believe we've met," he heard himself say, and the lips in that serene face twitched just the tiniest bit.

"No, we haven't," she replied. "It took TRC a while to catch up with you."

"Excuse me?" He blinked. "TRC?"

"Oh, he's *good*," Thvarstar said over Yawen's cochlear implant. "Not too smart, if he thinks he can convince us he's just a particularly brilliant indigene who doesn't have a clue about the Temporal Security Statutes, but smooth. Very smooth."

"Oh, shut up," she subvocalized back, never taking her eyes off "Mystery Martinus."

"What?" Thvarstar asked innocently. "I know how trusting and credulous you are. I wouldn't want you to be taken in by his 'who me?' act."

Yawen snorted, holding the laser sight's dot rock steady on Martinus's chest. Her forefinger pressed an unobtrusive button on the side of her weapon, activating the remote cardio monitor.

"All right," she said out loud, "are you trying to convince me that you think I'm stupid enough to believe you never heard of the TRC?"

"Young lady," Martinus said, "the last thing I'm trying to do is to convince you that you're stupid. Unfortunately, I don't have the least idea what you're talking about, aside from the fact that you're obviously from the future."

"Well, *that* was unexpected," Thvarstar murmured. "Kind of hard for him to play the innocent indigene bystander if he recognizes that *we're* from the future!"

"Yeah," Yawen agreed. "And if he recognizes that, he should damned well recognize the uniform, too. But look at that pulse rate. It's pretty damn steady for someone looking into the business end of a needler, and it didn't even flicker." She shook her head mentally. "But that's ridiculous. He can't be telling the *truth*, can he?"

"No way," Thvarstar replied promptly. "No way. Unless... You don't think he could be from another strand, do you?"

"Another strand?"

"Yes." The AI's tone was considerably grimmer. "Another strand that's discovered temporal translocation."

Yawen's eyes narrowed at that chilling possibility. So far as anyone back home knew, the Alpha Line was the only one which had discovered the secret of time travel, and she prayed to all of humanity's varied gods that there was no actual basis for Thvarstar's suggestion. The mayhem that the Alpha Line alone could wreak on the timestream was bad enough, but if it turned out there was another future—well, *present* from her and Thvarstar's perspective—civilization mucking about in Earth's past...

"Do you think that's why we didn't pick up any temporal resonance from his chronoport?" she subvocalized unhappily. "Because it uses some principle we don't even know about?"

"Now, now. Let's not panic," the AI admonished. "Physics are physics, Yawen. Somebody might have a different technology for manipulating them, but they'd still have to obey the same physical laws. Which means there's a 'bump' of temporal resonance wherever he stashed whatever he used as a chronoport. But this looks like it might just turn out to be just a *little* more complicated than they briefed us to expect."

"No! You *think*?" Yawen shot back, then gave herself a mental shake.

"So," the young woman behind the gun said, "you admit that you know I'm a time traveler, but you never heard of the Temporal Restoration Corps? Or, I suppose, the Temporal Security Statutes?"

"No," Padway said cautiously. "I mean, from your outfit and that weapon of yours, you're obviously not from around here. But I never saw a uniform quite like yours, and that gun of yours is unlike anything I ever saw back home."

"Back home?" the woman repeated.

"Sure. Back in the twentieth century." Padway shrugged. "The only thing I can figure out is that you must be from somewhere beyond the twentieth century. Somewhere where they've figured out how to tame time travel."

"What?" She blinked.

"Well you're certainly not from anywhere *earlier* than the twentieth century," Padway pointed out. "Unless—" His eyes went suddenly wide, and he drew a deep breath. "Unless you're from a twentieth century in a timeline when the Dark Ages didn't fall. My God. Did I pull it off after all?!"

Yawen's jaw tightened at the hope blazing in Martinus's brown eyes. "Vishnu!" Thvarstar said. "He's just *admitted* it!"

Yawen nodded numbly. The penalty for inducing a temporal discontinuity was death. Of course, they had him dead to rights already, based on the entire host of discontinuities they'd already catalogued. But no one just out and admitted they'd committed a capital offense!

"Of course the Dark Ages fell," the woman said, and Padway's heart seemed to stop. He stared at her, stricken by a pang of despair deeper than any threat from her weapon could have produced.

All of this. Everything he'd done. All the effort, all the help he'd won from friends and allies like Urias and Belisarius and Thomasus. *All* of that . . . and "of course" the darkness had fallen. It had all been for *nothing*.

Yawen winced as fiery hope turned to ashes and dust in Martinus's eyes. "Something's not right here," she subvocalized. "I mean, *seriously* not right. Even if he's from another strand with time travel, he must know the Dark Ages were inevitable? Without someone introducing a discontinuity, at—"

Despite herself, she lowered her weapon slightly and shook her head. "You really believed you could prevent the Dark Ages?" she asked, her tone almost compassionate. "That's what—" she took one hand from her pistol and waved it at the villa around them "—all of this is about. You thought you could prevent the Dark Ages from falling . . . and that we'd let you get away with that?"

"What?" He blinked those shocked eyes. "What are you talking about, 'get away' with it? Why shouldn't you? I'm trying to *help* these people, and all the people who'll come *after* them! God only knows how many lives I can save, how many mistakes I can prevent!"

"Interesting that you should bring God into it." There was more bite in her voice this time. "I mean, considering the fact that that's exactly who you're playing at being here—God."

"I'm an agnostic," Padway snapped back at her. "I'm not trying to play God. I'm only doing the best I can, given the mess I found myself in."

"That's rich. Next I suppose you're going to tell me that someone forced you into the chronoport at gunpoint!"

"What the hell is a *chronoport*?" Padway demanded.

"Well, maybe your strand calls it something else. You know, your time machine, whatever your people call it!"

"*Time machine?*" Padway stared at her. "Listen, lady, I don't know how *you* got here, but *I* didn't climb aboard any time machines. I mean, it's pretty obvious since you're here and you're obviously from sometime after the twentieth century, that you've got a—what did you call it? A chronoport? But I sure as hell didn't have one, and if I *had had* one, I'd've headed back to 1939 so fast it would make your head spin!"

"What?" She deflected the laser dot from his chest, raising the needler's muzzle and taking her finger out of the trigger guard.

"What makes you think for a minute I wouldn't have?" Padway demanded. "The sixth century is full of emperors with megalomania, senile kings, muscle-bound 'noblemen' who think with their swords, religious fanatics who want to burn each other at the stake, tooth decay, fleas and lice and ticks, and now the damned Black Death! You think anyone who was sane would voluntarily maroon himself here?"

"Then what are you doing here?" she demanded. "I mean, how did you get here if you don't even know what a chronoport is?"

"I fell down Tancredi's damned staircase," Padway told her, and she blinked.

She stared at him for seconds that seemed like hours, then, slowly, she lowered her weapon and slid it into the holster at her hip.

Padway took that as the first good sign from the last fifteen minutes of his life.

"Let's take this slowly," she said, sinking into a facing chair.

"I'm fine with that," he replied. "As long as you're not pointing any guns at me, that is. But if any of my people wander out here and see you, they're going to have a lot of questions, and some of those aren't going to do my efforts to live down the 'sinister sorcerer' label a bit of good."

"Oh, don't worry about that." She waved a dismissive hand. "I've generated a temporal bubble."

"Temporal bubble?" he repeated carefully.

"Look at the fountain," she suggested, and he did.

His jaw dropped as he realized the fountain was frozen. Individual droplets of water gleamed in the last orange rays of the sunset, hovering in midair.

"You mean no time is passing outside this 'bubble' of yours?"

"No, I mean—" she began, then stopped and shrugged. "No, that's not exactly what's happening, but it will do as an approximation. Now tell me how you got here."

"And then when I'm done, you'll shoot me?" He actually managed a smile, and she shook her head.

"Honesty compels me to admit that I can't *promise* I won't," she said. "But from what you've said so far, and assuming you're telling me the truth, this situation is clearly a lot more...complicated than my superiors thought when they sent me back to deal with it. Which means we're going to have to make a judgment call."

"We?"

"My...crewmate and I. You haven't met him."

"Oh." Padway considered that for a moment, then shrugged. "All right," he said. "First, my name is Martin Padway, and I am—was—an archaeologist. I was passing through Rome in 1939, headed for Lebanon for a dig—one I hoped I could get a doctoral thesis out of—when Professor Tancredi started babbling about this wild theory about something he called the 'trunk of time.' I figured he was a lunatic, of course, but he insisted that it actually existed and people could slide down it under the right circumstances and at what I guess you'd call the right 'nexus.' Like I say, I thought he was crazy! But then something funny happened on my way to the Coliseum. As nearly as I can tell, I got struck by lightning, and the next thing I knew I was in 535 A.D. with nothing but the clothes I was wearing and what I had in my pockets.

"So—"

It was a good thing she'd deployed the bubble generator, Yawen thought, the better part of a subjective hour later.

She leaned back against the chair's comfortably padded backrest—another of "mysterious Martinus's" innovations—and shook her head slowly.

"What do you think?" she subvocalized. "I think he's telling the truth."

Thvarstar sounded as if he didn't want to believe his own conclusions, and Yawen didn't blame him. For a lot of reasons.

She looked at the man in front of her. The man who,

single-handedly, without any support technology at all, had engineered what had to be the biggest temporal discontinuity she'd ever heard of. The man who had imagined, even for a moment, that he could change the course of an entire planet's history.

Preposterous, of course. Except that he'd done it. And that was the problem.

"Martinus," she said after a moment, deliberately using the Latin version of his name, "first, let me tell you that I am *deeply* impressed—awed, really—by what you've accomplished here. I can't begin to imagine what it must've been like to arrive here, with no understanding of the processes and nothing but the contents of your brain. And to see what you've done, the potential for the things you still hope to do. Well, it's . . . it's pretty mind-boggling, really."

"But you assumed I must be from your own time," Padway said slowly, "and you were prepared to shoot me dead for making those changes." His tone made the sentence a question, and she nodded soberly. "Why?" he asked. "*Why?*"

"Because temporal inertia must be conserved," she said. "It's not really inertia, you understand, but without getting into twelve-dimensional math, that's about the clearest layperson's term I can come up with.

"When changes like the ones you've made here are big enough, when they have sufficient impact, then what happens is exactly what your Professor Tancredi described. In fact, I'm astonished, maybe even flabbergasted, that someone in the first half of the twentieth century had actually worked all that out. We can't change our own past; if we try, we split off another universe—what we call a 'strand' where I—come from. There's a reason we call it that instead of simply calling it an 'alternate universe,' because, so far as we can tell, a damned near infinite number of alternate universes already exist. The problem is that the strands that get split off as the result of a temporal dislocation in any given universe are like . . . like unraveling individual strands of a rope. Each of them diverts a tiny portion of what we think of as that temporal inertia I mentioned. Any one of them isn't a significant problem, but enough of them in a relatively brief period of time—say the last 160,000 years or so—definitely could become just that. If enough temporal inertia gets diverted into those subsidiary strands, the central cord snaps. And then the future—the present, I come from, an entire universe—simply ceases to exist."

"That sounds...bad," Padway said with a crooked smile, and Yawen astonished herself with a chuckle.

"One way to put it," she agreed.

"But what happens to the...the unraveled strands?" he asked, leaning forward intently, his eyes bright with the scholar she knew now that he had been.

"There are competing theories about that," she said. "For what I imagine are fairly obvious reasons, no one's been in any hurry to give any of them a real-world test, you understand."

"Oh, indeed I do!"

"Well, one theory is that the 'unraveled strands' turn into central cords of their own. They become full-fledged universes in their own rights, immune to the collapse of the original trunk from which they branched. The strongest competing theory is that when their original universe collapses, they get sucked into the temporal equivalent of a black hole."

"Pardon?"

"The term hadn't been coined before he...left," Thvarstar told her. "Einstein had predicted them, but the original term was 'completely collapsed gravitational object,' I think."

"No wonder they came up with a better one," she muttered back, then returned her attention to Padway.

"It's something Einstein predicted," she said, watching his expression, and smiled when he nodded. "Basically, an object so massive that its gravity prevents even light from escaping it. Well, according to the second leading theory, when the central cord of the universe snaps, all of the temporal energy in that universe—and any of its unraveled strands—falls back down what I guess you'd call the equivalent of Professor Tancredi's staircase, to the basement. And when it gets there, there's something called a Big Bang, and a new universe explodes out of the wreckage of the old one.

"In either case, it's what you might call a Bad Thing for the original universe. In the second case, it's equally bad for the unraveled strands. Unfortunately, chronoports aren't that hard to build—or steal—if you're really determined, and there are always megalomaniacs, people with delusions of godhood, who think that if they could only shape their own universe, everything would be perfect. Some are altruists, some are would-be gods looking for worshippers, and some of them are like—well, like your own time's Hitler," she said as Thvarstar offered her the name.

"Hitler?" Padway frowned. "Adolf Hitler? He was actually important enough you remember him in your own time?"

"What time in 1939 did you come back from?" Yawen asked with a frown.

"May," Padway replied "May of 1939."

Yawen pursed her lips while Thvarstar poured a quick condensation of one of history's worst wars into her ear.

"You're telling me there was a war, after all?" Padway asked, and she nodded.

"Oh, yes, there was," she said softly. "It didn't end well for Hitler, but there were millions of dead by the time it was over." She shook her head. "He was the kind of human monster that makes me wish we *could* change history without consequences. Unfortunately, we can't. Or, rather, we probably could...in a single case, or a half-dozen cases, maybe even a hundred cases. But as soon as you make an exception for one intervention, you open the door to all those others, and sooner or later—"

"I...understand," Padway murmured.

"At any rate," she resumed, more briskly, "a hundred and fifty years ago, about sixty years before I was born, the Solar Senate enacted the Temporal Security Statutes and created the Temporal Restoration Corps to deal with infractions. It's our responsibility to find the lunatics willing to play fast and loose with something like this and stop them."

"You mean by going back to a time before they made the changes and preventing them?"

"No, we can't do that. Until they've made their changes, there's no alternate strand, only our own 'main trunk,' so we don't know to go looking for them until it's too late to stop them. In theory we could go back to that exact same temporal locus in our universe, but in practical terms, no one's navigation is that precise. Which means we're always a reactive force, I'm afraid."

"So how do you stop them?"

"Normally, the initial discontinuity when their chronoport departs the main strand is easily detectable. In those cases, we travel back to that moment and insert ourselves into their new strand. And then, as soon as possible, we kill them."

"Excuse me?"

"We kill them. The sentence for violating the Statutes is death, Martinus. There's no wiggle room there. And killing them—and, sometimes, if they've had time to enlist the aid of the local indigenes, killing *them*, as well—is the simplest and most definitive way of terminating the discontinuity their new strand represents. If we do it right, soon enough, the strand is simply reabsorbed into the main trunk as if it never happened."

"And an entire potential universe dies," Padway said very, very quietly.

"Yes," she acknowledged unflinchingly.

"Are there ever exceptions?" he asked carefully.

"For the perpetrators, the criminals? No. Occasionally, however, a strand is so well established that it can't be reabsorbed, no matter what we do. In those instances, we remove the disruptions that might create additional discontinuities, and allow those strands to develop. It's not ideal, but to be perfectly honest, I think that quite often our TRC agents breathe a sigh of relief when it happens. What we do is necessary, and we know it, but that doesn't mean we have to *like* it."

"So your laws don't leave you any choice but to kill me, and maybe all my friends, but at least you won't kill this universe." He sighed. "I guess that's something." His smile was bittersweet. "At least I succeeded in that much. In this universe, Darkness *won't* fall, even if I'm not here to see it."

"Yes, I think you can assume at least that much, Martinus." She nodded, her eyes compassionate. "Not many human beings can say they've accomplished something that monumental, especially with no more resources than you had when you arrived here."

"I hope you won't mind if I say that's a bit of a cold comfort?" Padway asked tartly.

"No, I won't mind at all. In your place, I'd feel exactly the same way."

"Then I suppose we might as well get it over with." Padway managed a smile. "And at least this way I'll find out one way or the other about my agnosticism."

"True," she said, smiling back at him. She reached into the side pocket of her tunic.

And vanished.

✦   ✦   ✦

Martin Padway sat very, very still, looking at the chair Captain Clasen-Hematti had occupied. It was empty, and he shook himself, then looked around wildly.

The courtyard fountain burbled and chuckled happily to him, the sun had settled visibly lower, and he swallowed. Wherever she'd gone, she must have taken that "temporal bubble" of hers with her.

Assuming she was ever actually here, he thought. *Assuming I haven't finally cracked under the strain and started imagining time travelers from the far-distant future! But there's no way I'd have that kind of technobabble buried in my subconscious ... is there?*

He reached out a trembling hand for the still half-full brandy snifter. The brandy it contained was immeasurably better than his original crude product. It deserved to be savored properly.

He gulped its contents like water, then coughed as the alcohol burned way down his esophagus and exploded in his stomach.

Well, that certainly felt real enough, anyway!

He looked at that empty chair for a moment longer, then pushed himself shakily to his feet, wondering what happened next. What did he—

"Excuse me, Martinus," a female voice which had become all too familiar said from behind him, and he whirled so quickly he would have fallen if a slender, strong hand hadn't darted out and caught his elbow.

"Don't *do* that!" he exclaimed. "If you're going to shoot me, just go ahead and *shoot* me! Don't *startle* me to death, damn it!"

"Oh, I'm not going to shoot you!" she assured him.

"But you said—"

"But I said that violation of the Statutes carried the death penalty. It occurred to me that your case was somewhat outside the scope of the Statutes, however, so I went home to present the case to my superiors. They spent about ten years examining this timeline, looking at everything you've done in what you might call excruciating detail, and then they decided I was right."

"Right about what?" He looked at her narrowly.

"What happened to you should be impossible according to all our current theories of temporal physics. Couldn't happen. But it *did*, and that's conclusive evidence that there's a major hole in our own understanding of temporal mechanics. Unfortunately this isn't something that we can afford to be wrong about. And

even if we killed you and every one of your . . . associates here in
the sixth century, the odds that this strand would be reabsorbed
are relatively low. So I got the Commission to designate this a
protected strand."

"You won't terminate it?"

"No," she said gently. "It's too important for that. Instead, we'll
study it—study it very, very carefully. And, if the changes you've
introduced are sufficient, this truly will be the only strand we're
familiar with in which Darkness never fell on Western Europe."

"Well," he said softly. "That's something. That's really something . . . even if I won't be here to see it."

"Oh, you will be." She reached out and across to squeeze his
shoulder. "We wouldn't think of depriving this strand of 'Mysterious Martinus.' In fact, since the strand's already unraveled,
and whatever inertia it's absorbed has already been diverted, my
superiors think that preventing the Dark Ages is . . . a worthwhile
goal. We would never have done something like this on purpose,
but now that you've—well, forced our hand, I suppose—we want
to see how far it goes."

"What?"

"We want to see how far it goes," she repeated, squeezing his
shoulder again. "And, under the circumstances, the Commission
feels you've earned the right to see the same thing. So they're
waiting for you."

"Waiting . . . ?"

"Back home. They're waiting for you, in the True Present."

"Waiting for me to *what*?"

"To come home so you can receive the antigerone treatments—
Martinus, I'm more than twice your age, so there's no reason
you have to be stuck in a decrepit hulk—and your own neural
implants. If you want it, we'll partner you with an AI like Thvarstar as well. Oh, I'm sorry. You still haven't been introduced to
him. He's the crewmate I was talking about the last time I was
here. And then, once we've brought your education up to speed,
you'll be put in charge of steering this strand."

Padway sank back into his chair.

"*Steering* this strand?"

"Well, I *have* spent ten years studying you, Martinus. Whatever you may say, you're not the sort who wants to leave a job
half-done, and you really care about these people. So I managed

to get the Commission to sign off on letting you return here, once you've been properly kitted up, for another... oh, fifty or sixty years. About the maximum these people could expect from a normal lifetime. You'll age, but only cosmetically, thanks to the antigerone treatments. And you'll have that time to continue doing what you've done."

Her eyes twinkled as his jaw dropped, and she squeezed his shoulder a third time.

"You won't get any more physical resources," she told him gently, "but you won't have to abandon the friends you care about, and if you take the position, I think you'll find you have a rather more complete technical library to consult."

He stared at her, mouth open, and the twinkle in her eyes became a broad grin.

"Interested?" she asked.

VIA ROMA

ROBERT SILVERBERG

Robert Silverberg's Roma Eterna series of stories assumes that Christianity never emerged and the Roman Empire not only did not fall, but extended its reach throughout the world—not necessarily in a good way, as a naïve visitor from the provinces will discover. The story is set in A.U.C. 2063, and the author explains, "A.U.C. is Latin for 'From the founding of the city,' meaning dating from 753 B.C., so A.U.C. 2603 means that the story is taking place in the equivalent of 1850 A.D."

◇◇◇◇◇

A.U.C. 2603

A carriage is waiting for me, by prearrangement, when I disembark at the port in Neapolis after the six-day steamer voyage from Britannia. My father has taken care of all such details for me with his usual efficiency. The driver sees me at once—I am instantly recognizable, great strapping golden-haired barbarian that I am, a giant Nordic pillar towering over this busy throng of small swarthy southern people running to and fro—and cries out to me, "Signore! Signore! Venga qua, signore."

But I'm immobilized in that luminous October warmth, staring about me in wonder, stunned by the avalanche of unfamiliar sights and smells. My journey from the dank rainy autumnal chill of my native Britannia into this glorious Italian land of endless summer has transported me not merely to another country but, so it seems, to another world. I am overwhelmed by the intense light, the radiant shimmering air, the profusion of unknown tropical-looking trees. By the vast sprawling city stretching before me along the shores of the Bay of Neapolis. By the lush green hills just beyond, brilliantly bespeckled with the white winter

35

villas of the Imperial aristocracy. And then too there is the great
dark mountain far off to my right, the mighty volcano, Vesuvius
itself, looming above the city like a slumbering god. I imagine
that I can make out a faint gray plume of pale smoke curling
upward from its summit. Perhaps while I am here the god will
awaken and send fiery rivers of red lava down its slopes, as it
has done so many times in the immemorial past.

No, that is not to happen. But there will be fire, yes: a fire
that utterly consumes the Empire. And I am destined to stand
at the very edge of it, on the brink of the conflagration, and be
altogether unaware of everything going on about me: poor fool,
poor innocent fool from a distant land.

"*Signore! Per favore!*" My driver jostles his way to my side
and tugs impatiently at the sleeve of my robe, an astonishing
transgression against propriety. In Britannia I surely would strike
any coachman who did that; but this is not Britannia, and customs evidently are very different here. He looks up imploringly.
I'm twice his size. In comic Britannic he says, "You no speak
Romano, *signore?* We must leave this place right away. Is very
crowded, all the people, the luggage, the everything, I may not
remain at the quay once my passenger has been found. It is the
law. *Capisce, signore? Capisce?*"

"*Si, si, capisco,*" I tell him. Of course I speak Roman. I spent
three weeks studying it in preparation for this journey, and it
gave me no trouble to learn. What is it, after all, except a mon-
grelized and truncated kind of bastard Latin? And everyone in
the civilized world knows Latin. "*Andiamo, si.*"

He smiles and nods. "*Allora. Andiamo!*"

All around us is chaos—newly arrived passengers trying to
find transportation to their hotels, families fighting to keep from
being separated in the crush, peddlers selling cheap pocket-watches
and packets of crudely tinted picture postcards, mangy dogs
barking, ragged children with sly eyes moving among us looking
for purses to pick. The roaring babble is astonishing. But we are
an island of tranquility in the midst of it all, my driver and I.
He beckons me into the carriage: a plush seat, leather paneling,
glistening brass fittings, but also an inescapable smell of garlic.
Two noble auburn horses stand patiently in their traces. A porter
comes running up with my luggage and I hear it being thumped
into place overhead. And then we are off, gently jouncing down

the quay, out into the bustling city, past the marble waterfront palaces of the customs officials and the myriad other agencies of the Imperial government, past temples of Minerva, Neptune, Apollo, and Jupiter Optimus Maximus, and up the winding boulevards toward the district of fashionable hotels on the slopes that lie midway between the sea and the hills. I will be staying at the Tiberius, on Via Roma, a boulevard which I have been told is the grand promenade of the upper city, the place to see and be seen.

We traverse streets that must be two thousand years old. I amuse myself with the thought that Augustus Caesar himself may have ridden through these very streets long ago, or Nero, or perhaps Claudius, the ancient conqueror of my homeland. Once we are away from the port, the buildings are tall and narrow, grim slender tenements of six and seven stories, built side by side with no breathing space between them. Their windows are shuttered against the midday heat, impenetrable, mysterious. Here and there among them are broader, shorter buildings set in small gardens: huge squat structures, gray and bulky, done in the fussy baroque style of two hundred years ago. They are the palatial homes, no doubt, of the mercantile class, the powerful importers and exporters who maintain the real prosperity of Neapolis. If my family lived here, I suppose we would live in one of those.

But we are Britannic, and our fine airy home sits on a great swath of rolling greensward in the sweet Cornish country, and I am only a tourist here, coming forth from my remote insignificant province for my first visit to great Italia, now that the Second War of Reunification is at last over and travel between the far-flung sectors of the Empire is possible again.

I stare at everything in utter fascination, peering so intensely that my eyes begin to ache. The clay pots of dazzling red and orange flowers fastened to the building walls, the gaudy banners on long posts above the shops, the marketplaces piled high with unfamiliar fruits and vegetables in green and purple mounds. Hanging down along the sides of some of the tenement houses are long blurry scrolls on which the dour lithographed portrait of the old Emperor Laureolus is displayed, or of his newly enthroned young grandson and successor, Maxentius Augustus, with patriotic and adoring inscriptions above and below. This is Loyalist territory: the Neapolitans are said to love the Empire more staunchly than the citizens of Urbs Roma itself.

We have reached the Via Roma. A grand boulevard indeed, grander, I would say, than any in Londin or Parisi: a broad carriageway down the middle bordered with the strange, unnaturally glossy shrubs and trees that thrive in this mild climate, and on both sides of the street the dazzling pink and white marble façades of the great hotels, the fine shops, the apartment buildings of the rich. There are sidewalk cafés everywhere, all of them frantically busy. I hear waves of jolly chatter and bursts of rich laughter rising from them as I pass by, and the sound of clinking glasses. The hotel marquees, arrayed one after the next virtually without a break, cry out the history of the Empire, a roster of great Imperial names: the Hadrianus, the Marcus Aurelius, the Augustus, the Maximilianus, the Lucius Agrippa. And at last the Tiberius, neither the grandest nor the least consequential of the lot, a white-fronted building in the Classical Revival style, well situated in a bright district of elegant shops and restaurants.

The desk clerk speaks flawless Britannic. "Your passport, sir?"

He gives it a haughty sniff. Eyes my golden ringlets and long drooping mustachio, compares them with the closer-cropped image of my passport photo, decides that I am indeed myself, Cymbelin Vetruvius Scapulanus of Londin and Caratacus House in Cornwall, and whistles up a *facchino* to carry my bags upstairs. The suite is splendid, two lofty-ceilinged rooms at the corner of the building, a view of the distant harbor on one side and of the volcano on the other. The porter shows me how to operate my bath, points out my night-light and my cabinet of liqueurs, officiously tidies my bedspread. I tip the boy with a gold solidus—never let it be said that a Scapulanus of Caratacus House is ungenerous—but he pockets it as coolly as if I have tossed him a copper.

When he is gone, I stand a long while at the windows before unpacking, drinking in the sight of the city and the sparkling bay. I have never beheld anything so magnificent: the wide processional avenues, the temples, the amphitheaters, the gleaming palatial towers, the teeming marketplaces. And this is only Neapolis, the second city of Italia! Next to it, our cherished Londin is a mere muddy provincial backwater. What will great Roma be like, if this is Neapolis?

I feel an oddly disconcerting and unfamiliar sensation that I suspect may be an outbreak of humility. I am a rich man's son, I can trace my ancestry more or less legitimately back to kings of ancient Britain, I have had the benefits of a fine education, with high Cantabrigian honors in history and architecture. But what does any of that matter here? I'm in Italia now, the heartland of the imperishable Empire, and I am nothing but a brawny bumptious Celt from one of the outer edges of the civilized world. These people must think I wear leather kilts at home and rub the grease of pigs into my hair. I can see that I may be going to find myself out of my depth in this land. Which will be a new experience for me; but is that not why I have come here to Italia, to Roma Mater—to open myself to new experiences?

The shops of the Via Roma are closed when I go out for an afternoon stroll, and there is no one to be seen anywhere, except in the crowded cafés and restaurants. In the heat of this place, businesses of all sorts shut down at midday and reopen in the cooler hours of early evening. The windows display an amazing array of merchandise from every part of the Empire, Africa, India, Gallia, Hispania, Britannia, even Hither Asia and the mysterious places beyond it, Khitai and Cipangu, where the little strange-eyed people live: clothing of the latest fashions, antique jewelry, fine shoes, household furnishings, costly objects of all sorts. Here is the grand abundance of Imperium, indeed. With the war finally at an end, shipments of luxury goods must converge constantly on Italia from all its resubjugated provinces.

I walk on and on. Via Roma seems endless, extending infinitely ahead of me, onward to the vanishing point of the horizon. But of course it *does* have an end: the street's own name announces its terminal point, Urbs Roma itself, the great capital city. It isn't true, the thing they always say in Italia, that all roads lead to Roma, but this is one that actually does: I need only keep walking northward and this boulevard will bring me eventually to the city of the Seven Hills. There's time for that, though. I must begin my conquest of Italia in easy stages: Neapolis and its picturesque environs first, then a gradual advance northward to meet the formidable challenge of the city of the Caesars.

People are emerging from the cafés now. Some of them turn and stare openly at me, the way I might stare at a giraffe or elephant parading in the streets of Londin. Have they never seen a Briton before? Is yellow hair so alien to them? Perhaps it is my height and the breadth of my shoulders that draws their scrutiny, or my golden earring and the heavy Celtic Revival armlet that I affect. They nudge each other, they whisper, they smile.

I return their smiles graciously as I pass by. *Good afternoon, fellow Roman citizens*, I am tempted to say. But they would probably snicker at my British-accented Latin or my attempts at their colloquial Roman tongue.

There is a message waiting for me at the hotel. My father, bless him, has posted letters of introduction ahead to certain members of the Neapolitan aristocracy whom he has asked to welcome me and ease my entry into Roman society. Before leaving the hotel for my walk I had sent a message announcing my arrival to the people I was meant to meet here, and already there has been a reply. I am invited in the most cordial terms to dine this very evening at the villa of Marcellus Domitianus Frontinus, who according to my father owns half the vineyards between Neapolis and Pompeii and whose brother Cassius was one of the great heroes of the recently concluded war. A carriage will pick me up at the Tiberius at the eighteenth hour.

I am suffused with a strange joy. They are willing to make the visiting barbarian feel welcome on his first night in the mother country. Of course Frontinus ships ten thousand cases of his sweet white wines to my father's warehouses in Londin every year and that is a far from inconsiderable bit of business. Not that business matters will be mentioned this evening. For one thing I know very little of my father's commercial dealings; but also, and this is much more to the point, we are patricians, Frontinus and I, and we must behave that way. He is of the ancient Senatorial class, descended from men who made and unmade Caesars a thousand years ago. And I carry the blood of British kings in my veins, or at least my father says I do and my own name—Cymbelin—proclaims it. Caratacus, Cassevelaunus, Tincommius, Togodumnus, Prasutagus: at one time or another I have heard my father claim descent from each of those grand old Celtic chieftains, and Queen Cartamandua of the Brigantes for good measure.

Well, and Cartamandua expediently signed a treaty with the Roman invaders of her country, and sent her fellow monarch Caratacus to Roma in chains. But all that was a long time ago, and we Britons have been pacified and repacified on many occasions since then, and everyone understands that the power and the glory will reside, now and always, in the great city that lies at the other end of the Via Roma from here. Frontinus will be polite to me, I know: if not for the sake of the heroic though unvictorious warriors who are my putative ancestors, then for the ten thousand cases of wine that he means to ship to Londin next year. I will dine well tonight, I will meet significant people, I will be offered easy entree to the great homes of Neapolis and, when I am ready to go there, the capital as well.

I bathe. I shave. I oil my ringlets, and not with the grease of pigs; and I select my clothing with great care, a silken Byzantine tunic and matching neckerchief, fine leggings of scarlet Aegyptian linen, sandals of the best Syrian workmanship. With, of course, my golden earring and my massive armlet to provide that interestingly barbaric touch for which they will value me more highly.

The carriage is waiting when I emerge from the hotel. A Nubian driver in crimson and turquoise; white Arabian horses; the carriage itself is of ebony inlaid with strips of ivory. Worthy, I would think, of an Emperor. But Frontinus is only a wealthy patrician, a mere southerner at that. What do the Caesars ride in, I wonder, if this is the kind of vehicle a Frontinus sends to pick up visiting young men from the backward provinces?

The road winds up into the hills. A cloud has drifted over the city and the early evening sunlight tumbles through it like golden rain. The surface of the bay is ablaze with light. Mysterious gray islands are visible in the distance.

The villa of Marcellus Domitianus Frontinus is set in a park so big it takes us fifteen minutes to reach the house once we are past the colossal iron gate. It is a light and graceful pavilion, the enormous size of which is carefully masked by the elegance of its design, set on the very edge of a lofty slope. There is a look of deceptive fragility about it, as though it would be sensitive to the slightest movements of the atmosphere. The view from its portico runs from Vesuvius in the east to some jutting cape far off down the other shore of the bay. All around it are marvelous shrubs and trees in bloom, and the fragrance they exhale is the fragrance of unthinkable wealth. I begin to wonder how much those ten thousand cases of wine can matter to this man.

Yet Frontinus himself is earthy and amiable, a stocky balding man with an easy grin and an immediately congenial style.

He is there to greet me as I step down from the carriage. "I am Marcello Domiziano," he tells me, speaking Roman, grinning broadly as he puts out his hand. "Welcome to my house, dear friend Cymbelin!"

Marcello Domiziano. He uses the Roman, not the Latin, form of his name. In the provinces, of course, we pretentiously allow ourselves Latin names, mingling them to some degree with Britannic or Gallic or Teutonic localisms; but here in Italia the only people who have the privilege of going by names in the ancient Latin mode are members of the Senatorial and Imperial families and high military officers, and the rest must employ the modern Roman form. Frontinus rises above his own privilege of rank: I may call him Marcello, the way I would one of his field hands. And he will call me Cymbelin. Very swiftly we are dear friends, or so he wants me to feel, and I have barely arrived.

The gathering is under way already, on a breeze-swept open patio with a terrazzo floor, looking outward toward the city center far below. Fifteen, perhaps twenty people, handsome men, stunning women, everyone laughing and chattering like the people in the sidewalk cafés.

"My daughter, Adriana," Frontinus says. "Her friend Lucilla, visiting from Roma."

They are extraordinarily beautiful. The two of them surround me and I am dazzled. I remember once in Gallia, at a great villa somewhere near Nemausus, I was led by my host into the heart of a mirror maze that he had had built for his amusement, and instantly I felt myself toppling dizzily forward, vanishing between the infinitely reduplicated images, and had to pull myself back with an effort, heart pounding, head spinning.

It is like that now, standing between these two girls. Their beauty dazes me, their perfume intoxicates me. Frontinus has moved away, leaving me unsure of which is the daughter and which is the friend; I look from one to the other, confused.

The girl to my left is full-bodied and robust, with sharp features, pale skin, and flaming red hair arrayed close to her skull in tight coils, an antique style that might have been copied from some ancient wall painting. The other, taller, is dark and slender, almost frail, with heavy rows of blue faience beads about her throat and shadowy rings painted beneath her eyes. For all her flimsiness she is very sleek, soft-skinned, with a glossy Aegyptian look about her. The red-haired one must be Frontinus's daughter,

I decide, comparing her sturdy deep-chested frame to his; but no, no, she is the visitor from Roma, for the taller, darker one says, speaking not Roman but Latin, and in a voice smooth as Greek honey, "You do honor to our house, distinguished sir. My father says that you are of royal birth."

I wonder if I am being mocked. But I see the way she is measuring me with her eyes, running over my length and breadth as though I am a statue in some museum's hall of kings. The other one is doing the same.

"I carry a royal name, at any rate," I say. "Cymbelin—you may know him as Cunobelinus, in the history books. Whose son was the warrior king Caratacus, captured and pardoned by the first Emperor Claudius. My father has gone to great pains to have our genealogy traced to their line."

I smile disarmingly; and I see that they take my meaning precisely. I am describing the foolish pretensions of a rich provincial merchant, nothing more.

"How long ago was that, actually?" asks the redhead, Lucilla.

"The genealogical study?"

"The capturing and pardoning of your great ancestor."

"Why—" I hesitate. Haven't I just said that it was in the time of Claudius the First? But she flutters her eyes at me as though she is innocent of any historical information. "About eighteen centuries ago," I tell her. "When the Empire was still new. Claudius the First was the fourth of the Caesars. The fifth, if you count Julius Caesar as an Emperor. Which I think is the proper thing to do."

"How precise you are about such things," Adriana Frontina says, laughing.

"About historical matters, yes. About very little else, I'm afraid."

"Will you be traveling widely in Italia?" asks Lucilla.

"I'll want to see the area around Neapolis, of course. Pompeii and the other old ruins, and a few days on the isle of Capreae. Then up to Roma, certainly, and maybe farther north—Etruria, Venetia, even as far up as Mediolanum. Actually, I want to see it all."

"Perhaps we can tour it together," Lucilla says. Just like that, bluntly, baldly. And now there is no flutter of innocence whatever in her wide-set, intelligent eyes, only a look of unmistakable mischief.

Of course I have heard that the women of Roma are that way. I am startled, all the same, by her forwardness, and for the moment I can find no reply; and then all the others come flocking around me. Marcellus Frontinus bombards me with introductions, reciting name after name, spilling them forth so quickly that it's impossible for me to match name to face.

"Enrico Giunio, the Count of Pausylipon, and Countess Emilia. My son, Druso Tiberio, and his friend Ezio. Quintillo Fabio Puteolano. Vitellio di Portofino; his wife, Claudia; their daughter, Crispina. Traiano Gordiano Tertullo, of Capreae—Marco Ulpio Africano—Sabina Metella Arboria—" A blur of names. There is no end to them. One alone out of all of them registers with real impact on me: "My brother, Cassio," Frontinus says. A slender, olive-skinned man with eyes like bits of polished coal: the great war hero, this is, Cassius Lucius Frontinus! I begin to salute him, but Frontinus rattles out four more introductions before I can. People seem to be materializing out of thin air. To Adriana I whisper, "Has your father invited all of Neapolis here tonight?"

"Only the interesting ones," she says. "It isn't every day that a British king visits us." And giggles.

Swarms of servants—slaves?—move among us, bringing things to eat and drink. I am cautious in the first few rounds, reminding myself that this is only my first day here and that the fatigue of my journey may lead me into embarrassments, but then, to avoid seeming impolite, I select a goblet of wine and a small meat-cake, and hold them without tasting them, occasionally lifting them to my mouth and lowering them again untouched.

The high lords and ladies of Neapolitan society surround me in swirling clusters, peppering me with questions to which they don't really appear to be expecting answers. Some speak in Roman, some in Latin. How long will I be here? Will I spend my entire time in Neapolis? What has aroused my interest in visiting Italia? Is the economy of Britannia currently flourishing? Does everyone speak only Britannic there, or is Latin widely used also? Is there anything in Britannia that a traveler from Italia would find rewarding to see? How does British food compare with Italian food? Do I think that the current Treaty of Unity will hold? Have I been to Pompeii yet? To the Greek temples at Paestum? On and on. It is a bombardment. I make such replies as I can, but the questions overlap my answers in a highly exhausting way.

I am grateful for my stout constitution. Even so, after a time I become so weary that I begin to have trouble understanding their quick, idiomatic Roman, and I revert entirely to the older, purer Latin tongue, hoping it will encourage them to do the same. Some do, some don't.

Lucilla and Adriana remain close by my side throughout the ordeal, and I am grateful for that also.

These people think of me as a new toy, I realize. The novelty of the hour, to be examined in fascination for a little while and then discarded.

The wind off the bay has turned chilly with the coming of evening, and somehow, almost imperceptibly, the gathering has moved indoors and upstairs, to a huge room overlooking the atrium that will apparently be our banqueting hall.

"Come," Adriana says. "You must meet Uncle Cassio."

The famous general is far across the room, standing with arms folded, listening with no show of emotion while his brother and another man carry on what seems to be a fierce argument. He wears a tightly cut khaki uniform and his breast is bedecked with medals and ribbons. The other man, I remember after a moment, is the Count of Pausylipon, whom Frontinus had so casually referred to as "Enrico Giunio." He is gaunt, tall—nearly as tall as I am—hawk-faced, animated: his expression seems close to apoplectic. Marcello Domiziano is just as excited, neck straining upward, face pushed close to the other's, arms pinwheeling in emphatic gesticulations. I get the sense that these two have been bitterly snarling and snapping at each other over some great political issue for years.

They are speaking, I gather, of nothing less than the destiny of Roma itself. The Count of Pausylipon appears to be arguing that it is of the highest importance that the Empire should continue to survive as a single political entity—something that I did not think anyone seriously doubted, now that Reunification had been accomplished. "There's a reason why Roma has lasted so long," the Count was saying. "It's not just about power—the power of one city over an entire continent. It's about stability, coherence, the supremacy of a system that values logic, efficiency, superb engineering, planning. The world is the better for our having ruled it so long. We have brought light where only the darkness of barbarism would have existed otherwise."

These did not seem to me like controversial propositions. But I could see by the expression on the florid face of Marcello Domiziano and his obvious impatience to respond that there must be some area of strong disagreement between the two men, not in any way apparent to me. And Adriana, leaning close to me as she leads me across the room, whispers something that amidst all the noise I am unable clearly to make out, but which obscures what Marcello Domiziano has just said to the Count.

Despite all the furor going on at his elbow, it appears almost as though the famous general is asleep on his feet—a knack that must be useful during lulls in long battles—except that every few moments, in response, I suppose, to some provocative remark by one combatant or the other, his eyelids widen and a brilliant, baleful glare is emitted by those remarkable coal-bright eyes. I feel hesitant at joining this peculiar little group. But Adriana steers me over to them.

Frontinus cries, "Yes, yes, Cymbelin! Come meet my brother!" He has noticed my hesitation also. But perhaps he would welcome an interruption of the hostilities.

Which I provide. The dispute, the discussion, whatever it is, evaporates the moment I get there, turning into polite vaporous chitchat. The Count, having calmed himself totally, an impressive display of patrician self-control, offers me a lofty, remote nod of acknowledgment, gives Adriana and Lucilla a pat on the shoulder apiece, and excuses himself to go in search of a fresh drink. Frontinus, still a little red in the face but cheerful as ever, commends me to his brother's attention with an upturned palm. "Our British friend," he says.

"I am honored, your Excellence," I say, making a little bow to Cassius Lucius Frontinus.

"Oh, none of that, now," says Uncle Cassio. "We aren't in the camp." He speaks in Latin. His voice is thin and hard, like the edge of a knife, but I sense that he's trying to be genial.

For a moment I am giddy with awe, simply at finding myself in his presence. I think of this little man—and that is what he is, little, as short as his brother and very much slighter of build—striding untiringly from Dacia to Gallia and back in seven-league boots, putting out the fires of secession everywhere. The indomitable general, the savior of the Empire.

There will be fire of a different sort ablaze in the Empire

soon, and I am standing very close to its source. But I have no awareness of that just yet.

Cassius Frontinus surveys me as though measuring me for a uniform. "Tell me, are all you Britons that big?"

"I'm a bit larger than average, actually."

"A good thing. We came very close to invading you, you know, very early in the war. It wouldn't have been any picnic, facing a whole army of men your size."

"Invading Britannia, sir?" Lucilla asks.

"Indeed," he says, giving the girl a quick chilly smile. "A preemptive strike, when we thought Britannia might be toying with joining the rebellion."

I blink at him in surprise and some irritation. This is a sore place for us: why is he rubbing it?

Staunchly I say, "That would never have happened, sir. We are Loyalists, you know, we Britons."

"Yes. Yes, of course you are. But the risk was there, after all. A fifty-fifty chance is the way it seemed to us then. It was a touchy moment. And the High Command thought, let's send a few legions over there, just to keep them in line. Before your time, I suppose."

I'm still holding my goblet of wine, still untasted. Now, nervously, I take a deep draught.

Against all propriety I feel impelled to defend my race. With preposterous stiffness I say, "Let me assure you, general, that I am not as young as you may think, and I can tell you that there was never the slightest possibility that Britannia would have gone over to the rebels. None."

A flicker of—amusement?—annoyance?—in those terrible eyes, now.

"In hindsight, yes, certainly. But it looked quite otherwise to us, for a while, there at the very beginning. Just how old were you when the war broke out, my lad?"

I hate being patronized. I let him see my anger.

"Seventeen, sir. I served in the Twelfth Britannic Legion, under Aelius Titianus Rigisamus. Saw action in Gallia and Lusitania. The Balloon Corps."

"Ah." He isn't expecting that. "Well, then. I've misjudged you."

"My entire nation, I would say. Whatever rumors of British disloyalty you may have heard in that very confused time were nothing but enemy fabrications."

"Ah, indeed," says the general. "Indeed." His tone is benign, but his eyes are brighter and stonier than ever and his jaws barely move as he says the words.

Adriana Frontina, looking horrified at the growing heat of our exchanges, is frantically signaling me with her eyes to get off the subject. Her red-haired friend Lucilla, though, merely seems amused by the little altercation. Marcellus Frontinus has turned aside, probably not coincidentally, and is calling instructions to some servants about getting the banquet under way.

I plunge recklessly onward, nonetheless. "Sir, we Britons are just as Roman as anyone in the Empire. Or do you think we still nurse private national grievances going back to the time of Claudius?"

Cassius Frontinus is silent a moment, studying me with some care.

"Yes," he says, finally. "Yes, I do, as a matter of fact. But that's beside the point. Everybody who got swept up into the Empire once upon a time and never was able to find their way out again has old grievances buried somewhere, no matter how Roman they claim to be now. The Teutons, the Britons, the Hispaniards, the Frogs, everyone. That's why we've had two nasty breakups of the system in less than a century, wouldn't you say? But no, boy, I didn't mean to impugn the loyalty of your people, not in the slightest. This has all been highly unfortunate. A thousand pardons, my friend."

He glances at my goblet, which I have somehow drained without noticing.

"You need another drink, is that not so? And so do I." He snaps his fingers at a passing servitor. "Boy! Boy! More wine, over here!"

I have a certain sense that my conversation with the great war hero Cassius Lucius Frontinus has not been a success, and that this might be a good moment to withdraw. I shoot a help-less glance at Adriana, who understands at once and says, "But Cymbelin has taken enough of your time, Uncle. And look, the praefectus urbi has arrived: we really must introduce our guest to him."

Yes. They really must, before I make a worse botch of things. I bow again and excuse myself, and Adriana takes me by one arm and Lucilla seizes the other, and they sweep me away off to the opposite side of the great hall.

"Was I very horrid?" I ask.

"Uncle likes men who show some spirit," Adriana says. "In the army nobody dares talk back to him at all."

"But to be so rude—he the great man that he is, and I just a visitor from the provinces—"

"He was the one that was rude," says Lucilla hotly. "Calling your people traitors to the Empire! How could he have said any such thing!" And then, in a lower voice, purring directly into my ear: "I'll take you to Pompeii tomorrow. It won't be nearly so boring for you there."

She calls for me at the hotel after breakfast, riding in an extraordinarily grand quadriga, mahogany-trimmed and silk-tasseled and gilded all over, drawn by two magnificent white horses and two gigantic duns. It makes the one that Marcellus Frontinus sent for me the night before seem almost shabby. I had compared that one to the chariot of an Emperor; but no, I was altogether wrong: surely this is closer to the real thing.

"Is this what you traveled down in from Roma?" I ask her.

"Oh, no, I came by train. I borrowed the chariot from Druso Tiberio. He goes in for things of this sort."

At the party I had had only the briefest of encounters with young Frontinus and was highly unimpressed with him: a soft young man, pomaded and perfumed, three or four golden rings on each hand, languid movements and delicate yawns, distinctly a prince. Shamelessly exchanging melting glances all evening long with his handsome friend Ezio, who seemed as stupid as a gladiator and probably once was one.

"What can a quadriga like this cost?" I ask. "Five million sesterces? Ten million?"

"Very likely even more."

"And he simply *lends* it to you for the day?"

"Oh, it's only his second best one, wouldn't you know? Druso's a rich man's son, after all, very spoiled. Marcello doesn't deny him a thing. I think it's terrible, of course."

"Yes," I say. "Dreadful."

If Lucilla picks up the irony in my voice, she gives no sign of it.

"And yet, if he's willing to lend one of his pretty chariots to his sister's friend for a day or two—"

"Why not take it, eh?"

"Why not indeed."

And so off we go down the coast road together, this lovely voluptuous red-haired stranger from Roma and I, riding toward Pompeii in a quadriga that would have brought a blush to the cheek of a Caesar. Traffic parts for us on the highway as though it *is* the chariot of a Caesar, and the horses streak eastward and then southward with the swiftness of the steeds of Apollo, clip-clopping along the wide, beautifully paved road at a startling pace.

Lucilla and I sit chastely far apart, like the well-bred young people that we are, chatting pleasantly but impersonally about the party.

"What was all that about," she says, "the quarrel that you and Adriana's uncle were having last night?"

"It wasn't a quarrel. It was—an unpleasantness."

"Whatever. Something about the Roman army invading Britannia to make sure you people stayed on our side in the war. I know so little about these things. You weren't *really* going to secede, were you?"

We have been speaking Roman, but if we are going to have this discussion I must use a language in which I feel more at home. So I switch to Latin and say, "Actually, I think it was a pretty close thing, though it was cruel of him to say so. Or simply boorish."

"Military men. They have no manners."

"It surprised me all the same. To fling it in my face like that—!"

"So it was true?"

"I was only a boy when it was happening, you understand. But yes, I know there was a substantial anti-Imperial faction in Londin fifteen or twenty years ago."

"Who wanted to restore the Republic, you mean?"

"Who wanted to pull out of the Empire," I say. "And elect a king of our own blood. If such a thing as our own blood can be said still to exist in any significant way among Britons, after eighteen hundred years as Roman citizens."

"I see. So they wanted an independent Britannia."

"They saw a chance for it. This was only about twenty years after the Empire had finished cleaning up the effects of the first collapse, you know. And then suddenly a second civil war seemed likely to begin."

"That was in the East, wasn't it?"

I wonder how much she really knows about these matters. More than she is letting on, I suspect. But I have come down from Cantabrigia with honors in history, after all, and I suppose she is trying to give me a chance to be impressive.

"In Syria and Persia, yes, and the back end of India. Just a little frontier rebellion, not even white people that were stirring up the fuss: ten legions could have put the whole thing down. But the Emperor Laureolus was already old and sick—senile, in fact—and no one in the administration was paying attention to the outer provinces, and the legions weren't sent in until it was too late. So there was a real mess to deal with, all of a sudden. And right in the middle of that, Hispania and Gallia and even silly little Lusitania decided to secede from the Empire again, too. So it was 2563 all over again, a second collapse even more serious than the first one."

"And Britannia was going to pull out also, this time."

"That was what the rabble was urging, at any rate. There were some noisy demonstrations in Londin, and posters went up outside the proconsul's palace telling him to go back to Roma, things like that: 'Britannia for the Britons!' Throw the Romans out and bring back the old Celtic monarchy, is what people were yelling. Well, of course, we couldn't have that, and we shut them up very quickly indeed, and when the war began and our moment came, we fought as bravely as any Romans anywhere."

"'We'?" she says.

"The decent people of Britannia. The intelligent people."

"The propertied people, you mean?"

"Well, of course. We understood how much there was to lose—not just for us, for everyone in Britannia—if the Empire should fall. What's our best market? Italia! And if Britannia, Gallia, Hispania, and Lusitania managed to secede, Italia would lose its access to the sea. It would be locked up in the middle of Europa with one set of enemies blocking the land route to the east and the other set closing off the ocean to the west. The heart of the Empire would wither. We Britons would have no one to sell our goods to, unless we started shipping them westward to Nova Roma and trying to peddle them to the redskins. The breakup of the Empire would cause a worldwide depression— famine, civil strife, absolute horror everywhere. The worst of the suffering would have fallen on the people who were yelling loudest for secession."

She gives me an odd look.

"Your own family claims royal Celtic blood, and you have a fancy Celtic name. So it would seem that your people like to look back nostalgically to the golden days of British freedom before the Roman conquest. But even so you helped to put down the secessionist movement in your province."

Is she mocking me too? I am so little at ease among these Romans.

A trifle woodenly I say, "Not I, personally. I was still only a boy when the anti-Imperial demonstrations were going on. But yes, for all his love of Celtic lore my father has always believed that we had to put the interests of Roman civilization in general ahead of our petty little nationalistic pride. When the war did reach us, Britannia was on the Loyalist side, thanks in good measure to him. And as soon as I was old enough, I joined the legions and did my part for the Empire."

"You love the Emperor, then?"

"I love the Empire. I believe the Empire is a necessity. As for this particular Emperor that we have now—" I hesitate. I should be careful here. "We have had more capable ones, I suppose."

Lucilla laughs. "My father thinks that Maxentius is an utter idiot!"

"Actually, so does mine. Well, but Emperors come and go, and some are better than others. What's important is the survival of the Empire. And for every Nero, there's a Vespasianus, sooner or later. For every Caracalla, there's a Titus Gallius. And for every weak and silly Maxentius—"

"Shh," Lucilla says, pointing to our coachman then to her ears. "We ought to be more cautious. Perhaps we're saying too much that's indiscreet, love. We don't want to do that."

"No. Of course not."

"*Doing* something indiscreet, now—"

"Ah. That's different."

"Very different," she says. And we both laugh.

We are passing virtually under the shadow of great Vesuvius now. Imperceptibly we have moved closer to each other while talking, and gradually I have come to feel the pressure of her warm thigh against mine.

Now, as the chariot takes a sharp turn of the road, she is thrown against me. Ostensibly to steady her, I slip my arm around her shoulders and she nestles her head in the hollow of my neck. My hand comes to rest on the firm globe of her breast. She lets it remain there.

We reach the ruins of Pompeii in time for a late lunch at a luxurious hostelry just at the edge of the excavation zone. Over a meal of grilled fish and glittering white wine we make no pretense of hiding our hunger for one another. I am tempted to suggest that we skip the archaeology and go straight to our room.

But no, no chance of that, a guide that she has hired is waiting for us after lunch, an excitable little bald-headed Greek who is bubbling with eagerness to convey us into the realm of antiquity. So off we go into the torrid Pompeiian afternoon, full of wine and lust, and he marches us up one dry stony street and down the next, showing us the great sights of the city that the volcano engulfed eighteen hundred years ago in the second month of the reign of the Emperor Titus.

It's terribly fascinating, actually. We modern Romans have the illusion that we still continue to design our cities and houses very much in the style of the ancients; but in fact the changes, however gentle they may have been from one century to the next, have been enormous, and Pompeii—sealed away under volcanic debris eighteen centuries ago and left untouched until its rediscovery just a few decades ago—seems truly antique. Our bubbly Greek shows us the homes of the rich men with their sumptuous paintings and statuary, the baths, the amphitheater, the forum. He takes us into the sweaty little whorehouse, where we see vivid murals of heavy-thighed prostitutes energetically pleasuring their clients, and Lucilla giggles into my ear and lightly tickles the palm of my hand with her fingertip. I'm ready to conclude the tour right then and there, but of course it can't be done: there is ever so much more to see, our relentless guide declares.

Outside the Temple of Jupiter Lucilla asks me, all innocence, "What gods do you people worship in Britannia? The same that we do?"

"The very same, yes. Jupiter, Juno, Apollo, Mithras, Cybele, all the usual ones, the ones that you have here."

"Not special prehistoric pagan gods of your own?"

"What do you imagine we are? Savages?"

"Of course, darling! Of course! Great, lovely golden-haired savages!"

There is a gleam in her eye. She is teasing, but she means what she says, as well. I know she does.

And she too has hit a vulnerable point; for despite all our Roman airs, we Britons are *not* really as much like these people as we would like to think, and we *do* have our own little lingering ancient allegiances. Not I myself, particularly; for such religious needs as I may have, Jupiter and Mercury are quite good enough. But I have friends at home, quite close friends, who sacrifice most sincerely to Branwen and Velaunus, to Rhiannon and Brighida, to Ancasta, to the Matres. And even I have gone—once, at least—to the festival of the Llewnasadh, where they worship Mercury Lugus under his old British name of Llew.

But it is all too foolish, too embarrassing, worshiping those crude old wooden gods in their nests of straw. Not that Apollo and Mercury seem any less absurd to me, or Mithras, or any of the dozens of bizarre Eastern gods that have been going in and out of fashion in Roma for centuries, Baal and Marduk and Jehovah and the rest. They are all equally meaningless to me. And yet there are times when I feel a great vacancy inside of me, as I look up at the stars, wondering how and why they all were made, and not knowing, not having even the first hint.

I don't want to speak of such things with her. These are private matters.

But her playful question about our local gods has wounded me. I am abashed; I am red-cheeked with shame at my own Britishness, which I have sensed almost from the start is one of the things about me, perhaps the most important thing, that makes me interesting to her.

We leave the ruins, finally.

We return to our hotel. We go to our room. Our suite has a terrace overlooking the excavations, a bedroom painted with murals in the Pompeiian style, a marble bath big enough for six. We undress each other with deliberate lack of haste. Lucilla's body is strongly built, broad through the hips and shoulders, full in buttock and breast and thigh: to me an extremely beautiful body, but perhaps she inwardly fears that it lacks elegance. Her skin is marvelous, pale as fine silk, with the lightest dusting of charming pink freckles across her chest and the tops of her shoulders, and—an oddity that I find very diverting—her pubic hair is black as night, the starkest possible contrast to the fiery crimson hair higher up.

She sees the direction of my gaze.

"I don't dye it," she informs me. "It just came that way, I don't know why."

"And this?" I say, placing my finger lightly on the tattoo of a pine tree that runs along the inside of her right thigh. "A birthmark, is it?"

"The priests of Atys put it there, when I was initiated."

"The Phrygian god?"

"I go to his temple, yes. Now and then. In springtime, usually."

So she has indeed played a little game with me.

"Atys! A devotee of Atys of Phrygia! Oh, Lucilla, Lucilla! You had the audacity to tell me that you think Britons are savages because some of us worship pagan gods. While all the time you had the mark of Atys on your own skin, right next to your—your—"

"To my what, love? Go on, say its name."

I say it in Britannic. She repeats it, savoring the word, so strange to her ears, so barbaric.

"Now kiss it," she says.

"Gladly," I tell her, and I drop to my knees and do. Then I sweep her up in my great barbaric arms and carry her to the bath, and lower her gently into it, and lie down beside her myself. We soak for a time; and then we wash each other, laughing; and then, still wet, we spring from the tub and race toward the bed. She is looking for savagery, and I give her savagery, all right, hearty barbarian caresses that leave her gasping in unintelligible bursts of no doubt obscene Roman; and what she gives me in return is the subtle and artful Roman manner of loving, tricks going back to Caesar's time, cunning ripplings of the interior muscles and sly strokes of the fingertips that drive me to the edge of madness; and no sooner have we done with each other than we find ourselves beginning all over again.

"My wild man," she murmurs. "My Celt!"

From Pompeii we proceed down the coast to Surrentum, a beautiful seaside town set amid groves of orange and lemon trees. We tell our driver to wait for us there for a couple of days, and take the ferry across to the romantic isle of Capreae, playground of Emperors. Lucilla has wired ahead to book a room for us at one of the best hotels, a hilltop place called the Punta Tragara that has, she says, a magnificent view of the harbor. She has been to Capreae before. With whom, I wonder, and how many times.

Lucilla and I lie naked on the terrace of our room, reclining on thick sheepskin mats, enjoying the mild autumn evening. The sky and the sea are the same shade of gray-blue. It's hard to tell where the boundary lies between the one and the other. Thickly wooded cliffs rise vertically from the water just across from us. Heavy-winged birds swoop through the dusk. In town, far below, the first lights of evening begin to shimmer.

"I don't even know your name," I say, after a while.

"Of course you do. It's Lucilla."

"You know what I mean. The rest of it."

"Lucilla Junia Scaevola," she says.

"Scaevola? Related to the famous *Consul* Scaevola, by any chance?"

I'm only making idle talk. Scaevola is hardly an uncommon Roman name, of course.

"He's my uncle Gaius," she says. "You'll get to meet him when we go up to Roma. Adriana adores him, and so will you."

Her casual words leave me thunderstruck. Consul Scaevola's niece, lying naked here beside me?

Gods! These girls and their famous uncles! Uncle Gaius, Uncle Cassius. I am in heady company. The whole Roman world knows Gaius Junius Scaevola—chosen again and again as Consul, three terms, perhaps four, the most recent time just a couple of years before. By all accounts he's the second most powerful man in the realm, the great strong figure who stands behind the wobbly young Emperor Maxentius and keeps him propped up. *My uncle Gaius*, this one says, so very simply and sweetly. I'll have quite a lot to tell my father when I get back to Cornwall.

Consul Scaevola's niece rears up above me and dangles her breasts in my face. I kiss their pink patrician tips and she drops down on top of me like one of those fierce swooping birds descending on its prey.

In the cool of the morning we take a long hike up one of the hills behind town to the Villa Jovis, the Imperial palace that has been there since the time of Tiberius. He used to have his enemies thrown from the edge of the cliff there.

Of course we can't get very close to it, since it's still in use, occupied by members of the Imperial family whenever they visit Capreae. Nobody seems to be in residence right now but the gates are heavily guarded anyway. We can see it rising grandly from the summit of its hill, an enormous pile of gleaming masonry surrounded by elaborate fortifications.

"I wonder what it's like in there," I say. "But I'll never know, I guess."

"I've been inside it," Lucilla tells me.

"You have?"

"They claim that some of the rooms and furnishings go all the way back to Tiberius's reign. There's an indoor swimming pool with the most absolutely obscene mosaics all around it, and that's where he's supposed to have liked to diddle little boys and girls. But I think it's all mostly a fake put together in medieval times, or even later. The whole place was sacked, you know, when the Byzantines invaded the Western Empire six hundred years ago. It's pretty certain that they carried the treasures of the early Emperors off to Constantinopolis with them, wouldn't you think?"

"How did you happen to see it?" I ask. "You were traveling with your uncle, I suppose."

"With Flavius Rufus, actually."

"Flavius Rufus?"

"Flavius Caesar. Emperor Maxentius's third brother. He loves southern Italia. Comes down here all the time."

"With you?"

"Once in a while. Oh, silly, silly! I was *sixteen*. We were just friends!"

"And how old are you now?"

"Twenty-one," she says. Six years younger than I am, then.

"Very close friends, I suppose."

"Oh, don't be such a fool, Cymbelin!" There is laughter in her eyes. "You'll meet him, too, when we're in Roma."

"A royal prince?"

"Of course! You'll meet *everyone*. The Emperor's brothers, the Emperor's sisters, the Emperor himself, if he's in town. I grew up at court, don't you realize that? In my uncle's household. My father died in the war."

"I'm sorry."

"Commanded the Augustus Legion, in Syria, Aegyptus, Palaestina. Palaestina's where he died. You've heard of the Siege of Aelia

Capitolina? That's where he was killed, right outside the Temple of
the Great Mother just as the city was falling to us. He was standing near some old ruined stone wall that survives from the temple
that was there before the present one, and a sniper got him. Cassius
Frontinus delivered the funeral oration himself. And afterward my
uncle Gaius adopted me, because my mother was dead, too, had
killed herself the year before—that's a long story, a scandal at the
court of the old Emperor—"

My head is swimming.

"Anyway, Flavius is like a brother to me. You'll see. We came
down here and I stayed the night in the Villa Jovis. Saw all
the naughty mosaics in Tiberius's swimming pool, swam in it,
even—there was a gigantic feast afterward, wild boar from the
mountains here, mountains of strawberries and bananas, and you
wouldn't believe how much wine—oh, cheer up, Cymbelin, you
didn't think I was a *virgin*, did you?"

"That isn't it. Not at all."

"Then what is it?"

"The thought that you really know the royals. That you're still
so young and you've done so many astonishing things. And also
that the man I was arguing with the other night was actually
Cassius Lucius Frontinus the famous general, and that you're the
niece of Gaius Junius Scaevola the Consul, and that you've been
the mistress of the Emperor's brother, and—don't you see, Lucilla,
how hard all this is for me? How bewildering?"

"My poor confused barbarian!"

"I wish you wouldn't call me that. Even if it's more or less
true."

"My gorgeous Celt, then. My beautiful blond-haired Briton.
That much is all right to say, isn't it?"

We hire one of the little one-horse carriages that are the
only permissible vehicles on Capreae and ride down to the beach
to spend the afternoon swimming naked in the warm sea and
sunning ourselves on the rocky shore. Though it is late in the
day and late also in the year, Lucilla's flawless skin quickly turns
rosy, and she's hot and glowing when we return to our room.

Two days, two unforgettable nights, on Capreae. Then back
to Surrentum, where our charioteer is dutifully waiting for us at
the ferry landing, and up to Neapolis again, an all-day drive. I
am reluctant to part from her at my hotel, urging her to spend

the night with me there, too, but she insists that she must get back to the villa of Frontinus.

"And I?" I say. "What do I do? I have to dine alone, I have to go to bed alone?"

She brushes her lips lightly across mine and laughs. "Did I say that? Of course you'll come with me to Frontinus's place! Of *course!*"

"But he hasn't invited me to return."

"What a fool you can be sometimes, Cymbelin. *I* invite you. I'm Adriana's guest. And you're mine. Go upstairs, pack up the rest of your things, tell the hotel you're checking out. Go on, now!"

And so it is. In Druso Tiberio's absurdly splendid quadriga we ride back up the hill to the villa of Marcellus Domitianus Frontinus, where I am greeted with apparently unfeigned warmth and no trace of surprise by our jolly host and given a magnificent suite of rooms overlooking the bay. Uncle Cassio is gone, and so are the other house guests who were there on the night of the party, and I am more than welcome.

My rooms just happen to adjoin those of Lucilla. That night, after a feast of exhausting excess at which Druso Tiberio and his gladiator playmate Ezio behave in a truly disgusting way while the elder Frontinus studiedly turns his attention elsewhere, I hear a gentle tapping at my door as I am preparing for bed.

"Yes?"

"It's me."

Lucilla. "Gods be thanked! Come in!"

She wears a silken robe so sheer she might as well have been naked. In one hand she carries a little candelabrum, in the other a flask of what appears to be wine. She is still tipsy from dinner, I see. I take the candelabrum from her before she sets herself afire, and then the flask.

"We could invite Adriana in, too," she says coyly.

"Are you crazy?"

"No. Are you?"

"The two of you—?"

"We're best friends. We share everything."

"No," I say. "Not this."

"You *are* provincial, Cymbelin."

"Yes, I am. And one woman at a time is quite enough for me."

She seems disappointed. I realize that she has promised to

provide me to Adriana for tonight. Well, this is Imperial Italia, where the old traditions of unabashed debauchery evidently are very much alive. But though I speak of myself as Roman, I'm not as Roman as all that, I suppose. Adriana Frontina is extraordinarily beautiful, yes, but so is Lucilla, and Lucilla is all I want just now, and that is that. Simple provincial tastes. No doubt I'll live to regret my decision; but this night I am unwavering in my mulish simplicity.

Lucilla, disappointed or not, proves passionate enough for two. The night passes in a sleepless haze. We go at each other wildly, feverishly. She teaches me another new trick or two, and claps her hands at her own erotic cleverness. There are no women like this in Britannia: none that are known to me, at any rate.

At dawn we stand together on the balcony of my bedroom, weary with the best of all possible wearinesses, relishing the sweet cool breeze that rises from the bay.

"When do you want to go north?" she asks.

"Whenever you do."

"What about tomorrow?"

"Why not?"

"I warn you, you may be shocked by a few of the things you see going on in Urbs Roma."

"Then I'll be shocked, I suppose."

"You're very easily shocked, aren't you, Cymbelin?"

"Not really. Some of this is new to me, that's all."

Lucilla chuckles. "I'll educate you in our ways, never fear. It'll all get less frightening as you get used to it. You poor darling barbarian."

"You know I asked you not to—"

"You poor darling Celt, I mean," Lucilla says. "Come with me to Roma, love. But remember: when in Roma, it's best to do as the Romans do."

"I'll try," I promise.

Yet another chariot is put at our disposal for the journey: this one Ezio's, which he drove down in alone from Urbs Roma. He's going back north next week with Druso Tiberio, and they'll ride in one of his, but Ezio's chariot has to be returned to the capital somehow, too. So we take it. It's not nearly as grand as the one Lucilla and I had just been using, but it's far more imposing than you would expect someone like Ezio to own. A gift from Druso Tiberio, no doubt.

The whole household turns out to see us off. Marcello Domiziano urges me to think of his villa as his home whenever I am
in Neapolis. I invite him to be my family's guest in Britannia.
Adriana gives Lucilla a more than friendly hug—I begin to wonder
about them—and kisses me lightly on the cheek. But as I turn
away from her I see a smoldering look in her eyes that seems
compounded out of fury and regret. I suspect I have made an
enemy here. But perhaps the damage can be repaired at a later
time: it would be pleasant enough work to attempt it.

Our route north is the Via Roma, and we must descend into
town to reach it. Since we have no driver, I will be the charioteer, and Lucilla sits beside me on the box. Our horses, a pair of
slender, fiery Arabians, are well matched and need little guidance
from me. The day is mild, balmy, soft breezes: yet another bright,
sunny, summer-like day here in the eighth month of the year.
I think of my homeland, how dark and wet it must be by now.

"Does winter ever reach Italia?" I ask. "Or have the Emperors
made special arrangements with the gods?"

"Oh, it gets quite cold, quite wet," Lucilla assures me. "You'll
see. Not so much down here, but in Roma itself, yes, the win-
ters can be extremely vile. You'll still be here at the time of the
Saturnalia, won't you?"

That's still two months away. "I hadn't really given it much
thought. I suppose I will."

"Then you'll see how cold it can get. I usually go to someplace
like Sicilia or Aegyptus for the winter months, but this year I'm
going to stay in Roma." She snuggles cozily against me. "When
the rains come we'll keep each other warm. Won't that be nice,
Cymbelin?"

"Lovely. On the other hand, I wouldn't mind seeing Aegyptus,
you know. We could take the trip together at the end of the year.
The Pyramids, the great temples at Menfe—"

"I have to stay in Italia this winter. In or at least near Roma."

"You do? Why is that?"

"A family thing," she says. "It involves my uncle. But I mustn't
talk about it."

I take the meaning of her words immediately.

"He's going to be named Consul again, isn't he? *Isn't* he?"

She stiffens and pulls her breath in quickly, and I know that
I've hit on the truth.

"I mustn't say," she replies, after a moment.

"That's it, though. It has to be. The new year's Consuls take office on the first of Januarius, and so of course you'll want to be there for the ceremony. What will this be, the fourth time for him? The fifth, maybe."

"Please, Cymbelin."

"Promise me this, at least. We'll stay around in Roma until he's sworn in, and then we'll go to Aegyptus. The middle of January, all right? I can see us now, heading up the Nilus from Alexandria in a barge for two—"

"That's such a long time from now. I can't promise anything so far in advance." She puts her hand gently on my wrist and lets it linger there. "But we'll have as much fun as we can, won't we, even if it's cold and rainy, love?"

I see that there's no point pressing the issue. Maybe her Januarius is already arranged, and her plans don't include me: a trip to Africa with one of her Imperial friends, perhaps, young Flavius Caesar or some other member of the royal family. Irrational jealousy momentarily curdles my soul; and then I put all thought of January out of my mind. This is October, and the gloriously beautiful Lucilla Junia Scaevola will share my bed tonight and tomorrow night and so on and on at least until the Saturnalia, if I wish it, and I certainly do, and that should be all that matters to me right now.

We are passing the great hotels of the Via Roma. Their resplendent façades shine in the morning sun. And then we begin to climb up out of town again, into the suburban heights, a string of minor villas and here and there an isolated hill with some venerable estate of the Imperial family sprawling around its summit. After a time we go down the far side of the hills and enter the flat open country beyond, heading through the fertile plains of Campania Felix toward the capital city in the distant north.

We spend our first night in Capua, where Lucilla wants me to see the frescoes in the Mithraeum. I attempt to draw on my letter of credit to pay the hotel bill, but I discover that there will be no charge for our suite: the magic name of Scaevola has opened the way for us. The frescoes are very fine, the god slaying a white bull with a serpent under its feet, and there is a huge amphitheater here, too—the one where Spartacus spurred the revolt of the gladiators—but Lucilla tells me, as I gawk in provincial awe, that the one in Roma is far more impressive. Dinner is brought to us in our room, breast of pheasant and some thick, musky wine, and afterward we soak in the bath a long while and then indulge in the nightly scramble of the passions. I can easily endure this sort of life well through the end of the year and some distance beyond.

Then in the morning it is onward, northward and westward along the Via Roma, which now has become the Via Appia, the ancient military highway along which the Romans marched when they came to conquer their neighbors in southern Italia. This is sleepy agricultural country, broken here and there by the dark cyclopean ruins of dead cities that go back to pre-Roman times, and by hilltop towns of more recent date, though themselves a thousand years old or more. I feel the tremendous weight of history here.

Lucilla chatters away the slow drowsy hours of our drive with talk of her innumerable patrician friends in the capital, Claudio and Traiano and Alessandro and Marco Aureliano and Valeriano and a few dozen more, nearly all of them male, but there are a few female names among them, too, Domitilla, Severina, Giulia, Paolina, Tranquillina. High lords and ladies, I suppose. Sprinkled through the gossip are lighthearted references to members of the Imperial family who seem to be well known to her, close companions, in fact—not just the young Emperor, but his four brothers and three sisters, and assorted Imperial cousins and more distant kin.

I see more clearly than I have ever realized before how vast an establishment the family of our Caesars is, how many idle princes and princesses, each one with a great array of palaces, servitors, lovers and hangers-on. Nor is it only a single family, the cluster of royals who sit atop our world. For of course we have had innumerable dynasties occupying the throne during the nineteen centuries of the Empire, most of them long since extinct but many of the past five hundred years still surviving at least in some collateral line, completely unrelated to each other but all of them nevertheless carrying the great name of Caesar and all staking their claim to the public treasury. A dynasty can be overthrown but somehow the great-great-great-grandnephews, or whatever, of someone whose brother was Emperor long ago can still manage, so it seems, to claim pensions from the public purse down through all the succeeding epochs of time.

It's clear from the way she talks that Lucilla has been the mistress of Flavius Caesar and very likely also of his older brother, Camillus Caesar, who holds the title of Prince of Constantinopolis, though he lives in Roma; she speaks highly also of a certain Roman count who bears the grand name of Nero Romulus Claudius Palladius, and there is a special tone in her voice when she tells me of him that I know comes into women's voices when they are speaking of a man with whom they have made love.

Jealousy of men I have never even met surges within me. How can she have done so much already, she who is only twenty-one? I try to control my feelings. This is Roma; there is no morality here as I understand the word; I must strive to do as the Romans do, indeed.

Despite myself I try to ask her about this Nero Romulus Claudius Palladius, but already she has moved along to a sister of the Emperor whom she's sure I'll adore. Severina Floriana is her name. "We went to school together. Next to Adriana, she's my best friend in the world. She's absolutely beautiful—dark, sultry, almost Oriental-looking. You'd think she was an Arab. And you'd be right, because her grandmother on her mother's side came from Syria. A dancing-girl, once upon a time, so the story goes—"

And on and on. I wonder if I am to be offered to Severina Floriana also.

It is the third day of our journey now. As the Via Appia nears the capital we begin to encounter the Imperial tombs, lining the road on both sides. Lucilla seems to know them all and calls them off for me.

"There's the tomb of Flavius Romulus, the big one on the left—and that one is Claudius IX—and Gaius Martius, there—that's Cecilia Metella, she lived in the time of Augustus Caesar—Titus Gallius—Constantinus V—Lucius and Arcadius Agrippa, both of them—Heraclius III—Gaius Paulus—Marcus Anastasius—"

The weight of antiquity presses ever more heavily on me.

"What about the earliest ones?" I ask. "Augustus, Tiberius, Claudius—"

"You'll see the Tomb of Augustus in the city. Tiberius? Nobody seems to remember where he was buried. There are a lot of them in Hadrianus's tomb overlooking the river, maybe ten of them,

Antoninus Pius, Marcus Aurelius, a whole crowd of dead Emperors in there. And Julius Caesar himself—there's a great tomb for him right in the middle of the Forum, but the archaeologists say it isn't really his, it was built six hundred years later—oh, look, Cymbelin—do you see, there? The walls of the city right ahead of us! Roma! Roma!"

And so it is, Urbs Roma, the great mother of cities, the capital of the world, the Imperial metropolis: its white marble-sheathed walls, built and rebuilt so many times, rise suddenly before me. Roma! The boy from the far country, humbled by the grandeur of it all, is shaken to the core. A shiver of awe goes through me so convulsively that it is transmitted through the reins to the horses, one of which glances back at me in what I imagine to be contempt and puzzlement.

Roma the city is like a palimpsest, a scroll that has been written on and cleaned and written on again, and again and again: and all the old texts show through amidst the newest one. Two thousand years of history assail the newcomer's bedazzled eye in a single glance. Nothing ever gets torn down here, except occasionally for the sake of building something even more grand on its site. Here and there can still be seen the last quaint occasional remnants of the Roma of the Republic—the First Republic, I suppose I should say now—with the marble Roma of Augustus Caesar right atop them, and then the Romas of all the later Caesars, Hadrianus's Roma and Septimius Severus's Roma and the Roma of Flavius Romulus, who lived and ruled a thousand years after Severus, and the one that the renowned world-spanning Emperor Trajan VII erected upon all the rest in the great years that followed Flavius's reuniting of the Eastern and Western Empires. All these are mixed together in the historic center of the city, and then too in a frightful ring surrounding them rise the massive hideous towers of modern times, the dreary office buildings and apartment houses of the Roma of today.

But even they, ugly as they are, are ugly in an awesomely grand Roman way. Roma is nothing if not grand: it excels at everything, even at ugliness.

Lucilla guides me in, calling off the world-famous sights as we pass them one by one: the Baths of Caracalla, the Circus Maximus, the Temple of the Divine Claudius, the Tower of Aemilius Magnus, even the ponderous and malproportioned Arch of Triumph that the Byzantine Emperor Andronicus erected in the year 1952 to mark the short-lived Greek victory in the Civil War, and which the Romans have allowed to remain as an all too visible reminder of the one great defeat in their history. But just at the opposite end of the avenue from it is the Arch of Flavius Romulus, too, five times the size of the Arch of Andronicus, to signify the final defeat of the Greeks after their two centuries of Imperial dominion.

The traffic is stupefying and chaotic. Chariots everywhere, horse-drawn trams, bicycles, and something that Lucilla says is very new, little steam-driven trains that run freely on wheels instead of tracks. There seem to be no rules: each vehicle goes wherever it pleases, nobody giving any signals, each driver attempting to intimidate those about him with gestures and curses. At first I have trouble with this, not because I am easily intimidated but because we Britons are taught early to be courteous to one another on the highways; but quickly I see that I have no choice but to behave as they do. *When in Roma*, et cetera—the old maxim applies to every aspect of life in the capital.

"Left here. Now right. You see the Colosseum, over there? Bigger than you thought, isn't it? Turn right, turn right! That's the Forum down there, and the Capitol up on that hill. But we want to go the other way, over to the Palatine—it's the hill up there, you see? The one covered with palaces."

Yes. Enormous Imperial dwellings, two score or even more of them, all higgledy-piggledy, cheek by jowl. Whole mountains of marble must have been leveled to build that incomprehensible maze of splendor.

And we are heading right into the midst of it all. The entrance to the Palatine is well patrolled, hordes of Praetorians everywhere, but they all seem to know Lucilla by sight and they wave us on in. She tries to explain to me which palace is whose, but it's all a hopeless jumble, and even she isn't really sure. Underneath what we see, she says, are the original palaces of the early Imperial days, those of Augustus and Tiberius and the Flavians, but of course nearly every Emperor since then has wanted to add his own embellishments and enhancements, and by now the whole hill is a crazy quilt of Imperial magnificence and grandiosity in twenty different styles, including a few very odd Oriental and pseudo-Byzantine structures inserted into the mix in the twenty-fourth century by some of the weirder monarchs of the Decadence. Towers and arcades and pavilions and gazebos and colonnades and domes and basilicas and fountains and peculiar swooping vaults jut out everywhere.

"And the Emperor himself?" I ask her. "Where in all that does he live?"

She waves her hand vaguely toward the middle of the heap. "Oh, he moves around, you know. He never stays in the same place two nights in a row."

"Why is that? Is he the restless type?"

"Not at all. But Actinius Varro makes him do it."

"Who?"

"Varro. The Praetorian Prefect. He worries a lot about assassination plots."

I laugh. "When an Emperor is assassinated, isn't it usually his own Praetorian Prefect who does it?"

"Usually, yes. But the Emperor always thinks that his prefect is the first completely loyal one, right up till the moment the knife goes into his belly. Not that anyone would want to assassinate a foolish fop like our Maxentius," she adds.

"If he's as incompetent as everyone says, wouldn't that be a good reason for removing him, then?"

"What, and make one of his even more useless brothers Emperor in his place? Oh, no, Cymbelin. I know them all, believe me, and Maxentius is the best of the lot. Long life to him, I say."

"Indeed. Long life to Emperor Maxentius," I chime in, and we both enjoy a good laugh.

The particular palace we are heading for is one of the newest on the hill: an ornate, many-winged guest pavilion, much bedizened with eye-dazzling mosaics, brilliant wild splotches of garish yellows and uninhibited scarlets. It had been erected some fifty years before, she tells me, early in the reign of the lunatic Emperor Demetrius, the last Caesar of the Decadence. Lucilla has a little apartment in it, courtesy of her good friend, Prince Flavius Rufus. Apparently a good many non-royal members of the Imperial Roman social set live up here on the Palatine. It's more convenient for everyone that way, traffic being what it is in Roma and the number of parties being so great.

The beginning of my stay in the capital is Neapolis all over again: there is a glittering social function for me to attend on

my very first night. The host, says Lucilla, is none other than the
famous Count Nero Romulus Claudius Palladius, who is terribly
eager to meet me.

"And who is he, exactly?" I ask.

"His grandfather's brother was Count Valerian Apollinaris.
You know who he was?"

"Of course." One doesn't need a Cantabrigian education to
recognize the name of the architect of the modern Empire, the
great five-term Consul of the First War of Reunification. It was
Valerian Apollinaris who had dragged the frayed and crumbling
Empire out of the sorry era known as the Decadence, put an
end to the insurrections in the provinces that had wracked the
Empire throughout the troubled twenty-fifth century, restored
the authority of the central government, and installed Laureolus
Caesar, grandfather of our present Emperor, on the throne. It
was Apollinaris who—acting in Laureolus's name, as an unofficial
Caesar standing behind the true one—had instituted the Reign
of Terror, that time of brutal discipline that had, for better or
for worse, brought the Empire back to some semblance of the
greatness that it last had known in the time of Flavius Romulus
and the seventh Trajan. And then perished in the Terror himself,
along with so many others.

I know nothing of this grand-nephew of his, this Nero Romulus
Claudius Palladius, except what I've heard of him from Lucilla.
But she conveys merely by the way she utters his name, his full
name every time, that he has followed his ancestor's path, that
he too is a man of great power in the realm.

And indeed it is obvious to me right away, when Lucilla and
I arrive at Count Nero Romulus's Palatine Hill palace, that my
guess is correct.

The palace itself is relatively modest: a charming little building on the lower slope of the hill, close to the Forum, that I am
told dates from the Renaissance and was originally built for one
of the mistresses of Trajan VII. Just as Count Nero Romulus
has never bothered to hold the Consulate or any of the other
high offices of the realm, Count Nero Romulus doesn't need a
grand edifice to announce his importance. But the guest list at
his party says it all.

The current Consul, Aulus Galerius Bassanius, is there. So
are two of the Emperor's brothers, and one of his sisters. And

also Lucilla's uncle, the distinguished and celebrated Gaius Junius Scaevola, four times Consul of Roma and by general report the most powerful man in the Empire next to Emperor Maxentius himself—*more* powerful than the Emperor, many believe.

Lucilla introduces me to Scaevola first. "My friend Cymbelin Vetruvius Scapulanus from Britannia," she says, with a grand flourish. "We met at Marcello Domiziano's house in Neapolis, and we've been inseparable ever since. Isn't he splendid, Uncle Gaius?"

What does one say, when one is a mere artless provincial on his first night in the capital and one finds oneself thrust suddenly into the presence of the greatest citizen of the realm?

But I manage not to stammer and blurt and lurch. With reasonable smoothness, in fact, I say, "I could never have imagined, when I set out from Britannia to see the fatherland of the Empire, Consul Scaevola, that I would have the honor to encounter the father of the country himself!"

At which he smiles amiably and says, "I think you rank me too highly, my friend. It's the Emperor who's the father of the country, you know. As it says right here." And pulls a shiny new sestertius piece from his purse and holds it up so I can see the inscriptions around the edge, the cryptic string of abbreviated Imperial titles that all the coinage has carried since time immemorial. "You see?" he says, pointing to the letters on the rim of the coin just above the eye-brows of Caesar Maxentius. "P.P., standing for 'Pater Patriae.' There it is. Him, not me. Father of the country." Then, with a wink to take the sting out of his rebuke, such as it had been, he says, "But I appreciate flattery as much as the next man, maybe even a little more. So thank you, young man. Lucilla's not being too much trouble for you, is she, now?"

I'm not sure what he means by that. Perhaps nothing.

"Hardly," I say.

I realize that I'm staring. Scaevola is a gaunt, wiry man of middle height as well, perhaps fifty years old, balding, with his remaining thin strands of hair—red hair, like Lucilla's—pulled taut across his scalp. His cheekbones are pronounced, his nose is sharp, his chin is strong; his eyes are a very pale, icy gray-blue, the blue of a milky-hued sapphire. He looks astonishingly like Julius Caesar, the famous portrait that is on the ten-denarius postage stamp: that same expression of utterly unstoppable determination that arises out of infinite resources of inner power.

He asks me a few questions about my travels and about my homeland, listens with apparent interest to my replies, wishes me well, and efficiently sends me on my way.

My knees are trembling. My throat is dry.

Now I must meet my host the Count, and he is no easy pudding either. Nero Romulus Claudius Palladius is every bit as imposing as I had come to expect, a suave, burnished-looking man of about forty, tall for a Roman and strongly built, with a dense, flawlessly trimmed black beard, skin of a rich deep tone, dark penetrating eyes. He radiates an aura of wealth, power, self-assurance, and—even I am capable of detecting it—an almost irresistible sensuality.

"Cymbelin," he says immediately. "A great name, a romantic name, the name of a king. Welcome to my house, Cymbelin of Britannia." His voice is resonant, a perfectly modulated basso, the voice of an actor, of an opera singer. "We hope to see you here often during your stay in Roma."

Lucilla, by my side, is staring at him in the most worshipful way. Which should trigger my jealousy; but I confess I feel such awe for him myself that I can scarcely object that she is under his spell.

He rests his hand lightly on my shoulder. "Come. You must meet some of my friends." And takes me around the room. Introduces me to the incumbent Consul, Galerius Bassanius, who is younger and more frivolously dressed than I would have thought a Consul would be, and to some actors who seem to expect that I would recognize their names, though I don't and have to dissemble a little, and to a gladiator whose name I do recognize—who wouldn't, considering that he is the celebrated Marcus Sempronius Diodorus, Marcus the Lion-Slayer?—and then to a few flashy young ladies, with whom I make the appropriate flirtatious banter even though Lucilla has more beauty in her left elbow alone than any one of them does in her entire body.

We pass now through an atrium where a juggler is performing and onward to a second room, just as crowded as the first, where the general conversation has an oddly high-pitched tone and people are standing about in strangely stilted postures. After a moment I understand why.

There are royals in here. Everyone is on best court behavior.

Two princes of the blood, no less. Lucilla has me meet them both.

The first is Camillus Caesar, the Prince of Constantinopolis, eldest of the Emperor's four brothers. He is plump, lazy-looking, with oily skin and an idle, slouching way of holding himself. If Gaius Junius Scaevola is a Julius Caesar, this man is a Nero. But for all his soft fleshiness I can make out distinct traces of the familiar taut features that mark the royal family: the sharp, fragile, imperious nose, the heroic chin, above all the chilly eyes, blue as Arctic ice, half hidden though they are behind owlish spectacles. It is as if the stern face of old Emperor Laureolus has somehow become embedded in the meaty bulk of this wastrel grandchild of his.

Camillus is too drunk, even this early in the evening, to say very much to me. He gives me a sloppy wave of his chubby hand and loses interest in me immediately.

Onward we go to the next oldest of the royals, Flavius Rufus Caesar. I am braced to dislike him, aware as I am that he has had the privilege of being Lucilla's lover when she was only sixteen, but in truth he is charming, affable, a very seductive man. About twenty-five, I guess. He too has the family face; but he is lean, agile-looking, quick-eyed, probably quick-witted as well. Since from all I have heard his brother Maxentius is a buffoon and a profligate, it strikes me as a pity that the throne had not descended to Flavius Rufus instead of the other one when their old grandfather finally had shuffled off the scene. But the eldest heir succeeds: it is the ancient rule. With Prince Florus dead three years before his father Laureolus, the throne had gone to Florus's oldest son Maxentius, and the world might be very different today had not that happened. Or perhaps I am overestimating the younger prince. Had Lucilla not told me Maxentius was the best of the lot?

Flavius Rufus—who plainly knows that I am Lucilla's current amusement, and who just as plainly isn't bothered by that—urges me to visit him toward the end of the year at the great Imperial villa at Tibur, a day's journey outside Roma, where he will be celebrating the Saturnalia with a few hundred of his intimate friends.

"Oh, and bring the redhead, too," Flavius Rufus says cheerfully. "You won't forget her, now, will you?"

He blows her a kiss, and gives me a friendly slap on the palm of my hand, and returns to the adulation of his entourage. I am pleased and relieved that our meeting went so well.

Lucilla has saved the best of the family for last, though.

The dearest friend of her childhood, her schoolmate, her honorary kinswoman: the Princess Severina Floriana, sister of the Emperor. Before whom I instantly want to throw myself in utter devotion, she is so overpoweringly beautiful.

As Lucilla had said, Severina Floriana is dark, torrid-looking, exotic. There is no trace of the family features about her—her eyes are glossy black, her nose is a wanton snub, her chin is elegantly rounded—and I know at once that she must not be full sister to the Emperor, that she has to be the child of some subsidiary wife of Maxentius's father: royals may have but one wife at a time, like the rest of us, but it is well known that often they exchange one wife for another, and sometimes take the first one back later on, and who is to say them nay? If Severina's mother looked anything like Severina, I can see why the late Prince Florus was tempted to dally with her.

I was glib enough when speaking with Junius Scaevola and Nero Romulus Claudius Palladius, but I am utterly tongue-tied before Severina Floriana. Lucilla and she do all the talking, and I stand to one side, looming awkwardly in silence like an ox that Lucilla has somehow happened to bring to the party. They chatter of Neapolis's social set, of Adriana, of Druso Tiberio, of a host of people whose names mean nothing to me; they speak of me, too, but what they are talking is the rapid-fire Roman of the capital, so full of slang and unfamiliar pronunciations that I can scarcely understand a thing. Now and again Severina Floriana directs her gaze at me—maybe appraisingly, maybe just out of curiosity at Lucilla's newest acquisition; I can't tell which. I try to signal her with my eyes that I would like a chance to get to know her better, but the situation is so complex and I know I am being reckless—how dare I even *think* of a romance with a royal princess, and how rash, besides, inviting the rage of Lucilla Scaevola by making overtures to her own friend right under her nose—!

In any case I get no acknowledgment from Severina of any of my bold glances.

Lucilla marches me away, eventually. We return to the other room. I am numb.

"I can see that you're fascinated with her," Lucilla tells me. "Isn't that so?"

I make some stammering reply.

"Oh, you can fall in love with her if you like," Lucilla says airily. "I won't mind, silly! Everyone falls in love with her, anyway, so why shouldn't you? She's amazingly gorgeous, I know. I'd take her to bed myself, if that sort of thing interested me a little more."

"Lucilla—I—"

"This is *Roma*, Cymbelin! Stop acting like such a simpleton!"

"I'm here with you. You are the woman I'm here with. I'm absolutely crazy about you."

"Of course you are. And now you're going to be obsessed with Severina Floriana for a while. It's not in the least surprising. Not that you made much of a first impression on her, I suspect, standing there and gawking like that without saying a word, although she doesn't always ask that a man have a mind, if he's got a nice enough body. But I think she's interested. You'll get your chance during Saturnalia, I promise you that." And she gives me a look of such joyous wickedness that I feel my brain reeling at the shamelessness of it all.

Roma! Roma! There is no place on Earth like it.

Silently I vow that one day soon I will hold Severina Floriana in my arms. But it is a vow that I was not destined to be able to keep; and now that she is dead I think of her often, with the greatest sadness, recreating her exotic beauty in my mind and imagining myself caressing her the way I might dream of visiting the palace of the Queen of the Moon.

Lucilla gives me a little push toward the middle of the party and I stagger away on my own, wandering from group to group, pretending to a confidence and a sophistication that at this moment is certainly not mine.

There is Nero Romulus in the corner, quietly talking with Gaius Junius Scaevola. The true monarchs of Roma, they are, the men who hold the real Imperial power. But in what way it is divided between them, I can't even begin to guess.

The Consul, Bassanius, smirking and primping between two male actors who wear heavy makeup. What is he trying to do, reenact the ancient days of Nero and Caligula?

The gladiator, Diodorus, fondling three or four girls at once.

A man I haven't noticed before, sixty or even seventy years old, with a face like a hatchet blade and skin the color of fine walnut, holding court near the fountain. His clothing, his jewelry, his bearing, his flashing eyes, all proclaim him to be a man of substance and power. "Who's that?" I ask a passing young man, and get a look of withering scorn. He tells me, in tones that express his wonder at my ignorance, that that is Leontes Atticus, a name that means nothing to me, so that I have to ask a second question, and my informant lets me know, even more contemptuously, that Leontes Atticus is merely the wealthiest man in the Empire. This fierce-eyed parched-looking Greek, I learn, is a shipping magnate who controls more than half the ocean trade with Nova Roma: he takes his fat percentage on most of the rich cargo that comes to us from the savage and strange New World far across the sea.

And so on and on, new guests arriving all the time, a glowing assembly of the great ones of the capital crowding into the room, everyone who is powerful or wealthy or young, or if possible all three at once.

There is fire smoldering in this room tonight. Soon it will burst forth. But who could have known that then? Not I, not I, certainly not I.

Lucilla spends what seems like an hour conversing with Count Nero Romulus, to my great discomfort. There is an easy intimacy about the way they speak to each other that tells me things I'm not eager to know. What I fear is that he is inviting her to spend the night here with him after the party is over. But I am wrong about that. Ultimately Lucilla returns to my side and doesn't leave it for the rest of the evening.

We dine on fragrant delicacies unknown to me. We drink wines of startling hues and strange piquant flavors. There is dancing; there is a theatrical performance by mimes and jugglers and contortionists; some of the younger guests strip unabashedly naked and splash giddily in the palace pool. I see couples stealing away into the garden, and some who sink into embraces in full view.

"Come," Lucilla says finally. "I'm becoming bored with this. Let's go home and amuse each other in privacy, Cymbelin."

It's nearly dawn by the time we reach her apartments. We make love until midday, and sink then into a deep sleep that holds us in its grip far into the hours of the afternoon, and beyond them, so that it is dark when we arise.

So it goes for me, then, week after week, autumn in Roma, the season of pleasure. Lucilla and I go everywhere together: the

theater, the opera, the gladiatorial contests. We are greeted with
deference at the finest restaurants and shown to the best tables.
She takes me on a tour of the monuments of the capital—the
Senate House, the famous temples, the ancient Imperial tombs. It
is a dizzying time for me, a season beyond my wildest fantasies.

Occasionally I catch a glimpse of Severina Floriana at some
restaurant, or encounter her at a party. Lucilla goes out of her
way to give us a chance to speak to each other, and on a couple
of these occasions Severina and I do have conversations that
seem to be leading somewhere: she is curious about my life in
Britannia, she wants to know my opinion of Roma, she tells me
little gossipy tidbits about people on the other side of the room.

Her dark beauty astounds me. We fair-haired Britons rarely
see women of her sort. She is a creature from another world,
blue highlights in her jet-black hair, eyes like mysterious pools of
night, skin of a rich deep hue utterly unlike that of my people,
not simply the olive tone that so many citizens of the eastern
Roman world have, but something darker, more opulent, with a
satiny sheen and texture. Her voice, too, is enchanting, husky
without a trace of hoarseness, a low, soft, fluting sound, musical
and magnificently controlled.

She knows I desire her. But she playfully keeps our encounters
beyond the zone where any such thing can be communicated,
short of simply blurting it out. Somehow I grow confident, though,
that we will be lovers sooner or later. Which perhaps would have
been the case, had there only been time.

On two occasions I see her brother the Emperor, too.

Once is at the opera, in his box: he is formally attired in the
traditional Imperial costume, the purple toga, and he acknowl-
edges the salute of the audience with a negligent wave and a
smile. Then, a week or two later, he passes through one of the
Palatine Hill parties, in casual modern dress this time, with a
simple purple stripe across his vest to indicate his high status.

At close range I am able to understand why people speak so
slightingly of him. Though he has the Imperial bearing and the
Imperial features, the commanding eyes and the nose and the
chin and all that, there is something about the eager, uncertain
smile of Caesar Maxentius that negates all his Imperial pretensions. He may call himself Caesar, he may call himself Augustus,
and Pater Patriae and Pontifex Maximus and all the rest; but

when you look at him, I discover to my surprise and dismay, he simpers and fails to return your gaze in any steady way. He should never have been given the throne. His brother Flavius Rufus would have been ever so much more regal.

Still, I have met the Emperor, such as he is. It is not every Briton who can say that; and the number of those who can will grow ever fewer from now on.

I send a message home by wire, every once in a while. *Having incredibly good time, could stay here forever but probably won't.* I offer no details. One can hardly say in a telegram that one is living in a little palace a stone's throw from the Emperor's official residence, and sleeping with the niece of Gaius Junius Scaevola, and attending parties with people whose names are known throughout the Empire, and hobnobbing with His Imperial Majesty himself once in a while, to boot.

The year is nearing its end, now. The weather has changed, just as Lucilla said it would: the days are darker and of course shorter, the air is cool, rain is frequent. I haven't brought much of a winter wardrobe with me, and Lucilla's younger brother, a handsome fellow named Aquila, takes me to his tailor to get me outfitted for the new season. The latest Roman fashions seem strange, even uncouth, to me: but what do I know of Roman fashion? I take Aquila's praise of my new clothes at face value, and the tailor's and Lucilla's also, and hope they're not all simply having sport with me.

The invitation that Flavius Rufus Caesar extended to Lucilla and me that first night—to spend the Saturnalia at the Imperial villa at Tibur—was, I discover, a genuine one. By the time December arrives I have forgotten all about it; but Lucilla hasn't, and she tells me, one evening, that we are to leave for Praeneste in the morning. That is a place not far from Roma, where in ancient and medieval times an oracle held forth in the Cave of Destiny until Trajan VII put an end to her privileges. We will stay there for a week or so at the estate of a vastly rich Hispanic merchant named Scipio Lucullo, and then go onward to nearby Tibur for the week of the Saturnalia itself.

Scipio Lucullo's country estate, even in these bleak days of early winter, is grand beyond my comprehension. The marble halls, the pools and fountains, the delicate outer pavilions, the animal chambers where lions and zebras and giraffes are kept, the collections of statuary and paintings and objects of art, the baths, everything is on an Imperial scale. But there is no Imperial heritage here. Lucullo's place was built, someone tells me, only five years ago, out of the profits of his gold mines in Nova Roma, ownership of which he attained by scandalous bribery of court officials during the disastrous final days of the reign of old Caesar Laureolus. His own guests, though they don't disdain his immense hospitality, regard his estate as tawdry and vulgar, I discover.

"I'd be happy to live in such tawdriness," I tell Lucilla. "Is that a terribly provincial thing to say?"

But she only laughs. "Wait until you see Tibur," she says.

And indeed I discover the difference between mere showiness and true magnificence when we move along to the famous Imperial villa just as the Saturnalia week is about to begin.

This is, of course, the place that the great Hadrianus built for his country pleasures seventeen centuries ago. In his own time it was, no doubt, a wonder of the world, with its porticos and fountains and reflecting pools, its baths both great and small, its libraries both Greek and Roman, its nymphaeum and triclinium, its temples to all the gods under whose spell Hadrianus fell as he traveled the length and breadth of the Roman world.

But that was seventeen centuries ago; and seventeen centuries of Emperors have added to this place, so that the original villa of Hadrianus, for all its splendor, is only a mere part of the whole, and the totality must surely be the greatest palace in the world, a residence worthy of Jupiter or Apollo. "You can ride all day and not see the whole thing," Lucilla says to me. "They don't keep it all open at once, of course. We'll be staying in the oldest wing, what they still call Hadrianus's Villa. But all around us you'll see the parts that Trajan VII added, and Flavius Romulus, and the Khitai Pavilions that Lucius Agrippa built for the little yellow-skinned concubine that he brought back from Asia Ultima. And if there's time—oh, but there won't be time, will there—?"

"Why not?" I ask.

She evades my glance. It is my first clue to what is to come.

All day long the great ones of Roma arrive at the Imperial villa for Flavius Rufus's Saturnalia festival. By now I don't need to have their names whispered to me. I recognize Atticus the shipping tycoon, and Count Nero Romulus, and Marco Tullio Garofalo, who is the president of the Bank of the Imperium, and

Diodorus the gladiator, and the Consul Bassanius, and pudgy, petulant Prince Camillus, and dozens more. Carriages are lined up along the highway, waiting to disgorge their glittering passengers.

One who does not arrive is Gaius Junius Scaevola. It's unthinkable that he hasn't been invited; I conclude therefore that my guess about his being named Consul once more for the coming year is correct, and that he has remained in Roma to prepare for taking office. I ask Lucilla if that's indeed why her uncle isn't here, and she says, simply, "The holiday season is always a busy time for him. He wasn't able to get away."

He *is* going to be Consul once again! I'm sure of it.

But I'm wrong. The day after our arrival I glance at the morning newspaper, and there are the names of the Consuls for the coming year. His Imperial Majesty has been pleased to designate Publius Lucius Gallienus and Gaius Acacius Aufidius as Consuls of the Realm. They will be sworn into office at noon on the first of Januarius, weather permitting, on the steps of the Capitol building.

Not Scaevola, then. It must be important business of some other kind, then, that keeps him from leaving Roma in the closing days of the year.

And who are these Consuls, Gallienus and Aufidius? For both, it will be their first term in that highest of governmental offices next to that of the Emperor.

"Boyhood friends of Maxentius," someone tells me, with a dismissive sniff. "Schoolmates of his."

And someone else says, "Not only don't we have a real Emperor any more, we aren't even going to have Consuls now. Just a bunch of lazy children pretending to run the government."

That seems very close to treasonous, to me—especially considering that this very villa is an Imperial palace, and we are all here as guests of the Emperor's brother. But these patricians, I have been noticing, are extraordinarily free in their criticisms of the royal family, even while accepting their hospitality.

Which is abundant. There is feasting and theatricals every night, and during the day we are free to avail ourselves of the extensive facilities of the villa, the heated pools, the baths, the libraries, the gambling pavilions, the riding paths. I float dreamily through it all as though I have stumbled into a fairy-tale world, which is indeed precisely what it is.

At the party the third night I finally find the courage to make a mild approach to Severina Floriana. Lucilla has said that she would like to spend the next day resting, since some of the biggest events of the week still lie ahead; and so I invite Severina Floriana to go riding with me after breakfast tomorrow. Once the two of us are alone, off in some remote corner of the property, perhaps I will dare to suggest some more intimate kind of encounter. Perhaps. What I am attempting to arrange, after all, is a dalliance with the Emperor's sister. Which is such an extraordinary idea that I can scarcely believe I am engaged in such a thing.

She looks amused and, I think, tempted by the suggestion.

But then she tells me that she won't be here tomorrow. Something has come up, she says, something trifling but nevertheless requiring her immediate attention, and she must return briefly to Urbs Roma in the morning.

"You'll be coming back here, won't you?" I ask anxiously.

"Oh, yes, of course. I'll be gone a day or two at most. I'll be here for the big party the final night, you can be sure of that!" She gives me a quick impish glance, as though to promise me some special delight for that evening, by way of consolation for this refusal now. And reaches out to touch my hand a moment. A spark as though of electricity passes from her to me. It is all that ever will; I have never forgotten it.

Lucilla remains in our suite the next day, leaving me to roam the villa's grounds alone. I lounge in the baths, I swim, I inspect the galleries of paintings and sculpture, I drift into the gambling pavilion and lose a few solidi at cards to a couple of languid lordlings.

I notice an odd thing that day. I see none of the people I had previously met at the parties of the Palatine Hill set in Roma. Count Nero Romulus, Leontes Atticus, Prince Flavius Rufus, Prince Camillus, Bassanius, Diodorus—not one of them seems to be around. The place is full of strangers today.

And without Lucilla by my side as I make my increasingly uneasy way among these unknowns, I feel even more of an outsider here than I really am: since I wear no badge proclaiming me to be the guest of Junius Scaevola's niece, I become in her absence merely a barely civilized outlander who has somehow wangled his way into the villa and is trying with only fair success to pretend to be a well-bred Roman. I imagine that they are laughing at me behind my back, mocking my style of dress, imitating my British accent.

Nor is Lucilla much comfort when I return to our rooms. She is distant, abstracted, moody. She asks me only the most perfunctory questions about how I have spent my day, and then sinks back into lethargy and brooding.

"Are you not feeling well?" I ask her.

"It's nothing serious, Cymbelin."

"Have *I* done something to annoy you?"

"Not at all. It's just a passing thing," she says. "These dark winter days—"

But today hasn't been dark at all. Cool, yes, but the sun has been a thing of glory all day, illuminating the December sky with a bright radiance that makes my British heart ache. Nor is it the bad time of month for her; so I am mystified by Lucilla's gloomy remoteness. I can see that no probing of mine will produce a useful answer, though. I'll just have to wait for her mood to change.

At the party that night she is no more ebullient than before. She floats about like a wraith, indifferently greeting people who seem scarcely more familiar to her than they are to me.

"I wonder where everyone is," I say. "Severina told me she had to go back to Roma to take care of something today. But where's Prince Camillus? Count Nero Romulus? Have they gone back to Roma, too? And Prince Flavius Rufus—he doesn't seem to be at his own party."

Lucilla shrugs. "Oh, they must be here and there, somewhere around. Take me back to the room, will you, Cymbelin? I'm not feeling at all partyish, tonight. There's a good fellow. I'm sorry to be spoiling the fun like this."

"Won't you tell me what's wrong, Lucilla?"

"Nothing. *Nothing.* I just feel—I don't know, a little tired. Low-spirited, maybe. Please. I want to go back to the room."

She undresses and gets into bed. Facing that party full of strangers without her is too daunting for me, and so I get into bed beside her. I realize, after a moment, that she's quietly sobbing.

"Hold me, Cymbelin," she murmurs.

I take her into my arms. Her closeness, her nakedness, arouse me as always, and I tentatively begin to make love to her, but she asks me to stop. So we lie there, trying to fall asleep at this strangely early hour, while distant sounds of laughter and music drift toward us through the frosty night air.

The next day things are worse. She doesn't want to leave our suite at all. But she tells me to go out without her: makes it quite clear, in fact, that she wants to be alone.

What a strange Saturnalia week this is turning into! How little jollity there is, how much unexplained tension!

But explanations will be coming, soon enough.

At midday, after a dispiriting stroll through the grounds, I return to the room to see whether Lucilla has taken a turn for the better.

Lucilla is gone.

There's no trace of her. Her closets are empty. She has packed and vanished, without a word to me, without any sort of warning, leaving no message for me, not the slightest clue. I am on my own in the Imperial villa, among strangers.

Things are happening in the capital this day, immense events, a convulsion of the most colossal kind. Of which we who remain at the Imperial villa will remain ignorant all day, though the world has been utterly transformed while we innocently swim and gamble and stroll about the grounds of this most lavish of all Imperial residences.

It had, in fact, begun to happen a couple of days before, when certain of the guests at the villa separately and individually left Tibur and returned to the capital, even though Saturnalia was still going on and the climactic parties had not yet taken place. One by one they had gone back to Roma, not only Severina Floriana but others as well, all those whose absences I had noticed.

What pretexts were used to lure Prince Flavius Rufus, Prince Camillus, and their sister Princess Severina away from the villa may never be known. The two newly appointed Consuls, I was told, had received messages in the Emperor's hand, summoning them to a meeting at which they would be granted certain high privileges and benefits of their new rank. The outgoing Consul, Bassanius, still was carrying a note ostensibly from the Praetorian Prefect, Actinius Varro, when his body was found, telling him that a conspiracy against the Emperor's life had been detected and that his presence in Roma was urgently required. The note was a forgery. So it went, one lie or another serving to pry the

lordlings and princelings of the Empire away from the pleasures
of the Saturnalia at Tibur, just for a single day.

Certain other party guests who returned to Roma, that day
and the next, hadn't needed to be lured. They understood perfectly
well what was about to happen and intended to be present at the
scene during the events. That group included Count Nero Romulus; Atticus, the shipowner; the banker Garofalo; the merchant
from Hispania, Scipio Lucullo; Diodorus the gladiator; and half
a dozen other patricians and men of wealth who were members
of the conspiracy. For them the jaunt to Tibur had been a way
of inducing a mood of complacency at the capital, for what was
there to fear with so many of the most powerful figures of the
realm off at the great pleasure dome for a week of delights? But
then these key figures took care to return quickly and quietly to
Roma when the time to strike had arrived.

On the fatal morning these things occurred, as all the world
would shortly learn:

A squadron of Marcus Sempronius Diodorus's gladiators
broke into the mansion of Praetorian Prefect Varro and slew him
just before sunrise. The Praetorian Guard then was told that the
Emperor had discovered that Varro was plotting against him,
and had replaced him as prefect with Diodorus. This fiction was
readily enough accepted; Varro had never been popular among
his own men and the Praetorians are always willing to accept a
change in leadership, since that usually means a distribution of
bonuses to insure their loyalty to their new commander.

With the Praetorians neutralized, it was an easy matter for
a team of gunmen to penetrate the palace where Emperor Maxentius was staying that night—the Vatican, it was, a palace on
the far side of the river in the vicinity of the Mauseoleum of
Hadrianus—and break into the royal apartments. The Emperor,
his wife, and his children fled in wild panic through the hallways,
but were caught and put to death just outside the Imperial baths.

Prince Camillus, who had reached the capital in the small
hours of the night, had not yet gone to bed when the conspira-
tors reached his palace on the Forum side of the Palatine. Hearing them slaughtering his guards, the poor fat fool fled through
a cellar door and ran for his life toward the Temple of Castor
and Pollux, where he hoped to find sanctuary; but his pursuers
overtook him and cut him down on the steps of the temple.

As for Prince Flavius Rufus, he awakened to the sound of gunfire and reacted instantly, darting behind his palace to a winery that he kept there. His workmen were not yet done crushing the grapes of the autumn harvest. Jumping into a wooden cart, he ordered them to heap great bunches of grapes on top of him and to wheel him out of the city, concealed in that fashion. He actually succeeded in reaching Neapolis safely a couple of days later and proclaimed himself Emperor, but he was captured and killed soon after—with some help, I have heard, from Marcellus Domitianus Frontinus.

Two younger princes of the royal house still survived—Prince Augustus Caesar, who was sixteen and off in Parisi at the university, and Prince Quintus Fabius, a boy of ten, I think, who dwelled at one of the Imperial residences in Roma. Although Prince Augustus did live long enough to proclaim himself Emperor and actually set out across Gallia with the wild intention of marching on Roma, he was seized and shot in the third day of his reign. Those three days, I suppose, put this young and virtually unknown Augustus into history as the last of all the Emperors of Roma.

What happened to young Quintus Fabius, no one knows for sure. He was the only member of the Imperial family whose body never was found. Some say that he was spirited out of Roma on the day of the murders wearing peasant clothes and is still alive in some remote province. But he has never come forth to claim the throne, so if he is still alive to this day, he lives very quietly and secretively, wherever he may be.

All day long the killing went on. The assassination of Emperors was of course nothing new for Roma, but this time the job was done more thoroughly than ever before, an extirpation of root and branch. Royal blood ran in rivers that day. Not only was the immediate family of the Caesars virtually wiped out, but most of the descendants of older Imperial families were executed, too, I suppose so that they wouldn't attempt to put themselves forward as Emperors now that the line of Laureolus was essentially extinct. A good many former Consuls, certain members of the priestly ranks, and others suspected of excessive loyalty to the old regime, including two or three dozen carefully selected Senators, met their deaths that day as well.

And at nightfall the new leaders of Roma gathered at the Capitol to proclaim the birth of the Second Republic. Gaius Junius

Scaevola would hold the newly devised rank of First Consul for Life—that is to say, Emperor, but under another name—and he would govern the vast entity that we could no longer call the Empire through a Council of the Senate, by which he meant his little circle of wealthy and powerful friends, Atticus and Garofalo and Count Nero Romulus and General Cassius Frontinus and half a dozen others of that sort.

Thus, after nineteen hundred years, was the work of the great Augustus Caesar finally undone.

Augustus himself had pretended that Roma was still a Republic, even while gathering all the highest offices into a single bundle and taking possession of that bundle, thus making himself absolute monarch; and that pretense had lasted down through the ages. I am not a king, Augustus had insisted; I am merely the First Citizen of the realm, who humbly strives, under the guidance of the Senate, to serve the needs of the Roman people. And so it went for all those years, though somehow it became possible for many of the First Citizens to name their own sons as their successors, or else to select some kinsman or friend, even while the ostensible power to choose the Emperor was still in the hands of the Senate. But from now on it would be different. No one would be able to claim the supreme power in Roma merely because he was the son or nephew of someone who had held that power. No more crazy Caligulas, no more vile Neros, no more brutish Caracallas, no more absurd Demetriuses, no more weak and foppish Maxentiuses. Our ruler now would truly be a First Citizen—a Consul, as in the ancient days before the first Augustus—and the trappings of the monarchy would at last be abandoned.

All in a single day, a day of blood and fire. While I lounged in Tibur, at the villa of the Emperors, knowing nothing of what was taking place.

On the morning of the day after the revolution, word comes to the villa of what has occurred in Roma. As it happens, I have slept late that day, after having drunk myself into a stupor the night before to comfort myself for the absence of Lucilla; and the villa is virtually deserted by the time I rouse myself and emerge.

That alone is strange and disconcerting. Where has everyone gone? I find a butler, who tells me the news. Roma is in flames, he says, and the Emperor is dead along with all his family.

"*All* his family? His brothers and sisters too?"

"Brothers and sisters too. Everyone."

"The Princess Severina?"

The butler looks at me without sympathy. He is very calm; he might be speaking of the weather, or next week's chariot races. In the autumn warmth he is as chilly as a winter fog.

"The whole lot, is what I hear. Every last one, and good riddance to them. Scaevola's the new Emperor. Things will all be very different now, you can be sure of that."

All this dizzies me. I have to turn away and take seven or eight gasping breaths before I have my equilibrium again. Overnight our world has died and been born anew.

I bathe and dress and eat hurriedly, and arrange somehow for a carriage to take me to Roma. Even in this moment of flux and madness, a purse full of gold will get you what you want. There are no drivers, so I'll have to find my way on my own, but no matter. Insane though it may be to enter the capital on this day of chaos, Roma pulls me like a magnet. Lucilla must be all right, if her uncle has seized the throne; but I have to know the fate of Severina Floriana.

I see flames on the horizon when I am still an hour's ride from the city. Gusts of hot wind from the west bring me the scent of smoke: a fine dust of cinders seems to be falling, or am I imagining it? No. I extend my arm and watch a black coating begin to cover it.

It's supreme folly to go to the capital now.

Should I not turn away, bypass Roma and head for the coast, book passage to Britannia while it's still possible to escape? No. No. I must go there, whatever the risks. If Scaevola is Emperor, Lucilla will protect me. I will continue on to Roma, I decide. And I do.

The place is a madhouse. The sky streams with fire. On the great hills of the mighty, ancient palaces are burning; their charred marble walls topple like falling mountains. The colossal statue of some early Emperor lies strewn in fragments across the road. People run wildly in the streets, screaming, sobbing. Squads of wild-eyed soldiers rush about amongst them, shouting furiously and incoherently as they try to restore order without having any idea of whose orders to obey. I catch sight of a rivulet of crimson in the gutter and think for a terrible moment that it is blood;

but no, no, it is only wine running out of a shattered wineshop, and men are falling on their faces to lap it from the cobblestones.

I abandon my chariot—the streets are too crazy to drive in—and set out on foot. The center of the city is compact enough. But where shall I go? I wonder. To the Palatine? No: everything's on fire up there. The Capitol? Scaevola will be there, I reason, and—how preposterous this sounds to me now—he can tell me where Lucilla is, and what has become of Severina Floriana.

Of course I get nowhere near the Capitol. The entire governmental district is sealed off by troops. Edicts are posted in the streets, and I pause to read one, and it is then I discover the full extent of the alteration that this night has worked: that the Empire is no more, the Republic of the ancient days has returned. Scaevola now rules, but has the title not of Emperor but of First Consul.

As I stand gaping and dazed in the street that runs past the Forum, I am nearly run down by a speeding chariot. I yell a curse at its driver; but then, to my great amazement, the chariot stops and a familiar ruddy face peers out at me.

"Cymbelin! Good gods, is that you? Get in, man! You can't stand around out there!"

It's my robust and jolly host from Neapolis, my father's friend, Marcellus Domitianus Frontinus. What bad luck for him, I think, that he's come visiting up here in Roma at a time like this. But I have it all wrong, as usual, and Marcellus Domitianus very quickly spells everything out for me.

He has been in on the plot from the beginning—he and his brother the general, along with Junius Scaevola and Count Nero Romulus, were in fact the ringleaders. It was necessary, they felt, to destroy the Empire in order to save it. The current Emperor was an idle fool, the previous one had been allowed to stay on the throne too long, the whole idea of a quasi-hereditary monarchy had been proved to be a disaster over and over again for centuries, and now was the time to get rid of it once and for all. There was new restlessness in all the provinces and renewed talk of secession. Having just fought and won a Second War of Reunification, General Cassius Frontinus had no desire to launch immediately into a third one, and he had without much difficulty convinced his brother and Scaevola that the Caesars must go. Must in fact be put where they would never have the opportunity of reclaiming the throne.

Ruthless and bloody, yes. But better to scrap the incompetent and profligate royal family, better to toss out the empty, costly pomp of Imperial grandeur, better to bring back, at long last, the Republic. Once again there would be government by merit rather than by reason of birth. Scaevola was respected everywhere; he would know the right things to do to hold things together.

"But to *kill* them—to murder a whole family—!"

"A clean sweep, that's what we needed," Frontinus tells me. "A total break with the past. We can't have hereditary monarchs in this modern age."

"All the princes and princesses are dead too, then?"

"So I hear. One or two may actually have gotten away, but they'll be caught soon enough, you can be sure of that."

"The Princess Severina Floriana?"

"Can't say," Frontinus replies. "Why? Did you know her?"

Color floods to my cheeks. "Not very well, actually. But I couldn't help wondering—"

"Lucilla will be able to tell you what happened to her. She and the princess were very close friends. You can ask her yourself."

"I don't know where Lucilla is. We were at Tibur together this week, at the Imperial villa, and then—when everything started happening—"

"Why, you'll be seeing Lucilla five minutes from now! She's at the palace of Count Nero Romulus—you know who he is, don't you?—and that's exactly where we're heading."

I point toward the Palatine, shrouded in flames and black gusts of smoke behind us.

"Up there?"

Frontinus laughs. "Don't be silly. Everything's destroyed on the Palatine. I mean his palace by the river." We are already past the Forum area. I can see the somber bulk of Hadrianus's Mausoleum ahead of us, across the river. We halt just on this side of the bridge. "Here we are," says Frontinus.

I get to see her one last time, then, once we have made our way through the lunatic frenzy of the streets to the security of Nero Romulus's well-guarded riverfront palace. I hardly recognize her. Lucilla wears no makeup and her clothing is stark and simple—peasant clothing. Her eyes are somber and red-rimmed. Many of her patrician friends have died this night for the sake of the rebirth of Roma.

"So now you know," she says to me. "Of course I couldn't tell you a thing about what was being planned."

It is hard for me to believe that this woman and I were lovers for months, that I am intimately familiar with every inch of her body. Her voice is cool and impersonal, and she has neither kissed me nor smiled at me.

"You knew—all along—what was going to happen?"

"Of course. From the start. At least I got you out of town to a safe place while it was going on."

"You got Severina to a safe place, too. But you couldn't keep her there, it seems."

Her eyes flare with rage, but I see the pain there, too.

"I tried to save her. It wasn't possible. They all had to die, Cymbelin."

"Your own childhood friend. And you didn't even try to warn her."

"We're *Romans*, Cymbelin. It had become necessary to restore the Republic. The royal family had to die."

"Even the women?"

"All of them. Don't you think I asked? Begged? No, said Nero Romulus. She's got to die with them. There's no choice, he said. I went to my uncle. You don't know how I fought with him. But nobody can sway his will, nobody at all. No, he said. There's no way to save her." Lucilla makes a quick harsh motion with her hand. "I don't want to talk about this anymore. Go away, Cymbelin. I don't even understand why Marcello brought you here."

"I was wandering around in the street, not knowing where to go to find you."

"Me? Why would you want to find me?"

It's like a blow in the ribs. "Because—because—" I falter and fall still.

"You were a very amusing companion," she says. "But the time for amusements is over."

"Amusements!"

Her face is like stone. "Go, Cymbelin. Get yourself back to Britannia, as soon as you can. The bloodshed isn't finished here. The First Consul doesn't yet know who's loyal and who isn't."

"Another Reign of Terror, then?"

"We hope not. But it won't be pretty, all the same. Still, the

First Consul wants the Second Republic to get off to the most peaceful possible—"

"The First Consul," I say, with anger in my voice. "The Second Republic."

"You don't like those words?"

"To kill the Emperor—"

"It's happened before, more times than you can count. This time we've killed the whole system. And will replace it at long last with something cleaner and healthier."

"Maybe so."

"Go, Cymbelin. We are very busy now."

And she turns away and leaves the room, as though I am nothing to her, only an inquisitive and annoying stranger. It is all too clear to me now that she had regarded me all along as a mere casual plaything, an amusing barbarian to keep by her side during the autumn season; and now it is winter and she must devote herself to more serious things.

And so I went. The last Emperor had perished and the Republic had come again, and I had slept amidst the luxurious comforts of the Imperial villa while it all was happening. But it has always been that way, hasn't it? While most of us sleep, an agile few create history in the night.

Now all was made new and strange. The world I had known had been entirely transformed in ways that might not be fully apparent for years—the events of these recent hours would be a matter for historians to examine and debate and assess, long after I had grown old and died—nor would the chaos at the center of the Empire end in a single day, and provincial boys like me were well advised to take themselves back where they belonged.

I no longer had any place here in Roma, anyway. Lucilla was lost to me—she will marry Count Nero Romulus to seal his alliance with her uncle—and whatever dizzying fantasies I might have entertained concerning the Princess Severina Floriana were best forgotten now, or the ache would never leave my soul. All that was done and behind me. The holiday was over. There would be no further tourism for me this year, no ventures into Etruria and Venetia and the other northern regions of Italia. I knew I must leave Roma to the Romans and beat a retreat back to my distant rainy island in the west, having come all too close to the flames that had consumed the Roma of the Emperors, having in fact been somewhat singed by them myself.

Except for the help that Frontinus provided, I suppose I might have had a hard time of it. But he gave me a safe-conduct pass to get me out of the capital, and lent me a chariot and a charioteer; and on the morning of the second day of the Second Republic I found myself on the Via Appia once more, heading south. Ahead of me lay the Via Roma and Neapolis and a ship to take me home.

I looked back only once. Behind me the sky was smudged with black clouds as the fires on the Palatine Hill burned themselves out.

71

DAVID BRIN

The late Eric Flint's Ring of Fire series, in which a modern West Virginia town has been catapulted back through time to seventeenth-century Europe, has been entertaining readers for over two decades, and other writers have gotten in on the fun. Best-selling writer David Brin provides an example of how exposure to twentieth-century fiction might influence a writer known for very different works in his original timeline.

◇◇◇◇◇

As deeply roiled and troubled as we all have been, ever since the Ring of Fire brought disruption to our time, sending all fixed notions a-tumble, how seldom have we pondered the greater picture—the "context" of it all, as up-timers so concisely put it?

I refer to the event itself, the very act of carving a town out of twentieth-century America and dropping it into the Germanies, three hundred and sixty-nine years earlier. Engrossed as we have been, in the consequential aftermath, we have tended to wave away the act itself! We beg the question, calling it simply an Act of God.

Indeed, as a Lutheran layman, I am inclined to accept that basic explanation. The event's sheer magnitude can only have had divine originating power. Take that as given.

As to the purpose of it all? That, too, remains opaque. And yet, one aspect by now seems clear to most down-timers. By winning an unbroken chain of successive victories, the Americans and their allies have at minimum forced a burden of proof upon those potentates who condemn up-timers as satanic beings. To many deeply religious folk, there is a rising sense of vindication, even blessing about them.

A consensus is growing that "America" was not named for

some Italian map-maker, *after all, but rather for "himmel-reich,"
or heavenly country. Or so goes the well-beloved rumor, nowadays,
spread especially by the Committees of Correspondence.*

*And yet, be that as it may, "the Will of God" leaves so many
other matters darkly unexamined, even by speculation! Indeed,
these appear to be ignored by the Grantvillers themselves.*

*Among those neglected questions, one has burned—especially
harsh and bright—in the mind of this humble observer.*

What happened to the village of Milda, *nestled in a bend
of the small river Leutra in Thuringia, when it was* erased from
our time and reckoning *by the Ring of Fire, replaced by fabulous
Grantville?*

*To many, the answer would seem obvious—that it was a
simple trade.*

A swap!

*And hence, the bemused neighbors of Grantville—West Virgin-
ians of the United States of America, in the year 2000—received, in
exchange for their departed metropolis, a few bewildered, terrified
seventeenth-century Germans, hopelessly archaic and primitive,
of no practical use at all, except as recipients of kindness and
largesse until—amid the welcoming spirit of that blissful nation,
they would merge, adapt and transform into boring-but-content
citizens. Of little import, other than as curiosities.*

A trade? A swap? Oh, perhaps it was so.

*Only, dear reader, let me endeavor to persuade you that—in the
immortal words of the up-time bard and balladeer Ira Gershwin—it
ain't necessarily so.*

Kurt, Baron von Wolfschild, stared down upon a long column
of refugees.

For that, clearly, they were, hundreds of them, shambling
with meager possessions balanced atop heads or strapped upon
backs. And, alongside the road, for as far as he could see with
his foggy spyglass, many articles the migrants had abandoned,
so that children might ride shoulders, instead. Those scattered
discards were punctuated by an occasional old man or woman,
shrilly insistent to be left behind, so that a family might live.

Such telltales were all too familiar to a knight whose own
demesne suffered this very same fate, not so long ago.

People... my tenants, villagers and farmers... who counted on

*my brothers and me to protect them. Cut down like wheat, or else
scattered to the wind.*

These fugitives were a grimy lot, as clouds of dust hovered in
both winding directions along the bone-dry road. *In a bone-dry
land,* he pondered, rising on his stirrups to scan every unfamiliar
horizon. This hilly countryside wasn't exactly a desert—Kurt had
seen the real thing, guarding a Genoese diplomatic mission to
Egypt, almost a decade ago. Here, trees and shrubs dotted every
slope. Indeed, some distance below, through a southern haze, he
could make out green and fertile fields. *At least, I think that's
south.* And far beyond, the shoreline of some lake or small sea.

Still, the scouts had not been drunk or lying. This was clearly
not the green-forested dampness of central Germany. Nor were
these Germans, shambling below on open-toed sandals. Both
women and men wore robelike garments and cloth headdresses,
scarves, or turbans—it was rare to spot exposed hair, except
among the weary-looking children.

Now, some of the more alert refugees appeared to take notice,
pointing uphill toward Kurt and his men—twenty *Landsknecht*
cavalry in battered helmets and cuirasses, with two dozen pikemen and ten arquebusiers marching up from behind. Murmurs
of worry arose from the dusty migrants.

Not that Kurt could blame them. His own company of mercenary guardsmen had a pretty clean record, protecting merchants
through the hellscape that recently stretched from Alps to Baltic.
But no civilian who still had any grip upon reality would be
placid at the sight of armed and armored men.

"What's that language they're gabbling?" complained the young
adventurer, Samuel Burns, from his oversized charger to Kurt's left.

The Hollander sergeant, Lucas Kuipers, shrugged broad shoulders, looking to his commander for orders.

Kurt listened carefully for a moment. "It . . . sounds a bit
like Hebrew . . . or Arabic . . . and neither. Perhaps something in
between. I can't speak either of them well enough to tell. You'd
better send a rider back to fetch Father Braun."

"Hebrew? So many Jews?" Burns shook his head.

"Braun won't want to come," Sergeant Kuipers said. "The villagers are terrified, since we all passed through the Mouth of Hell."

A good name for it, Kurt thought. Just over an hour ago, it
had seemed that Milda and its surroundings were, indeed, being

swallowed by some fiery gullet, amid a shaking, noise and painful brilliance that just had to be infernal.

"They think that it's the end time," Kuipers went on, in thickly accented Low German. "Especially after hearing what happened to Magdeburg. Half of the peasants seem bent on setting fire to their hovels, then throwing themselves on the flames."

Kurt shrugged. It was all right for the sergeant to raise a point. But a commander's silence should speak for itself. And so, with hardly a pause, Kuipers turned in his saddle to shout for a courier. *Two*, since one horse would be needed to bring the priest, if the Jesuit was wanted in such a hurry.

"*Gut.*" Kurt nodded. A sergeant who thinks is worth his weight in coppers. Maybe even silver.

Watching the riders depart, he only half listened as Kuipers began shouting at the infantry, arraying them in some kind of presentable order. Of course, the pikemen and arquebusiers weren't part of Kurt's *landsknecht* company, which had only been passing through Milda, escorting a small commercial caravan, when the calamity struck. These footmen were a motley assortment of local militia and grizzled veterans, augmented by deserters—from both Tilly's Catholic army and Protestant Magdeburgers—fleeing the atrocities to Milda's north. That siege, according to breathless reports, had come to an end as forces of the Austrian emperor and the Roman Church performed a feat of butchery surpassing the massacre of Cathars at Beziers in 1209. Perhaps even matching horror stories from the Crusades.

Hell's mouth, indeed. What more do we deserve, for allowing such things to happen, and murderers to enrich themselves?

The new infantry recruits seemed grateful to have found employment with Kurt's company, not the richest guard unit, by any means, but one that seemed at least free of taint from this latest soul-killing crime. Moreover, Kurt, Baron von Wolfschild had forbidden any man to ask religious questions of any other. There would be none of that.

Kurt watched the couriers gallop across a broad pasture, then ascend a rough, recently blazed trail over a shrubby hill, disappearing beyond the crest to where...

The terrain beyond that point was stark in Kurt's mind, if just out of sight. There, a new, shiny-smooth ridgeline jutted a few feet above the natural topography. A perfect circle, it seemed, a couple of imperial miles across, centered half a mile west of little Milda. Within, the pines and birches of Thuringia still trembled from recent disruption, in stark contrast to these slopes of cedar, cypress and scrub oak.

Now that I think on it. This does resemble the Levant…

From here, he could see the true extant of Milda's *plug*, taken fiercely out of Germany. A large hill or small mountain loomed on the other side. There, the circle's shiny-sheer boundary loomed *above* the plug, and even seemed to arc a little over one of Milda's hamlets, surrounding the local mill.

We'll have to survey water sources, not only for drinking but to reestablish the pond and millrace, he pondered, then shook his head over the strangeness of such thoughts. Clearly, he was keeping a shocked mind busy with pragmatic fantasies, rather than grappling with what's obvious…

…for example, that the refugees below could only be another group of damned beings, like the hapless Germans who had come to join them, through Hell's Mouth. This outer circle did not much resemble the description in Dante's *Inferno*. But then, Kurt's Latin had been rudimentary when he read it.

At a cry, he turned his head to see young Samuel pointing south, not at the refugees but upslope-east a way, where clusters of figures—several score, at least—were descending rapidly from a rocky passage, perhaps a narrow pass through the hills. An ideal lair for bandits, he realized.

Metal flashed in the sun. A woman screamed. Then another. And then several terrified men.

My heart. Should it be racing like this, if I am already dead? How could a corpse or damned soul feel this familiar mixture—of fear, loathing and exhilaration—that sweeps over me, before combat?

Hell or not, this situation offered a clear enough choice. Pure evil was afoot, and Kurt, Baron von Wolfschild had means at his disposal to deal with it. Indeed, he reckoned it unlikely that there was anything better to do.

"Sergeant. Please get the infantry moving. Cavalry on me.

"Then have the bugler announce us."

#

"Wow," John Dennis Flannery said as he turned a page, and noted the hash or pound symbol "#" denoting a minor scene break, at exactly the right moment in this story. His left-hand prosthetic slipped and the sheet went floating off his desk...to be caught by the author, who gently placed it atop the pile, face down.

"Wow," John repeated. "It's even better on second reading. The rhythms, the beat and tempo of prose. They're...very modern."

"Modern, truly? Like fictions of the twentieth century? I am so glad. I tried to break so many down-time habits of what you call 'flowery prose,' concentrating instead upon the main character's *point of view*."

"Right. The hardest thing for a novice to grok, even back in America. Point of view. Show us the world, the situation, through your protagonist's thoughts and senses. And especially through his *assumptions*. Things he takes for granted. Heinlein was the master of that technique."

"Yes, I studied and copied many of his story openings, until the method became clear to me."

"Only next you segue..." John used his right-hand claw to shift five more pages to the other pile... "into a seriously cool *battle scene*, during which the baron character coordinates his *landsknecht* cavalry and the Milda militia to defeat bandits bent on rape and murder. Thereby winning devotion from a few of the most important refugees. Of course anyone will recognize your inspiration."

"Of course. From the way Michael Stearns rallied his West Virginian mine workers to defeat a horde of Tilly's raiders, thus earning the admiration of his future wife. Do...do you think the *homage* is too blatant?"

"Who cares!" John shrugged. "It's seriously good action!"

"I am so relieved that you think so. I know that I can still be prolix and garrulous. For example in my prologue—"

"Oh, don't worry about that." John waved away the author's concern. "Prologues are supposed to be like that. Heck, it will help prove that the creator was an authentic down-timer, and not Jason Glazer or me, ghost-writing it.

"Still, what I want to know is *how* you picked up these techniques for point of view and action so quickly. How did you learn it all so fast?"

John's left hook clanked against his spectacles as he pushed them back a bit. They kept sliding down his nose and he wanted to see this fellow, who could be everything he and his partners were looking for.

Don't get your hopes up too high.

"The boardinghouse here in Grantville where I am staying... the landlord has a complete collection of *Analog* magazines, which he guards like a wolfhound! But I talked him into letting me read selected stories. Eventually, he warmed to me and began enthusiastically choosing—even explaining—the best ones for me."

"Old Homer Snider, yeah. He makes me wear gloves when I come over to copy a story for the zine. He must really like you."

The author wasn't wearing clerical garb, today. Just a downtime shirt and trousers, modeled on up-time jeans and a pullover.

"I believe he sees me as a...convert."

"To science fiction?" John laughed. "Yeah. I guess there's always been an aspect of proselytizing religion to—"

He cut off abruptly with a sharp hiss, as pain lanced up his arms from the stumps at both ends. Vision blurred for a few seconds, till he found his visitor leaning over him.

"Mein herr...Mr. Flannery. Shall I go for a doctor?"

John shook his head. "No, just...give me a second. It always passes."

The author returned to his seat and pretended to be busy with papers from a leather valise, till John finally shifted in his chair with a sigh.

"You can see why we're subsidized by the state, and by the USE Veterans' Foundation. A man who loses his legs can still do skilled tasks like machinery assembly. But a man without hands?" He lifted both arms, letting the question hang.

"Intellectual pursuits, of course." The visitor had a choked tightness in his throat.

"It's busy work."

"I beg to differ, Herr Flannery! What you are accomplishing, with your zine, is so much more than giving war amputees something to do!"

He gestured past John's office, piled high with manuscripts and proofs, toward the main workroom, where a dozen men and several women bustled about the tasks of a publishing house, one of just a few that had not moved from Grantville to the modern, bustling, capital city of Magdeburg. All but two of the staff bore major disabilities, yet hurried busily to meet deadlines.

"Well, my own disaster wasn't from battle, but a freak industrial..."

"Perhaps, as an up-timer, you underestimate the powerful effects that this literature is having, across Europe and beyond. Except in countries where it has been banned, for the insidious, underlying assumption of science fiction, that *change* is a permanent fact of life! And that any child, of no matter what mean background, can become an agent of change. No, Herr Flannery. You are still potent. Your 'hands' now guide minds upward, gently pushing them to ponder how things might be different than they are!"

"Well, that can be dangerous in these times. There are many out there, in both low and high places, who consider science fiction to be heretical, blasphemous, and radically revolutionary."

"Making you popular with the Committees of Correspondence, of course."

John shrugged. "A connection we don't publicly encourage. We get more than enough death threats. And, only last month, a crude pipe bomb. Fortunately, we discovered it in time. Still, I try to open all the packages myself since, as you can see, I have little left to lose."

He lifted both prosthetics into the light.

"Ah, but we shall soon put a stop to that!" commented a youthful voice from behind John. He turned to see Hercule Savinien casting a lanky shadow through the doorway. The sixteen-year-old editorial apprentice had survived Charles de La Porte's futile infantry advance at the Battle of Ahrensbök, with only a severe limp, thanks to twentieth-century field medicine. He now flourished a *poignard* dagger of considerable heft.

"An elegant blade like this may be obsolete for matters of honor," the young man said, in thickly accented English. "But it still can suffice as a letter-opener!"

John frowned, pretending more anger than he felt.

"Hercule, go stick that prodigious proboscis of yours into someone else's business. Unless you have some good reason to be bothering us?"

The boy's eyes flashed briefly with a mix of warning and fierce intelligence... but that heat swiftly lapsed into a tolerant grin.

"Jason and Jean-Baptiste have galleys for the next issue ready, when *monsieur l'editeur* will deign to look them over."

"Hm. And I assume *you* already have?"

"But of course." A gallic shrug. "The usual mix of TwenCen reprints and hack melodramas from my fellow primitives of this benighted era, who could not emulate Delaney or Verne, if their very lives depended on a *soupcon* of creative verve. If *you* had any *real* taste, you might look closer to home. Possibly in-house, for—"

"Your time will come. That is, if you drop some of your own preening pretentiousness. If you focus. Learn patience and craft, as the deacon here has done." John gestured toward his guest. "Now get out!"

Hercule Savinien's grin only widened as he delivered a flourished bow that would have served in any royal court—though conveying a shameless touch of wry sarcasm—and departed. John stared after the apprentice for an instant, then shook his head. Turning back to the visitor, he carefully used the artificial gripper of his right-hand prosthetic to shift, then pluck up the next page of the manuscript, having to clear his throat, before he spoke.

"Now, where were we? Ah, yes. What is...what's so cool about this story of yours—unlike so much of the 'sci-fi' we get submitted here—is that you've taken a speculative premise based upon our own shocking and strangely transformed world, *extrapolating* it into a plausible thought experiment of your very own.

"This notion, for example, that the Ring of Fire wasn't a simple *swap* of two land-plugs, one of them shifting *backward* to become powerful and destiny-changing, while the other one, shifted forward to the year 2000, would be inherently harmless, pathetically unimportant...I never realized how *smug* that image was. How self-important and based on unwarranted assumptions.

"In other words, how very *American!*" John laughed ruefully. "But you point out that it may not have been a swap, at all! It could instead be a *chain*. A sequence, shuttling a series of spheres of space-time ever-backward, one following the other, like—"

He shook his head, unable to come up with a metaphor. The visitor nodded, though with some reticence.

"At the Grantville high school, I never fail to attend Demonstration Tuesday. They once showed us a *laser*, whose magical medium is capped, at both ends, by inward facing mirrors. At the time, I was struck that perhaps the Ring of Fire was like such a device, only with *destiny* as the active medium..."

"Whoa. What a way-cool idea!" John reached for his pencil with the special grip-end.

"Only then, later the same night, it came to me in a dream... a dream that was so much more than..."

The author paused, staring into space, then shook himself in order to resume. "Well, it came to me that perhaps there might be mirror *after* mirror, after mirror...."

His voice trailed off again, as John scribbled.

"Huh. Of course the implicit paradoxes abound. We've assumed that either Grantville's arrival *changed* the former timeline, erasing and replacing the one we came from, or else it started a new, *branching* timestream that leaves the original one in place. The new one that received Grantville will gain advantages and get many boosts and head starts as a result, but also some losses. Either way, Grantville is making a huge difference.

"In contrast, Milda Village would have very little impact, arriving in the year 2000—at most a few hundred confused villagers and traders, farmers and soldiers with antique weapons and antiquated technologies...

"On the other hand, if Milda instead bounced *further back* in time, say another thousand years—"

"More like fifteen centuries."

"Yeah, in your story, more than fifteen hundred years...then it implies branching after branching of *multiple* timelines! Each one offering a technological boost to more-primitive ancestors... no offense?"

"None taken, Herr Flannery."

"In fact, why stop there? If you squint, you can envision *another* story about—"

John felt a tingle in his spine. A sense, soft but familiar, that he had just missed something important. He lifted his head from the notepad sketch that he had begun, depicting a trellis of possible histories. Now he looked, yet again at the author.

At his very distant facial expression.

John played back the conversation a bit. Then he twisted his hand-hook to put the pencil down.

"Tell me about your dream," he said.

Kurt had been pleased, day before yesterday, to find a market fair in this part of Thuringia. His troopers murmured happily as the small *landsknecht* company rode into Milda, escorting three cargo wagons and two carriages of merchant dignitaries. Perhaps, this close to Jena, the locals felt some normality, especially with a university town between them and the fighting.

It was a small fair—three or four tents where locals compared garden produce and bragged over samples of their winter piecework, while tapping barrels of home brew and betting on wrestling matches—plus a "theater" consisting of a painted backdrop behind a rickety stage, for pantomimes and palmers, preaching repentance while lacing songs and bawdy jokes amid stern morality plays.

The illusion was brave, but threadbare, and it lasted only till a breathless rider came racing through, panting news of Magdeburg.

At least thirty thousand dead and the whole city burned to the ground, with detachments of Tilly's killers now spreading even this way.

Half of the merchants wanted to turn around. The rest urged hurrying on to Jena. Their argument had raged on for hours, while a troupe of dispirited jugglers tried to herd everyone back to the little fairground for the midday highlight—a march of the local militia, with burnished pikes and laughably archaic matchlock muskets. Kurt's frantic employers made the local inn so depressing that his *Landsknechte* took their beers outside, perching on a fence to heckle as pot-bellied volunteers high stepped, trying to look martially impressive in review.

Well there's no laughing at them anymore, he now thought, watching by firelight as two of the farmer-soldiers got stitched by a pair of midwives. Beyond the circle of light, barely in view, were two more forms, shrouded and still—a tanner's apprentice and the miller's youngest son—who had been less lucky during the brief, nasty battle.

It's my fault, of course, he thought. *If only I'd ordered my cavalry to use their pistols sooner. But who knew so many bandits would be terrified by a little gunfire?*

At least none of his *Landsknechte* had been killed or injured. They now mingled freely with the militia men, who had fought a pitched battle with unexpected bravery. Still, the mercenary guardsmen were in a foul mood. The robbers had nothing of value to pillage, beyond short swords of questionable value, and most of the refugees had scattered in all directions, leaving only a couple of dozen to be collared and prodded uphill, past the Hell Mouth ring, all the way back to Milda, for questioning by Father Braun.

And our special guests, he added, peering past the coals at a cluster of people seated along the edge of the pantomime stage, where all the assembled Germans could see them. Two middle-aged men, three women and four children—all of them apparently of the same family—dressed better than the average refugee...plus an elderly fellow with gnarled hands and piercing eyes, to whom everyone deferred, as if he were an abbot or bishop.

Hours ago, during the bandit attack, both of the younger men and one woman had tried valiantly to rally other émigrés and prepare a defense—*it would have been futile, of course,* but at least they tried—when the robbers' attention had been drawn away by a phalanx of approaching Milda pikemen.

The foe never saw Kurt's cavalry till it was too late.

Unlike the involuntary ones, who huddled under the half-tent behind them, this family had required no urging to ascend toward Milda, eagerly and gratefully following the pikemen while helping the wounded. Without displaying any dread, they had crossed the Hell Mouth boundary, staring at the transplanted disk of Germany as afternoon waned and Kurt rode about swiftly, inspecting the perimeter, setting things in order for nightfall.

Now, the family sat, cross-legged but erect, apparently more curious than fearful. When offered food, they spurned all meats and sniffed at the boiled potatoes, till the youngest woman smiled—an expression like sunlight—then nodded gratefully and placed a bowl before the old man, who murmured a few words of blessing, then began to eat with slow care. Gently urging the frightened ones, she got first children and then other adults to join in.

A noblewoman of some kind, Kurt realized. Or at least a natural leader, as well as something of a beauty...if you ignored a deep scar that ran from her left ear down to the line of her jaw. At one point, her gaze briefly locked with Kurt's—as it had after the battle—measuring, as if *she* were the one here with real power. Then she went back to watching intently—whispering now and then into the old fellow's ear—as Father Braun reported, at tedious length, what he had learned.

"...and so, after this extensive philological comparison, I finally concluded that they speak *Aramaic,* a tongue quite similar to Hebrew, and hence confirming that most of the denizens of this region appear to be *Jews,* plus some Samaritans, Syrians..."

The rest of the cleric's recitation was drowned out by a mutter of consternation from those seated on makeshift benches and crowding in from all sides—a motley assortment of Milda residents, travelers, soldiers, teamsters, palmers, and shabby entertainers, almost all of those who were trapped here when the Hell Mouth snapped around Milda. Far too many to congregate within the small village inn.

Kurt frowned at the reaction. Not all of the murmurs were actively hateful. He figured most were only shocked to learn that a despised minority now apparently surrounded them, in great numbers. And at least some of these Jews were armed.

During his travels, Kurt had learned how most prejudices were as useful as a hymnal in a privy. *Anyway, we don't have time for this.* He stepped into the light, clearing his throat. Those nearby swiftly took the hint—from a nobleman and commander of their little army—to settle down. Certainly, the village headman and masters, seated on a front row bench, seemed happy to defer.

"What about our other guests?" Kurt pointed to a trio of grimy men who were clearly soldiers, staring fixedly at the coals, with bound wrists. Though clean-shaven—unlike most of the local males—they appeared to be in shock. As Kurt had felt earlier, when he inspected their confiscated weapons . . . short, *gladius*-style swords and skirted leather armor, of a type that looked so familiar.

"I was unable to gather much from those three," Braun said. "They were found wandering just outside the Hell Mouth, having apparently taken the brunt of it, near what seems to have been the outermost wall of some fortification."

Kurt had examined the wall in question, just before nightfall. Most of the stronghold must have been sliced away by the Hell Mouth, vanishing completely when Milda's plug of Thuringia displaced whatever had been here, before.

I wonder where that plug of land wound up, with its garrison of armed men. Perhaps they are now back where we came from?

If so, they would stand little chance against Tilly's raiders. From what he could tell, these locals had never heard of gunpowder.

"Well, never mind them. What else did you learn from the refugees?"

Braun nodded. "My smattering of Hebrew might not have sufficed. Certainly I doubted the testimony of my ears . . . until this young woman made my task much easier by speaking to me, at last, in rather good Latin."

The beauty with the scar. Kurt stepped forward and switched from German.

"*Est quod verum? Tu loqueris?* You speak Latin? Why did you not say so before?"

She whispered in the old man's ear. He nodded permission, and she met Kurt's gaze with confident serenity.

"*Et non petisti,*" she replied to his question. *You did not ask.*

Kurt's initial flare at her impertinence quickly tempered. Courage was acceptable coin, and he liked women who made eye-contact. So he nodded, with the faintest upturn at one corner of his mouth...then turned and motioned for the priest to continue.

Braun sighed, as if he dreaded coming to this part.

"With her help, I questioned every person about the *name* of this region, into which we find ourselves plunged. They all replied with great assurance and consistency."

"It's hell!" screamed one high-pitched voice, possibly a hysterical man.

The Jesuit shook his head.

"Nay, it is Judea."

Kurt nodded. He had already suspected as much, from the terrain, foliage, and much else. Around him, Catholics told their rosaries while other voices spoke in hushed tones of the Holy Land.

"Then it's *worse* than hell," cried the same pessimist. "Tomorrow we'll face a thousand Turks!"

Father Braun raised a hand.

"That might have been true, had a mere shift in *location* been the only aspect of what happened to us, today. Only there is more, far more shocking than that.

"It appears, my dear children, that—by some great wonder achievable only by divine will—we have also been transported through *time.*"

This brought on silence so deep that only the crackling logs spoke. Indeed, it seemed that most of the villagers and travelers and soldiers merely blinked, assuming that the priest had shifted to some non-Germanic tongue.

Kurt stepped closer to the firelight. *Someone* had to look and sound confident at this point, though his own calm was more a matter of numbness than *noblesse.* Anyway, he already had guessed the answer to his next question.

"What is the date then, Father?"

"Ahem. Well. There are discrepancies of calendar to take into account. It's difficult to narrow down precisely. That is…"

"Priest—" Kurt gave him the full-on baron-look.

The Jesuit threw his shoulders back, as if defying fate even to utter it aloud. In so doing, he revealed a build that must have once—in a former life—been that of a soldier.

"The date is seventy, or seventy-one, or two or three, or perhaps seventy-four years… after the birth of our lord. We stand above the valley where he dwelled as a child, within sight of the sea where he preached and fished for souls."

Kurt nodded, accepting the finality of a diagnosis, already known.

"And the poor people who we see, shambling along these roads in despair? What calamity do they flee?"

He was envisioning Magdeburg, only much, much worse.

Father Braun met his eyes.

"It is as you suppose, Baron von Wolfschild. They are escaping the wrath of the Roman emperor-to-be, Titus, who has, of late, burned the holy Temple itself. And the city of Jerusalem."

Jason was having none of it.

"Come on, Johnny. It's a great story! The fellow clearly studied Piper and de Camp, in all those *Analog* zines he read. He's a natural. Anyway, weren't we looking hard for some down-timers with talent?"

Before John could answer, Sister Maria Celeste emitted a curt cough. She had been adjusting the pads on Jason's wheelchair, which kept bunching up, he fidgeted so.

"And what am I, *signore*? Chopped kidney? I have submitted to you several fine *fantasies aeronatical dei mondi qui sopra*, based upon discoveries made by my father. Yet, all you have seen fit to publish of my work are a few short poems. While you endlessly encourage *those* two rascals to believe they hold promise, as writers!"

She nodded toward the front door of the Literary Home for Wounded Veterans… where a pair of figures dressed in black tried to seem innocuous, failing to conceal daggers at their hips. A nightly charade. Caught in the act, thirteen-year-old Jean-Baptiste murmured—"We're just goin' out for a—for some air, messieurs."

The older boy, Hercule Savinien, simply grinned, as if daring anyone to make something of their evening ritual. Again, the flourished bow.

"*Macht die Tür zu!*" one of the other vets shouted, unnecessarily, as the lads slammed the door behind them.

"Traps and snares and trip-wires." The nun shook her head. "Romantic dolts! They should be working for *Spy Magazine*, and not *Galaxy*." She turned her attentions to John, helping him to remove his prosthetics.

"Oh, what's the harm?" Jason said. "They think they're protecting us from assassins. And the wires are always gone, by morning. Anyway, now that your father has also moved to Grantville, won't you be too busy—"

"For writing? Typical man! Your condescension is insulting, as if a woman cannot develop her art while caring for others. I am tempted to report you to Gretchen Richter. Or, better yet, perhaps I will start up my *own* magazine. One dedicated to truly fabulous tales, unrestrained by your confining Rules of Extrapolative Storytelling!"

Despite her bellicose words, Maria Celeste's tone was as gentle as her caring touch, as she rubbed each of John's stumps, in turn.

"I..." He sighed. "I'll be your first investor."

Jason snorted. "Softie!"

Fortunately, conversation became impossible for a while, as the sixth member of their little commune—Vaclav Klimov—performed his own nightly ritual, cranking up the scratchy old stereo system with "Up on Cripple Creek," by The Band.

Jason muttered. "I swear I'll strangle Klimov, one of these days." Still, he tapped the armrest of his chair, keeping time to the song. And if this home for reclaimed lives were to have a nickname and an anthem, well, John figured they could do worse.

Sister Maria Celeste moved on, tending to the other fellows—efficiently, so she could return to the small cottage next to Grantville's new college, where her elderly father now both studied and taught. While Vaclav played DJ, swapping disks though a selection of blood-rousing tunes, John watched the door. And when the boys returned—pretending to be sneaky—he gave Hercule an eye roll.

I know what you're doing. And I know that you know that I know.

Almost lost under those eyebrows and behind that nose, Hercule's left eye winked. Then with a sweep, he was gone with his young friend. Leaving John to muse.

But do you know that I know your real secret, my young friend?

Caught up in a manhunt ordered by Cardinal Richelieu, just one year after Grantville arrived to upset Europe's teetering balance, scores of French subjects—mostly bewildered—had found themselves drafted into the army that Richelieu sent marching toward the Baltic. For the youngest of these involuntary recruits, like Jean-Baptiste, the duties of a drummer boy meant no lessening of hardship or danger. Indeed, the generals were under orders. These special levees were to be given places of honor. In the front ranks.

Given what a slaughterhouse Ahrensbök became, it was fortunate that Hercule and Jean-Baptiste...and Jason on the other side...got out with their lives. So many did not.

Fortunately for Jason's prospects of staying out of prison, Klimov only had the stamina to play DJ each night for half an hour or so. The evening serenade ended with another upbeat ode—"Joy to the World." After which peaceful quiet ensued. Soon, beyond the crackling fire, John was able to imagine no Grantville...no Germany roiling in change...no world wracked with upheaval. Only the universe, spinning on and on.

Or, rather...universes.

At last, Jason resumed where he had left off.

"It's one helluva yarn. That big battle at the edge of the Hell Mouth had my heart pounding! Roman siege ladders and catapults against pikes and matchlock muskets? That girl, hurrying back in the nick of time after fetching a *prince* and his men. A descendant of Judah freaking Macabee? Who would expect a seventeenth-century German writer to even know about that guy?"

"Well, in fact, even medieval Christians spoke of Macabee as one of the Nine Worthies," John said. "But I admit, it's solid stuff."

"Okay then. I say we publish it as a serial. As-is."

John sighed.

"No way. Not without removing some of the explicit names. And changing the afterword. And even so, we'd better brace for trouble."

"You're that afraid of fundamentalist terrorists? Screw 'em! We'll be doing our bit for freedom of speech."

"It's not that so much. Though this could unite both Protestant and Catholic extremists in fury." He shook his head. "No. What concerns me is how *sincere* this fellow seems to be. When he told me about his...dream...I could tell he was holding back. *Vision* might be the word he really meant."

John sat up and leaned toward his partner. "Look, I agree, he could be the first great down-timer science fiction author! I'd like nothing better. But we have to be careful, Jason. He needs guidance, and I don't just mean editorial."

"Because he thinks it may have been *more* than just a daydream? That it all really happened? Huh. It wouldn't be the first time."

"Exactly. Even in our own cynical, materialistic and scientific age, folks were human. And human beings tend to give great credence to their subjective imaginings. *Delusion* is our greatest talent! It can be among our finest gifts, when imagination takes us on grand journeys, that still leave us rooted in reality.

"But it's also been a curse. All of history was warped by *sincere* men and women, convinced that a delusion was real."

"Hmph. Yeah, well, science helps."

"Yes. Science teaches us to say the mantra of maturity—*I might be wrong.* But half of our citizens couldn't grasp that concept, even back in 2000. Picture how hard it is where we find ourselves. Here. Now.

"In fact, I do think this fellow gets it. He's hungry for knowledge and I've talked him into enrolling at the college. With any luck, we may squeak by and he'll become this generation's Asimov or Clarke, a creator of stirring thought-experiments. Instead of..."

John let his implication trail off. But, after a long pause, his partner finished the sentence for him.

"Instead of a prophet."

Lucilius Bassus was a canny old soldier. Kurt knew the type. The man wanted, above all, to achieve his assigned mission—the final pacification of Judea—with as little further fuss as possible. Bald, clean-shaven and a bit shriveled, wearing a white toga with red trim, the general eyed Kurt carefully while introducing his second in command, Lucius Flavius Silva, then offering Kurt a seat in his command tent.

Bassus raised an eyebrow but said nothing when Kurt motioned for Sarah to sit beside him on another camp stool. The rest of the Milda party remained outside, under a flag of truce, watching the highly ordered busy-ness of a disciplined Roman camp. Scowling, Lucius Flavius Silva remained standing in full leather armor, as his commander seated himself on a cushioned bench.

"I was told that your factotum would be a male priest," Bassus said, as servants mixed wine with water and served goblets. Sarah refused, with a soft smile.

"Father Braun is no longer with us," Kurt answered. While his Latin was improving, he still glanced at Sarah. She gave a slight nod. No correction needed, so far. "Our priest left suddenly, hurrying north, to Ephesus. This noblewoman has consented to help you..." he stumbled over the words. The correct grammar.

Sarah finished for him. "To help you, great Lucilius Bassus, to communicate with your loyal German auxiliaries," she said, gesturing an open hand toward Kurt.

That was the story the two of them had concocted, yesterday, after word came that the general had arrived in the Galilee with six fresh cohorts. The core of his legion, ready to advance and wipe out this infestation of strange barbarians. Only the messenger brought a codicil, that Bassus was willing to talk, first.

It's all one big misunderstanding, went the fabulous lie that Sarah translated into flawless Latin.

These aren't enemies. They are fierce German mercenaries who were attached to the Fifth Legion and left behind to garrison this area, when the Fifth returned to Macedonia. Apparently without properly informing the mighty Tenth.

It's not our fault that your centurion, Sextus Callus, attacked us, killing our Roman liaison officer and forcing us to defend ourselves!

Kurt left it to Sarah to spin out an elaborated version, while he tried to convey a best impression upon Bassus—that of a tough and wily, though semi-literate, soldier who cared, above all, about sparing his men further bloodshed, and getting them back to a distant homeland someday, with honor and pay.

Exactly like you, old man.

In terms of casualties, the Judean Revolt had been the worst war in Roman history. Moreover, while plunder from the Temple was being paraded before Vespasian and Titus, back home in the Forum, only the battered Tenth Legion *Fulminata* remained to do mopping up—eliminating half a dozen holdout fortresses still held by Jewish zealots. Saving the toughest nut—Masada—for last.

Kurt had feared the worst. A vengeful commander, prideful and overflowing with fury over the defeats that his subordinates suffered in these northern hills, starting with the small garrison that formerly resided where Milda now stood—charged with preparing a thousand slaves for transport to the wharves of Akko—all taken away by the Mouth of Hell.

Deprived of that expected income, Sextus Callus had come aggressively, ruthlessly, and obstinately—responding to every failure with double strength. The final loss, two weeks ago, cost Rome almost two entire cohorts, assailing the smooth walls of the Hell Mouth with siege ladders, arbalests, and catapults, in the face of pikes and limited gunfire. And better cavalry than they ever saw. Though far too few guns and horses to make the hardened, stubborn enemy flee.

Tough bastards, Sergeant Kuipers finally acknowledged, with soldierly respect, after the Sadducee prince Ezra and his band slammed upon the Roman rear, just in the nick of time, leaving only a handful of legionaries alive. Ezra had wasted no time, directing his Galilean recruits to arm themselves with captured weapons and armor.

Even victories stink to high heaven, wretched and odious to any decent person's senses. Only this time, while bodies were gathered for burning, with respect to Roman custom, Kurt's thoughts had roiled around how little gunpowder remained, a mere volley or two, with production slowed to a crawl as the new dam filled too slowly, behind Milda's rebuilt water mill.

There was so much to do, like expanding the smithy enough to make cannon...even recasting a church bell into a single two-pounder would be better than nothing, *which is what we now have.* If they could find one—he wasn't sure if church bells even existed in this day and age.

Or training locals to hold a pike without flinching and letting down the man next to you. Plus planning how to feed Milda's expanding population of ragged refugees. Teaching local farmers advanced, seventeenth-century technologies like the mold board plow, the horse collar, the wheelbarrow, could double production and eliminate any excuse for slavery—that is, if war could be kept off their backs.

And there were expeditions to send forth. Samuel Burns—now perhaps the only native English speaker on the planet—led a wagon and some guards to trade for sulfur, by the shores of the Dead Sea. Georg Stahl, the bravest merchant, volunteered to head east and find the Parthian trade route, seeking copper for a new distillery. While mad Johann Blisterfeld yammered about making a printing press and taking it (someday) to Alexandria, of all crazy ideas.

Finally, as if Kurt had too little cause to fret, there was Braun, raving that he had to run off. To Ephesus, of all places! Pursuing an angry old man who Braun deemed to be *more dangerous than all the world's legions.*

"All I did was read to him from the Epistles. And some of Revelations," the priest said, coming to realize what he had done, two full days after Sarah's uncle and brother departed on stolen horses.

The implications only dawned on Kurt himself some days after Braun departed. In fact, they made his head spin so fast that he pushed the entire matter out of his mind. Survival first. Survival first.

Now Kurt watched the Roman general's eyes, while Sarah spun their contrived tale. How the Fifth Legion must have neglected to inform the Tenth that German auxiliaries were holding these hills for Rome. (Shameful!) And how all their records and documentation had burned in the fighting. And that (alas, regrettably) Kurt had always left to others the tedious details of business—others who were now dead. And how he counted on Roman honor to live up to the mercenary's contract anyway! And how his men had not been paid in months, and would the general kindly see to making up the arrears?

What a ridiculously bold fabrication! And yet, on the plus side, what alternative explanation could there be, for a small army of Germans to appear in this far land? The savage folk who had destroyed the legions of Quinctillius Varus in the Teutoburg Forest, a few decades before. And hence Rome's most respected source of fierce auxiliaries?

He's not buying it, Kurt realized, watching the old general's face.

On the other hand, he is weighing the costs.

So, Lucilius Bassus, what are your options? You can bring the whole legion against us, an entrenched force of uncertain size, with weapons rumored to include hurled thunderbolts. And risk losing so many men that the Jewish Revolt might reignite across this land.

Or you could decide to be pragmatic. Accept a way to save face and salvage something from all this.

Sarah finished. In the ensuing silence, Kurt saw Lucius Flavius Silva scowling—even seething—exactly what Kurt would have expected of the man, whose infamy came down fifteen hundred years. But Silva wasn't the one who mattered. Not while Lucilius Bassus lived.

That figure sat completely still. At least a minute stretched. And another.

Finally, the general stood up and took a step forward, with outstretched arm.

"Dear comrade, please accept my deep regrets over the rash mistakes of Sextus Callus and his foolish centurions. This was entirely my fault. I should have sent Silva here, who can count his toes without referring to a wax board and who can tell a foe from an ally. Isn't that right, Silva?"

The younger officer blinked, then nodded. Though Kurt thought he could hear the grinding of teeth.

"Yes, General."

Kurt took the offered hand of Lucilius Bassus, not palm to palm but each gripping the other's forearm, bringing both men close to each other. Almost eye-to-eye. And the old man's grip was like iron. Only Sarah's presence, just behind him, gave Kurt the strength he needed to maintain that gaze contact...till Lucilius Bassus grunted, nodded, and let go.

"And now," the general asked. "I would appreciate your advice, Baron von Wolfschild, as to how I can turn my back upon the Galilee while duty calls my legion south."

"*C'est tout la? Mais il n'est pas complet!*" Jean-Baptiste complained after finishing the last page of the manuscript. "How can it end there? This will infuriate everyone, across the continent, demanding to know what happens next!"

Hercule nodded.

"I think, *mon cher ami*, that is the desired result."

The thirteen-year-old—though a veteran of war and privation—still had innocent eyes that now widened in delighted realization.

"Ah. The work of a devil, indeed. Readers will champ eagerly to buy the next issue. And some will fantasize stories of their own, that diverge, like the branchings of a river delta. Perhaps some will even write them, following the young Englishman to the Dead Sea, for example. Or Father Braun to Turkey and Greece, chasing after that mysterious old man. Do you have a clue who it might be?"

"I have suspicions. But I will leave that for you to divine. Or the author to reveal for himself."

"Bastard," Jean-Baptiste sallied. An accusation that Hercule accepted with a nod. In fact, though, he had read an earlier draft. The original version that contained some more details.

James had been the elderly Jew's name. A Jew... and a Christian... and a powder keg. Omitting that name was one of just a few places where John Flannery had put his foot down, demanding that vagueness replace specificity, for survival's sake.

Discretion, Hercule thought. *In my other life, I apparently had none. Though I should not be ashamed of it. My modest fame on that timeline was colorful, at least. But here, with this second chance, I must school myself, if my work is to achieve real importance.*

He blew out the candle, plunging their tiny attic room into darkness. Beyond the little window, he could see by moonlight the mighty towers of Grantville, one of them four stories high, and in his minds-eye he envisioned the sky city of Manhattan. The fabulous Paris of Zola and Rostand and Bardot.

There were muted, rustling sounds as the gay couple in the apartment below settled down for the night. Here in Grantville, that didn't seem to be a problem. And it drew Hercule to ponder the accounts told by his own biographers, so varied, so contradictory. *I cannot have been all of those things. Some must be mistaken. Anyway, I do like girls. Though, I also hate whenever anyone says don't-do-that.*

He shook his head. Life was open before him. Only that mattered. Stay bold! But maybe act less out of reflex. Make fewer mistakes.

From the pallet nearby, a soft voice asked:

"Have you read any of your own plays, yet?"

Exasperation.

"We agreed not to do that."

A long pause.

"I went and read one of yours," Jean-Baptiste admitted. "*L'Autre Monde.* The one about visiting the Moon? It's really good! I guess you always had it in you to be a science fiction author."

Such admiration in his voice. Oh, the irony.

"I also tried to read one of mine," the boy went on.

"*Bien? Alors* then, what did you think?"

"It was all manners and people playing tricks on each other in drawing rooms and trying to get sex. No action at all. I didn't understand or like it much."

"Well, you're just a kid. Your balls probably haven't dropped yet."

"You're only three years older!"

"But I was a soldier."

"So was I!"

"Drummer boy."

"Yeah? Well you have a great big—"

"Don't say it," Hercule warned, with a flash of the old, cold rage.

"I'm sorry," Jean-Baptiste murmured in a small voice. And Hercule remembered his oath, never to let the lad come to harm.

"Forget-about-it," he growled, in English. "Anyway, I agree with you."

"About what?"

"That we can both do better, this time around. Write better. Aim higher."

"I thought you said you weren't gonna read what we—"

"Well, I lied. I read it all."

Silence, then, in hushed tones...

"Is it true, then? Did you *invent* science fiction?"

"Invent...Nah. That other me wrote silly stuff, mostly."

Hercule stared at the ceiling, envisioning a very different moon and sun and planets, all aswarm with fanciful creatures.

"But fun," he added in a very low voice. "Way, way fun."

He turned his head toward Jean-Baptiste. To that dim shadow across the little room, he almost said: *"You have far more talent with words and drama and characters than I'll ever have. While I'm crazy enough to imagine or dare anything. Just think of what we could write together, combining your strengths with mine."*

But the words went unspoken.

Instead he commanded, gruffly, like a big brother.

"Allez dormir." Go to sleep.

Silence reigned for a time. Though the quiet had texture, as electric music played softly, somewhere across town. There were motor sounds, a brief glimmer of headlights passing in the night. Far distant, he thought there might be the drone of an aeroplane. Miracles, brought to this gritty, hopeless world from a marvelous future. A future now bound to change.

"Good night, Cyrano," his young friend whispered, breaking open their secret, for an instant.

And—also for a moment—he answered in kind.

"Sleep tight, Molière."

ISLANDS

A Belisarius Story

ERIC FLINT

David Drake and Eric Flint have collaborated on a series of novels in which opposing forces in the far future have sent electronic elements of change back in time to the Roman Empire, one to found a worldwide totalitarian state to endure to eternity, the other to thwart the tyrannical agent's plans. The legendary Roman general Belisarius, who also appeared in Lest Darkness Fall *in a crucial role, is the agent the forces of freedom have chosen to oppose the enemy. In this novella, by Flint alone, the focus is on one of Belisarius's adjutants—and his very remarkable wife.*

◇◇◇◇◇

Bukkur Island

He dreamed mostly of islands, oddly enough.

He was sailing, now, in one of his father's pleasure crafts. Not the luxurious barge-in-all-but-name-and-glitter which his father himself preferred for the family's outings into the Golden Horn, but in the phaselos which was suited for sailing in the open sea. Unlike his father, for whom sailing expeditions were merely excuses for political or commercial transactions, Calopodius had always loved sailing for its own sake.

Besides, it gave him and his new wife something to do besides sit together in stiff silence.

Calopodius' half-sleeping reverie was interrupted. Wakefulness came with the sound of his aide-de-camp Luke moving through the tent. The heaviness with which Luke clumped about was deliberate, designed to allow his master to recognize who had entered his domicile. Luke was quite capable of moving easily and lightly, as he had proved many times in the course of the savage fighting on the island. But the man, in this as so many things, had proven to be far more subtle than his rough and muscular appearance might suggest.

"It's morning, young Calopodius," Luke announced. "Time to clean your wounds. And you're not eating enough."

Calopodius sighed. The process of tending the wounds would be painful, despite all of Luke's care. As for the other—

"Have new provisions arrived?"

There was a moment's silence. Then, reluctantly: "No."

Calopodius let the silence lengthen. After a few seconds, he heard Luke's own heavy sigh. "We're getting very low, truth to tell. Ashot hasn't much himself, until the supply ships arrive."

Calopodius levered himself up on his elbows. "Then I will eat my share, no more." He chuckled, perhaps a bit harshly. "And don't try to cheat, Luke. I have other sources of information, you know."

"As if my hardest job of the day won't be to keep half the army from parading through this tent," snorted Luke. Calopodius felt the weight of Luke's knees pressing into the pallet next to him, and, a moment later, winced as the bandages over his head began to be removed. "You're quite the soldiers' favorite, lad," added Luke softly. "Don't think otherwise."

In the painful time that followed, as Luke scoured and cleaned and rebandaged the sockets that had once been eyes, Calopodius tried to take refuge in that knowledge. It helped. Some.

"Are there any signs of another Malwa attack coming?" he asked. Calopodius was perched in one of the bastions his men had rebuilt after the last enemy assault had overrun it—before, eventually, the Malwa had been driven off the island altogether. That had required bitter and ferocious fighting, however, which had inflicted many casualties upon the Roman defenders. His eyes had been among those casualties, ripped out by shrapnel from a mortar shell.

"After the bloody beating we gave 'em the last time?" chortled one of the soldiers who shared the bastion. "Not likely, sir!"

Calopodius tried to match the voice to a remembered face.

As usual, the effort failed of its purpose. But he took the time to engage in small talk with the soldier, so as to fix the voice itself in his memory. Not for the first time, Calopodius reflected wryly on the way in which possession of vision seemed to dull all other human faculties. Since his blinding, he had found his memory growing more acute along with his hearing. A simple instinct for self-preservation, he imagined. A blind man *had* to remember better than a seeing man, since he no longer had vision to constantly jog his lazy memory.

After his chat with the soldier had gone on for a few minutes, the man cleared his throat and said diffidently: "You'd best leave here, sir, if you'll pardon me for saying so. The Malwa'll likely be starting another barrage soon." For a moment, fierce good cheer filled the man's voice: "They seem to have a particular grudge against this part of our line, seeing's how their own blood and guts make up a good part of it."

The remark produced a ripple of harsh chuckling from the other soldiers crouched in the fortifications. That bastion had been one of the most hotly contested areas when the Malwa launched their major attack the week before. Calopodius didn't doubt for a moment that when his soldiers repaired the damage to the earthen walls they had not been too fastidious about removing all the traces of the carnage.

He sniffed tentatively, detecting those traces. His olfactory sense, like his hearing, had grown more acute also.

"Must have stunk, right afterward," he commented.

The same soldier issued another harsh chuckle. "That it did, sir, that it did. Why God invented flies, the way I look at it."

Calopodius felt Luke's heavy hand on his shoulder. "Time to go, sir. There'll be a barrage coming, sure enough."

In times past, Calopodius would have resisted. But he no longer felt any need to prove his courage, and a part of him—a still wondering, eighteen-year-old part—understood that his safety had become something his own men cared about. Alive, somewhere in the rear but still on the island, Calopodius would be a source of strength for his soldiers in the event of another Malwa onslaught. Spiritual strength, if not physical; a symbol, if nothing else. But men—fighting men, perhaps, more than any others—live by such symbols.

So he allowed Luke to guide him out of the bastion and down

the rough staircase which led to the trenches below. On the way, Calopodius gauged the steps with his feet.

"One of those logs is too big," he said, speaking firmly, but trying to keep any critical edge out of the words. "It's a waste, there. Better to use it for another fake cannon."

He heard Luke suppress a sigh. *And will you stop fussing like a hen?* was the content of that small sound. Calopodius suppressed a laugh. Luke, in truth, made a poor "servant."

"We've got enough," replied Luke curtly. "Twenty-odd. Do any more and the Malwa will get suspicious. We've only got three real ones left to keep up the pretense."

As they moved slowly through the trench, Calopodius considered the problem and decided that Luke was right. The pretense was probably threadbare by now, anyway. When the Malwa finally launched a full-scale amphibious assault on the island that was the centerpiece of Calopodius' diversion, they had overrun half of it before being beaten back. When the survivors returned to the main Malwa army besieging the city of Sukkur across the Indus, they would have reported to their own top commanders that several of the "cannons" with which the Romans had apparently festooned their fortified island were nothing but painted logs.

But how many? That question would still be unclear in the minds of the enemy.

Not all of them, for a certainty. When Belisarius took his main force to outflank the Malwa in the Punjab, leaving behind Calopodius and fewer than two thousand men to serve as a diversion, he had also left some of the field guns and mortars. Those pieces had wreaked havoc on the Malwa attackers, when they finally grew suspicious enough to test the real strength of Calopodius' position.

"The truth is," said Luke gruffly, "it probably doesn't really matter anyway. By now, the general's reached the Punjab." Again, the heavy hand settled on Calopodius' slender shoulder, this time giving it a little squeeze of approval. "You've already done what the general asked you to, lad. Kept the Malwa confused, thinking Belisarius was still here, while he marched in secret to the northeast. Did it as well as he could have possibly hoped."

They had reached one of the covered portions of the trench, Calopodius sensed. He couldn't see the earth-covered logs which gave some protection from enemy fire, of course. But the quality

of sound was a bit different within a shelter than in an open
trench. That was just one of the many little auditory subtleties
which Calopodius had begun noticing in the past few days.

He had not noticed it in days past, before he lost his eyes.
In the first days after Belisarius and the main army left Sukkur on their secret, forced march to outflank the Malwa in the
Punjab, Calopodius had noticed very little, in truth. He had had
neither the time nor the inclination to ponder the subtleties of
sense perception. He had been far too excited by his new and
unexpected command and by the challenge it posed.

Martial glory. The blind young man in the covered trench
stopped for a moment, staring through sightless eyes at a wall
of earth and timber bracing. Remembering, and wondering.

The martial glory Calopodius had sought, when he left a new
wife in Constantinople, had certainly come to him. Of that, he
had no doubt at all. His own soldiers thought so, and said so
often enough—those who had survived—and Calopodius was
quite certain that his praises would soon be spoken in the Senate.

Precious few of the Roman Empire's most illustrious families
had achieved any notable feats of arms in the great war against
the Malwa. Beginning with the great commander Belisarius himself, born into the lower Thracian nobility, it had been largely a
war fought by men from low stations in life. Commoners, in the
main. Agathius—the great hero of Anatha and the Dam—had
even been born into a *baker's* family, about as menial a position
as any short of outright slavery.

Other than Sittas, who was now leading Belisarius' cataphracts
in the Punjab, almost no Greek noblemen had fought in the Malwa
war. And even Sittas, before the Indus campaign, had spent the
war commanding the garrison in Constantinople which overawed
the hostile aristocracy and kept the dynasty on the throne.

Had it been worth it?

Reaching up and touching gently the emptiness which had
once been his eyes, Calopodius was still not sure. Like many
other young members of the nobility, he had been swept up
with enthusiasm after the news came that Belisarius had shattered the Malwa in Mesopotamia. Let the adult members of the
aristocracy whine and complain in their salons. The youth were
burning to serve.

And serve they had...but only as couriers, in the beginning. It hadn't taken Calopodius long to realize that Belisarius intended to use him and his high-born fellows mainly for liaison with the haughty Persians, who were even more obsessed with nobility of blood-line than Greeks. The posts carried prestige—the couriers rode just behind Belisarius himself in formation—but little in the way of actual responsibility.

Standing in the bunker, the blind young man chuckled harshly. "He used us, you know. As cold-blooded as a reptile."

Silence, for a moment. Then, Calopodius heard Luke take a deep breath.

"Aye, lad. He did. The general will use anyone, if he feels it necessary."

Calopodius nodded. He felt no anger at the thought. He simply wanted it acknowledged.

He reached out his hand and felt the rough wall of the bunker with fingertips grown sensitive with blindness. Texture of soil, which he would never have noticed before, came like a flood of dark light. He wondered, for a moment, how his wife's breasts would feel to him, or her belly, or her thighs. Now.

He didn't imagine he would ever know, and dropped the hand. Calopodius did not expect to survive the war, now that he was blind. Not unless he used the blindness as a reason to return to Constantinople, and spent the rest of his life resting on his laurels.

The thought was unbearable. *I am only eighteen! My life should still be ahead of me!*

That thought brought a final decision. Given that his life was now forfeit, Calopodius intended to give it the full measure while it lasted.

"Menander should be arriving soon, with the supply ships."

"Yes," said Luke.

"When he arrives, I wish to speak with him."

"Yes," said Luke. The "servant" hesitated. Then: "What about?"

Again, Calopodius chuckled harshly. "Another forlorn hope." He began moving slowly through the bunker to the tunnel which led back to his headquarters. "Having lost my eyes on this island, it seems only right I should lose my life on another. Belisarius' island, this time—not the one he left behind to fool the enemy. The *real* island, not the false one."

"There was nothing *false* about this island, young man," growled Luke. "Never say it. Malwa was broken here, as surely as it was on any battlefield of Belisarius. There is the blood of Roman soldiers to prove it—along with your own eyes. Most of all—"

By some means he could not specify, Calopodius understood that Luke was gesturing angrily to the north. "Most of all, by the fact that we kept an entire Malwa army pinned here for two weeks—by your cunning and our sweat and blood—while Belisarius slipped unseen to the north. *Two weeks.* The time he needed to slide a lance into Malwa's unprotected flank—we gave him that time. *We did. You did.*"

He heard Luke's almost shuddering intake of breath. "So never speak of a 'false' island again, boy. Is a shield 'false,' and only a sword 'true'? Stupid. The general did what he needed to do—and so did you. Take pride in it, for there was nothing false in that doing."

Calopodius could not help lowering his head. "No," he whispered.

But was it worth the doing?

"I know I shouldn't have come, General, but—"

Calopodius groped for words to explain. He could not find any. It was impossible to explain to someone else the urgency he felt, since it would only sound . . . suicidal. Which, in truth, it almost was, at least in part.

But . . .

"May—maybe I could help you with supplies or—or something."

"No matter," stated Belisarius firmly, giving Calopodius' shoulder a squeeze. The general's large hand was very powerful. Calopodius was a little surprised by that. His admiration for Belisarius bordered on idolization, but he had never really given any thought to the general's physical characteristics. He had just been dazzled, first, by the man's reputation; then, after finally meeting him in Mesopotamia, by the relaxed humor and confidence with which he ran his staff meetings.

The large hand on his shoulder began gently leading Calopodius off the dock where Menander's ship had tied up.

"I can still count, even if—"

"Forget that," growled Belisarius. "I've got enough clerks." With a chuckle: "The quartermasters don't have that much to count, anyway. We're on very short rations here."

Again, the hand squeezed his shoulder; not with sympathy, this time, so much as assurance. "The truth is, lad, I'm delighted to see you. We're relying on telegraph up here, in this new little fortified half-island we've created, to concentrate our forces quickly enough when the Malwa launch another attack. But the telegraph's a new thing for everyone, and keeping the communications straight and orderly has turned into a mess. My command bunker is full of people shouting at cross-purposes. I need a good officer who can take charge and *organize* the damn thing."

Cheerfully: "That's *you*, lad! Being blind won't be a handicap at all for that work. Probably be a blessing."

Calopodius wasn't certain if the general's cheer was real, or simply assumed for the purpose of improving the morale of a badly maimed subordinate. Even as young as he was, Calopodius knew that the commander he admired was quite capable of being as calculating as he was cordial.

But...

Almost despite himself, he began feeling more cheerful.

"Well, there's this much," he said, trying to match the general's enthusiasm. "My tutors thought highly of my grammar and rhetoric, as I believed I mentioned once. If nothing else, I'm sure I can improve the quality of the messages."

The general laughed. The gaiety of the sound cheered up Calopodius even more than the general's earlier words. It was harder to feign laughter than words. Calopodius was not guessing about that. A blind man aged quickly, in some ways, and Calopodius had become an expert on the subject of false laughter, in the weeks since he lost his eyes.

This was real. This was—

Something he could *do*.

A future which had seemed empty began to fill with color again. Only the colors of his own imagination, of course. But Calopodius, remembering discussions on philosophy with learned scholars in far-away and long-ago Constantinople, wondered if reality was anything *but* images in the mind. If so, perhaps blindness was simply a matter of custom.

"Yes," he said, with reborn confidence. "I can do that."

For the first two days, the command bunker was a madhouse for Calopodius. But by the end of that time, he had managed to bring some semblance of order and procedure to the way in which telegraph messages were received and transmitted. Within a week, he had the system functioning smoothly and efficiently.

The general praised him for his work. So, too, in subtle little ways, did the twelve men under his command. Calopodius found the latter more reassuring than the former. He was still a bit uncertain whether Belisarius' approval was due, at least in part, to the general's obvious feeling of guilt that he was responsible for the young officer's blindness. Whereas the men who worked for him, veterans all, had seen enough mutilation in their lives not to care about yet another cripple. Had the young nobleman not been a blessing to them instead of a curse, they would not have let sympathy stand in the way of criticism. And the general, Calopodius was well aware, kept an ear open to the sentiments of his soldiers.

Throughout that first week, Calopodius paid little attention to the ferocious battle which was raging beyond the heavily timbered and fortified command bunker. He traveled nowhere, beyond the short distance between that bunker and the small one—not much more than a covered hole in the ground—where he and Luke had set up what passed for "living quarters." Even that route was sheltered by soil-covered timber, so the continual sound of cannon fire was muffled.

The only time Calopodius emerged into the open was for the needs of the toilet. As always in a Belisarius camp, the sanitation arrangements were strict and rigorous. The latrines were located some distance from the areas where the troops slept and ate, and no exceptions were made even for the blind and crippled. A man who could not reach the latrines under his own power would either be taken there, or, if too badly injured, would have his bedpan emptied for him.

For the first three days, Luke guided him to the latrines. Thereafter, he could make the journey himself. Slowly, true, but he used the time to ponder and crystallize his new ambition. It was the only time his mind was not preoccupied with the immediate demands of the command bunker.

Being blind, he had come to realize, did not mean the end of life. Although it did transform his dreams of fame and glory into much softer and more muted colors. But finding dreams in the course of dealing with the crude realities of a latrine, he decided, was perhaps appropriate. Life was a crude thing, after all. A project begun in confusion, fumbling with unfamiliar tools, the end never really certain until it came—and then, far more often than not, coming as awkwardly as a blind man attends to his toilet.

Shit is also manure, he came to understand. A man does what he can. If he was blind...he was also educated, and rich, and had every other advantage. The rough soldiers who helped him on his way had their own dreams, did they not? And their own glory, come to it. If he could not share in that glory directly, he could save it for the world.

When he explained it to the general—awkwardly, of course, and not at a time of his own choosing—Belisarius gave the project his blessing. That day, Calopodius began his history of the war against the Malwa. The next day, almost as an afterthought, he wrote the first of the *Dispatches to the Army* which would, centuries after his death, make him as famous as Livy or Polybius.

They had approached Elafonisos from the south, because Calopodius had thought Anna might enjoy the sight of the great ridge which overlooked the harbor, with its tower perched atop it like a hawk. And she had seemed to enjoy it well enough, although, as he was coming to recognize, she took most of her pleasure from the sea itself. As did he, for that matter.

She even smiled, once or twice.

The trip across to the island, however, was the high point of the expedition. Their overnight stay in the small tavern in the port had been...almost unpleasant. Anna had not objected to the dinginess of the provincial tavern, nor had she complained about the poor fare offered for their evening meal. But she had retreated into an even more distant silence—almost sullen and hostile—as soon as they set foot on land.

That night, as always since the night of their wedding, she performed her duties without resistance. But also with as much energy and enthusiasm as she might have given to reading a particularly dull piece of hagiography. Calopodius found it all quite frustrating, the more so since his wife's naked body was something which aroused him greatly. As he had suspected in the days before the marriage, his wife was quite lovely once she could be seen. And felt.

So he performed his own duty in a perfunctory manner. Afterward, in another time, he might have spent the occasion idly considering the qualities he would look for in a courtesan—now that he had a wife against whose tedium he could measure the problem. But he had already decided to join Belisarius' expedition to the Indus. So, before falling asleep, his thoughts were entirely given over to matters of martial glory. And, of course, the fears and uncertainties which any man his age would feel on the eve of plunging into the maelstrom of war.

The Euphrates

When trouble finally arrived, it was Anna's husband who saved her. The knowledge only increased her fury.

Stupid, really, and some part of her mind understood it perfectly well. But she still couldn't stop hating him.

Stupid. The men on the barge who were clambering eagerly onto the small pier where her own little river craft was tied up were making no attempt to hide their leers. Eight of them there were, their half-clad bodies sweaty from the toil of working their clumsy vessel up the Euphrates.

A little desperately, Anna looked about. She saw nothing beyond the Euphrates itself; reed marshes on the other bank, and a desert on her own. There was not a town or a village in sight. She had stopped at this little pier simply because the two sailors she had hired to carry her down to Charax had insisted they needed to take on fresh water. There was a well here, which was the only reason for the pier's existence. After taking a taste of the muddy water of the Euphrates, Anna couldn't find herself in disagreement.

She wished, now, that she'd insisted on continuing. Not that her insistence would have probably done much good. The sailors had been civil enough, since she employed them at a small town in the headwaters of the Euphrates. But they were obviously not overawed by a nineteen-year-old girl, even if she did come from the famous family of the Melisseni.

She glanced appealingly at the sailors, still working the well. They avoided her gaze, acting as if they hadn't even noticed the men climbing out of the barge. Both sailors were rather elderly, and it was clear enough they had no intention of getting into a fracas with eight rivermen much younger than themselves—all of whom were carrying knives, to boot.

The men from the barge were close to her, and beginning to spread out. One of them was fingering the knife in a scabbard attached to his waist. All of them were smiling in a manner which even a sheltered young noblewoman understood was predatory.

Now in sheer desperation, her eyes moved to the only other men on the pier. Three soldiers, judging from their weapons and gear. They had already been on the pier when Anna's boat drew up, and their presence had almost been enough to cause the sailors to pass by entirely. A rather vicious-looking trio, they were. Two Isaurians and a third one whom Anna thought was probably an Arab. Isaurians were not much better than barbarians; Arabs might or might not be, depending on where they came from. Anna suspected this one was an outright bedouin.

The soldiers were lounging in the shade of a small pavilion they had erected. For a moment, as she had when she first caught sight of them, Anna found herself wondering how they had gotten there in the first place. They had no boat, nor any horses or camels—yet they possessed too much in the way of goods in sacks to have lugged them on their own shoulders. Not through this arid country, with their armor and weapons. She decided they had probably traveled with a caravan, and then parted company for some reason.

But this was no time for idle speculation. The rivermen were very close now. The soldiers returned Anna's beseeching eyes with nothing more than indifference. It was clear enough they had no more intention of intervening than her own sailors.

Still—they *could*, in a way which two elderly sailors couldn't. Pay them.

Moving as quickly as she could in her elaborate clothing—and cursing herself silently, again, for having been so stupid as to make this insane journey without giving a thought to her apparel—Anna walked over to them. She could only hope they understood Greek. She knew no other language.

"I need help," she hissed.

The soldier in the center of the little group, one of the Isaurians, glanced at the eight rivermen and chuckled.

"I'd say so. You'll be lucky if they don't kill you after they rob and rape you."

His Greek was fluent, if heavily accented. As he proceeded to demonstrate further. "Stupid noblewoman. Brains like a chicken. Are you some kind of idiot, traveling alone down this part of Mesopotamia? The difference between a riverman here and a pirate—" He turned his head and spit casually over the leg of the other Isaurian. His brother, judging from the close resemblance.

"I'll pay you," she said.

The two brothers exchanged glances. The one on the side, who seemed to be the younger one, shrugged. "We can use her boat to take us out of Mesopotamia. Beats walking, and the chance of another caravan...But nothing fancy," he muttered. "We're almost home."

His older brother grunted agreement and turned his head to look at the Arab. The Arab's shrug expressed the same tepid enthusiasm. "Nothing fancy," he echoed. "It's too hot."

The Isaurian in the middle lazed to his feet. He wasn't much taller than Anna, but his stocky and muscular build made him seem to loom over her.

"All right. Here's the way it is. You give us half your money and whatever other valuables you've got." He tapped the jeweled necklace around her throat. "The rivermen can take the rest of it. They'll settle for that, just to avoid a brawl."

She almost wailed. Not quite. "I *can't*. I need the money to get to—"

The soldier scowled. "Idiot! We'll keep them from taking your boat, we'll leave you enough—just enough—to get back to your family, and we'll escort you into Anatolia."

He glanced again at the rivermen. They were standing some few yards away, hesitant now. "You've no business here, girl," he growled quietly. "Just be thankful you'll get out of this with your life."

His brother had gotten to his feet also. He snorted sarcastically. "Not to mention keeping your precious hymen intact. That ought to be worth a lot, once you get back to your family."

The fury which had filled Anna for months boiled to the surface. "I don't *have* a hymen," she snarled. "My husband did for that, the bastard, before he went off to war."

Now the Arab was on his feet. Hearing her words, he laughed aloud. "God save us! An abandoned little wife, no less."

The rivermen were beginning to get surly, judging from the scowls which had replaced the previous leers. One of them barked something in a language which Anna didn't recognize. One of the Aramaic dialects, probably. The Isaurian who seemed to be the leader of the three soldiers gave them another glance and an idle little wave of his hand. The gesture more or less indicated: *relax, relax—you'll get a cut.*

That done, his eyes came back to Anna. "Idiot," he repeated. The word was spoken with no heat, just lazy derision. "Think you're the first woman got abandoned by a husband looking to make his fortune in war?"

"He already *has* a fortune," hissed Anna. "He went looking for fame. Found it too, damn him."

The Arab laughed again. "Fame, is it? Maybe in your circles! And what is the name of this paragon of martial virtue? Anthony the Illustrious Courier?"

The other three soldiers shared in the little laugh. For a moment, Anna was distracted by the oddity of such flowery phrases coming out of the mouth of a common soldier. She remembered, vaguely, that her husband had once told her of the poetic prowess of Arabs. But she had paid little attention, at the time, and the memory simply heightened her anger.

"He *is* famous," Anna insisted. A certain innate honesty forced her to add: "At least in Constantinople, after Belisarius' letter was read to the Senate. And his own dispatches."

The name *Belisarius* brought a sudden little stillness to the group of soldiers. The Isaurian leader's eyes narrowed.

"Belisarius? What's the general got to do with your husband?"

"And what's his name?" added the Arab.

Anna tightened her jaws. "Calopodius. Calopodius Saronites."

The stillness turned into frozen rigidity. All three soldiers' eyes were now almost slits.

The Isaurian leader drew a deep breath. "Are you trying to tell us that you are the wife of *Calopodius the Blind*?"

For a moment, a spike of anguish drove through the anger. She didn't really understand where it came from. Calopodius had always seemed blind to her, in his own way. But...

Her own deep breath was a shaky thing. "They say he is blind now, yes. Belisarius' letter to the Senate said so. *He* says it himself, in fact, in his letters. I—I guess it's true. I haven't seen him in many months. When he left..."

One of the rivermen began to say something, in a surly tone

of voice. The gaze which the Isaurian now turned on him was nothing casual. It was a flat, flat gaze. As cold as a snake's and just as deadly. Even a girl as sheltered as Anna had been all her life understood the sheer physical menace in it. The rivermen all seemed to shuffle back a step or two.

He turned his eyes back to Anna. The same cold and flat gleam was in them. "If you are lying..."

"Why would I lie?" she demanded angrily. "And how do you expect me to prove it, anyway?"

Belatedly, a thought came to her. "Unless..." She glanced at the little sailing craft which had brought her here, still piled high with her belongings. "If you can *read* Greek, I have several of his letters to me."

The Arab sighed softly. "As you say, 'why would you lie?'" His dark eyes examined her face carefully. "God help us. You really don't even understand, do you?"

She shook her head, confused. "Understand what? Do you know him yourself?"

The Isaurian leader's sigh was a more heartfelt thing. "No, lass, we didn't. We were so rich, after Charax, that we left the general's service. We"—he gestured at his brother—"I'm Illus, by the way, and he's Cottomenes—had more than enough to buy us a big farm back home. And Abdul decided to go in with us."

"I'm sick of the desert," muttered the Arab. "Sick of camels, too. Never did like the damn beasts."

The Arab was of the same height as the two Isaurian brothers— about average—but much less stocky in his frame. Still, in his light half-armor and with a spatha scabbarded to his waist, he seemed no less deadly.

"Come to think of it," he added, almost idly, "I'm sick of thieves too."

The violence which erupted shocked Anna more than anything in her life. She collapsed in a squat, gripping her knees with shaking hands, almost moaning with fear.

There had been no sign; nothing, at least, which she had seen. The Isaurian leader simply drew his spatha—so quick, so quick!—took three peculiar little half steps and cleaved the skull of one of the rivermen before the man even had time to do more than widen his eyes. A second or two later, the same spatha tore open another's throat. In the same amount of time, his brother and the Arab gutted two other rivermen.

Then—

She closed her eyes. The four surviving rivermen were desperately trying to reach their barge. From the sounds—clear enough, even to a young woman who had never seen a man killed before— they weren't going to make it. Not even close. The sounds, wetly horrid, were those of a pack of wolves in a sheep pen.

Some time later, she heard the Isaurian's voice. "Open your eyes, girl. It's over."

She opened her eyes. Catching sight of the pool of blood soaking into the planks of the pier, she averted her gaze. Her eyes fell on the two sailors, cowering behind the well. She almost giggled, the sight was so ridiculous.

The Isaurian must have followed her gaze, because he began chuckling himself. "Silly looking, aren't they? As if they could hide behind that little well."

He raised his voice. "Don't be stupid! If nothing else, we need you to sail the boat. Besides—" He gestured at the barge. "You'll want to loot it, if there's anything in that tub worth looting. We'll burn whatever's left."

He reached down a hand. Anna took it and came shakily to her feet.

Bodies everywhere. She started to close her eyes again.

"Get used to it, girl," the Isaurian said harshly. "You'll see plenty more of that where you're going. Especially if you make it to the island."

Her head felt muzzy. "Island? What island?"

"*The* island, idiot. 'The Iron Triangle,' they call it. Where your husband is, along with the general. Right in the mouth of the Malwa."

"I didn't know it was an island," she said softly. Again, honesty surfaced. "I'm not really even sure where it is, except somewhere in India."

The Arab had come up in time to hear her last words. He was wiping his blade clean with a piece of cloth. "God save us," he half-chuckled. "It's not really an island. Not exactly. But it'll do, seeing as how the general's facing about a hundred thousand Malwa."

He studied her for a moment, while he finished wiping the blood off the sword. Then, sighed again. "Let's hope you learn *something*, by the time we get to Charax. After that, you'll be on your own again. At least—"

He gave the Isaurian an odd little look. The Isaurian shrugged. "We were just telling ourselves yesterday how stupid we'd been, missing out on the loot of Malwa itself. What the hell, we may as well take her the whole way."

His brother was now there. "Hell, yes!" he boomed. He bestowed on Anna a very cheerful grin. "I assume you'll recommend us to the general? Not that we deserted or anything, but I'd *really* prefer a better assignment this time than being on the front lines. A bit dicey, that, when the general's running the show. Not that he isn't the shrewdest bastard in the world, mind you, but he *does* insist on fighting."

The other two soldiers seemed to share in the humor. Anna didn't really understand it, but for the first time since she'd heard the name of Calopodius—spoken by her father, when he announced to her an unwanted and unforeseen marriage—she didn't find it hateful.

Rather the opposite, in fact. She didn't know much about the military—nothing, really—but she suspected . . .

"I imagine my husband needs a bodyguard," she said hesitantly. "A bigger one than whatever he has," she added hastily. "And he's certainly rich enough to pay for it."

"Done," said the Isaurian leader instantly. "Done!"

Not long afterward, as their ship sailed down the river, Anna looked back. The barge was burning fiercely now. By the time the fire burned out, there would be nothing left but a hulk carrying what was left of a not-very-valuable cargo and eight charred skeletons.

The Isaurian leader—Illus—misunderstood her frown. "Don't worry about it, girl. In this part of Mesopotamia, no one will care what happened to the bastards."

She shook her head. "I'm not worrying about *that*. It's just—"

She fell silent. There was no way to explain, and one glance at Illus' face was enough to tell her that he'd never understand.

Calopodius hadn't, after all.

"So why the frown?"

She shrugged. "Never mind. I'm not used to violence, I guess."

That seemed to satisfy him, to Anna's relief. Under the circumstances, she could hardly explain to her rescuers how much she hated her husband. Much less why, since she didn't really understand it that well herself.

Still, she wondered. Something important had happened on that pier, something unforeseen, and she was not too consumed by her own anger not to understand that much. For the first time in her life, a husband had done something other than crush her like an insect.

She studied the surrounding countryside. So bleak and dangerous, compared to the luxurious surroundings in which she had spent her entire life. She found herself wondering what Calopodius had thought when he first saw it. Wondered what he had thought, and felt, the first time he saw blood spreading like a pool. Wondered if he had been terrified, when he first went into a battle.

Wondered what he thought now, and felt, with his face a mangled ruin.

Another odd pang of anguish came to her, then. Calopodius had been a *handsome* boy, even if she had taken no pleasure in the fact.

The Isaurian's voice came again, interrupting her musings. "Weird world, it is. What a woman will go through to find her husband."

She felt another flare of anger. But there was no way to explain; in truth, she could not have found the words herself. So all she said was: "Yes."

The Iron Triangle

The next day, as they sailed back to the mainland, he informed Anna of his decision. And for the first time since he met the girl, she came to life. All distance and ennui vanished, replaced by a cold and spiteful fury which completely astonished him. She did not say much, but what she said was as venomous as a serpent's bite.

Why? he wondered. He would have thought, coming from a family whose fame derived from ancient exploits more than modern wealth, she would have been pleased.

He tried to discover the source of her anger. But after her

initial spate of hostile words, Anna fell silent and refused to answer any of his questions. Soon enough, he gave up the attempt. It was not as if, after all, he had ever really expected any intimacy in his marriage. For that, if he survived the war, he would find a courtesan.

As always, the sound of Luke's footsteps awakened him. This time, though, as he emerged from sleep, Calopodius sensed that other men were shuffling their feet in the background.

He was puzzled, a bit. Few visitors came to the bunker where he and Luke had set up their quarters. Calopodius suspected that was because men felt uncomfortable in the presence of a blind man, especially one as young as himself. It was certainly not due to lack of space. The general had provided him with a very roomy bunker, connected by a short tunnel to the great command bunker buried beneath the small city which had emerged over the past months toward the southern tip of the Iron Triangle. The Roman army called that city "the Anvil," taking the name from the Punjabi civilians who made up most of its inhabitants.

"Who's there, Luke?" he asked.

His aide-de-camp barked a laugh. "A bunch of boys seeking fame and glory, lad. The general sent them."

The shuffling feet came nearer. "Begging your pardon, sir, but we were wondering—as he says, the general sent us to talk to you—" The man, whoever he was, lapsed into an awkward silence.

Calopodius sat up on his pallet. "Speak up, then. And who are you?"

The man cleared his throat. "Name's Abelard, sir. Abelard of Antioch. I'm the hecatontarch in charge of the westernmost bastion at the fortress of—"

"You had hot fighting yesterday," interrupted Calopodius. "I heard about it. The general told me the Malwa probe was much fiercer than usual."

"Came at us like demons, sir," said another voice. Proudly: "But we bloodied 'em good."

Calopodius understood at once. The hecatontarch cleared his throat, but Calopodius spoke before the man was forced into embarrassment.

"I'll want to hear all the details!" he exclaimed forcefully. "Just give me a moment to get dressed and summon my scribe.

We can do it all right here, at the table there. I'll make sure it goes into the next dispatch."

"Thank you, sir," said Abelard. His voice took on a slightly aggrieved tone. "T'isn't true, what Luke says. It's neither the fame nor the glory of it. It's just...your *Dispatches* get read to the Senate, sir. Each and every one, by the Emperor himself. And then the Emperor—by express command—has them printed and posted all over the Empire."

Calopodius was moving around, feeling for his clothing. "True enough," he said cheerfully. "Ever since the old Emperor set up the new printing press in the Great Palace, everybody—every village, anyway—can get a copy of something."

"It's our families, sir," said the other voice. "They'll see our names and know we're all right. Except for those who died in the fighting. But at least..."

Calopodius understood. Perfectly. "Their names will exist somewhere, on something other than a tombstone."

Charax

"I *can't*," said Dryopus firmly. Anna glared at him, but the Roman official in charge of the great port city of Charax was quite impervious to her anger. His next words were spoken in the patient tone of one addressing an unruly child.

"Lady Saronites, if I allowed you to continue on this—" he paused, obviously groping for a term less impolite than *insane* "—headstrong project of yours, it'd be worth my career." He picked up a letter lying on the great desk in his headquarters. "This is from your father, demanding that you be returned to Constantinople under guard."

"My father has no authority over me!"

"No, he doesn't." Dryopus shook his head. "But your husband *does*. Without his authorization, I simply can't allow you to continue. I certainly can't detail a ship to take you to Barbaricum."

Anna clenched her jaws. Her eyes went to the nearby window. She couldn't see the harbor from here, but she could visualize it easily enough. The Roman soldiers who had all-but-formally arrested her when she and her small party arrived in the great port city of Charax on the Persian Gulf had marched her past it on their way to Dryopus' palace.

For a moment, wildly, she thought of appealing to the Persians who were now in official control of Charax. But the notion died as soon as it came. The Aryans were even more strict than Romans when it came to the independence of women. Besides—

Dryopus seemed to read her thoughts. "I should note that *all* shipping in Charax is under Roman military law. So there's no point in your trying to go around me. No ship captain will take your money, anyway. Not without a permit issued by my office."

He dropped her father's letter back onto the desk. "I'm sorry, but there's nothing else for it. If you wish to continue, you will have to get your husband's permission."

"He's all the way up the Indus," she snapped angrily. "And there's no telegraph communication between here and there."

Dryopus shrugged. "There is between Barbaricum and the Iron Triangle. And by now the new line connecting Barbaricum and the harbor at Chabahari may be completed. But you'll still have to wait until I can get a ship there—and another to bring back the answer."

Anna's mind raced through the problem. On their way down the Euphrates, Illus had explained to her the logic of travel between Mesopotamia and India. During the winter monsoon season, it was impossible for sailing craft to make it to Barbaricum. Taking advantage of the relatively sheltered waters of the Gulf, on the other hand, they could make it as far as Chabahari—which was the reason the Roman forces in India had been working so hard to get a telegraph line connecting Chabahari and the Indus.

So if *she* could get as far as Chabahari . . . She'd still have to wait, but if Calopodius' permission came she wouldn't be wasting weeks here in Mesopotamia.

"Allow me to go as far as Chabahari then," she insisted.

Dryopus started to frown. Anna had to fight to keep from screaming in frustration.

"Put me under guard, if you will!"

Dryopus sighed, lowered his head, and ran his fingers through thinning hair. "He's not likely to agree, you know," he said softly.

"He's my husband, not yours," pointed out Anna. "You don't know how he thinks." She didn't see any reason to add: *no more than I do.*

His head still lowered, Dryopus chuckled. "True enough. With that young man, it's always hard to tell."

He raised his head and studied her carefully. "Are you *that* besotted with him? That you insist on going into the jaws of the greatest war in history?"

"He's my *husband*," she replied, not knowing what else to say.

Again, he chuckled. "You remind me of Antonina, a bit. Or Irene."

Anna was confused for a moment, until she realized he was referring to Belisarius' wife and the Roman Empire's former head of espionage, Irene Macrembolitissa. Famous women, now, the both of them. One of them had even become a queen herself.

"I don't know either one," she said quietly. Which was true enough, even though she'd read everything ever written by Macrembolitissa. "So I couldn't say."

Dryopus studied her a bit longer. Then his eyes moved to her bodyguards, who had been standing as far back in a corner as possible.

"You heard?"

Illus nodded.

"Can I trust you?" he asked.

Illus' shoulders heaved a bit, as if he were suppressing a laugh. "No offense, sir—but if it's worth *your* career, just imagine the price *we'd* pay." His tone grew serious: "We'll see to it that she doesn't, ah, escape on her own."

Dryopus nodded and looked back at Anna. "All right, then. As far as Chabahari."

On their way to the inn where Anna had secured lodgings, Illus shook his head. "If Calopodius says 'no,' you realize you'll have wasted a lot of time and money."

"He's my *husband*," replied Anna firmly. Not knowing what else to say.

The Iron Triangle

After the general finished reading Anna's message, and the accompanying one from Dryopus, he invited Calopodius to sit down at the table in the command bunker.

"I knew you were married," said Belisarius, "but I know none of the details. So tell me."

Calopodius hesitated. He was deeply reluctant to involve the general in the petty minutia of his own life. In the little silence that fell over them, within the bunker, Calopodius could hear the artillery barrages. As was true day and night, and had been for many weeks, the Malwa besiegers of the Iron Triangle were shelling the Roman fortifications—and the Roman gunners were responding with counter-battery fire. The fate of the world would be decided here in the Punjab, some time over the next few months. That, and the whole future of the human race. It seemed absurd—grotesque, even—to waste the Roman commander's time...

"Tell me," commanded Belisarius. For all their softness, Calopodius could easily detect the tone of command in the words.

Still, he hesitated.

Belisarius chuckled. "Be at ease, young man. I can spare the time for this. In truth—" Calopodius could sense, if not see, the little gesture by which the general expressed a certain ironic weariness. "I would enjoy it, Calopodius. War is a means, not an end. It would do my soul good to talk about ends, for a change."

That was enough to break Calopodius' resistance.

"I really don't know her very well, sir. We'd only been married for a short time before I left to join your army. It was—"

He fumbled for the words. Belisarius provided them.

"A marriage of convenience. Your wife's from the Melisseni family."

Calopodius nodded. With his acute hearing, he could detect the slight sound of the general scratching his chin, as he was prone to do when thinking.

"An illustrious family," stated Belisarius. "One of the handful of senatorial families which can actually claim an ancient pedigree without paying scribes to fiddle with the historical records. But a family which has fallen on hard times financially."

"My father said they wouldn't even have a pot to piss in if their creditors ever really descended on them." Calopodius sighed. "Yes, General. An illustrious family, but now short of means. Whereas my family, as you know..."

"The Saronites. Immensely wealthy, but with a pedigree that needs a *lot* of fiddling."

Calopodius grinned. "Go back not more than three generations, and you're looking at nothing but commoners. Not in the official records, of course. My father can afford a *lot* of scribes."

"That explains your incredible education," mused Belisarius.

"I had wondered, a bit. Not many young noblemen have your command of language and the arts." Calopodius heard the scrape of a chair as the general stood up. Then, heard him begin to pace about. That was another of Belisarius' habits when he was deep in thought. Calopodius had heard him do it many times, over the past weeks. But he was a bit astonished that the general was giving the same attention to this problem as he would to a matter of strategy or tactics.

"Makes sense, though," continued Belisarius. "For all the surface glitter—and don't think the Persians don't make plenty of sarcastic remarks about it—the Roman aristocracy will overlook a low pedigree as long as the 'nobleman' is wealthy *and* well educated. Especially—as you are—in grammar and rhetoric."

"I can drop three Homeric and biblical allusions into any sentence," chuckled Calopodius.

"I've noticed!" laughed the general. "That official history you're writing of my campaigns would serve as a Homeric and biblical commentary as well." He paused a moment. "Yet I notice that you don't do it in your *Dispatches to the Army.*"

"It'd be a waste," said Calopodius, shrugging. "Worse than that, really. I write those for the morale of the soldiers, most of whom would just find the allusions confusing. Besides, those are really *your* dispatches, not mine. And you don't talk that way, certainly not to your soldiers."

"They're *not* my dispatches, young man. They're yours. I approve them, true, but you write them. And when they're read aloud by my son to the Senate, Photius presents them as *Calopodius'* dispatches, not mine."

Calopodius was startled into silence.

"You didn't know? My son is almost eleven years old, and quite literate. And since he *is* the Emperor of Rome, even if Theodora still wields the actual power, he insists on reading them to the Senate. He's very fond of your dispatches. Told me in his most recent letter that they're the only things he reads which don't bore him to tears. His tutors, of course, don't approve."

Calopodius was still speechless. Again, Belisarius laughed. "You're quite famous, lad." Then, more softly; almost sadly: "I can't give you back your eyes, Calopodius. But I *can* give you the fame you wanted when you came to me. I promised you I would."

The sound of his pacing resumed. "In fact, unless I miss my

guess, those *Dispatches* of yours will someday—centuries from now—be more highly regarded than your official history of the war." Calopodius heard a very faint noise, and guessed the general was stroking his chest, where the jewel from the future named Aide lay nestled in his pouch. "I have it on good authority," chuckled Belisarius, "that historians of the future will prefer straight narrative to flowery rhetoric. And—in my opinion, at least—you write straightforward narrative even better than you toss off classical allusions."

The chair scraped as the general resumed his seat. "But let's get back to the problem at hand. In essence, your marriage was arranged to lever your family into greater respectability, and to provide the Melisseni—discreetly, of course—a financial rescue. How did you handle the dowry, by the way?"

Calopodius shrugged. "I'm not certain. My family's so wealthy that a dowry's not important. For the sake of appearances, the Melisseni provided a large one. But I suspect my father *loaned* them the dowry—and then made arrangements to improve the Melisseni's economic situation by linking their own fortunes to those of our family." He cleared his throat. "All very discreetly, of course."

Belisarius chuckled drily. "Very discreetly. And how did the Melisseni react to it all?"

Calopodius shifted uncomfortably in his chair. "Not well, as you'd expect. I met Anna for the first time three days after my father informed me of the prospective marriage. It was one of those carefully rehearsed 'casual visits.' She and her mother arrived at my family's villa near Nicodemia."

"Accompanied by a small army of servants and retainers, I've no doubt."

Calopodius smiled. "Not such a small army. A veritable host, it was." He cleared his throat. "They stayed for three days, that first time. It was very awkward for me. Anna's mother—her name's Athenais—barely even tried to disguise her contempt for me and my family. I think she was deeply bitter that their economic misfortunes were forcing them to seek a husband for their oldest daughter among less illustrious but much wealthier layers of the nobility."

"And Anna herself?"

"Who knows? During those three days, Anna said little. In the course of the various promenades which we took through the grounds of the Saronites estate—God, talk about chaperones!—she seemed distracted to the point of being almost rude. I couldn't really get much of a sense of her, General. She seemed distressed by something. Whether that was her pending marriage to me, or something else, I couldn't say."

"And you didn't much care. Be honest."

"True. I'd known for years that any marriage I entered would be purely one of convenience." He shrugged. "At least my bride-to-be was neither unmannerly not uncomely. In fact, from what I could determine at the time—which wasn't much, given the heavy scaramangium and headdress and the elaborate cosmetics under which Anna labored—she seemed quite attractive."

He shrugged again. "So be it. I was seventeen, General." For a moment, he hesitated, realizing how silly that sounded. He was only a year older than that now, after all, even if...

"You were a boy then; a man, now," filled in Belisarius. "The world looks very different after a year spent in the carnage. I know. But then—"

Calopodius heard the general's soft sigh. "Seventeen years old. With the war against Malwa looming ever larger in the life of the Roman Empire, the thoughts of a vigorous boy like yourself were fixed on feats of martial prowess, not domestic bliss."

"Yes. I'd already made up my mind. As soon as the wedding was done—well, and the marriage consummated—I'd be joining your army. I didn't even see any reason to wait to make sure that I'd provided an heir. I've got three younger brothers, after all, every one of them in good health."

Again, silence filled the bunker and Calopodius could hear the muffled sounds of the artillery exchange. "Do you think that's why she was so angry at me when I told her I was leaving? I didn't really think she'd care."

"Actually, no. I think..." Calopodius heard another faint noise, as if the general were picking up the letters lying on the table. "There's this to consider. A wife outraged by abandonment—or glad to see an unwanted husband's back—would hardly be taking these risks to find him again."

"Then why is she doing it?"

"I doubt if she knows. Which is really what this is all about, I suspect." He paused; then: "She's only a year older than you, I believe."

Calopodius nodded. The general continued. "Did you ever wonder what an eighteen-year-old girl wants from life? Assuming she's high-spirited, of course—but judging from the evidence, your Anna is certainly that. Timid girls, after all, don't race off on their own to find a husband in the middle of a war zone."

Calopodius said nothing. After a moment, Belisarius chuckled. "Never gave it a moment's thought, did you? Well, young man, I suggest the time has come to do so. And not just for your own sake."

The chair scraped again as the general rose. "When I said I knew nothing about the details of your marriage, I was fudging a bit. I *didn't* know anything about what you might call the 'inside' of the thing. But I knew quite a bit about the 'outside' of it. This marriage is important to the Empire, Calopodius."

"Why?"

The general clucked his tongue reprovingly. "There's more to winning a war than tactics on the battlefield, lad. You've also got to keep an eye—always—on what a future day will call the 'home front.'" Calopodius heard him resume his pacing. "You can't be *that* naïve. You must know that the Roman aristocracy is not very fond of the dynasty."

"*My* family is," protested Calopodius.

"Yes. Yours—and most of the newer rich families. That's because their wealth comes mainly from trade and commerce. The war—all the new technology Aide's given us—has been a blessing to you. But it looks very different from the standpoint of the old landed families. You know as well as I do—you *must* know—that it was those families which supported the Nika insurrection a few years ago. Fortunately, most of them had enough sense to do it at a distance."

Calopodius couldn't help wincing. And what he wasn't willing to say, the general was. Chuckling, oddly enough.

"The Melisseni came *that* close to being arrested, Calopodius. Arrested—the whole family—and all their property seized. If Anna's father Nicephorus had been even slightly less discreet... the truth? His head would have been on a spike on the wall of the Hippodrome, right next to that of John of Cappadocia's. The only thing that saved him was that he *was* discreet enough—barely—and the Melisseni are one of the half-dozen most illustrious families of the Empire."

"I didn't know they were that closely tied..."

Calopodius sensed Belisarius' shrug. "We were able to keep it quiet. And since then, the Melisseni seem to have retreated from any open opposition. But we were delighted—I'm speaking of Theodora and Justinian and myself, and Antonina for that matter—when we heard about your marriage. Being tied closely to the Saronites will inevitably pull the Melisseni into the orbit of the dynasty. Especially since—as canny as your father is—they'll start getting rich themselves from the new trade and manufacture."

"Don't tell them that!" barked Calopodius. "Such work is for plebeians."

"They'll change their tune, soon enough. And the Melisseni are very influential among the older layers of the aristocracy."

"I understand your point, General." Calopodius gestured toward the unseen table, and the letters atop it. "So what do you want me to do? Tell Anna to come to the Iron Triangle?"

Calopodius was startled by the sound of Belisarius' hand slapping the table. "Damn fool! It's time you put that splendid mind of yours to work on *this*, Calopodius. A marriage—if it's to work—needs grammar and rhetoric also."

"I don't understand," said Calopodius timidly.

"I know you don't. So will you follow my advice?"

"Always, General."

Belisarius chuckled. "You're more confident than I am! But..." After a moment's pause: "Don't *tell* her to do anything, Calopodius. Send Dryopus a letter explaining that your wife has your permission to make her own decision. And send Anna a letter saying the same thing. I'd suggest..."

Another pause. Then: "Never mind. That's for you to decide."

In the silence that followed, the sound of artillery came to fill the bunker again. It seemed louder, perhaps. "And that's enough for the moment, young man. I'd better get in touch with Maurice. From the sound of things, I'd say the Malwa are getting ready for another probe."

Calopodius wrote the letters immediately thereafter. The letter to Dryopus took no time at all. Neither did the one to Anna, at first. But Calopodius, for reasons he could not determine, found it difficult to find the right words to conclude. Grammar and rhetoric seemed of no use at all.

In the end, moved by an impulse which confused him, he simply wrote:

Do as you will, Anna. For myself, I would like to see you again.

Chabahari

Chabahari seemed like a nightmare to Anna. When she first arrived in the town—city, now—she was mainly struck by the chaos in the place. Not so long ago, Chabahari had been a sleepy fishing village. Since the great Roman-Persian expedition led by Belisarius to invade the Malwa homeland through the Indus valley had begun, Chabahari had been transformed almost overnight into a great military staging depot. The original fishing village was now buried somewhere within a sprawling and disorganized mass of tents, pavilions, jury-rigged shacks—and, of course, the beginnings of the inevitable grandiose palaces which Persians insisted on putting anywhere that their grandees resided.

Her first day was spent entirely in a search for the authorities in charge of the town. She had promised Dryopus she would report to those authorities as soon as she arrived.

But the search was futile. She found the official headquarters easily enough—one of the half-built palaces being erected by the Persians. But the interior of the edifice was nothing but confusion, a mass of workmen swarming all over, being overseen by a handful of harassed-looking supervisors. Not an official was to be found anywhere, neither Persian nor Roman.

"Try the docks," suggested the one foreman who spoke Greek and was prepared to give her a few minutes of his time. "The noble sirs complain about the noise here, and the smell everywhere else."

The smell *was* atrocious. Except in the immediate vicinity of the docks—which had their own none-too-savory aroma—the entire city seemed to be immersed in a miasma made up of the combined stench of excrement, urine, sweat, food—half of it seemingly rotten—and, perhaps most of all, blood and corrupting flesh. In addition to being a staging area for the invasion, Chabahari was also a depot where badly injured soldiers were being evacuated back to their homelands.

Those of them who survive this horrid place, Anna thought

angrily, as she stalked out of the "headquarters." Illus and Cot-tomenes trailed behind her. Once she passed through the aivan onto the street beyond—insofar as the term "street" could be used at all for a simple space between buildings and shacks, teeming with people—she spent a moment or so looking south toward the docks.

"What's the point?" asked Illus, echoing her thoughts. "We didn't find anyone there when we disembarked." He cast a glance at the small mound of Anna's luggage piled up next to the building. The wharf boys whom Anna had hired to carry her belongings were lounging nearby, under Abdul's watchful eye.

"Besides," Illus continued, "it'll be almost impossible to keep your stuff from being stolen, in that madhouse down there."

Anna sighed. She looked down at her long dress, grimacing ruefully. The lowest few inches of the once-fine fabric, already ill-used by her journey from Constantinople, was now completely ruined. And the rest of it was well on its way—as much from her own sweat as anything else. The elaborate garments of a Greek noblewoman, designed for salons in the Roman Empire's capital, were torture in this climate.

A glimpse of passing color caught her eye. For a moment, she studied the figure of a young woman moving down the street. Some sort of Indian girl, apparently. Since the war had erupted into the Indian subcontinent, the inevitable human turbulence had thrown people of different lands into the new cauldrons of such cities as Chabahari. Mixing them up like grain caught in a thresher. Anna had noticed several Indians even in Charax.

Mainly, she just envied the woman's clothing, which was infi-nitely better suited for the climate than her own. By her senatorial family standards, of course, it was shockingly immodest. But she spent a few seconds just *imagining* what her bare midriff would feel like, if it didn't feel like a mass of spongy, sweaty flesh.

Illus chuckled. "You'd peel like a grape, girl. With your fair skin?"

Anna had long since stopped taking offense at her "servant's" familiarity with her. That, too, would have outraged her family. But Anna herself took an odd little comfort in it. Much to her surprise, she had discovered over the weeks of travel that she was at ease in the company of Illus and his companions.

"Damn you, too," she muttered, not without some humor of

her own. "I'd toughen up soon enough. And I wouldn't mind shedding some skin, anyway. What I've got right now feels like it's gangrenous."

It was Illus' turn to grimace. "Don't even think it, girl. Until you've seen real gangrene..."

A stray waft of breeze from the northwest illustrated his point. That was the direction of the great military "hospital" which the Roman army had set up on the outskirts of the city. The smell almost made Anna gag.

The gag brought up a reflex of anger, and, with it, a sudden decision.

"Let's go there," she said.

"*Why?*" demanded Illus.

Anna shrugged. "Maybe there'll be an official there. If nothing else, I need to find where the telegraph office is located."

Illus' face made his disagreement clear enough. Still—for all that she allowed familiarity, Anna had also established over the past weeks that she *was* his master.

"Let's go," she repeated firmly. "If nothing else, that's probably the only part of this city where we'd find some empty lodgings."

"True enough," said Illus, sighing. "They'll be dying like flies, over there." He hesitated, then began to speak. But Anna cut him off before he got out more than three words.

"I'm not insane, damn you. If there's an epidemic, we'll leave. But I doubt it. Not in this climate, this time of year. At least... not if they've been following the sanitary regulations."

Illus' face creased in a puzzled frown. "What's that got to do with anything? What regulations?"

Anna snorted and began to stalk off to the northwest. "Don't you read *anything* besides those damned *Dispatches*?"

Cottomenes spoke up. "No one does," he said. Cheerfully, as usual. "No soldier, anyway. Your husband's got a way with words, he does. Have you ever tried to *read* official regulations?"

Those words, too, brought a reflex of anger. But, as she forced her way through the mob toward the military hospital, Anna found herself thinking about them. And eventually came to realize two things.

One. Although she was a voracious reader, she *hadn't* ever read any official regulations. Not those of the army, at any rate. But she suspected they were every bit as turgid as the regulations which officials in Constantinople spun out like spiders spinning webs.

Two. Calopodius *did* have a way with words. On their way down the Euphrates—and then again, as they sailed from Charax to Chabahari—the latest *Dispatches* and the newest chapters from his *History of Belisarius and the War* had been available constantly. Belisarius, Anna had noted, seemed to be as adamant about strewing printing presses behind his army's passage as he was about arms depots.

The chapters of the *History* had been merely perused on occasion by her soldier companions. Anna could appreciate the literary skill involved, but the constant allusions in those pages were meaningless to Illus and his brother, much less the illiterate Abdul. Yet they pored over each and every *Dispatch*, often enough in the company of a dozen other soldiers. One of them reading it aloud, while the others listened with rapt attention.

As always, her husband's fame caused some part of Anna to seethe with fury. But, this time, she also *thought* about it. And if, at the end, her thoughts caused her anger to swell, it was a much cleaner kind of anger. One which did not coil in her stomach like a worm, but simply filled her with determination.

The hospital was even worse than she'd imagined. But she did, not surprisingly, find an unused tent in which she and her companions could make their quarters. And she did discover the location of the telegraph office—which, as it happened, was situated right next to the sprawling grounds of the "hospital."

The second discovery, however, did her little good. The official in charge, once she awakened him from his afternoon nap, yawned and explained that the telegraph line from Barbaricum to Chabahari was still at least a month away from completion.

"That'll mean a few weeks here," muttered Illus. "It'll take at least that long for couriers to bring your husband's reply."

Instead of the pure rage those words would have brought to her once, the Isaurian's sour remark simply caused Anna's angry determination to harden into something like iron.

"Good," she pronounced. "We'll put the time to good use."

"How?" he demanded.

"Give me tonight to figure it out."

✧   ✧   ✧

It didn't take her all night. Just four hours. The first hour she spent sitting in her screened-off portion of the tent, with her knees hugged closely to her chest, listening to the moans and shrieks of the maimed and dying soldiers who surrounded it. The remaining three, studying the books she had brought with her—especially her favorite, Irene Macrembolitissa's *Commentaries on the Talisman of God*, which had been published just a few months before Anna's precipitous decision to leave Constantinople in search of her husband.

Irene Macrembolitissa was Anna's private idol. Not that the sheltered daughter of the Melisseni had ever thought to emulate the woman's adventurous life, except intellectually. The admiration had simply been an emotional thing, the heroine-worship of a frustrated girl for a woman who had done so many things she could only dream about. But now, carefully studying those pages in which Macrembolitissa explained certain features of natural philosophy as given to mankind through Belisarius by the Talisman of God, she came to understand the hard practical core which lay beneath the great woman's flowery prose and ease with classical and biblical allusions. And, with that understanding, came a hardening of her own soul.

Fate, against her will and her wishes, had condemned her to be a wife. So be it. She would begin with that practical core; with concrete truth, not abstraction. She would steel the bitterness of *a* wife into the driving will of *the* wife. The wife of Calopodius the Blind, Calopodius of the Saronites.

The next morning, very early, she presented her proposition.

"Do any of you have a problem with working in trade?"

The three soldiers stared at her, stared at each other, broke into soft laughter.

"We're not senators, girl," chuckled Illus.

Anna nodded. "Fine. You'll have to work on speculation, though. I'll need the money I have left to pay the others."

"What 'others'?"

Anna smiled grimly. "I think you call it 'the muscle.'"

Cottomenes frowned. "I thought *we* were 'the muscle.'"

"Not anymore," said Anna, shaking her head firmly. "You're promoted. All three of you are now officers in the hospital service."

"*What* 'hospital service'?"

Anna realized she hadn't considered the name of the thing. For a moment, the old anger flared. But she suppressed it easily enough. This was no time for pettiness, after all, and besides—it was now a *clean* sort of anger.

"We'll call it Calopodius' Wife's Service. How's that?"

The three soldiers shook their heads. Clearly enough, they had no understanding of what she was talking about.

"You'll see," she predicted.

It didn't take them long. Illus' glare was enough to cow the official "commander" of the hospital—who was as sorry-looking a specimen of "officer" as Anna could imagine. And if the man might have wondered at the oddness of such glorious ranks being borne by such as Illus and his two companions—Abdul looked as far removed from a *tribune* as could be imagined—he was wise enough to keep his doubts to himself.

The dozen or so soldiers whom Anna recruited into the Service in the next hour—"the muscle"—had no trouble at all believing that Illus and Cottomenes and Abdul were, respectively, the *chiliarch* and two *tribunes* of a new army "service" they'd never heard of. First, because they were all veterans of the war and could recognize others—and knew, as well, that Belisarius promoted with no regard for personal origin. Second—more importantly—because they were wounded soldiers cast adrift in a chaotic "military hospital" in the middle of nowhere. Anna—Illus, actually, following her directions—selected only those soldiers whose wounds were healing well. Men who could move around and exert themselves. Still, even for such men, the prospect of regular pay meant a much increased chance at survival.

Anna wondered, a bit, whether walking-wounded "muscle" would serve the purpose. But her reservations were settled within the next hour, after four of the new "muscle"—at Illus' command— beat the first surgeon into a bloody pulp when the man responded to Anna's command to start boiling his instruments with a sneer and a derogatory remark about meddling women.

By the end of the first day, eight other surgeons were sporting cuts and bruises. But, at least when it came to the medical staff, there were no longer any doubts—none at all, in point of fact—as to whether this bizarre new "Calopodius' Wife's Service" had any actual authority.

Two of the surgeons complained to the hospital's commandant, but that worthy chose to remain inside his headquarters'
tent. That night, Illus and three of his new "muscle" beat the two
complaining surgeons into a still bloodier pulp, and all complaints
to the commandant ceased thereafter.

Complaints from the medical staff, at least. A body of perhaps twenty soldiers complained to the hospital commandant
the next day, hobbling to the HQ as best they could. But, again,
the commandant chose to remain inside; and, again, Illus—this
time using his entire corps of "muscle," which had now swollen
to thirty men—thrashed the complainers senseless afterward.

Thereafter, whatever they might have muttered under their
breath, none of the soldiers in the hospital protested openly when
they were instructed to dig real latrines, *away* from the tents—and
use them. Nor did they complain when they were ordered to help
completely immobilized soldiers use them as well.

By the end of the fifth day, Anna was confident that her authority in the hospital was well enough established. She spent a goodly
portion of those days daydreaming about the pleasures of wearing
more suitable apparel, as she made her slow way through the ranks
of wounded men in the swarm of tents. But she knew full well that
the sweat which seemed to saturate her was one of the prices she
would have to pay. Lady Saronites, wife of Calopodius the Blind,
daughter of the illustrious family of the Melisseni, was a figure
of power and majesty and authority—and had the noble gowns
to prove it, even if they were soiled and frayed. Young Anna, all
of nineteen years old, wearing a sari, would have had none at all.

By the sixth day, as she had feared, what was left of the money
she had brought with her from Constantinople was almost gone.
So, gathering her now-filthy robes in two small but determined
hands, she marched her way back into the city of Chabahari. By
now, at least, she had learned the name of the city's commander.

It took her half the day to find the man, in the *taberna* where
he was reputed to spend most of his time. By the time she did,
as she had been told, he was already half-drunk.

"Garrison troops," muttered Illus as they entered the tent
which served the city's officers for their entertainment. The tent
was filthy, as well as crowded with officers and their whores.

Anna found the commandant of the garrison in a corner, with a young half-naked girl perched on his lap. After taking half the day to find the man, it only took her a few minutes to reason with him and obtain the money she needed to keep the Service in operation.

Most of those few minutes were spent explaining, in considerable detail, exactly what she needed. Most of that, in specifying tools and artifacts—*more shovels to dig more latrines; pots for boiling water; more fabric for making more tents, because the ones they had were too crowded.* And so forth.

She spent a bit of time, at the end, specifying the sums of money she would need.

"Twenty solidi—a day." She nodded at an elderly wounded soldier whom she had brought with her along with Illus. "That's Zeno. He's literate. He's the Service's accountant in Chabahari. You can make all the arrangements through him."

The garrison's commandant then spent a minute explaining to Anna, also in considerable detail—mostly anatomical—what she could do with the tools, artifacts and money she needed.

Illus' face was very strained, by the end. Half with fury, half with apprehension—this man was no petty officer to be pounded with fists. But Anna herself sat through the garrison commander's tirade quite calmly. When he was done, she did not need more than a few seconds to reason with him further and bring him to see the error of his position.

"My husband is Calopodius the Blind. I will tell him what you have said to me, and he will place the words in his next *Dispatch.* You will be a lucky man if all that happens to you is that General Belisarius has you executed."

She left the tent without waiting to hear his response. By the time she reached the tent's entrance, the garrison commander's face was much whiter than the tent fabric and he was gasping for breath.

The next morning, a chest containing 100 solidi was brought to the hospital and placed in Zeno's care. The day after that, the first of the tools and artifacts began arriving.

Four weeks later, when Calopodius' note finally arrived, the mortality rate in the hospital was less than half what it had been when Anna arrived. She was almost sorry to leave.

In truth, she might not have left at all, except by then she was confident that Zeno was quite capable of managing the entire service as well as its finances.

"Don't steal anything," she warned him as she prepared to leave.

Zeno's face quirked with a rueful smile. "I wouldn't dare risk the Wife's anger."

She laughed, then; and found herself wondering through all the days of their slow oar-driven travel to Barbaricum why those words had brought her no anger at all.

And, each night, she took out Calopodius' letter and wondered at it also. Anna had lived with anger and bitterness for so long—"so long," at least, to a nineteen-year-old girl—that she was confused by its absence. She was even more confused by the little glow of warmth which the last words in the letter gave her, each time she read them.

"You're a strange woman," Illus told her, as the great battlements and cannons of Barbaricum loomed on the horizon.

There was no way to explain. "Yes," was all she said.

The first thing she did upon arriving at Barbaricum was march into the telegraph office. If the officers in command thought there was anything peculiar about a young Greek noblewoman dressed in the finest and filthiest garments they had ever seen, they kept it to themselves. Perhaps rumors of "the Wife" had preceded her.

"Send a telegram immediately," she commanded. "To my husband, Calopodius the Blind."

They hastened to comply. The message was brief:

Idiot. Address medical care and sanitation in next dispatch. Firmly.

The Iron Triangle

When Calopodius received the telegram—and he received it immediately, because his post was in the Iron Triangle's command and communication center—the first words he said as soon as the telegraph operator finished reading it to him were:

"God, I'm an idiot!"

Belisarius had heard the telegram also. In fact, all the officers in the command center had heard, because they had been waiting with an ear cocked. By now, the peculiar journey of

Calopodius' wife was a source of feverish gossip in the ranks of the entire army fighting off the Malwa siege in the Punjab. *What the hell is that girl doing, anyway?* being only the most polite of the speculations.

The general sighed and rolled his eyes. Then, closed them. It was obvious to everyone that he was reviewing all of Calopodius' now-famous *Dispatches* in his mind.

"We're both idiots," he muttered. "We've maintained proper medical and sanitation procedures *here*, sure enough. But..."

His words trailed off. His second-in-command, Maurice, filled in the rest.

"She must have passed through half the invasion staging posts along the way. Garrison troops, garrison officers—with the local butchers as the so-called 'surgeons.' God help us, I don't even want to think..."

"I'll write it immediately," said Calopodius.

Belisarius nodded. "Do so. And I'll give you some choice words to include." He cocked his head at Maurice, smiling crookedly. "What do you think? Should we resurrect crucifixion as a punishment?"

Maurice shook his head, scowling. "Don't be so damned flamboyant. Make the punishment fit the crime. Surgeons who do not boil their instruments will be boiled alive. Officers who do not see to it that proper latrines are maintained will be buried alive in them. That sort of thing."

Calopodius was already seated at the desk where he dictated his *Dispatches* and the chapters of the *History*. So was his scribe, pen in hand.

"I'll add a few nice little flourishes," his young voice said confidently. "This strikes me as a good place for grammar and rhetoric."

Barbaricum

Anna and her companions spent their first night in India crowded into the corner of a tavern packed full with Roman soldiers and all the other typical denizens of a great port city—longshoremen, sailors, petty merchants and their womenfolk, pimps and prostitutes, gamblers, and the usual sprinkling of thieves and other criminals.

Like almost all the buildings in Barbaricum, the tavern was a mudbrick edifice which had been badly burned in the great fires which swept the city during the Roman conquest. The arson had not been committed by Belisarius' men, but by the fanatic Mahaveda priests who led the Malwa defenders. Despite the still-obvious reminders of that destruction, the tavern was in use for the simple reason that, unlike so many buildings in the city, the walls were still standing and there was even a functional roof.

When they first entered, Anna and her party had been assessed by the mob of people packed in the tavern. The assessment had not been as quick as the one which that experienced crowd would have normally made. Anna and her party were... odd.

The hesitation worked entirely to her advantage, however. The tough-looking Isaurian brothers and Abdul were enough to give would-be cutpurses pause, and in the little space and time cleared for them, the magical rumor had time to begin and spread throughout the tavern. Watching it spread—so obvious, from the curious stares and glances sent her way—Anna was simultaneously appalled, amused, angry, and thankful.

It's her. Calopodius the Blind's wife. Got to be.

"Who started this damned rumor, anyway?" she asked peevishly, after Illus cleared a reasonably clean spot for her in a corner and she was finally able to sit down. She leaned against the shelter of the walls with relief. She was well-nigh exhausted.

Abdul grunted with amusement. The Arab was frequently amused, Anna noted with exasperation. But it was an old and well-worn exasperation, by now, almost pleasant in its predictability.

Cottomenes, whose amusement at life's quirks was not much less than Abdul's, chuckled his own agreement. "You're hot news, Lady Saronites. Everybody on the docks was talking about it, too. And the soldiers outside the telegraph office." Cottomenes, unlike his older brother, never allowed himself the familiarity of calling her "girl." In all other respects, however, he showed her a lack of fawning respect which would have outraged her family.

After the dockboys whom Anna had hired finished stacking her luggage next to her, they crowded themselves against a wall nearby, ignoring the glares directed their way by the tavern's usual habitués. Clearly enough, having found this source of incredible largesse, the dockboys had no intention of relinquishing it.

Anna shook her head. The vehement motion finished the last

work of disarranging her long dark hair. The elaborate coiffure under which she had departed Constantinople, so many weeks before, was now entirely a thing of the past. Her hair was every bit as tangled and filthy as her clothing. She wondered if she would ever feel clean again.

"*Why?*" she whispered.

Squatting next to her, Illus studied her for a moment. His eyes were knowing, as if the weeks of close companionship and travel had finally enabled a half-barbarian mercenary soldier to understand the weird torments of a young noblewoman's soul.

Which, indeed, perhaps they had.

"You're different, girl. What you do is *different*. You have no idea how important that can be, to a man who does nothing, day after day, but toil under a sun. Or to a woman who does nothing, day after day, but wash clothes and carry water."

She stared up at him. Seeing the warmth lurking somewhere deep in Illus' eyes, in that hard tight face, Anna was stunned to realize how great a place the man had carved for himself in her heart. *Friendship* was a stranger to Anna of the Melisseni.

"And what is an angel, in the end," said the Isaurian softly, "but something *different*?"

Anna stared down at her grimy garments, noting all the little tears and frays in the fabric.

"In *this*?"

The epiphany finally came to her, then. And she wondered, in the hour or so that she spent leaning against the walls of the noisy tavern before she finally drifted into sleep, whether Calopodius had also known such an epiphany. Not on the day he chose to leave her behind, all her dreams crushed, in order to gain his own; but on the day he first awoke, a blind man, and realized that sight is its own curse.

And for the first time since she'd heard Calopodius' name, she no longer regretted the life which had been denied to her. No longer thought with bitterness of the years she would never spend in the shelter of the cloister, allowing her mind to range through the world's accumulated wisdom like a hawk finally soaring free.

When she awoke the next morning, the first thought which came to her was that she finally understood her own faith—and never had before, not truly. There was some regret in the thought, of course. Understanding, for all except God, is also limitation. But with that limitation came clarity and sharpness, so different from the froth and fuzz of a girl's fancies and dreams.

In the gray light of an alien land's morning, filtering into a tavern more noisome than any she would ever have imagined, Anna studied her soiled and ragged clothing. Seeing, this time, not filth and ruin but simply the carpet of her life opening up before her. A life she had thought closeted forever.

"Practicality first," she announced firmly. "It is not a sin."

The words woke up Illus. He gazed at her through slitted, puzzled eyes.

"Get up," she commanded. "We need uniforms."

A few minutes later, leading the way out the door with her three-soldier escort and five dock urchins toting her luggage trailing behind, Anna issued the first of that day's rulings and commandments.

"It'll be expensive, but my husband will pay for it. He's rich."

"He's not here," grunted Illus.

"His name is. He's also famous. Find me a banker."

It took a bit of time before she was able to make the concept of "banker" clear to Illus. Or, more precisely, differentiate it from the concepts of "pawnbroker," "usurer" and "loan shark." But, eventually, he agreed to seek out and capture this mythological creature—with as much confidence as he would have announced plans to trap a griffin or a minotaur.

"Never mind," grumbled Anna, seeing the nervous little way in which Illus was fingering his sword. "I'll do it myself. Where's the army headquarters in this city? *They'll* know what a 'banker' is, be sure of it."

That task *was* within Illus' scheme of things. And since Barbaricum was in the actual theater of Belisarius' operations, the officers in command of the garrison were several cuts of competence above those at Chabahari. By midmorning, Anna had been steered to the largest of the many new moneylenders who had fixed themselves upon Belisarius' army.

An Indian himself, ironically enough, named Pulinda. Anna wondered, as she negotiated the terms, what secrets—and what dreams, realized or stultified—lay behind the life of the small and elderly man sitting across from her. How had a man from the teeming Ganges valley eventually found himself, awash with wealth obtained in whatever mysterious manner, a paymaster to the alien army which was hammering at the gates of his own homeland?

Did he regret the life which had brought him to this place? Savor it?

Most likely both, she concluded. And was then amused, when she realized how astonished Pulinda would have been had he realized that the woman with whom he was quarreling over terms was actually awash in good feeling toward him.

Perhaps, in some unknown way, he sensed that warmth. In any event, the negotiations came to an end sooner than Anna had expected. They certainly left her with better terms than she had expected.

Or, perhaps, it was simply that magic name of Calopodius again, clearing the waters before her. Pulinda's last words to her were: "Mention me to your husband, if you would."

By midafternoon, she had tracked down the tailor reputed to be the best in Barbaricum. By sundown, she had completed her business with him. Most of that time had been spent keeping the dockboys from fidgeting as the tailor measured them.

"You also!" Anna commanded, slapping the most obstreperous urchin on top of his head. "In the Service, cleanliness is essential."

The next day, however, when they donned their new uniforms, the dockboys were almost beside themselves with joy. The plain and utilitarian garments were, by a great margin, the finest clothing they had ever possessed.

The Isaurian brothers and Abdul were not quite as demonstrative. Not quite.

"We look like princes," gurgled Cottomenes happily.

"And so you are," pronounced Anna. "The highest officers of the Wife's Service. A rank which will someday"—she spoke with a confidence far beyond her years—"be envied by princes the world over."

The Iron Triangle

"Relax, Calopodius," said Menander cheerfully, giving the blind young officer a friendly pat on the shoulder. "I'll see to it she arrives safely."

"She's already left Barbaricum," muttered Calopodius. "Damnation, why didn't she *wait*?"

Despite his agitation, Calopodius couldn't help smiling when he heard the little round of laughter which echoed around him. As usual, whenever the subject of Calopodius' wife arose, every officer and orderly in the command had listened. In her own way, Anna was becoming as famous as anyone in the great Roman army fighting its way into India.

Most husbands, to say the least, do not like to discover that their wives are the subject of endless army gossip. But since, in his case, the cause of the gossip was not the usual sexual peccadilloes, Calopodius was not certain how he felt about it. Some part of him, ingrained with custom, still felt a certain dull outrage. But, for the most part—perhaps oddly—his main reaction was one of quiet pride.

"I suppose that's a ridiculous question," he admitted ruefully. "She hasn't waited for anything else."

When Menander spoke again, the tone in his voice was much less jovial. As if he, too, shared in the concern which—much to his surprise—Calopodius had found engulfing him since he learned of Anna's journey. Strange, really, that he should care so much about the well-being of a wife who was little but a vague image to him.

But... Even before his blinding, the world of literature had often seemed as real to Calopodius as any other. Since he lost his sight, all the more so—despite the fact that he could no longer read or write himself, but depended on others to do it for him.

Anna Melisseni, the distant girl he had married and had known for a short time in Constantinople, meant practically nothing to him. But *the Wife of Calopodius the Blind*, the unknown woman who had been advancing toward him for weeks now, she was a different thing altogether. Still mysterious, but not a stranger. How could she be, any longer?

Had he not, after all, written about her often enough in his own *Dispatches*? In the third person, of course, as he always spoke of himself in his writings. No subjective mood was ever inserted into his *Dispatches*, any more than into the chapters of his massive *History of the War*. But, detached or not, whenever he received news of Anna he included at least a few sentences detailing for the army her latest adventures. Just as he did for those officers and men who had distinguished themselves. And he was no longer surprised to discover that most of the army found a young wife's exploits more interesting than their own.

She's different.

"Difference," however, was no shield against life's misfortunes—misfortunes which are multiplied several times over in the middle of a war zone. So, within seconds, Calopodius was back to fretting.

"Why didn't she *wait*, damn it all?"

Again, Menander clapped his shoulder. "I'm leaving with the *Victrix* this afternoon, Calopodius. Steaming with the river flow, I'll be in Sukkur long before Anna gets there coming upstream in an oared river craft. So I'll be her escort on the last leg of her journey, coming into the Punjab."

"The Sind's not *that* safe," grumbled Calopodius, still fretting. The Sind was the lower half of the Indus river valley, and while it had now been cleared of Malwa troops and was under the jurisdiction of Rome's Persian allies, the province was still greatly unsettled. "Dacoits everywhere."

"Dacoits aren't going to attack a military convoy," interrupted Belisarius. "I'll make sure she gets a Persian escort of some kind as far as Sukkur."

One of the telegraphs in the command center began to chatter. When the message was read aloud, a short time later, even Calopodius began to relax.

"Guess not," he mumbled—more than a little abashed. "With *that* escort."

The Lower Indus

"I don't believe this," mumbled Illus—more than a little abashed. He glanced down at his uniform. For all the finery of the fabric and the cut, the garment seemed utterly drab matched against the glittering costumes which seemed to fill the wharf against which their river barge was just now being tied.

Standing next to him, Anna said nothing. Her face was stiff, showing none of the uneasiness she felt herself. Her own costume was even more severe and plainly cut than those of her officers, even if the fabric itself was expensive. And she found herself wishing desperately that her cosmetics had survived the journey from Constantinople. For a woman of her class, being seen with a face unadorned by anything except nature was well-nigh unthinkable. In *any* company, much less...

The tying-up was finished and the gangplank laid. Anna was able to guess at the identity of the first man to stride across it.

She was not even surprised. Anna had read everything ever written by Irene Macrembolitissa—several times over—including the last book the woman wrote just before she left for the Hindu Kush on her great expedition of conquest. *The Deeds of Khusrau*, she thought, described the man quite well. The Emperor of Persia was not particularly large, but so full of life and energy that he seemed like a giant as he strode toward her across the gangplank.

What am I doing here? she wondered. I never planned on such as this!

"So! You are the one!" were the first words he boomed. "To live in such days, when legends walk among us!"

In the confused time which followed, as Anna was introduced to a not-so-little mob of Persian officers and officials—most of them obviously struggling not to frown with disapproval at such a disreputable woman—she pondered on those words.

They seemed meaningless to her. Khusrau Anushirvan—"Khusrau of the Immortal Soul"—was a legend, not she.

So why had he said that?

By the end of that evening, after spending hours sitting stiffly in a chair while Iran's royalty and nobility wined and dined her, she had mustered enough courage to lean over to the emperor—sitting next to her!—and whisper the question into his ear.

Khusrau's response astonished her even more than the question had. He grinned broadly, white teeth gleaming in a square-cut Persian beard. Then, he leaned over and whispered in return:

"I am an expert on legends, wife of Calopodius. Truth be told, I often think the art of kingship is mainly knowing how to make the things."

He glanced slyly at his assembled nobility, who had not stopped frowning at Anna throughout the royal feast—but always, she noticed, under lowered brows.

"But keep it a secret," he whispered. "It wouldn't do for my noble *vurzurgan* to discover that their emperor is really a common manufacturer. I don't need another rebellion this year."

She *did* manage to choke down a laugh, fortunately. The effort, however, caused her hand to shake just enough to spill some wine onto her long dress.

"No matter," whispered the emperor. "Don't even try to remove the stain. By next week, it'll be the blood of a dying man brought back to life by the touch of your hand. Ask anyone."

She tightened her lips to keep from smiling. It was nonsense, of course, but there was no denying the emperor was a charming man.

But, royal decree or no, it was still nonsense. Bloodstains aplenty there had been on the garments she'd brought from Constantinople, true enough. Blood and pus and urine and excrement and every manner of fluid produced by human suffering. She'd gained them in Chabahari, and again at Barbaricum. Nor did she doubt there *would* be bloodstains on this garment also, soon enough, to match the wine stain she had just put there.

Indeed, she had designed the uniforms of the Wife's Service with that in mind. That was why the fabric had been dyed a purple so dark it was almost black.

But it was still nonsense. Her touch had no more magic power than anyone's. Her *knowledge*—or rather, the knowledge which she had obtained by reading everything Macrembolitissa or anyone else had ever written transmitting the Talisman of God's wisdom—now, *that* was powerful. But it had nothing to do with her, except insofar as she was another vessel of those truths.

Something of her skepticism must have shown, despite her effort to remain impassive-faced. She was only nineteen, after all, and hardly an experienced diplomat.

Khusrau's lips quirked. "You'll see."

✦　　　✦　　　✦

The next day she resumed her journey up the river toward Sukkur. The emperor himself, due to the pressing business of completing his incorporation of the Sind into the swelling empire of Iran, apologized for not being able to accompany her personally. But he detailed no fewer than four Persian war galleys to serve as her escort.

"No fear of dacoits," said Illus, with great satisfaction. "Or deserters turned robbers."

His satisfaction turned a bit sour at Anna's response.

"Good. We'll be able to stop at every hospital along the way then. No matter how small."

And stop they did. Only briefly, in the Roman ones. By now, to Anna's satisfaction, Belisarius' blood-curdling threats had resulted in a marked improvement in medical procedures and sanitary practices.

But most of the small military hospitals along the way were Persian. The "hospitals" were nothing more than tents pitched along the riverbank—mere staging posts for disabled Persian soldiers being evacuated back to their homeland. The conditions within them had Anna seething, with a fury that was all the greater because neither she nor either of the Isaurian officers could speak a word of the Iranian language. Abdul could make himself understood, but his pidgin was quite inadequate to the task of convincing skeptical—even hostile—Persian officials that Anna's opinion was anything more than female twaddle.

Anna spent another futile hour trying to convince the officers in command of her escort to send a message to Khusrau himself. Clearly enough, however, none of them were prepared to annoy the emperor at the behest of a Roman woman who was probably half-insane to begin with.

Fortunately, at the town of Dadu, there was a telegraph station. Anna marched into it and fired off a message to her husband.

Why Talisman medical precepts not translated into Persian? Instruct Emperor Iran discipline his idiots.

"Do it," said Belisarius, after Calopodius read him the message. The general paused. "Well, the first part, anyway. The Persian translation. I'll have to figure out a somewhat more diplomatic way to pass the rest of it on to Khusrau."

Maurice snorted. "How about hitting him on the head with a club? That'd be 'somewhat' more diplomatic."

By the time the convoy reached Sukkur, it was moving very slowly.

There were no military hospitals along the final stretch of the river, because wounded soldiers were kept either in Sukkur itself or had already passed through the evacuation routes. The slow pace was now due entirely to the native population.

By whatever mysterious means, word of the Wife's passage had spread up and down the Indus. The convoy was constantly approached by small river boats bearing sick and injured villagers, begging for what was apparently being called "the healing touch."

Anna tried to reason, to argue, to convince. But it was hopeless. The language barrier was well-nigh impassible. Even the officers of her Persian escort could do no more than roughly translate the phrase "healing touch."

In the end, not being able to bear the looks of anguish on their faces, Anna laid her hands on every villager brought alongside her barge for the purpose. Muttering curses under her breath all the while—curses which were all the more bitter since she was quite certain the villagers of the Sind took them for powerful incantations.

At Sukkur, she was met by Menander and the entire crew of the *Victrix*. Beaming from ear to ear.

The grins faded soon enough. After waiting impatiently for the introductions to be completed, Anna's next words were: "Where's the telegraph station?"

Urgent. Must translate Talisman precepts into native tongues also.

Menander fidgeted while she waited for the reply.

"I've got a critical military cargo to haul to the island," he muttered. "Calopodius may not even send an answer."

"He's my husband," came her curt response. "Of course he'll answer me."

✧   ✧   ✧

Sure enough, the answer came very soon.

Cannot. Is no written native language. Not even alphabet.

After reading it, Anna snorted. "We'll see about that."

You supposedly expert grammar and rhetoric. Invent one.

"You'd best get started on it," mused Belisarius. The general's head turned to the south. "She'll be coming soon."

"Like a tidal bore," added Maurice.

The Iron Triangle

That night, he dreamed of islands again.

First, of Rhodes, where he spent an idle day on his journey to join Belisarius' army while his ship took on supplies.

Some of that time he spent visiting the place where, years before, John of Rhodes had constructed an armaments center. Calopodius' own skills and interests were not inclined in a mechanical direction, but he was still curious enough to want to see the mysterious facility.

But, in truth, there was no longer much there of interest. Just a handful of buildings, vacant now except for livestock. So, after wandering about for a bit, he spent the rest of the day perched on a headland staring at the sea.

It was a peaceful, calm, and solitary day. The last one he would enjoy in his life, thus far.

Then, his dreams took him to the island in the Strait of Hormuz where Belisarius was having a naval base constructed. The general had sent Calopodius over from the mainland where the army was marching its way toward the Indus, in order to help resolve one of the many minor disputes which had erupted between the Romans and Persians who were constructing the facility. Among the members of the small corps of noble couriers who served Belisarius for liaison with the Persians, Calopodius had displayed a great deal of tact as well as verbal aptitude.

It was something of a private joke between him and the general. "I need you to take care of another obstreperous aunt," was the way Belisarius put it.

The task of mediating between the quarrelsome Romans and Persians had been stressful. But Calopodius had enjoyed the boat ride well enough; and, in the end, he had managed to translate Belisarius' blunt words into language flowery enough to slide the command through—like a knife between unguarded ribs.

Toward the end, his dreams slid into a flashing nightmare image of Bukkur Island. A log, painted to look like a field gun, sent flying by a lucky cannon ball fired by one of the Malwa gunships whose bombardment accompanied that last frenzied assault. The Romans drove off that attack also, in the end. But not before a mortar shell had ripped Calopodius' eyes out of his head.

The last sight he would ever have in his life was of that log, whirling through the air and crushing the skull of a Roman soldier standing in its way. What made the thing a nightmare was that Calopodius could not remember the soldier's name, if he had ever known it. So it all seemed very incomplete, in a way which was too horrible for Calopodius to be able to express clearly to anyone, even himself. Grammar and rhetoric simply collapsed under the coarse reality, just as fragile human bone and brain had collapsed under hurtling wood.

The sound of his aide-de-camp clumping about in the bunker awoke him. The warm little courtesy banished the nightmare, and Calopodius returned to life with a smile.

"How does the place look?" he asked.

Luke snorted. "It's hardly fit for a Melisseni girl. But I imagine it'll do for *your* wife."

"Soon, now."

"Yes." Calopodius heard Luke lay something on the small table next to the cot. From the slight rustle, he understood that it was another stack of telegrams. Private ones, addressed to him, not army business. "Any from Anna?"

"No. Just more bills."

Calopodius laughed. "Well, whatever else, she still spends money like a Melisseni. Before she's done, that banker will be the richest man in India."

Beyond a snort, Luke said nothing in response. After a moment, Calopodius' humor faded away, replaced by simple wonder.

"Soon, now. I wonder what she'll be like?"

The Indus

The attack came as a complete surprise. Not to Anna, who simply didn't know enough about war to understand what could be expected and what not, but to her military escort.

"What in the name of God do they think they're *doing?*" demanded Menander angrily.

He studied the fleet of small boats—skiffs, really—pushing out from the southern shore. The skiffs were loaded with Malwa soldiers, along with more than the usual complement of Mahaveda priests and their mahamimamsa "enforcers." The presence of the latter was a sure sign that the Malwa considered this project so near-suicidal that the soldiers needed to be held on a tight rein.

"It's an ambush," explained his pilot, saying aloud the conclusion Menander had already reached. The man pointed to the thick reeds. "The Malwa must have hauled those boats across the desert, hidden them in the reeds, waited for us. We don't keep regular patrols on the south bank, since there's really nothing there to watch for."

Menander's face was tight with exasperation. "But what's the *point* of it?" For a moment, his eyes moved forward, toward the heavily-shielded bow of the ship where the *Victrix*'s fire-cannon was situated. "We'll burn them up like so many piles of kindling."

But even before he finished the last words, even before he saw the target of the oncoming boats, Menander understood the truth. The fact of it, at least, if not the reasoning.

"*Why?* They're all dead men, no matter what happens. In the name of God, she's just a woman!"

He didn't wait for an answer, however, before starting to issue his commands. The *Victrix* began shuddering to a halt. The skiffs were coming swiftly, driven by almost frenzied rowing. It would take the *Victrix* time to come to a halt and turn around; time to make its way back to protect the barge it was towing.

Time, Menander feared, that he might not have.

"What should we do?" asked Anna. For all the strain in her voice, she was relieved that her words came without stammering. A Melisseni girl could afford to scream with terror; she couldn't. Not any longer.

Grim-faced, Illus glanced around the barge. Other than he and Cottomenes and Abdul, there were only five Roman soldiers on the barge—and only two of those were armed with muskets. Since Belisarius and Khusrau had driven the Malwa out of the Sind, and established Roman naval supremacy on the Indus with the new steam-powered gunboats, there had been no Malwa attempt to threaten shipping south of the Iron Triangle.

Then his eyes came to rest on the vessel's new feature, and his tight lips creased into something like a smile.

"God bless good officers," he muttered.

He pointed to the top of the cabin amidships, where a shell of thin iron was perched. It was a turret, of sorts, for the odd and ungainly looking "Puckle gun" which Menander had insisted on adding to the barge. The helmeted face and upper body of the gunner was visible, and Illus could see the man beginning to train the weapon on the oncoming canoes.

"Get up there—*now*. There's enough room in there for you, and it's the best armored place on the barge." He gave the oncoming Malwa a quick glance. "They've got a few muskets of their own. Won't be able to hit much, not shooting from skiffs moving that quickly—but keep your head *down* once you get there."

It took Anna a great deal of effort, encumbered as she was by her heavy and severe gown, to clamber atop the cabin. She couldn't have made it at all, if Abdul hadn't boosted her. Climbing over the iron wall of the turret was a bit easier, but not much. Fortunately, the gunner lent her a hand.

After she sprawled into the open interior of the turret, the hard edges of some kind of ammunition containers bruising her back, Anna had to struggle fiercely not to burst into shrill cursing.

I have got to design a new costume. Propriety be damned!

For a moment, her thoughts veered aside. She remembered that Irene Macrembolitissa, in her *Observations of India*, had mentioned—with some amusement—that Empress Shakuntala often wore pantaloons in public. Outrageous behavior, really, but... when *you're* the one who owns the executioners, you can afford to outrage public opinion.

The thought made her smile, and it was with that cheerful expression on her lips that she turned her face up to the gunner frowning down at her.

"Is there anything I can do to help?"

The man's face suddenly lightened, and he smiled himself.

"Damn if you aren't a prize!" he chuckled. Then, nodding his head. "Yes, ma'am. As a matter of fact, there is."

He pointed to the odd-looking objects lying on the floor of the turret, which had bruised Anna when she landed on them. "Those are called cylinders." He patted the strange looking weapon behind which he was half-crouched. "This thing'll wreak havoc, sure enough, as long as I can keep it loaded. I'm supposed to have a loader, but since we added this just as an afterthought..."

He turned his head, studying the enemy vessels. "Better do it quick, ma'am. If those skiffs get alongside, your men and the other soldiers won't be enough to beat them back. And they'll have grenades anyway, they're bound to. If I can't keep them off, we're all dead."

Anna scrambled around until she was on her knees. Then seized one of the weird-looking metal contraptions. It was not as heavy as it looked. "What do you need me to do? Be precise!"

"Just hand them to me, ma'am, that's all. I'll do the rest. And keep your head down—it's *you* they're after."

Anna froze for a moment, dumbfounded. "Me? *Why?*"

"Damned if I know. Doesn't make sense."

But, in truth, the gunner did understand. Some part of it, at least, even if he lacked the sophistication to follow all of the reasoning of the inhuman monster who commanded the Malwa empire. The gunner had never heard—and never would—of a man named Napoleon. But he was an experienced soldier, and not stupid even if his formal education was rudimentary. *The moral is to the material in war as three-to-one* was not a phrase the man would have ever uttered himself, but he would have had no difficulty understanding it.

Link, the emissary from the new gods of the future who ruled the Malwa in all but name and commanded its great army in the Punjab, had ordered this ambush. The "why" was self-evident to its superhuman intelligence. Spending the lives of a few soldiers and Mahaveda priests was well worth the price, if it would enable the monster to destroy *the Wife* whose exploits its spies reported. Exploits which, in their own peculiar way, had become important to Roman morale.

Cheap at the price, in fact. Dirt cheap.

The Iron Triangle

The battle on the river was observed from the north bank by a patrol of light Arab cavalry in Roman service. Being Beni Ghassan, the cavalrymen were far more sophisticated in the uses of new technology than most Arabs. Their commander immediately dispatched three riders to bring news of the Malwa ambush to the nearest telegraph station, which was but a few miles distant.

By the time Belisarius got the news, of course, the outcome of the battle had already been decided, one way or the other. So he could do nothing more than curse himself for a fool, and try not to let the ashen face of a blind young man sway his cold-blooded reasoning.

"I'm a damned fool not to have foreseen the possibility. It just didn't occur to me that the Malwa might carry *boats* across the desert. But it should have."

"Not your fault, sir," said Calopodius quietly.

Belisarius tightened his jaws. "Like hell it isn't."

Maurice, standing nearby, ran fingers through his bristly iron-gray hair. "We all screwed up. I should have thought of it, too. We've been so busy just being entertained by the episode that we didn't think about it. Not seriously."

Belisarius sighed and nodded. "There's still no point in me sending the *Justinian*. By the time it got there, it will all have been long settled—and there's always the chance Link might be trying for a diversion."

"You *can't* send the *Justinian*," said Calopodius, half-whispering. "With the *Victrix* gone—and the *Photius* down at Sukkur—the Malwa might try an amphibious attack on the Triangle."

He spoke the cold truth, and every officer in the command center knew it. So nothing further was said. They simply waited for another telegraph report to inform them whether Calopodius was a husband or a widower.

The Indus

Before the battle was over, Anna had reason to be thankful for her heavy gown.

As cheerfully profligate as he was, the gunner soon used up

the preloaded cylinders for the Puckle gun. Thereafter, Anna had to reload the cylinders manually with the cartridges she found in a metal case against the shell of the turret. Placing the new shells *into* a cylinder was easy enough, with a little experience. The trick was taking out the spent ones. The brass cartridges were hot enough to hurt her fingers, the first time she tried prying them out.

Thereafter, following the gunner's hastily shouted instructions, she started using the little ramrod provided in the ammunition case. Kneeling in the shelter of the turret, she just upended the cylinders—carefully holding them with the hem of her dress, because they were hot also—and smacked the cartridges loose.

The cartridges came out easily enough, that way—right onto her lap and knees. In a lighter gown, a less severe and formal garment, her thighs would soon enough have been scorched by the little pile of hot metal.

As it was, the heat was endurable, and Anna didn't care in the least that the expensive fabric was being ruined in the process. She just went about her business, brushing the cartridges onto the floor of the turret, loading and reloading with the thunderous racket of the Puckle gun in her ears, ignoring everything else around her.

Throughout, her mind only strayed once. After the work became something of a routine, she found herself wondering if her husband's mind had been so detached in battles. Not whether he had ignored pain—of course he had; Anna had learned that much since leaving Constantinople—but whether he had been able to ignore his continued existence as well.

She suspected he had, and found herself quite warmed by the thought. She even handed up the next loaded cylinder with a smile.

The gunner noticed the smile, and that too would become part of the legend. He would survive the war, as it happened; and, in later years, in taverns in his native Anatolia, whenever he heard the tale of how the Wife smote down Malwa boarders with a sword and a laugh, saw no reason to set the matter straight. By then, he had come to half-believe it himself.

Anna sensed a shadow passing, but she paid it very little attention. By now, her hands and fingers were throbbing enough to block out most sensation beyond what was necessary to keep reloading the cylinders. She barely even noticed the sudden burst of fiery light and the screams which announced that the *Victrix* had arrived and was wreaking its delayed vengeance on what was left of the Malwa ambush.

Which was not much, in truth. The gunner was a very capable man, and Anna had kept him well-supplied. Most of the skiffs now drifting near the barge had bodies draped over their sides and sprawled lifelessly within. At that close range, the Puckle gun had been murderous.

"Enough, ma'am," said the gunner gently. "It's over."

Anna finished reloading the cylinder in her hands. Then, when the meaning of the words finally registered, she set the thing down on the floor of the turret. Perhaps oddly, the relief of finally not having to handle hot metal only made the pain in her hands—and legs, too, she noticed finally—all the worse.

She stared down at the fabric of her gown. There were little stains all over it, where cartridges had rested before she brushed them onto the floor. There was a time, she could vaguely remember, when the destruction of an expensive garment would have been a cause of great concern. But it seemed a very long time ago.

"How is Illus?" she asked softly. "And the others? The boys?"

The gunner sighed. "One of the boys got killed, ma'am. Just bad luck—Illus kept the youngsters back, but that one grenade..."

Vaguely, Anna remembered hearing an explosion. She began to ask which boy it was, whose death she had caused, of the five urchins she had found on the docks of Barbaricum and conscripted into her Service. But she could not bear that pain yet.

"Illus?"

"He's fine. So's Abdul. Cottomenes got cut pretty bad."

Something to do again. The thought came as a relief. Within seconds, she was clambering awkwardly over the side of the turret again—and, again, silently cursing the impractical garment she wore.

Cottomenes was badly gashed, true enough. But the leg wound was not even close to the great femoral artery, and by now Anna had learned to sew other things than cloth. Besides, the *Victrix*'s boiler was an excellent mechanism for boiling water.

The ship's engineer was a bit outraged, of course. But, wisely, he kept his mouth shut.

The Iron Triangle

"It's not much," said Calopodius apologetically.

Anna's eyes moved over the interior of the little bunker where Calopodius lived. Where she would now live also. She did not fail to notice all the little touches here and there—the bright, cheery little cloths; the crucifix; even a few native handcrafts—as well as the relative cleanliness of the place. But . . .

No, it was not much. Just a big pit in the ground, when all was said and done, covered over with logs and soil.

"It's fine," she said. "Not a problem."

She turned and stared at him. Her husband, once a hand-some boy, was now a hideously ugly man. She had expected the empty eye sockets, true enough. But even after all the carnage she had witnessed since she left Constantinople, she had not once considered what a mortar shell would do to the *rest* of his face.

Stupid, really. As if shrapnel would obey the rules of poetry, and pierce eyes as neatly as a goddess at a loom. The upper half of his face was a complete ruin. The lower half was relatively unmarked, except for one scar along his right jaw and another puckerlike mark on his left cheek.

His mouth and lips, on the other hand, were still as she vaguely remembered them. A nice mouth, she decided, noticing for the first time.

"It's fine," she repeated. "Not a problem."

A moment later, two soldiers came into the bunker hauling her luggage. What was left of it. Until they were gone, Anna and Calopodius were silent. Then he said, very softly:

"I don't understand why you came."

Anna tried to remember the answer. It was difficult. And probably impossible to explain, in any event. *I wanted a divorce, maybe* . . . seemed . . . strange. Even stranger, though closer to the truth, would be: *or at least to drag you back so you could share the ruins of my own life.*

"It doesn't matter now. I'm here. I'm staying."

For the first time since she'd rejoined her husband, he smiled. Anna realized she'd never really seen him smile before. Not, at least, with an expression that was anything more than politeness.

He reached out his hand, tentatively, and she moved toward him. The hand, fumbling, stroked her ribs.

"God in Heaven, Anna!" he choked. "How can you *stand* something like that—in this climate? You'll drown in sweat."

Anna tried to keep from laughing; and then, realizing finally where she was, stopped trying. Even in the haughtiest aristocratic circles of Constantinople, a woman was allowed to laugh in the presence of her husband.

When she was done—the laughter was perhaps a bit hysterical—Calopodius shook his head. "We've got to get you a sari, first thing. I can't have my wife dying on me from heat prostration."

Calopodius matched deed to word immediately. A few words to his aide-to-camp Luke, and, much sooner than Anna would have expected, a veritable horde of Punjabis from the adjacent town were packed into the bunker.

Some of them were actually there on business, bringing piles of clothing for her to try on. Most of them, she finally understood, just wanted to get a look at her.

Of course, they were all expelled from the bunker while she changed her clothing—except for two native women whose expert assistance she required until she mastered the secrets of the foreign garments. But once the women announced that she was suitably attired, the mob of admirers was allowed back in.

In fact, after a while Anna found it necessary to leave the bunker altogether and model her new clothing on the ground outside, where everyone could get a good look at her new appearance. Her husband insisted, to her surprise.

"You're beautiful," he said to her, "and I want everyone to know it."

She almost asked how a blind man could tell, but he forestalled the question with a little smile. "Did you think I'd forget?"

But later, that night, he admitted the truth. They were lying side by side, stiffly, still fully clothed, on the pallet in a corner of the bunker where Calopodius slept. "To be honest, I can't remember very well what you look like."

Anna thought about it, for a moment. Then:

"I can't really remember myself."

"I wish I could see you," he murmured.

"It doesn't matter." She took his hand and laid it on her bare belly. The flesh reveled in its new coolness. She herself, on the other hand, reveled in the touch. And did not find it strange that she should do so.

"Feel."

His hand was gentle, at first. And never really stopped being so, for all the passion that followed. When it was all over, Anna was covered in sweat again. But she didn't mind at all. Without heavy and proper fabric to cover her—with nothing covering her now except Calopodius' hand—the sweat dried soon enough. That, too, was a great pleasure.

"I warn you," she murmured into his ear. "We're not in Constantinople any more. Won't be for a long time, if ever. So if I catch you with a courtesan, I'll boil you alive."

"The thought never crossed my mind!" he insisted. And even believed it was true.

AVE ATQUE VALE

SANDRA MIESEL

Three centuries after the Legions withdrew, England still remembered Rome. Now something more than a lingering memory has come to disrupt the life of an Anglo-Saxon nun.

◇◇◇◇◇

A soft summer night lay over the Kingdom of Essex. The wind from the North Sea had stilled, and mists rising from the marsh had turned the moon to a milky blur. Near the mouth of the River Colne, the Priory of St. Mary was at peace.

Elfleda the infirmarian wearily smoothed her patient's coarse blanket. This morning's ritual had overtaxed the old nun's weak heart, but the sleeping draught had finally brought Mildrith rest. All too soon it would be the eternal rest. For now, her shallow breathing was regular enough that Elfleda judged it safe to leave the infirmary. She carried the candle stub into her own room, carefully propping the connecting door ajar with a stick of kindling.

Just as she was about to unveil for bed, a man in shining armor walked out of the wall. Elfleda lurched backwards, too startled to scream.

"*Ave, Soror!*" said the vision. His arm raised in salute. "Hail Sister!"

"Saint Michael?" Elfleda gasped. Was he coming for Mildrith's soul? She reached for the wooden cross hanging on the wall. "Are you Saint Michael?"

"No, I am not." He came no closer.

Cross now in hand, she thrust it in his face. "*Vade, Satanas!*" she cried.

"I am not that one either." The figure lightly waved her hand away.

175

Holding the cross before her tightly shut eyes like a shield, Elfleda raced through a *Pater noster*. When she opened her eyes again, the vision was still there—and frowning.

"Neither am I an evil from which you require delivery," he said coolly. "When you attempt to use the Latin tongue, do try to speak it properly. Your accent is barbarous."

Her pride flared. "Who—or what—are you to correct me?" Elfleda squinted in the light of her guttering candle, craning her neck for a better look at the vision. The lean, angular face under a plumed helmet was clean-shaven, not old but accustomed to all weathers.

"Come, now. Tell me your name," she demanded. "I will tell you mine: I am Sister Elfleda, daughter of Elfwald. I am no spell-caster who would bind you." Naming herself first could put her in his power but she was willing to risk it.

The figure squared his shoulders and recited as if answering a roll call: "I am the shade of Gaius Aurelius Perennis, once *signifer* of the Ninth Legion Hispana, serving in the Imperial Province of Brittannia."

"Oh!" cried Elfleda. "A Roman!" Her eyes grew wide with awe. "Are you the ghost of some lost martyr from the elder days? Have you come to show us where your bones lie so we can honor them?" She'd heard such stories about forgotten saints.

"I am not one of your Christian saints." Each word was a hammer stroke. "I was never even a Christian!"

"Mind your voice." *Heathen*, she silently added, pointing at the sickroom.

"Only you can hear me. And I can hear anything you say, however softly."

Elfleda flushed.

Ignoring her embarrassment, Gaius continued. "There is no lost grave to reveal. My remains, all that's left of me, is already being honored—right in this place. That decorated box your sisterhood enshrined this morning with so much ceremony contains my incorrupt head."

"A false relic?" She covered her face with her hands. "No! That can't be! Our reliquary was a gift from the King of Mercia."

"Woman, don't you think I know my own head?" Then his voice turned gentle. "A moment ago, you would've believed me without question had I claimed to be a Christian saint. But when

I told the truth, you couldn't accept it. I am a Roman and my honor requires me to be truthful."

Elfleda retreated across the room. She sat down heavily on her cot, bowed low by shock. "I sense that you speak true. Why then have you come? To trouble the peace of this holy house? To mock our faith? To rob me of sleep?" She raised her eyes to meet his gaze. "Tell me."

"I want to be buried with the ancient rites of my fathers. Otherwise, I must stay bound to my severed head until that lump of tanned skin over brown bone turns to dust. For twenty generations and more I have lingered on Earth, a doomed phantom stretching forth my hands to the shade of the Opposite Shore, never able to cross over...to whatever lies beyond."

"Never to reach the bright meads of Paradise.... My pity, warrior, my deepest pity." Elfleda sighed. "What rites or prayers would bring you peace? If our old chaplain were still living, he would know." Surely the Father Almighty had a resting place for heathens who had not known him.

"I don't ask for pomp and a roaring pyre," he said. "A small libation, blood sprinkled from a sacrifice, then..."

"No!" Elfleda sprang up. "Never! I cannot do such heathen deeds, even out of kindness."

"You needn't believe in any of it; just do it."

"That's what Roman rulers said to the martyrs. But holy virgins died in torment rather than burn one pinch of incense on your altars." She crossed her arms defiantly across her chest.

"So, you see yourself as a holy virgin."

"A virgin, yes. Holy is for heaven to judge." A holy nun would not be talking to a ghost, Elfleda thought. She ought to confess this night's work in the next Chapter of Faults but knew in her heart that that wasn't likely to happen.

"Your virginity I confirm." Gaius passed his hand through her body as Elfleda swung a fist at him.

"Keep your unclean paws to yourself!" she hissed. Further imprecations were cut off by the sound of a bell. "Time for Matins."

Elfleda charged through her assailant's shade, glanced at sleeping Mildrith, and left by the sickroom door. Head bowed, arms thrust in her ample sleeves, she joined a line of other nuns emerging from their dormitory. They processed to the chapel following the Prioress and her lantern.

Gaius marched beside them, striding through the wooden posts upholding the cloister roof. "I foresee a long siege," he muttered. "Let the battle be joined."

Osyth the prioress led her community into the candlelit chapel, black figures casting shadows on the whitewashed wooden walls. The line split in two as ten nuns took their places in opposing rows of prayer stalls. Elfleda gazed at Mildrith's empty place, then turned toward Hildelith the chantress standing at her lectern. All the sisters offered the customary silent *Pater noster* that began Matins.

Hildelith, a stocky woman with a powerful voice, intoned: "*Domine, labia mea aperies.*"

With the others, Elfleda opened her lips and announced the Lord's praise.

As the psalms and prayers unrolled, Elfleda's attention wandered. Prolonged lack of sleep was starting to take its toll and she began to nod. Rote memory pulled her along, praying more out of habit than heart. However imperfectly, she would last to the end of the Hour: "O Lord make haste to help me." Was Gaius still here? Heaven forbid he would mock the nuns—or worse, profane the chapel. Elfleda tried harder to focus her eyes. Then she spied him, a patch of brightness where the wall should be dark.

Gaius circled the room slowly behind the stalls and paused before the wooden aumbry cabinet where the Sacrament and sacred vessels were reserved. Although he raised his hand briefly as if to touch it, he moved quickly towards the altar and stared awhile at the whalebone and silver box that held his skull. He passed the sacristy door and spent the rest of the service peering over—and sometimes through—Hildelith's shoulder at their fine new choirbook. Was the proud Roman struggling to match script to sound? Elfleda hid a tight smile.

How welcome was the last *Amen* of Matins!

Dispensed from Lauds and Prime to tend Mildrith, Elfleda was relieved to find the old sister's condition much improved. She dosed, fed, washed, and dressed her in time for the community's morning assembly in the Chapter House. Mildreth's entry on Elfleda's arm drew smiles all around.

Seeing this welcome eased Elfleda's weariness; she hadn't lost nights of sleep in vain. But was sleep also well lost over a Roman ghost?

Mother Osyth bestowed a kiss of peace on Mildrith. "Besides expert care," she nodded at Elfleda, "perhaps Sister's turn for the better is an early blessing sent by the nameless saint of our new relic. If he would deign to shower our priory with miracles, pilgrims would come. Their offerings could rebuild our chapel in more seemly form." As they all well knew, the plain little wooden building was supposed to have been replaced years earlier. But income from the Priory's estates upriver barely sufficed to keep the community alive. "Our esteemed new intercessor," the prioress continued, "came to us unidentified. Surely, he deserves a better name than Saint Ignotus. I am open to suggestions. Speak freely."

And speak the nuns did, with proposals that failed to persuade the group. Elfleda pondered: did she dare? Yes, she did.

"Mother," she asked, "perhaps we could call him Saint Perennis, 'the enduring one'? After all, his head seems to have lasted hundreds of years undecayed."

Saint Perennis he became. Only Elfleda heard Gaius chuckle. Later, Elfleda was taking her midday meal when Gaius appeared before her in the refectory. He inspected her bread, ale, and green pottage. Did the sight of simple food stir regret? She touched her forefinger to her lips. They were observing silence while one sister read a passage from the Bible aloud. Burghild, not their most fluent lector, was plowing a jagged furrow through the First Book of Kings wherein Solomon turns away from the Lord by offering heathen sacrifices to please his foreign women.

The story must have annoyed Gaius, for he vanished before Elfleda's eyes. She took a bite of bread and mused that she could make herself wiser than Solomon by not performing the Roman's ritual. That was a worthy ambition.

Gaius reappeared later that afternoon as Elfleda was weeding her herb garden.

"Have you no slaves for such tasks?" He stood in a bed of Saint-John's-wort.

She dusted earth from her hands before answering. "Our bondman Cedd and his wife Pega do the heaviest work, but we all lend a hand as needed. Even Mother Osyth. Didn't you notice Sister Leoba, our youngest, serving food? These herbs and all the healing plants are mine to tend."

"A few I recognize." He pointed to a plant with small, spiky leaves: "*Rosmarinum*, 'dew of the sea.' I can almost recall the scent and taste. What do you use it for?"

"Besides cooking, it soothes the nerves, keeps moths away, and..." she broke off a sprig and waved it at him. "It's the herb of remembrance."

"Yes." He nodded. "Memory is all I have left of life. Would you cast some in my grave when you bury my head?"

Elfleda made a show of pulling more weeds and dropping them in her basket. To change the subject, she asked, "Why am I the only one who can see and hear you?"

"I think you must be my descendent, from a child I got on some *Britanna* wench long ago."

"*You?* My longfather? Impossible!" Elfleda sprang to her feet, knocking the basket over. My people came with Hengist and Horsa!"

"Hold onto that pride of lineage if it pleases you." Gaius shrugged. "At least they were successful pirates, unlike the waves of Saxon rabble that we built forts along the coast to repel. But Rome left and the rabble got through."

"The children of what you call rabble now dwell in settled Christian kingdoms."

"You're still barbarous. Look around you. You live in shelters of wood and thatch. My legion's barracks was built of stone, with a red tile roof."

"How cozy." Elfleda spat out her reply. "Our Priory will rise in stone someday. Your Empire fell, despite all that stonework. Where now are your Caesars?"

"Where now are your ring-giving lords? Your kingdoms will fall in their turn, when new barbarians invade. There are always more barbarians than civilized men."

"Did barbarians or civilized men kill you?"

"That I will tell you in due time. In either case I'd be dead by now howsoever I died."

"All things are passing; God only will stay." Elfleda quoted a proverb.

"Does your god care about passing things...or people?"

"He cared enough to come down to us so he could bring us to his Heavenly Kingdom."

"So you say." Gaius paused, acknowledging her conviction. "Our gods only visit Earth to bed mortals—or make them fight." He turned away and vanished.

Elfleda gathered up the weeds. They were too lush to burn but would serve as fodder. She carried the basket to the cowshed.

The rest of the day passed without another visit from Gaius. Refreshed by a normal span of sleep, Elfleda prayed and sang her way through the day's Hours with proper attention. She came cheerfully to her afternoon tasks in the infirmary workroom.

She was using a stone mortar and pestle to crush flaxseeds when Gaius appeared. "What is that oily mess?" he asked.

"It's going to become a poultice for a boil on Sister Wynflaed's eye. Watch as I add an infusion of chamomile flowers." Elfleda was flushed with effort by the time the mixture became a smooth paste. She scraped it into a small clay pot and set it on the bench beside a vessel filled with greenish liquid. "This is elder-leaf wash, to cleanse her eyes before applying the poultice. She's coming by before Vespers and I'll show her how to use it." She began tearing a piece of clean cloth into strips for bandages.

Gaius surveyed her neat shelves of labeled jars, her bunches of drying herbs, and her brazier, and her bronze tools hanging from pegs. "Not unlike what a legionary *medicus* would have," he said.

"Am I to take that as a compliment?"

"You could." He bent down to peer at something murky gently simmering in a pot hanging over her brazier.

"That's leek, wine, and salts of ox-gall," she explained, continuing to scour her implements clean. "It will become an eye salve in case Sister's boil doesn't heal cleanly."

"How did you learn this art?"

"I followed a local healer around from the time I could toddle." Elfleda smiled. "That's not a usual pastime for a thane's daughter . . . an extra daughter. So rather than have me sit in his hall unwed, my father sent me here because his earl was kin to Mother Osyth. Both our families are from Mercia." She put her mortar and pestle away and sat on a tall stool by the bench. "Thus, I get to serve the Lord of Heaven and still use my healing skills."

"No regrets for not marrying?"

"Do you regret your oath as a soldier?"

"It was my calling."

"And this is mine."

"My calling was in my blood," Gaius explained. "My father was a centurion, so he had the means to pay for my education.

That led to my appointment as *signifer*—standard-bearer—in the first cohort of the Ninth Legion. I expected to serve with honor and advance to higher rank."

"But you died too soon," Elfleda broke in. "Where did you fall?"

"My legion was being transferred from Eboracum—you call it York—to build a wall along the northern border of Britannia. I was sent out with too small a detachment of guards to bring the men already working at the west end their pay. We were ambushed by a war band of Selgovae, the very tribesmen the wall was intended to restrain. The bright enamelwork on my belt must have made them think I was someone special. They spared me and dragged me off to their village. I expected to get my belly slit so they could examine my entrails...which would've been quicker than what they did do."

"Perhaps they doubted the quality of your entrails."

Gaius scowled. His armor vanished. Ghastly wounds briefly gaped across his face and body.

Elfleda shuddered. "Forgive my cruel jest," she begged and turned away her face in shame.

Acknowledging her with a slight nod, Gaius continued. "After the savages had had their sport, they hung my severed head from my own standard and sank both in a bog as an offering to their gods."

"But how did your head become a relic?" she asked.

"By a series of foolish mistakes by a peat cutter, farmer, monk, abbot, and king who assumed that an incorrupt head had to be that of a holy martyr."

"Burial in a peat bog preserves things. People sometimes store butter that way."

"Yes, the dim-witted peat cutter dug me up thinking he's found a ball of butter. The monks, on the other hand, treated me as a holy treasure. They wrapped my head in figured silk and sealed it in that fancy box. I watched it made. The fellow who wrought it was not without skill, but what a waste of whalebone and silver." He fumed. "Dead bodies should be burned or at least buried, not dismembered and kept as trophies!"

"But saints aren't ordinary dead," Elfleda objected. "Their bodies—or even pieces of their bodies—make them present to us in a special way and link us to their life in the Kingdom of Heaven."

"How many times must I explain that I don't want to be one of your saints—or even deified like a Roman Emperor?" His words marched out like heavy footfalls. "I simply want my head to be interred according to ancestral custom."

"And how many times must I explain why that's impossible," Elfleda snapped back, springing to her feet. "I cannot and will not perform heathen ceremonies. Moreover, in order to bury your head—with or without ceremonies—I'd first have to steal the reliquary or break it open and switch your skull with a stone."

"That would be dishonorable." Gaius sighed. "Is there no way to enlighten your Prioress? She seems intelligent...." He tactfully did not add "for a barbarian."

"Mother Osyth can't see you and she wouldn't believe my testimony...wouldn't *want* to believe my testimony. She badly needs the relic to work miracles to draw us new patronage. She understands why Mercia sent this gift—it's a bribe so she will influence her son if he becomes King of Essex."

"The Prioress has a son?" Gaius exclaimed. "I thought this was a house of virgins."

"We do count widows among us. Mother was once queen to Sighere of Essex but after she gave him a son, she begged leave to take the veil. He agreed and gave her land for the Priory."

"What kind of man would do that?"

"A generous one," said Elfleda.

"I see: once he has his son, what further use is the woman?"

Elfleda continued as if she had not heard. "Sighere also feared for his soul because he had fallen away from the Faith for a time. He's dead now and two kinsmen are ruling jointly until his son comes of age."

"My head's not just a relic; it's a royal gaming piece as well." He groaned. "I can't even fall on my sword to escape the impasse because I'm already dead. It's a jest worthy of some god or other."

Elfleda stretched out a consoling hand but it passed through his shoulder.

"It's almost time for Vespers. Sister Wynflaed will be coming for her medicines."

"I will return," said Gaius and vanished.

But he appeared the next day and every day thereafter as the flowery summer weeks flowed by. Days lengthened; quarrels dwindled. Both Elfleda and Gaius admitted that further dispute was pointless. But it pained her to see him standing among bees gathering honey he could never taste from blossoms whose fragrance he could never enjoy. Now she prayed with new fervor for a solution. It was no longer a battle of wills but a matter of this man's salvation.

Gaius continued to follow Elfleda on her daily round, listening to her chant the Hours, watching her treat the small hurts and ills of her community. Her ministrations were not limited to the Priory: once a tenant farmer walked miles to have her set his broken arm. Elfleda found the ghost's presence an unspoken reproach. She tried to counter such thoughts with friendliness. At least she could offer the comfort of human speech to one bereft of it year after long year while tethered to a bog.

While the bright jewel of the heavens continued its climb, a shadow crept across Elfleda's busy days: Mildrith's heart continued to fail. Lungwort tea soothed her coughing somewhat but none of Elfleda's tonics gave her strength and her badly swollen legs resisted every remedy. She returned to the infirmary bed and Elfleda was dispensed from the night Offices to watch over her.

Gaius shared these watches. "Not all battles can be won, Elfleda. Man arms himself in vain against the march of Death."

"I know she's dying, Gaius. That is our common fate: dust we are and to dust we shall return. What you don't understand is that Sister Mildrith is the real heart of the Priory. She taught us all, even Mother, because she had been trained at the royal monastery of Chelles in Frankland. I—and I think the other sisters—are torn between sorrow over losing her and joy that she will enter soon into Life Eternal. But we will stay strong beside her. As the proverb says: 'No weary mind can withstand Fate nor sad heart offer help.'"

"Your ranks will hold steady to the end," said Gaius.

Osyth also took note of Mildrith's decline. She had the reliquary of Saint Perennis taken from the chapel and placed beside Mildrith's sickbed as a source of blessing, if not healing. Concerned lest her beloved daughter die without the sacraments, Osyth dispatched Cedd with a message to Byrhtstan, their earl, requesting the loan of a priest. Invoking her royal connections, she reminded him that no Mass had been said at the Priory since Pentecost despite his promise to find them a new chaplain.

Cedd duly returned with a priest named Wulfmar who clearly resented being called abruptly from a comfortable position to tend nuns. He brought as acolyte his gangly son Wulfred, a youth already training to follow his father's path.

Rumor traveled with them. Cedd had arrived just as Byrhtstan was about to ride off to the royal hall in Maldon. The kings had summoned him for counsel after reports of strange ships lingering along the coast and even off Mersea Island by the Colne. He instantly agreed to Osyth's request lest discussion delay him.

The Prioress ordered Cedd to keep news of strangers quiet but the priest shared it anyway. To distract everyone, Osyth kept them busy preparing for the Vigil of Saint John, three days hence. The nuns cleansed every building in the Priory. They gathered wood for a bonfire and flowers for garlands.

"What are you celebrating?" Gaius asked Elfleda, watching her tidy the infirmary.

"The birthday of Saint John, Christ our King's own thane of glory, who lost his head for offending a king." She glanced at Gaius, in case mention of beheading bothered him. "Joy is greater for it falls at Midsummer, when the sun lingers longest in his sun-stead. We'll light a bonfire to salute him. Its ashes will make the garden fruitful. There will be wine and sweet cakes...."

"Something like our Vestalia in Rome," Gaius interrupted. "You're holding festival when you ought to be worrying about raiders from the sea?" Gaius snapped. "Look around you. You're far from any settlement but only a mile from a river inlet. You have no wall, no palisade, not even a ditch lined with pointed sticks. A legion on the march pitched camps more secure than this place."

"Should we worry? This land's been at peace for many years. The Priory is hallowed ground. It needs no warriors."

"No? Never? One song you chant to your god thanks him for training hands for battle and fingers for war."

"Ah. You're paying attention to our Psalms. Did you notice another one where the Lord of All promises to break the bow, snap the spear, and burn the shields with fire?" Elfleda softened her tone. "Nevertheless, I admit we did have warriors who were sainted, like Edwin and Oswald of Northumbria."

"You may yet have cause to wish they were here." Gaius left her.

✧   ✧   ✧

The next day Mildrith's condition suddenly worsened. Her long-resisted death was at hand. The new priest Wulfmar administered the last rites with minimal correctness, but the sacred words carried their own power regardless. The whole community gathered 'round the tiny old woman's bed to bid her farewell. One by one they kissed her deeply wrinkled cheeks and stroked her twisted, mottled fingers. Osyth tucked strands of sparse white hair back under her cap and blessed her.

Mildrith's eyes fluttered open. With blue-tinged lips she thanked her sisters for their love and begged their forgiveness for her failures in loving them. Pointing towards the reliquary beside her bed, she thanked the saint for comforting her as a shining glow of presence. "Sent me good thoughts...and..." Her words trailed off in fits of wet coughing. Only those kneeling closest could hear her whisper, "Into Thy hands, Lord..." The steady murmur of prayers for the dying could not mask her gasps for breath until they ceased.

Elfleda felt for a pulse and gently drew the covers over Mildrith's peaceful face.

"Eternal rest grant to her, O Lord," the priest intoned.

"And let perpetual light shine upon her," the nuns responded.

It was Elfleda's duty to wash Mildrith's body and prepare it for burial. She placed a wooden cross in the dead woman's folded hands and shrouded her tightly in white linen. Her mortal remains were now an anonymous bundle lying on the pallet that would serve as her bier. Before she yielded to tears, Gaius appeared.

"When do you bury her?" he asked.

"Tomorrow, on St. John's Day. Mother has decided to honor her with burial in the chapel floor, rather than our cemetery. Cedd is digging the grave now. We'll take turns keeping watch here until the service begins tomorrow morning."

Elfleda continued: "You didn't mention that you were visiting Mildrith."

"I didn't think it was necessary. I spoke to her even though she couldn't hear me."

"But she sensed you were there and felt comforted." Elfleda smiled at him. "That was a miracle of sorts as well as a good deed, a work of mercy."

Gaius deflected her compliment. "What do you think became of the old one's spirit?"

"Saint Michael, standard-bearer of the Almighty, has led her into Paradise where eternal light will shine upon her. But this body that we bury will rise again, remade and immortal on the Last Day."

Gaius shook his head. "I was taught that the reward of virtue is to be freed from the fetters of the body. Those who have served their community will have a place marked out for them in the starry heavens."

It was Elfleda's turn to be puzzled. "Is this what you expect to happen if the ceremonies you crave were performed?

"I would like to become a star."

"God who made the stars calls each one by name." She thought to herself: And even they must fall and be remade at the End.

Later, Elfleda approached Osyth in her parlor with a special request.

"Mother, may I speak? You saw how the relic of Saint Perennis eased Mildrith's passing. Because she became so attached to it, would it not be fitting to bury it with her? The reliquary would still be with us in the chapel, although hidden from sight."

Osyth smiled but shook her head. "You have a caring heart, daughter. We thank Saint Perennis for his tenderness towards Mildrith, but he is not meant to be hers alone. His relic belongs to the Priory, now and in days to come. Our sisters and our visitors deserve to see the reliquary itself, not merely its burial spot. That said," she continued, "I have decided to honor Mildrith another way. I will have her buried in the coffin already prepared against my own time of dying."

"That is a singular privilege. I bow to your judgment, Mother," Elfleda said with a sigh and left.

Afterwards, Elfleda walked over to the chapel to view the open grave. Cedd had piled the spoil dirt on a large canvas sheet and stacked the paving stones lifted from that part of the floor.

When Gaius appeared beside her, she gave him a rueful smile and said: "I tried my best to get you buried."

"I heard. Thank you for the effort. But I'd still need a libation and a blood sacrifice. Also, there's the matter of the ferryman's fee."

"What's that?"

"The shades of the dead must pay for passage over the Hateful River that divides this world from the next."

"That's taking a long way round to become a star." Elfleda was confused. "How much does this passage cost?"

"A small coin will do, even a barbarous token."

"I can't help you there. I've taken a vow of poverty. I haven't a single *sceatta*, much less a *denarius*."

"How do you know what a *denarius* is?" It was his turn to be puzzled.

"It's in the Gospel. Maybe we're not such barbarians after all."

As she turned away from him to hide a grin of triumph, something bluish green caught her eye in the dirt pile. Elfleda bent down and dug out a corroded metal disk. "This looks like copper," she said, holding it up for Gaius to see.

"By the size, I'd say that was an *as*, worth about one third of a *denarius*."

"Whose image and whose inscription?"

He peered at the coin. "It's too worn to tell."

"But enough Roman money, I suppose, to pay your way?" Elfleda scraped at it with her fingernails. "But starting from this you think you could make yourself into a star? Go try." She flipped it into the open grave.

Gaius laughed harder and harder. "'*Ab as se creavit.*'" He could barely get the words out between loud guffaws.

"What? Are you saying: 'the Abbot hid'? That doesn't make any sense."

"Don't try to understand, Elfleda." He regained his composure. "I was quoting from Petronius, a Latin author you most assuredly have never read."

Elfleda had never heard Gaius laugh before.

Afterwards, she pondered whether laughter beside a grave was fitting. Mildrith had had as happy a death as anyone could wish: she fought the good fight, finished the course, kept the faith. Since for her Death has lost its sting, why not laugh? Or at least not weep.

The next morning dawned shrouded in dense fog as if Nature herself mourned. But Elfreda and the others were tearless as they filed into their stalls for the funeral. Gytha the sacristan had decked the chapel in festive array. Spotless white linens covered the candle-lit altar and long white curtains edged with embroidery hung behind it. There were bunches of Saint-John's-wort in bowls around the sanctuary and heaped on the black pall that covered

Mildrith's coffin. The golden flowers were like pools of sunshine brought indoors on what should have been the sun's brightest day.

The funeral proceeded with stately calm. Mildrith's coffin was lowered into her grave, facing east to await her resurrection on the Last Day. As Wulfmar the priest handed Elfleda the reliquary, she could sense Gaius standing behind her. She joined Osyth and the other nuns, who were now holding lighted candles, to line up alongside the grave. The priest sprinkled the body with holy water from a brass bucket held by his son. He bestowed a final blessing upon Mildrith's head. But just as he bid her eternal rest: "*Requiem aeternam...*"

A wild swarm of armed men burst through all three doors of the chapel yelling: "Die, Christers! By Woden's spear, die!"

As screaming women tried to flee, the invaders' swords and axes took a fearful toll. Wulfmar was the first to die, cut down from behind while other brutes dragged his son and Osyth away. Cedd swung his spade like a weapon. He lost his hand and then his life. Pega fell skewered beside him.

One grinning brute tried to seize the reliquary from Elfleda. She held on despite the voice of Gaius shouting: "Drop the damn box and run!"

The hands that wrenched it away flung her backwards to crash against another fighter. His axe stroke scraped the top of her head rather than taking it off. She sprawled senseless underfoot.

Elfleda awakened on the edge of the canvas ground cloth, half blinded by dirt and dried blood.

Gaius knelt beside her, pleading, "Don't wake up."

She tried to raise her pounding head but it hurt too much.

"Why did you have to wake up? I was hoping you'd pass without further pain."

Groaning with effort, Elfleda managed to push herself up on her forearms and turn her face toward him. She spat out grit and blinked her eyes clear.

"I didn't want you to die like them."

Her vision cleared enough that she could make out bloody bodies and body parts strewn over the chapel floor. The bodies of the nuns that were still in one piece had their skirts pulled over their heads. The stench gagged her. She felt bile scalding her throat but there was nothing in her stomach to vomit.

"God have mercy!" Her head dropped back to the earth.

"Forgive me, Elfleda, for failing you, for failing to notice the pirates creeping through the mist. I am only a helpless shade, not the man I was." He slammed his fist silently into the floor.

"Nothing to forgive." She raised herself higher on her elbows. "Where's the reliquary?"

He pointed to the smashed box near her. "But my head is over there." It lay a few feet from the foot of the grave. "Since it wasn't a treasure, he pitched it away. It bounced off the wall and rolled back. He did get that piece of silk for his trouble, though."

"I wouldn't have recognized that dirty lump as a human head. It looks like a clod of earth."

Rolling over clumsily, Elfleda tried to move closer but found to her horror that she couldn't control her feet or rise on her right knee.

"What happened?"

"You were trampled. Possibly more than once."

"Then I'll have to crawl." She clenched her teeth and proceeded to do so, inch by agonizing inch. "I'm going to bury you, one way or another." She came near blacking out again but Gaius kept her going with a stream of encouraging words. When she finally reached the head, she almost knocked it into the grave before getting a good grip. She laced her fingers through the hair still present on the preserved flesh and nestled it between her breasts.

Before Elfleda could do anything else, a pirate holding a sword and a silver chalice reeled out of the sacristy. He must have found the Communion wine, she thought.

"Uh? Live 'un? Whatcha got, girlie?"

Elfleda slumped down on the head like a hen on a nest. As the pirate lunged to jab her left arm with his sword, his wine sloshed over her.

"Hel take ya, bitch!" He slashed her back wide open and kicked her into the grave, still clutching the precious head.

Elfreda fell backwards with a crash onto Mildrith's coffin. Her blood welled across the wood and dripped on golden flowers. Gaius stood beside her, sunk halfway into the earth. He stretched his shadowy hand towards her cheek as she gasped through bloody foam: "...commend...our spirits."

"*Vale. In pace, vale.*" Willing her to go in peace, he bowed low to catch her last life's breath as she breathed it forth. Could he at least salute her before she soared off to her heaven? Or would they remain lost shades together?

While Gaius kept his station in the grave, the angry pirate returned from the sacristy, drunker than before. Knocking the lighted altar candles askew, he grabbed one and threw it at Elfleda's body.

"Burn, Christer bitch!" He staggered out, still clutching his empty chalice.

Her veil caught, then her robe, then the leathery relic. Little by little, the shade of Gaius Aurelius Perennis flickered and fluttered, slowly beginning to diffuse away out like mist burnt off by the sun. It was not alone.

The scattered candles set the altar fittings on fire. Sparks fell on corpses' woolen garments, flew up to the thatched ceiling and kindled what they touched until the whole chapel burned as one giant bonfire. The flames of its passing blazed up to heaven's stars, lofting a pair of spirits into Saint Michael's bright-mailed arms.

A DIFFICULT UNDERTAKING

HARRY TURTLEDOVE

Harry Turtledove is a renowned creator of alternate histories, including his Videssos Cycle, which includes twelve novels and such shorter tales is this one. About it, the author has written, "It's set a few hundred years before the events in The Videssos Cycle, and well to the east of anything that happened there. Like a good deal of what happens in Videssos, it has a real historical model—in this case from the pages of that most accomplished historian, Anna Comnena." In this part of the series, a leader and his troops are trapped in a fortress, and food is running out. Trapped like a bird in a cage, you might say, though this bird has a trick or two in mind.

◇◇◇◇◇

Ulror Raska's son stood in the topmost chamber of the tall watchtower, staring out to sea. Like most Halogai, he was tall and fair. His shining hair hung in a neat braid that reached the small of his back, but there was nothing effeminate about him. His face, hard-featured to begin with, had been battered further by close to half a century of carousing and war. His shoulders were wide as a bear's. Until a few weeks ago, his belly had bulged over his belt. It did not bulge any more. No one inside the fortress of Sotevag was fat any more.

Staring out to sea kept Ulror from thinking about the Videssian army that sat outside the walls of the fortress. The sea ran east forever from Sotevag. Looking at it, Ulror could feel free for a while, even if these southern waters were warm and blue, not like the chill, whitecap-flecked Bay of Haloga he had watched so often from the battlements of his own keep.

Of course, in the north the harvest failed one year in three. Even when it did not, there was never enough, nor enough land, not with every family running to three, five, seven sons. And so the Halogai hired on as mercenaries in Videssos and the lesser kingdoms, and manned ships and raided when they saw the chance.

Ulror smacked a big fist into his open palm in frustrated rage. By the gods, this chance had looked so good! With Videssos convulsed as two rival emperors battled, the island of Kalavria, far from the Empire's heartland, should have been easy to seize, to make a place where Halogai could settle freely, could live without fear of starving—it even reminded Ulror of his own district of Namdalen, if one could imagine Namdalen without snow. Chieftains whose clans had hated each other for generations joined in building and crewing the fleet.

The really agonizing thing was that, over much of the island, the men from the far north had managed to establish themselves. And here sat Ulror, under siege. He would not have admitted it to any of his warriors, but he expected Sotevag to fall. If it did, the Videssians would probably mop up the rest of the Halogai, one band at a time.

Damn Kypros Zigabenos anyway!

Kypros Zigabenos stood staring up at the walls of Sotevag, wondering how he was ever going to take the stronghold. His agile mind leapt from one stratagem to another, and unfailingly found flaws in each. From where he stood, the fortress looked impregnable. That was unfortunate, for he was all too likely to lose his head if it held.

An eyebrow quirked in wry amusement. Zigabenos had a long, narrow, mobile face, the kind that made him look younger than his forty-five years. Hardly any gray showed in his dark hair or in the aristocratic fringe of beard tracing the angle of his jaw.

He brushed a speck of lint from the sleeve of his brocaded robe. To wear the rich samite in the field was the mark of a fop, but he did not care. What was the point to civilization, if not the luxuries it made possible?

That they destroyed the opportunity to create such things was to him reason enough to oppose the Halogai. As individuals he valued highly many of the northerners, Ulror not least among them. Certainly Ulror was a better man than the fool and the butcher who each claimed to be rightful Avtokrator of the Videssians.

Both those men had called on him for aid. In a way, he thanked the good god Phos for the arrival of the Halogai. Their attack gave him the perfect excuse to refuse to remove men from Kalavria to take part in internecine strife. He would have done the same, though, if the invaders had not come.

But either the butcher or the fool would be able to rule Videssos, once the internal foe was vanquished. The Empire had survived for close to a thousand years; it had seen bad Emperors before. The eternal bureaucracy, of which Zigabenos was proud to be a part, held Videssos together when leadership faltered.

And that was something the Halogai, were their chieftains the best leaders in the world—and some came close—could never do. They knew nothing of the fine art of shearing a flock without flaying it. Like any barbarians, if they wanted something they took it, never caring whether the taking ruined in a moment years of patient labor.

For that Zigabenos would fight them, all the while recognizing and admiring their courage, their steadiness, aye, even their wit. When Ulror had sensibly decided to stand siege at Sotevag rather than risk his outnumbered, harried troops in a last desperate battle, Zigabenos had shouted to him up there on the battlements: "If you're so great a general, come out and fight!"

Ulror had laughed like one of his heathen gods. "If you're so great a general, Videssian, make me!"

The taunt still rankled. Zigabenos had surrounded the fortress, had even succeeded in cutting it off from the sea. The Halogai would not escape that way, or gain fresh supplies. But the storerooms and cisterns of Sotevag were full, thanks in no small measure to Zigabenos's own exertions the year before. Now he could not afford to wait and starve Ulror out. While he sat in front of Sotevag with forces he had scraped together from all over Kalavria, the northerners could do as they would through the rest of the island. Yet trying to storm the fortress would be hellishly expensive in men and materiel.

Damn Ulror Raska's son, anyway!

"They're stirring around down there," said Flosi Wolf's-Pelt, brushing back from his eyes the thick locks of gray hair that gave him his sobriquet.

"Aye." Ulror's eyes narrowed in suspicion. Till now, Zigabenos had been content to let hunger do his work for him. Like many Videssian generals, he played at war as if it were a game where the object was to win while losing as few pieces as possible. Ulror despised that style of fighting; he craved the hot, clean certainty of battle.

But there was no denying that what Zigabenos did, he did very well. He had chivvied Ulror's Halogai halfway across Kalavria, never offering combat unless the odds were all in his favor. He had even forced Ulror to dance to his tune and go to earth here like a hunted fox.

So why was he changing his way of doing things, when it had worked so well for him up to now?

Ulror pondered that as he watched the Videssians deploy. They moved smartly and in unison, as if they were puppets animated by Zigabenos's will alone. The Halogai lacked that kind of discipline. Even as the horns called them to their places on the battlements of Sotevag castle, they came out of the great hall in straggling groups of different sizes, getting in each other's way as they went to their assigned sections of the wall.

A single man rode past the palisade the Videssians had thrown up around Sotevag. He came within easy bowshot of the walls, his head bare so the defenders could recognize him. Ulror's lip twisted. Zigabenos might favor a spineless kind of warfare, but he was no coward.

"Your last chance, northerners," the Videssian general called, speaking the Haloga tongue badly but understandably. He did not bellow, as Ulror would have; still, his voice carried. "Surrender the fortress and yield up your commander, and you common soldiers will not be harmed. By Phos I swear it." Zigabenos drew a circle over his breast—the sun sign, symbol of the Videssian god of good. "May Skotos drag me down to hell's ice if I lie."

Ulror and Flosi looked at each other. Zigabenos had offered those same terms at the start of the siege, and been answered with jeers. No commander, though, could be sure how his troops would stand up under privation....

An arrow buried itself in the ground a couple of strides in front of Zigabenos's horse. The beast snorted and sidestepped. The Videssian general, a fine rider, brought it back under control. Even then, he did not retreat. Instead he asked, "Is that your final reply?"

"Aye!" the Halogai yelled, shaking their fists and brandishing weapons in defiance.

"No!" Ulror's great shout overrode the cries of his men. "I have another."

Zigabenos looked his way, suddenly alert. The northern chieftain understood that look, and knew the Videssian thought he was about to turn his coat. Rage ripped through him. "The gods curse you, Zigabenos!" he roared. "The only way you'll get me out of Sotevag is stinking in my coffin!"

His men raised a cheer; the more bravado a Haloga showed in the face of danger, the more his fellows esteemed him. Zigabenos sat impassive until quiet returned. He gave Ulror the Videssian salute, his clenched fist over his heart. "That can be arranged," he said. He wheeled his horse, showing the northerners his back.

Ulror bit his lip. In his own cold-blooded way, Zigabenos had style.

The palisade drew near. The space between Zigabenos's shoulder blades stopped itching. If that had been he in the fortress, no enemy commander who exposed himself would have lived to return to his troops. The Haloga notion of honor struck him as singularly naive.

Yet the trip up to the walls had been worth making. When the northerners once fell into corruption, they wallowed in it. They reminded the Videssian general of a man never exposed to some childhood illness, who would die if he caught it as an adult. His own troops, no more brave or honorable than they had to be, would never sink to the depths of a Haloga who abandoned his code of conduct.

No time for such reverie now, he told himself reproachfully. The trumpeters and fifemen were waiting for his signal. He nodded. As the martial music rang out, his command echoed it: "Forward the palisade!"

Half the Videssian soldiers picked up the stakes and brush surrounding the castle of Sotevag and moved ahead, toward the fortress walls. The rest of the men—the better archers in the army—followed close behind, their bows drawn.

The Halogai began shooting to harass the advance. The range was long and the stuff of the palisade gave some protection.

Nevertheless, here and there a man dropped. The dead lay where they had fallen; the wounded were dragged to the rear, where the priests would tend them with healing magic.

Zigabenos gave a quiet order. The musicians sent it to the troops, who halted and began emplacing the palisade once more. "Give them a volley!" the general said. "From now on, they keep their heads down!"

The thrum of hundreds of bowstrings released together was the only pleasant note in the cacophony of war. Arrows hissed toward Sotevag. The Halogai dove for cover. Shouts of fury and screams showed that not all reached it.

One by one, the northerners reappeared, some standing tall and proud, others peering over the top of the battlements. Zigabenos gauged the moment. "Another!" he shouted.

The Halogai vanished again. "Marksmen only, from now on," the general commanded. "If you see a good target, shoot at it. Try not to waste arrows, though."

He had expected a furious answering fire from the besieged warriors, but it did not come. They were shooting back, but picking their marks as carefully as their foes. That made him want to grind his teeth. Ulror had learned too much, fighting against Videssians. Most of his countrymen would never have thought about saving arrows for a later need.

Zigabenos shook his head in reluctant admiration. He sighed, regretting the need to kill such a man. A race with the restless energy of the Halogai might go far, allied to Videssian canniness. Unfortunately, he knew the first place it would head for: Videssos the city, the great imperial capital. No lesser goal could sate such a folk. And so he would do his duty, and try to make sure it never came into being.

He waved. An aide appeared at his elbow. "Sir?"

"Muster the woodworkers. The time has come to build engines."

"I grow to hate the sounds of carpentry," Ulror said. The Videssian artisans were a quarter-mile away, out of reach of any weapons from inside Sotevag, but there were so many of them and they were chewing up so much timber that the noise of saw, hammer, axe, and adze was always present in the fortress.

"Not I," Flosi Wolf's-Pelt said.

"Eh? Why not?" Ulror looked at his companion in surprise.

"When the building noises stop, they'll be finished. Then they'll start using their toys."

"Oh. Aye." Ulror managed a laugh, as any northerner should in the face of danger, but even he could hear how grim it sounded. Frustrated, he shook his head until his braid switched like a horse's tail. "By the gods, I'd give two thumb's-widths off my prong for a way to strike at those accursed siege engines."

"A sally?" Flosi's eyes lit at the prospect; his hand went to the hilt of his sword.

"No," Ulror said reluctantly. "Look how openly the carpenters are working out there. See the cover off to the flanks? Zigabenos wants to tempt us into the open, so he can slaughter us at his leisure. I'll not give him his triumph so cheap."

Flosi grunted. "There's no honor in such tricks."

"True, but they work all the same." Ulror had lost too many men to ambushes to doubt that. Such tactics were of a piece with the rest of the way the Videssians made war, seeking victory at the least cost to themselves. To counter them, a man had to fight the same way, regardless of how much it went against his grain.

Flosi, though, still wanted to strike a blow at the enemy. "What of using sorcery on their engines?"

That had not occurred to Ulror. Battle magic almost always failed; in the heat of combat, men's emotions flamed strong enough to weaken the bite of spells. Only the most powerful wizards went to war, save as healers or diviners. And the one Haloga with Ulror who knew something of magic, Kolskegg Cheese-Curd, had a better reputation as tosspot than sorcerer.

When Ulror said as much to Flosi, his comrade snorted in disgust. "What do we lose by trying? If you don't aim to fight, why not throw yourself off the wall and have done?"

"I aim to fight," Ulror growled, pointing down into the outer ward, where men chopped logs and filled barrels with earth to build makeshift barriers if the walls should be breached.

"Defense," Flosi said scornfully.

Nettled, Ulror opened his mouth to snarl back, but stopped with his angry words still unspoken. How could he blame Flosi for wanting to hurt the Videssians? He wanted to himself. And who could say? Maybe Kolskegg could take the imperials by surprise. Ulror made for the stairwell, to track down the wizard. Behind him, Flosi nodded in satisfaction.

Kolskegg Cheese-Curd was a big, pockmarked man who, like Ulror, had been fat before the siege of Sotevag began. Now his skin was limp and saggy, like a deflated bladder. Something seemed to have gone out of his spirit, too, when the castle's ale casks ran dry. Living on well-water was torment for him.

His eyes widened in alarm as Ulror explained what he required. "You must be mad!" he burst out. "A hundredth part of such a magic would burn out my brain!"

"No great loss, that," Ulror growled. "How do you have the nerve to call yourself a wizard? What *are* you good for, anyway?"

"My skill at divination is not of the worst." Kolskegg eyed Ulror warily, as if wondering how much trouble that admission would get him into.

"The very thing!" the Haloga chieftain said, slapping him on the back. Kolskegg beamed, until Ulror went on, "Divine me a way to slip out of Zigabenos's clutches."

"But—my art is tyromancy," Kolskegg quavered, "reading the future in the patterns curds make as they separate out in new cheese. Where can I get milk?"

"One of the last two jennies foaled the other day. The colt went into the stewpot, of course, but we still need the mother for hauling wood and earth. She may not have dried up yet."

"Ass's milk?" Kolskegg's lip curled. Even poor sorcerers had standards.

"What better, for you?" Ulror said brutally. Losing patience, he grabbed Kolskegg by the arm and half-led, half-dragged him down to the ward, where the donkey was dragging a log up to the wall. The beast's ribs showed through its mangy coat; it was plainly on its last legs. It gave a sad bray as Kolskegg squeezed a few squirts of milk into a bowl.

"Butcher it," Ulror told his men; if they waited any longer, no meat would be left on those sad bones.

Seeming more confident once he had sniffed and tasted the milk, Kolskegg took Ulror back to his pack, which lay on top of his straw pallet. He rummaged in it until he found a small packet of whitish powder. "Rennet," he explained, "made from the stomach lining of young calves."

"Just get on with it," Ulror said, faintly revolted.

Kolskegg sat cross-legged in the dry rushes on the floor. He began a low, whining chant, repeating the same phrase over and over. Ulror had seen other wizards act thus, to heighten their concentration. His regard for Kolskegg went up a notch.

He noticed Kolskegg was not blinking. All the sorcerer's attention focused on the chipped earthenware bowl in front of him. Ulror tried to find meaning in the swirling pattern of emerging curds as the rennet coagulated the milk, but saw nothing there he could read.

Kolskegg stiffened. White showed round the irises of his staring blue eyes. "A coffin!" he said hoarsely. "A coffin and the stench of the grave. Only through a death is there escape." His eyes rolled up altogether and he slumped over in a faint.

Ulror's lips skinned back from his teeth in a humorless grin. Too well he remembered his roar of defiance to Zigabenos. The gods had a habit of listening to a man when he least wanted them to.

"I wish Skotos would drag that heathen down to the ice of hell now, instead of waiting for him to live out his span of days," Kypros Zigabenos said furiously, watching from the Videssian lines as Ulror dashed along the battlements of Sotevag, his blond braid flapping behind him. The barbarian ignored the hail of stones and darts with which the imperials were pounding the fortress. Buoyed by his spirit, the defenders stayed on the walls, shooting back with what they had and rushing to repair the damage from the bombardment.

Then, because he was an honest man—not always an advantage in Videssian service—Zigabenos felt he had to add, "But oh, he is a brave one."

"Sir?" said the servant who fetched him a cup of wine.

"Eh? Nothing." Zigabenos was irritated that anyone should have heard his mumblings. Still, he wished with all his heart for one of the Videssian missiles to dash out Ulror's brains.

Quite simply, the man was too good. Aye, he had let himself be penned here, but only as an alternative to worse. If ever he escaped, he might yet find a way to rally the Halogai and rape Kalavria away from the Empire. He was worth an army to the northerners, just as Zigabenos, without false modesty, assessed his own similar value to Videssos.

He snapped his fingers in happy inspiration. At his shout, a runner came trotting up. He sent the man over to the stone-throwers and ballistae. One by one, the siege engines stopped.

Zigabenos took up a white-painted shield—a badge of truce or parley—and walked toward Sotevag's battered walls.

"Ulror!" he called. "Ulror, will you speak with me?"

After a minute or so, the northern chieftain shouted back, "Aye, if you'll talk so my men understand us."

"As you wish," Zigabenos said in the Haloga tongue. Another ploy wasted; he had deliberately used Videssian before to try to make Ulror's warriors doubt their leader. Very well, let them hear: "Come out of the fortress and I will still guarantee all your lives. And I pledge better for you, Ulror: a fine mansion, with a stipend to support a large band of retainers."

"And where will this fine mansion be? Here on the island?"

"You deserve better than this backwater, Ulror. What do you say to a residence at the capital, Videssos the city?"

Ulror was silent so long, Zigabenos's hopes began to rise. At last the northerner asked, "Will you give me a day's leave to think on it?"

"No," Zigabenos said at once. "You'll only use it to strengthen your defenses. Give me your answer."

Ulror boomed laughter. "Oh, how I wish you were a fool. I think I will decline your gracious invitation. With civil war in the Empire, even if by some mischance I reached the capital alive, I'd last about as long as a lobster's green shell when you throw him in the boiling pot."

The Videssian general felt like snarling, but his face never showed it. "You have my personal guarantee of your safety," he said.

"Aye, and that's good as silver so long as I'm on the island, and worth nothing soon as I sail west, since both Emperors hate you for not sending 'em men."

Too good by half, Zigabenos thought. Without another word, he turned and walked away. But Ulror was still in the lobster pot. It remained only to bring him to the boil.

The cat crawled forward, its timber sides and roof covered with green hides to keep them from being burned. Fire arrows streaked from the Videssian archers toward bales of straw the Halogai had hung on the side of the wall to deaden the impact of the battering ram the cat protected. The northerners dumped pails of water and sewage, snuffing out the flames before they took hold.

Then the imperials manhandled their shed up to the base of

the wall. The Halogai pelted it with boulders and spears, trying to create rifts in the hide covering through which boiling water and red-hot sand might find their way.

"There!" Ulror cried, pointing, and another stone thudded home. The din was indescribable. Through it all, though, Ulror heard the commands of the Videssian underofficer in the cat, each order delivered as calmly as if on parade.

He could not fathom that kind of courage. The hazards of the field—aye, he had their measure. This siege was harder, but here he had had no good choice. But how men could hold their wits about them advancing turtle-fashion into danger, knowing they would die if their shell was broken, was beyond him.

Like so many Halogai, he scorned the discipline Videssos imposed on her troops; no free man would let himself be used so. Now he saw what such training was worth. His own men, he knew, would have broken under the punishment the imperials were taking. Yet they stolidly labored on.

Rather than hearing the ram strike the wall, Ulror felt it through the soles of his feet. Chains rattled in the cat below as the Videssians drew their great iron-faced log back for another stroke. The wall shook again. Ulror could see the spirit oozing out of his warriors. They had gaily faced the chance of arrow or flying stone, but this methodical pounding stole the manhood from them. He wondered if he could make them fight in the breach. He had no great hope of it.

Just when he was telling himself he should have made what terms he could with Zigabenos, shrieks replaced the stream of orders coming from the cat. One of the smoking cauldrons the Halogai tipped down on it had found a breach of its own.

When the ram's rhythm missed a beat, the northerners above seemed to realize their doom was not inevitable after all. Ulror bellowed encouragement to them. They redoubled their efforts, working like men possessed.

Three soldiers grunted to lift a huge stone to a crenelation, then shoved it out and down onto the cat. The shed's sloping roof and thick sides had sent other boulders bouncing aside, but this one struck square on the midline. Along with the crash, Ulror heard a metallic snap as a chain holding the ram to the roof of the cat broke. Shouts of pain from the imperials it injured in its fall and curses from the rest were as sweet music in his ears.

Like a wounded animal, the shed began to limp away. Videssian shieldsmen stood at its open front, where the ram had swung.
They protected their comrades from the missiles the Halogai
rained on them. Whenever one was shot, another took his place.
That was bravery Ulror could grasp. Even as he let fly at them,
he hoped they would safely reach their own line. Zigabenos, he
thought, would want them to fall to the arrows like so many
quail. That was sensible, but he did not have the stomach for it.

The Halogai danced with joy as the cat withdrew, their heavy
boots clumping on the stone walkways and stairs. "A victory,"
Flosi Wolf's-Pelt said.

"Aye, or so the lads think, anyway," Ulror answered quietly.
"Well, that's worth something of itself, I suppose. It'll take their
minds off the stale donkey tripes—the last of them left—and the
handful of barley meal they'll be eating tonight."

"We hurt the cat," Flosi protested.

"So we did, and they hurt the wall. Which do you think the
easier to repair?"

Flosi grimaced and turned away.

High overhead, a seagull screeched. Ulror envied the bird its
freedom. Not too many gulls came near Sotevag anymore. If they
did, the Halogai shot them and ate them. Their flesh was tough
and salty and tasted strongly of fish, but hungry men did not
care. Ulror had stopped asking about the meat that went into the
stewpots. He did know he had seen fewer rats lately.

Watching the gull wheel in the sky and glide away was suddenly more than Ulror could bear. He slammed his fist against
the stone of the battlement, cursed at the pain. Ignoring Flosi's
startled look, he rushed down the stairs and into the outer ward.

Kolskegg Cheese-Curd had been making what looked like a
mousetrap out of sticks and leather thongs. He put the contrap-
tion aside as his chieftain bore down on him, asked warily, "Is
there something I might do for you?"

"Aye, there is." Ulror hauled his reluctant wizard to his feet;
his belly might be gone, but he still kept his bull strength. Paying
no attention to the protests Kolskegg yammered, he dragged him
through the gatehouse into the keep, and on into the chamber
he had taken for himself.

The goose-feather mattress had belonged to the Videssian who
once commanded here. So did the silk coverlet atop it, now sadly

stained. Ulror flopped down on the bed with a sigh of relief, waved Kolskegg to a chair whose delicacy proclaimed it also to be imperial work.

Once Kolskegg had made himself comfortable, Ulror came to the point with his usual directness. "That was a true divination you gave me—that the only way I would leave Sotevag would be in my coffin?"

The wizard licked his lips, but had to answer, "Aye, it was."

To his surprise, his chieftain grunted in satisfaction. "Good. If Zigabenos's priests read the omens, they should learn the same, not so?"

"Aye." Kolskegg had been a warrior long enough to know not to volunteer more than he was asked.

"All right, then," Ulror said. "Give me a spell to turn me to the seeming of a corpse, stench and all, to let me get away. Then when I'm outside, you can take it off, or arrange in the first place for it to last only so long, or whatever you think best." He nodded, pleased at his own ingenuity.

The wizard's face, though, went chalky white. "Have mercy!" he cried. "I am nothing but a miserable diviner. Why do you set me tasks to strain the powers of the greatest adepts? I cannot do this; he who trifles with death in magic courts it."

"You are the only sorcerer I have," Ulror said implacably. "And you will do it."

"I cannot." As a weak man will, Kolskegg sounded querulous in his insistence.

"You will," Ulror told him. "If you do not, Sotevag will surely fall. And if the Videssians take me alive, I will tell them you worked your charms through their dark god Skotos. Once they believe that, you will wish you died fighting. No demon could serve you worse than their inquisitors."

Kolskegg shivered, for Ulror was right. As dualists, the imperials hated their deity's evil rival and dealt with legendary savagery with anyone who dared revere him. "You would not—" the wizard began, and stopped in despair. Ulror would.

The Haloga commander said nothing more. He waited, bending Kolskegg to his will with silence. Under his unwinking stare, the wizard's resolve melted like snow in springtime. "I will try," he said at last, very low. "Maybe at midnight, a spell I know might serve. It is, after all, only a seeming you seek."

He spoke more to reassure himself than for any other reason, Ulror judged. That was all right. "Midnight it is," Ulror said briskly. "I'll see you here then." He did not put any special warning in his voice. He had done his job properly, and did not need to.

The wizard returned at the hour he had set, stumbling in the darkness as he approached Ulror's door. Inside, the chieftain had a tallow dip lit. Not many lights burned in Sotevag at night; tallow and olive oil could be eaten, if a man was hungry enough.

Even in the red, flickering light, Kolskegg looked pale. "I wish I had a beaker of ale," he muttered under his breath. He fumbled in his pouch, finally digging out a chain that held a black stone with white veins. "An onyx," he said, hanging it round Ulror's neck. "The stone for stirring up terrible fantasms."

"Get on with it," Ulror said. He spoke more harshly than he had intended; Kolskegg's nervousness was catching.

The wizard cast a powder into the flame of the tallow dip, which flared a ghastly green. Kolskegg began a slow, rhymeless chant full of assonances. The stone he had set on Ulror's breast grew cold, so he could feel its chill through his tunic. He could also feel the little hairs at the nape of his neck prickling upright.

The chant droned on. Kolskegg began singing faster and faster, as if he wanted to get through the incantation as quickly as he could. In the end, his own fear of what he was doing undid him. His tongue slipped, so that when he meant to intone "thee," "me" came out instead.

Had he been wearing the onyx, the spell might have possessed him as he intended it to possess Ulror: as an unpleasant but impermanent illusion. But the Holga chieftain had the magical focus, not his wizard. Before Kolskegg could do more than gasp in horror at his blunder, the transformation struck him.

Ulror gagged on the stench that filled his chamber. He staggered outside and was sick against the wall of the keep. Several of his warriors rushed over, asking if he was all right.

One had the wit to offer a bucket of water. He rinsed his mouth, spat, rinsed again. The sour taste remained. His men began exclaiming over the graveyard reek that followed him into the inner ward.

"You will find a lich—not a fresh one—inside," he told them. "Treat poor Kolskegg with respect; he showed more courage dying at my order than ever he did in life."

✧　　✧　　✧

As was his privilege, even after midnight, the blue-robed priest burst past Zigabenos's bodyguard and into the tent of the Videssian general. "Sorcery!" he cried, the firelight gleaming from his shaved pate. "Sorcery most foul!"

"Huh?" Zigabenos sat up with a start. He was glad he'd sent the kitchen wench back to her tavern instead of keeping her for the night. He enjoyed his vices, but had learned long since not to flaunt them.

His wits returned with their usual rapidity. "Say what you mean, Bonosos. Are the Halogai assailing us with magic?"

"Eh? No, your illustriousness. But they play at wizardry even so, a wizardry that stinks of Skotos." The priest spat on the ground in rejection of the wicked god, his faith's eternal enemy.

"The conjuration was not aimed against us? You are certain of that?"

"I am," Bonosos said reluctantly. "Yet it was strong, and of a malefic nature. It was not undertaken to curry favor with us."

"I hardly expected it would be," Zigabenos said; he had no intention of letting a priest out-irony him. "Still, so long as they do not send a blast our way, the Halogai are welcome to play at whatever they wish. Maybe it will go awry and eat them up, and save us the trouble."

"May the lord of the great and good mind hear and heed your prayer," Bonosos said, drawing Phos's sun sign on his breast.

Zigabenos did the same; his own piety, though he did not let it interfere with whatever he had to do, ran deep. After a moment he said, "Bonosos, I hope you had a reason for disturbing my rest, other than merely to tell me the Halogai have some fribbling spell afoot."

"Hardly fribbling." Bonosos's glare was wasted; to Zigabenos, he was only a silhouette in the doorway. But there was no mistaking the abhorrence in the priest's voice as he went on, "The conjuration smacked of necromancy."

"Necromancy!" Zigabenos exclaimed, startled. "You must be mistaken."

Bonosos bowed. "Good evening, sir. I tell the truth. If you do not care to hear it, that is none of my affair." He spun on his heel and stalked away.

Stiff-necked old bastard, the Videssian general thought as he settled back under his silk coverlet, and mad as a loon besides.

The Halogai inside Sotevag had too many other things to worry about to bother with corpse-raising or anything like it.

Or did they? Zigabenos suddenly remembered Ulror's howl of defiance from the battlements. The northerner must have taken that for prophecy as well as brag. Zigabenos laughed out loud, admiring Ulror's ingenuity in trying to get around his own oath. Unfortunately for the Haloga, he thought, there was no way around it. The northerners fought bravely and, under Ulror's command, resourcefully. Against siege engines, however, bravery and resource only counted for so much. In a week, maybe less, maybe a day or two more, he would be inside Sotevag. And then Ulror's boast would be fulfilled in the most literal way imaginable.

Still chuckling, Zigabenos rolled over and went back to sleep.

After a sleepless night, Ulror stared out to sea, watching the rising sun turn the water to a flaming sheet of molten gold and silver. He regretted Kolskegg's death, and regretted even more that it had been in vain. Now, impaled on his own rash words, he found nothing else to do but face the prospect of dying.

He did not fear death. Few Halogai did; they lived too close to it, both at home and in battle on distant shores. But he bitterly regretted the waste. If only he could get free, rally the Halogai all across Kalavria...In pursuing him, Zigabenos really had concentrated his own forces too much—provided the northerners moved against him in unison. If not, he would go on dealing with them piecemeal, methodical as a cordwainer turning out boots.

Ulror ground his teeth. All he, all any of the Halogai, wanted was a steading big enough for a free man to live on and to pass down to his sons; a good northern woman to wife, with perhaps two or three of these island wenches to keep a bed warm of nights; a chance to enjoy the luxuries the imperials took for granted: wine grown on a man's own holding, a bathtub, wheat bread instead of loaves of rye or oats. If the Empire's god would grant him so much, he might even give worship to Phos along with his own somber deities.

Unless Zigabenos made a mistake, though, none of that would happen. And Zigabenos was not in the habit of making mistakes.

As had happened a few days before, a gull gave its raucous call high over Sotevag. This time the frustration was more than the Haloga chieftain could bear. Without conscious thought, in one smooth motion he reached over his shoulder for an arrow, set it to his bow, and let fly. His rage lent power to the shot. The bird's cry abruptly cut off. It fell with a thud to the dirt of the outer ward. Ulror stared malevolently at the dead gull—miserable, stinking thing, he thought.

"Good shooting," one of his warriors called, ambling over to pick up the bird and carry it off to be cooked.

"Hold!" Ulror shouted suddenly, rushing for a stairway. "That seagull's mine!" The warrior gaped at him, certain he had lost his mind.

An orderly came dashing into the tent, interrupting Zigabenos's breakfast. Paying no attention to the Videssian general's glare, he said breathlessly, "Sir, there's sign of truce over the main gatehouse of Sotevag!"

Zigabenos stood up so quickly that he upset the folding table in front of him. He ignored his valet's squawk of distress and hurried out after the orderly to see this wonder for himself.

It was true. Above the gate, a white shield hung on a spear. "They turned coward at the end," the orderly said, "when they saw what our engines were about to do to them."

"I wonder," Zigabenos said. It was not like Ulror to give in so tamely. What sort of scheme could the Haloga chieftain have come up with? No one had spied him on the walls for several days now. Was he planning a last desperate sally, hoping to slay Zigabenos and throw the Videssian army into confusion?

To forestall that, the general approached the fortress in the midst of a squadron of shieldsmen, enough to get him out of danger no matter what the Halogai tried. When he was within hailing distance, he called, "Well, Ulror? What have you to say to me?"

But it was not Ulror who came to stand by the northerners' truce shield. A raw-boned Haloga with gray hair took that place instead. He stared down at Zigabenos in silence for a long moment, then asked, "Have you honor, imperial?"

Zigabenos shrugged. "If you need the question, would you trust the answer?"

A harsh chuckle. "Summat to that. All right, be it so. You'll do what you promised before, let the rest of us go if we yield you Sotevag and bring out Ulror?"

The Videssian general had all he could do not to cry out for joy. In exchange for Ulror, he was willing, nay eager, to let a few hundred barbarians of no special importance keep their lives. He was too old a hand, however, to let his excitement show. After a suitable pause, he demanded, "Show me Ulror now, so I may see you have him prisoner."

"I cannot," the Haloga said.

Zigabenos turned to leave. "I am not a child, for you to play tricks on."

"He is dead," the northerner replied, and Zigabenos stopped. The northerner went on, "He took a fever a week ago, but fought on with it, as any true man would. He died four nights past. Now that he is gone, we ask ourselves why we must sell our lives dear, and find no answer."

"You need not, of course," Zigabenos said at once. No wonder the Halogai had tried necromancy, he thought. But Ulror was tricksy, and who knew how far he would go to lend verisimilitude to a ploy? The Videssian general declared, "I will abide by my terms, save that I add one condition: as each man of yours leaves Sotevag, my wizards will examine him, to be sure he is not Ulror in sorcerous disguise."

The Haloga spokesman spat. "Do what you please. Victors always do. But I have told you you will not find him among them."

They haggled over details for the next hour. Zigabenos was lenient. Why not, with the one great northern chieftain gone and Sotevag about to return to imperial hands?

When noon came, the long-shut fortress gates swung open. As had been agreed, the Halogai came out two by two, in armor and carrying their weapons. They were all skinny, and many wounded. They could not help looking out toward the imperial lines; if Zigabenos wanted to betray them, he could. He did not want to. He expected to fight their countrymen again, and fear of a broken truce would only lead the Halogai to fight to the end from then on.

The Videssian general stood outside the gates with a pair of priests. The blue-robes had anointed their eyes with a paste made from the gall of a male cat and the fat of a pure white hen, an ointment that let them pierce illusion. They examined each emerging northerner, ready to cry out if they spied Ulror behind a veil of magic.

The gray-haired Haloga with whom Zigabenos had dickered came limping out. The general gave him a formal salute. He had developed some respect for this Flosi Wolf's-Pelt, for his spirit, his courage, and his blunt honesty. What sprang from those, though, was easy to anticipate. When the time came, he knew he would beat Flosi. With Ulror he had never been sure.

Flosi looked through him as if he did not exist.

The moment Zigabenos had been waiting for finally came. A dozen Halogai dragged a rough-built coffin behind them on a sledge. "Ulror is inside?" the general asked one of them.

"Aye," the man said.

"Check it," Zigabenos snapped to the priests who flanked him.

They peered at the coffin with their sorcerously enhanced vision. "That is truly Ulror Raska's son within," Bonosos declared.

So Ulror had been a prophet after all, Zigabenos thought, and look what it gained him. Something else occurred to the Videssian general. "Is the rascal dead?"

Bonosos frowned. "A spell to ascertain that will take some little time to prepare, and in any case I mislike touching on death with my sorcery—see how such an unholy effort profited the northerner here. I suggest you make your own examination to satisfy yourself. If he is four days dead, you will know it."

"Something in the air, you mean. Yes, I take your point." Zigabenos chuckled. He added, "Who would expect such plain sense from a priest?" Bonosos's frown turned to scowl. The Videssian general approached the coffin. "Pry up the top of the lid, you," he told one of the northerners.

Shrugging, the Haloga drew his sword and used it to lever up the coffin lid; nails squealed in protest. Through the narrow opening Zigabenos saw Ulror's face, pale and thin and still. The death smell welled out, almost thick enough to slice. "Shut it," Zigabenos said, coughing. He drew Phos's sun-circle on his breast, then saluted the coffin with the same formality he had offered Flosi.

Seeing how exhausted the pallbearers were, Zigabenos said kindly, "If you like, we will bury him for you here."

The Halogai drew themselves up; even in privation, they were proud men. One said, "I thank you, but we care for our own."

"As you wish." Zigabenos waved them on.

When the last northerner had left Sotevag castle, the general sent in a crack platoon to search it from top to bottom. No matter what the priests said, no matter what he had seen and smelled, maybe Ulror had found a way to stay behind and then drop over the walls and escape. Zigabenos did not see how, but he took no chances where Ulror was concerned.

Only when the platoon's lieutenant reported back to him that Sotevag was empty of life did he truly begin to believe he had won.

Hungry, worn, and battered as they were, the Halogai traveled slowly. Still, Kalavria was not a large island; by the end of the second day after they left Sotevag, they were at the end of the central uplands. They camped next to a swift, cool stream.

As the warriors shared the half-ripe fruits and nuts they had gathered on their march and hunters went into the undergrowth after rabbits, Flosi went up to Ulror's coffin. Wrinkling his nose at the stench emanating from it, he pried up the ends of a couple of boards with his dagger.

The coffin shook, as with some internal paroxysm. The boards Flosi had loosened flew up. Ulror scrambled out. The first thing he did was to dive into the water and scrub himself from head to foot with sand from the streambank. When he came splashing out, streaks of the mixture of chalk and grease with which he had smeared his face remained on it, but his natural ruddy color dominated once more.

One of his warriors threw a ragged cloak around him. "Food!" he boomed. "After two days with nothing but three stinking seagulls for company, even the rubbish we were eating back at Sotevag would taste good."

Flosi brought him some of their meager fare. He wolfed it down. One by one, the hunters returned. Fresh meat, even a couple of bites' worth, roasted over an open fire was the most delicious thing he had ever eaten.

His belly was still growling after all the food was gone, but he had grown used to that in Sotevag. He looked around again and again, admiring the stream, the trees, the little clearing in which the Halogai were camped. "Free," he breathed.

"Aye." Flosi still did not seem to believe it. "I thought we were ruined when your magicking with Kolskegg failed."

"And I." Ulror longed for wine, but after a moment he realized triumph was a sweeter, headier brew. He laughed. "We get so used to using sorcery for our ends, we forget what we can do without it. Once I thought of the scheme, my biggest worry was that Zigabenos would attack before the birds got ripe enough to use."

"A good thing you whitened your face, even so."

"Oh, indeed. Zigabenos is too canny for me to dare miss a trick against him," Ulror said. A swirl of the breeze brought the carrion reek his way. He grimaced. "I was afraid of one other thing, too. He might have noticed something wrong if he'd heard my 'corpse' puking its guts out."

"So he might." Flosi allowed himself a rare smile. He rose and started over to the opened coffin. "The birds have served their purpose. I'll toss them in the creek."

"Eh? Don't do that," Ulror exclaimed.

"Why not? What do you want them for? I wouldn't eat the smelly things if I'd stood siege for years, not a couple of months. Throw 'em away and have done."

"I have a better plan," Ulror said.

"What's that?"

"I'm going to send one back to Zigabenos behind a shield of truce." Ulror's eyes glowed with mischief. "I wish I could be there to see his face when he finds out how"—he grinned a huge grin; it felt monstrous good to be able to joke again—"how he's been gulled."

"Gulled, eh?" Kypros Zigabenos nodded at the noisome pile of feathers the smirking Haloga herald set before him. He would not give the barbarian the satisfaction of showing he felt anything at all at finding Ulror alive and free. Never in his life, though, had he come so close to dishonoring a truce shield. The northerner would never know by how little he had missed the lash, the thumbscrews, the red-hot bronze needles, and the rest of the ingenious torments the Videssians had devised over the centuries.

But only a vicious fool struck at the bearer of bad news. And so Zigabenos, his heart a cold stone in his breast, poured wine for the Haloga and laughed politely to hear how Ulror had duped him.

"Wait here a moment, if you will," he said to the warrior, and stepped out of his tent to speak to one of his guards. The man blinked in surprise, then saluted and hurried away, stringing his bow as he trotted.

Zigabenos returned to his unwelcome guest, refilled the fellow's cup, and went on with the urbane conversation he had briefly interrupted. Behind his smiling mask, he felt desperation building. He had staked too great a part of the imperial forces on Kalavria to finishing Ulror here. The Videssians scattered over the rest of the island were ragtag and bobtail. With his victorious army as a core, they would have sufficed. Now the Halogai would mop up, not he.

And then they would come for him. He wondered how fast his artisans could repair the damage his own engines had done to Sotevag, and what sort of supplies he could bring in. The Halogai were impetuous, impatient. They might not have the staying power to conduct a siege of their own.

But with Ulror leading them, they might.

The sentry with whom Zigabenos had spoken stuck his head into the tent. "I have one, your excellency."

"Very good. Bring it in." The general drew himself up straighter in his chair. Sometimes one won, sometimes one lost; no sane man expected nothing but triumph in his life. But win or lose, style mattered. He prayed the day might never come when he failed to meet misfortune with aplomb.

The bird the Videssian soldier brought in was smaller than the one Ulror had sent, with a deeply forked tail and a black cap. It was still warm. Zigabenos picked it up and ceremoniously offered it to the Haloga. "I hope you will be so kind as to present this to your master, with my compliments."

The northerner looked at him as if he had gone mad. "Just the bird, or shall I say something?"

"The latter." Zigabenos was an imperial, a man of anciently civilized race, and of high blood as well. This grinning blond lout here would never understand, but somehow he felt Ulror might appreciate the spirit in which he sent his message. "Tell him one good tern deserves another."

THE WANDERING WARRIORS

ALAN SMALE AND RICK WILBER

By now, the reader should be used to the notion of present-day or so folks suddenly pitched back in time, who try to change the past. This time, when a whole baseball team are temporally transported, the results are a bit wackier. Batter up!

◇◇◇◇◇

1
July 1946

It was a steamy July night. We were filling up the tank of our old Ford Transit bus at Ambler's Texaco in Dwight, Illinois, when Quentin Williams, one of our two "Cubans" on the Warriors, had the great idea of getting off the dependable concrete of Route 66 and taking the back roads down to Decatur.

We were all standing around, some of the players smoking and a few spitting out tobacco juice from their chaw while a few of us—me, included—drank cold pop from the station's icebox. Sure, we were tired. The doubleheader on Sunday had gone extra innings both games, and we'd finally had to call the second game a draw when it got too dark to play—ten hours of baseball on a hot Illinois summer day that had started at noon and ended with us driving off into the darkness. And all for a total of maybe two hundred bucks, split eleven ways. But that's how it was for the Wandering Warriors.

I was stiff and my knees were sore after a full day catching, so I was a little disagreeable. As I opened up the side hood to tinker with the distributor cap, I said I wasn't sure it was a great idea to get off the main road and drive through the night on narrow two-lane blacktop. I mentioned that a wrong turn or two and we might wind up in Indiana or Missouri or anywhere else and then we'd have to spend all morning driving back to where we were supposed to be in time for the noon game in Decatur. And the Decatur Dukes were supposed to be pretty good this year, and so were we, so there'd be a nice crowd. We'd make three or four times as much money as we had in Kankakee. Let's play it safe, I said, and stick to the main highway.

Then I slammed the hood down, climbed into the driver's seat, and turned the key to start up the old Transit. It backfired once—the distributor cap still wasn't quite right—and then settled into a nice rumble.

"Professor," Quentin said from the front row behind me, laughing, "you got no sense of adventure. Plus," he said, "this will get us to that hotel in Decatur an hour faster, so we can get some sleep before we do this all over again tomorrow."

Quentin liked the Prairie Hotel in Decatur because our two "Cubans" and our two Jews—me being one of them—got rooms with no trouble there. It wasn't like that in some of the towns we played in farther south. Sure, the Major Leagues broke the color line during the war when the Negro vets started coming home. But at the level we played and the towns we played in, it wasn't so simple as that.

There were little mumblings of agreement in the back of the bus. Quentin loved maps and thought of himself as our navigator, and the guys trusted him. He was smart as a whip. Hell, like me, he even read the newspaper every day, which really impressed the guys. Plus, a shorter drive and more sleep sounded good to the Wandering Warriors.

I sighed and rolled my eyes and said, "Quentin, I'll talk to the driver, but that map of yours better get us there in the dark." He laughed. I was the driver. And the owner. And the catcher. Quentin was our ace and he'd won sixteen on the season. We had a good understanding. I laughed with him, and about five miles down Route 66, I took a left when Quentin said to, and that's how it all began.

At first the road was fine, two-lane and not wide; but it was paved and there was no traffic, so we moved along at a pretty decent clip, fields of knee-high corn on both sides of this good farmland. Every now and then, the road curved and the head-lights would pick out a farmhouse or a barn in the distance, but mostly we saw telephone poles and corn. Lots of corn. And the land was flat as a pancake, the way Illinois can be.

The road wound its way south, and us with it, for nearly an hour before Quentin said to me, "Take a right up there, Professor," and next road I saw, I did just that. It was narrower, but still paved. The old Ford occupied most of that concrete. We'd have had to pull over and squeeze by if there'd been anybody coming the other way; but there wasn't, just fields of wheat now in the headlights, and some soybeans here and there, a mist rising from the fields as it started to sneak up on midnight.

I liked driving the bus, even at night on back roads in Illinois. Being on the road was necessary to the game I spent all summer playing, like a child; and driving the bus was part and parcel with catching and hitting and running the bases: a comfort, a happiness. I'd played the game for money when I was younger, and I'd done all right, though in my naïveté I hadn't realized what it all meant. Then the war had come, and I'd done what they asked of me—odd and mysterious though it often was—and when it was over, so was my career as a spy and as a ballplayer. So now I played for the joy of it. I didn't dare tell my players any of this. They'd have ribbed me unmercifully.

I'd always been a good backstop as a kid in St. Louis; soft hands, strong arm, good hitting. I played for University City High School, where I was head of the class in school as well as sports, and did well enough to be the starting catcher for the college nine at Washington U. there in St. Louis, where I took my degree in Literature and then sailed through the doctorate in Classical Languages. Then, at twenty-five, I showed up at a tryout in Springfield, Illinois, and they gave me a contract, catchers being hard to find. In three years, I climbed through the minors and on to the big club, the competition tougher at every level, so I went from star to starter to journeyman; but I made the team, a backup catcher for the White Sox. That's where I stayed for six good years, playing in fifty or sixty games a season, hitting a respectable mid two-hundreds, handling a favorite pitcher or two. Good glove, not much of an arm, decent bat but not enough power. Solid. That was me, and I was happy to be there. The Professor, the guys called me when a local reporter caught on to my education, and the nickname stuck.

And then came the war, and I wound up working in Intelligence on one little island after another as we fought our way to Japan. I spoke Japanese, and that made me useful as an interrogator when we had prisoners. But we didn't have many, the Japanese preferring death to surrender, and so even though I was right behind the front lines I had time to play some catch with the Marines and even work up an exhibition game every now and then. That kept me busy and pleased the Marines. It was good to think about balls and strikes instead of the carnage that surrounded us.

After the armistice with Germany and the victory over the Japanese, I came home and took a job teaching Latin and Greek at Northwestern, and that teaching job left my summers free. I liked teaching, and I liked being a scholar; but I missed playing ball, and I come from a family that made its money in real estate, so I could spend money when I wanted. So I put together the Wandering Warriors, a name that I never explained to the others. We played in the Midwest Semipro League, from Davenport to Kankakee to Decatur to Carbondale to Paducah and then back up north to Crystal City and Hannibal and then Cedar Rapids and then over to Rockford. Round and round we traveled, staying on the circuit, playing one or two or three games in each town, and winding up having played sixty games before the summer came to an end.

There were just eleven of us and we knew we needed one more pitcher and a good utility infielder, but we hadn't found the right people for that yet. But we got by with eleven. I did the catching, and Quentin did the bulk of the pitching. He had a rubber arm, it seemed. Not much of a fastball, but a nice sinker and a good curveball and generally more junk than most hitters at this level could even imagine. Plus, he was a great guy and the closest thing I had to a best friend.

"How far, Quentin?" I asked him after some time.

"Another left," he said, "in about a mile. Ten miles on that, and we'll be there."

"Sure enough," I said, and slowed down some so we could see the road when we got to it. Which we did, but it wasn't much, just a dirt road with ruts. "You sure?"

"That's what the map shows," he said. He was using his Zippo to light up the map every now and again. That Zippo got him through some dark nights in Guadalcanal during the war, so I took that left.

It was slow going, maybe ten miles an hour, maybe less. I could have pointed out to Quentin that the more roundabout way on better roads would've gotten us there sooner; but he's our ace and he wins about all the time. His ball moves all over the place and he needs me back there behind the plate to catch that thing. And his curveball sometimes falls off the table and gets into the dirt, and he needs me for that too.

I was thinking about that, thinking about what a good battery we made, me and Quentin, positive and negative and all that, when the road went up a little rise, and when we crested that it dropped down steeply and there was a river, pretty good sized so maybe the Sangamon or the Mackinaw. And that was where the road stopped.

"Quentin?" I asked him.

"Oh, hell, Professor," he said, "this don't show on the map. I thought there'd be a bridge. Can we back our ass out of here?"

The mist was thicker near this water and getting thicker still. "We're here for the night, I think, Quentin," I said.

The guys were grumbling, wondering what the hell we'd gotten into. There were some pointed remarks as I opened the door and me and Quentin dug the flashlight out of the glove box and walked on down to the river. No bridge and never had been one, it looked like to me. But when Quentin shined his light across the river, we could see a good-sized ferry.

"You see that?" Quentin asked me.

"I do," I said, "but not for long in this damn river fog." And as I said that it disappeared into the darkness and the mist.

"Someone'll be there in the morning, I suspect," said Quentin.

I reached over to slap him on the back and say, "Heck, yes, Quentin, someone'll be there at first light, for sure, and we'll be at that old bandbox of a ballpark in Decatur not long after that. It'll all work out fine."

"I'm damn sorry, Professor," he said, but I told him not to worry, we'd get our sleep on the bus. Wouldn't be the first time or the last time we'd done that.

"Sure enough," he said, and we walked back with the bad news, told the guys how it was, and that we might as well get as comfortable as we could and try to get some sleep.

We were lucky the night was pretty cool. I took my duffel outside and sat on it, leaning back against a front tire. Quentin joined me and handed me his newspaper and his Zippo. I took a look at the headlines. Hitler's invasion of Spain and Portugal was going to end sometime soon with the fall of Lisbon. Part of the Armistice was that the exhausted Brits got to keep Gibraltar, so Hitler was about done for now, I figured. Maybe, in a year or two, he'd turn his attention again to England, but for now the Royal Navy and the overworked RAF would ensure the peace. And then there was Russia, still in turmoil after Stalin's assassination, but soon enough there'd be trouble there. Sure, we were at peace, but it wasn't going to last. At least we'd beaten the Japanese with that superbomb, and as long as we had that and the Germans and Russians didn't, we'd be okay. Fingers crossed. I wished freedom well, but I wasn't all that optimistic.

But here, now, in Illinois, we were a long way from being at war. Our only worry was getting some shut-eye in a bus by a sleepy summer river as the fog thickened. Tomorrow the Wandering Warriors came to town in Decatur, Illinois, for a three-game stint. We'd put on a show and maybe get ourselves back into first place if we won two out of the three. I figured we'd make about thirty dollars a man by way of pay. It wasn't much, but it kept us going.

I folded up the paper and set it on the ground. "We'll get 'em tomorrow," I said to Quentin.

"Sure we will," he said back. And then we both did our best to get comfortable. Quentin can sleep anywhere, but it took me a while and then, eventually, I drifted off.

2

Quentin

I was the last to wake, as always, but even before I woke up proper, I knew everything was wrong. I'd got chilled in the middle of the night and climbed up into the bus to stay warm. That seemed like a good idea at the time, but now the old Transit was swaying under me like I was all at sea, and I hadn't felt that way since those troop ships on the Pacific. I didn't like it then, and didn't now.

It was daylight and bright outside, but the wrong sort of bright, and I was all hot and sweaty, but it was somehow a different hot, with dusty smells in the air I couldn't place. I heard the Professor shouting, and he doesn't do that. He's a man who gets all quiet when he's angry and glares into your face instead of giving you what-for straight out.

Worst of all, I couldn't make out *what* he was shouting.

So I'm calling out, "All right!" and "What the heck now?" and getting to my feet and stumbling down the bus, which I'm alone on, bumping back and forth off the seat backs. The windows are damp with all our night sweat, and I'm peering and squinting and trying to make out who's who out there.

Then a blade flashed in the sunlight, and suddenly I was wideawake. I lunged for the nearest bag—Jimmy's, I think—and grabbed up a bat and jumped down the steps and out the front door of that bus real fast.

I expected good ol' boys, small-town know-nothings who don't take kindly to strangers camping by their land and even less kindly to folks of a darker hue such as myself and Walter. I had no doubts I'd be jumping into a fracas.

Was I expecting Romans, like from that Ben-Hur movie I snuck into as a little bitty kid? No. I was not.

Romans.

I stopped dead in my tracks and said a very bad word that I generally only whisper when I'm alone, in case the Lord gets angry.

Last night's fog had cleared. The river was still there, and the ferry, only now it was on this side of the river. But around us was no farmland, no corn, nothing but grass and olive trees, a whole orchard of them surrounding us. The dirt road under the bus led right to the water where that ferryboat had pulled up. It was short and wooden with low sides and places to tie off horses and a big oar at each end where the ferryman would stand and propel that thing. There'd been no Illinois ferry like that in a long time.

As for the sixteen Roman soldiers squaring off against the Professor and the others, they had helmets with plumes, and metal armor that covered their chests and arms in segments, and those odd kilty-skirty Roman things with the metal chains hanging down like an apron. Bare legs and leather sandals, and they all had short swords. Behind them stood a dozen folks egging on the soldiers, dressed in rough linen tunics, three of them carrying—I swear to God—pitchforks. Simple farm folk if I ever saw any, but not in shirts or denims or boots.

Six of those Roman soldiers had been pushing the bus around, trying to get it to move, I guess, and when they saw me come out the door of it they drew their swords and came at me.

I wondered for a second if we'd stumbled into some movie

being made in the middle of Nowhere, Illinois, but then I heard the Professor standing up to them all with his head high and his chin thrust out, shouting in Latin, which I knew was Latin because he used it all the time to cuss at us when we needed it, and he liked to read to us sometimes from some book written by Julius Caesar himself way back a couple of thousand years ago, about battles with Vercingetorix and those wild Gauls and all.

The Roman with the sideways helmet plume who was shouting back in the same language looked strong and muscular, as if he could take any three of us down single-handed and then pitch a no-hitter right after with his other arm. And to be honest, our guys, standing behind the Professor, looked nine different kinds of terrified. The Wandering Warriors had wandered mighty far, and that was the truth.

That Roman who seemed in charge of things shouted at the six who were coming at me, and they stopped dead in their tracks. He barked another command, and in two seconds they were over with the others, so that the two sides, us and them, were now facing off twenty feet from the bus and nobody was even looking at me anymore. So when the Professor stepped forward, hands spread wide for calm and still spouting Latin, and the Roman leader upped and raised his sword high, there was no way my bat and me could get there in time to help. I'd been in hand-to-hand combat on Ie Shima so I mighta been useful too.

Instead, I jumped back up into the bus, put my hand on the ignition key, and turned it, and that engine started up with a loud backfire. The Professor had been working on the timing of that engine for a week now, and I was glad he hadn't been able to fix it.

That backfire cut through the babble of voices like all get-out. The Warriors all flinched like startled coneys, but they'd been hearing that backfire for days and weren't shook up by it. But the Romans, dear Lord, the Romans *threw* themselves back away from me and that old Ford Transit. The soldiers leaped, and the farm folk who had brought them ran, hands high and eyes rolling.

Well, I turned the engine off and stepped back outside the bus and said out loud, "Yes sirree, that is more like it. A little respect for the Professor. That is all we ask."

The Professor didn't even glance at me. He was still steel-eyeing that Roman in charge, trying to stare him down, intimidate him like he was the pitcher for a team we hated.

The Roman looked at me again, all uncertain, and at the bus, and lowered his sword. Then the two of them jabber-jawed away for what seemed like ten minutes, the Professor in his Julius Caesar Latin and the Roman in his rough, gritty version of the same. But they understood each other good enough, I could see that.

Then the Romans put their swords away and the Professor turned to the guys. "Get your stuff from the bus," he said. "Get your gloves and bats, bring the ball bag, all of that. And lock up behind you. We'll be taking a little walk with these boys to see what's what."

Jimmy shook his head, not understanding, on the verge of crying. "What about the game? The Dukes are expecting us. The game. This can't be happening!"

The Professor took a good look around, and down at the ground and up at the sky, and then he pinched his own arm so hard I could see the white mark.

Then he shook his head. "Jimmy," he said, "and you others, you all just keep it together and don't fret. I think we have a really, *really* long time ahead of us before that Decatur game begins."

"We're leaving the bus here?" asked young Davey.

The Professor wiped sweat from his forehead. "Best save the gas," is all he said.

We gathered up our things and started walking down to the river to the ferry. As we walked I looked at the guys, and it was sure that they didn't have a clue. They were all rattled and confused and scared, and probably not one in three with any idea how far we'd come, where we'd been brought to and why, and just how impossible this all was. Me, I believed the Professor had things in hand. Or I hoped so.

Romans beside and behind us, we went across on that ferry and then started walking, following a rough track between fields. I saw scrawny cows and a few pigs, real small. The Professor looked lost in thought, as if he was doing math. I didn't want to disturb those thoughts, but I just had to step up beside him.

"I'm sorry, Professor," I said.

"For what?" he said, irritated. "For firing up the bus and likely saving our lives?"

"Nope, for me gettin' us stranded here in God-knows-where-and-when."

He shook his head, and his voice softened. "You'll have to

explain that to me, Quentin, because you have lost me and that's the truth."

"Because I was the one insisted we leave Route 66 behind and take them back roads," I said.

The Professor upped and laughed. It was the one moment in the whole adventure that I thought maybe he'd lost his marbles. It was a high, wild laugh and the Roman soldiers marching by our side and behind us clutched their sword hilts like they meant business.

"Hey, don't do that, Professor, you're making these guys nervous."

He said, "And to think that all morning I've been sure this all was *my* fault."

"And you figure that how?" I asked.

The Professor shrugged. "Maybe because we're in Ancient Rome and I speak Latin? That feels like we must be here because of me. But for my life I can't fathom why."

I nearly said to him, "You'll work it out, Professor." But I didn't, because that would've put all this on him and made him frown even harder.

So instead, I asked him, "Where are these Roman bruisers takin' us? What's next?"

About then we climbed to the top of that low ridge and there it was, a Roman road, right in front us, heading off both right and left. It was raised about a foot, had rocks along the sides and then smoothed out rocks on the top. It was about perfect to walk on.

We got up on there, and then the Professor looked over at me and said, "See that post over there, Quentin?"

I looked and I did see a post, a stone post maybe three feet tall, with some marks scratched into it.

"I do," I said. "What's it say?"

"That's called a millarium, Quentin, and the Romans used them to tell people how far it was to the next important place. A milestone."

"How far to what?" I asked.

"Unless I'm mistaken, Quentin, that sign means we're on the Appian Way, the most famous Roman road of them all. I'd say we're headed to Rome."

"Well, hell," I said, "I ain't never been to Rome, Professor." And he laughed. I added, "What are they going to do with us, do you think, when we get there?"

"Well, Quentin," he said, tugging up a bit on the duffel bag he was carrying that had all his catching gear, "I hope maybe we're going to play some ball."

I grinned at him. "Damnation, Professor, why didn't you tell us that a little sooner?"

3
The Professor

The Appian Way! I knew the guys were terrified by all this, but for me it was all the excitement without—yet, anyway—any of the real danger. The Romans were calm, we weren't in slave chains, we were headed to Rome herself, and the centurion in charge seemed to have something definite in mind.

I had questions, a lot of them, like why was a centurion in charge of a dozen-plus soldiers and a few carts with civilian types walking along beside them. Centurions had eighty or a hundred legionaries under their command. And was it an accident they'd come across us in the morning? I'd asked the centurion that, and he'd just said he was under orders. His Latin and mine weren't quite on the same page, so I wasn't sure what he meant by that. But it was obvious that he wasn't all that surprised to find us, though the old Ford Transit's backfire had certainly shocked the hell out of the guy. I had to smile at that.

"What's so funny?" Quentin asked me. "You grinning about all this, Professor?"

I looked at him. My ace pitcher, a guy who'd fought at Iwo and Ie Shima and Saipan and was ready to land on Honshu when the bomb ended that war. A real hero. Amazing, really, that a guy like Quentin, sharp as a tack and a genuine war hero, couldn't stay at the team hotel in Paducah each time we went there. You had to wonder what he'd been fighting for.

"You daydreaming, Professor?" he was asking me.

I smiled again. "No," I said, "I was just thinking about you starting up the Transit, Quentin. These Romans about jumped out of those fancy uniforms."

"They sure enough did, Professor, but they don't seem too worried now. We're all marching along pretty good. And this duffel bag ain't all that good for carrying, you know?"

"I know." I shifted mine around some. "Let's try and keep

up for another half hour or so and then I'll ask the centurion up there for a break, okay?"

Quentin nodded and then drifted back in line to tell the others, and I upped the pace a bit to catch up with the centurion. But it wasn't easy; he was used to moving along smartly, and I had my duffel slung over my shoulder. Plus, I had to admit, a lot of catching over the years had slowed me down. My knees didn't take nicely to all this walking. But I did get up there, finally, only to have his bodyguards cross their pila in front of me to make sure of my intentions. The centurion was up at the front, chatting with one of his officers as I got there, the two of them looking at something the centurion was holding.

I spoke up. "A word, please?"

He turned to look at me and frowned, waved the bodyguards off, and as I approached to within about ten feet of him, with not a bit of warning, he upped and threw what he was holding straight at my head.

I should've ducked or dodged it, but in that less-than-split-second, something clicked in my brain and I reached up with my left hand and caught it.

I wasn't wearing my catcher's mitt, of course. If it had been a rock with some edges on it, I might have wound up with a nasty cut. Instead, it just stung a bit. Like Quentin's fastball on a good day. Which made sense, since the thing he'd thrown at me was one of our baseballs. And the whole group of Romans marching along there laughed and nodded when I tossed it in the air and then lobbed it back to that centurion.

4
Quentin

Well, that was it for hilarity. They waved the Professor back, and we never did get our break. If anything, they upped the pace. Some of our guys were panting, and even for me it was bringing back bad memories of the Marine Corps. As for the Professor, I could tell his legs were causing him trouble, though that frown on his face may not have been all about his knees.

And then the walls of Rome came in sight, and I could see the fear growing in the guys' eyes. They were muttering, looking around for a way out of this mess.

"Don't," I said in warning, "don't even give that a thought." And then I hustled up to walk next to the Professor. "Hey, me and the guys, we was wondering if this is really such a good idea."

"I'll talk to 'em," he said, and we both dropped back. "Fellows," he said, "You got to stay calm here, now, you hear me? No one makes a break for it, you hear? Don't make trouble, not now. You won't outrun these troops. We all stay together. This will be fine. We're a team. We came here together, and we'll leave together too." He gestured ahead of us and grinned. "Besides, we split up now, you guys'll miss out on the glory that's Rome."

"Heads down, now, guys," I added quietly. "Just you keep on walking. Don't fret. Don't think too much. We'll get through this OK."

And so, not thinking too much, we walked through those massive gates and into the Eternal City.

Truth be told, I . . . was expecting more. Streets paved with marble and gold, maybe. Grand men in togas and laurel wreaths striding the streets. Chariots? I'd seen those movies and listened to the Professor talk about Rome so much that the real thing was kind of a letdown at first.

Mostly, it looked dirty and poor. Grimy streets of rough stone, strewn with garbage and lined by high walls. Surly men in linen tunics and sandals. Clothes, knees, and faces filthy. The women looked unhappy and hard-bitten too. No one smiled—mostly they were watching the soldiers go by and looking worried about that.

Then the walls gave way to what looked like tenements, six stories high on either side of us, and right away the muck in the streets at our feet grew even worse. It smelled like bathrooms, and the end of the day at the market when the food is going rotten.

"Glory?" Danny Felton muttered rebelliously. Danny had a mouth on him, and we'd have to keep an eye on that. Good glove at third base, and a strong arm. But a short fuse. I shot him a look, but I knew what he meant. If Rome had any glory, it must be behind all those stout wooden doors that hid the homes away from the poor working stiffs.

The Professor was striding along in a trance, his face unreadable. I thought perhaps he hadn't heard Danny's sass. But then he nodded once and smiled thinly. "Just you wait a moment, oh Danny-boy. Glory's coming."

I started to feel my own fear squirming in my gut. I thought I was done with that, after surviving Iwo and Ie Shima and coming home in one piece. All I wanted to do after that was play some baseball, you know? I loved pitching, I loved being in control, painting some corners, moving somebody off the plate, keeping 'em guessing. And then your world turns upside down and you're walking along like it's just another day in ancient Rome and you realize that you never had any control at all in this world. You don't know anything. You're the one doing the guessing.

I wondered if maybe me and the Professor had been wrong after all. Perhaps we should've all made a big old break for it while we still had some countryside around us.

Then we took a right turn, and uh-oh. *Here* came the marble.

"What the—" said Danny, and I glared quickly at his profanity, but . . . oh Danny-boy.

5
The Professor

I knew pretty much everything there was to know about the Colosseum, but in all the photographs it's two thousand years old and broken down, a heap of old stone that looks like it was sliced diagonally with a giant rusty gladius. Seeing it whole was mind-blowing. Curved walls a hundred fifty feet high lined with arches all around and all grand and golden and shiny and busy-looking.

And hell, Quentin and the guys recognized that thing straight off. I could feel their terror rise. My boys might not be all that well read, but every single one of them had heard of *gladiators*.

If the legionaries had tried to march us straight into that giant arena of stone and gold, the Warriors would have broken. I know it. All the discipline in the world couldn't have stopped some of them from bolting, and then the rest would've tried to follow. And God alone knows what would have happened next.

But they didn't. The centurion looked at me, and damn him, he *winked*, and then we turned and instead walked into the building next door, a low square functional-looking block with porticos across the front.

I heard Quentin murmuring calming things, and I could feel everyone relax. Bobby Gamin, our left fielder, even cracked a funny about feasting and couches and such. I wasn't surprised,

Bobby loved to go to the movies and I'm sure he'd seen *Quo Vadis* and *Ben-Hur* and plenty of Caesar and Cleopatra movies. The Claudette Colbert version of Cleo was a hoot, and the Vivien Leigh wasn't bad. Not accurate, I'd always thought, but not bad. It occurred to me that I was about to get a chance to see just how accurate all those movies and novels and history books had been.

Which wouldn't help me much if we all were dead. Unlike Bobby, I was far from relaxed.

No, we weren't going into the Colosseum. At least, not yet. Instead, Rome's soldier-boys were escorting us into the Ludus Magnus. Otherwise known as?

The Great Gladiatorial Training School.

And as we walked in the door, two legionaries grabbed my arms and half-lifted, half-dragged me away from my team.

Instant pandemonium. I heard Walter, our shortstop, shouting "Hey!", heard the other guys start to move, heard a fight breaking out behind me, and then the soldiers had me around the corner and bumping up the stairs before I could even call out and tell them to be calm, not to get themselves hurt.

6
The Professor

I smelled her before I saw her. Oils and sweet unguents and rose water and maybe some powder. Either that, or Rome's Gladiatorial Training School kept a perfumery on the premises.

I'd stopped struggling two floors below; it would help nobody if I got myself killed or injured. Now the legionaries and I stood outside an open doorway with daylight and all those sweet aromas spilling out of it, so when the soldiers let me go, I smoothed down the ruffled clothes that I'd slept and hiked twenty miles in, in the vain hope of making myself a tiny bit presentable.

Then came a brisk command from inside the room in a low alto voice that was obviously used to being obeyed immediately. And, immediately, they marched me in.

To my right was a big open window that overlooked the circular courtyard in the center of the Ludus Magnus. There, a dozen groups of men battled with sword and shield, trident and net, whips, spears, and various other weapons. It looked like a giant brawl, but amid the grunts and the clamor of steel meeting steel, the voices that wafted up here to the third-floor overlook were focused, businesslike, even cheerful. This was not battle. This was practice.

But much as I wanted to look at the living history exhibit out in the training arena, I wanted to look at the noblewoman to my left even more.

The Romans I had seen so far had the olive skin common to many Italians. This woman's skin was two shades darker than that. Her hair was auburn, shoulder-length but coiffed into tight curls that hugged her head and looked as if they'd been arranged strand by strand. Perhaps they had; she was obviously rich enough to be able to spare the time.

Her eyes were large, penetrating, and rimmed with kohl. Her face was angular but beautiful. She looked commanding and confident, but I also saw something else in those eyes: an intense intelligence and curiosity. She looked about thirty years old.

I was willing to bet that the essences and fragrances her slaves had artfully applied to her hair and body today cost more than my whole team earned in a year. Do I need to add that she was dressed magnificently, in fine white linens hemmed with gold and silver threads, ornamented with what might have been gems?

I tore my eyes away. I was staring. And so I missed the gesture she must have made to the legionaries, because they saluted and withdrew, leaving us alone together.

Well, that was unexpected.

Under her stern gaze I did what anyone would have done, which was to drop my eyes, bow, and say a polite, "Good afternoon," to her in Latin.

She half-smiled, half-cringed, perhaps at my pronunciation. "Huh. So *you* are..."

And, just like that, she addressed me by name. My real name, not just Professor, which is what everyone calls me.

My mouth dropped open. No one on my team calls me by my real name. Hell, most of them don't even know it. She couldn't have heard it from any of the boys, even if she'd been with us.

My heart was hammering, fit to burst by now, but I tried to stay calm and merely nodded. "The same, ma'am." Then realized I'd stupidly said that in English, and in Latin repeated the sentiment: "Yes. That is my name."

Again, she cringed, but hey, she had a hell of an accent of her own. Far from schoolbook or church Latin, that was sure.

I bowed again. "And, please, what is yours?"

There must have been politer ways of asking, but I was lucky I could drag any Latin at all to mind at this precise moment.

"I am Domna," she said simply.

In Latin, *Domna* just means "Lady," so that was far from helpful. But I looked again and thought about it a trifle longer, and then said: "*Julia* Domna?"

Domna looked shocked, though whether at my knowledge or my over-familiarity wasn't clear. Then she inclined her head.

I smiled at her, and she shook her head slightly in amazement. I expect the people around her were trained not to meet her eye. I was not well-trained. "And, if you'll forgive me: how is your husband Septimius? And your sons?"

Now her face hardened and she looked as if she wanted to kill me. I backed off, literally; I stepped away three paces and lowered my gaze. "My apologies. *Many* apologies, Domna. I did not know. Severus is fallen?"

"He is," she said curtly and, turning her back, walked away from me.

Well. I hoped my clumsiness hadn't broken anything. But at least I now knew where—or *when*—we were.

The Colosseum was built and complete by 80 A.D., so I'd known we were later than that. Styles of Roman dress had started changing in the fourth and fifth centuries, but that still gave me a wide window.

But if this was Julia Domna, and her husband Septimius Severus had died recently enough for her to be shocked at the mere mention of it, then this was 211 A.D., or perhaps 212.

I fervently hoped it was 211. After old Septimius struck out, the next Emperor up to bat would be Caracalla, who was almost as nutty and violent as Caligula. If *he* was anywhere around here, we'd all have to be very careful indeed.

But then I remembered I had a much more bizarre problem at hand, because Julia Domna *knew who I was.*

"So it was you," I said to her back. "Julia Domna? You brought us here. Picked us up right out of time. Out of the years. To your year. To your place. To Rome."

It was the only way I could think to put it in Latin. But

Domna did not respond, and so I stepped to the window and looked out at the gladiatorial practice. Trying to match her calmness, maintain some initiative.

Trying not to be desperately afraid that we would all end up down there or across the road in the Colosseum, me and Quentin and Walter and Enos and Jake and all the guys, with swords in our hands, swinging them like bats because that was what we knew, while brawny and utterly ruthless brutes like those in the courtyard below me rushed at us and hacked our lives away.

7
Quentin

The Romans stopped our little rebellion with an ease that bordered on contempt, and threw us into a pen. That's what I'd have to call it: a big square room, featureless in every way, just a few small windows up too high for any of us to see out of. They threw our bags in after us. At first, we just sat there, scared and angry. But time passed and nothing seemed to be going on, and then more time passed until Walter grabbed a ball and, still sitting down, started throwing it against a wall so it bounced back to him; just like you do when you're a kid. And then he stood up and started throwing it harder, so it came back on the short hop, which he backhanded and then flipped the ball into the air, caught it with his right hand and did it all over again.

Pretty soon Danny joined, and then so did I, and then Jake grabbed a bat and we started playing pepper and flipping the ball around like you do to each other, behind the back and all that, showing off for the fans. We had a good game, everybody loosening up and getting involved in one way or another. This was all weird as it could be; but, hell, we were ballplayers. It wasn't long before we were wisecracking, like you do, and flipping the ball all over the place. It took our minds off the trouble we were in.

And so, when the Professor came back to us, we looked like his Wandering Warriors, about ready to get out there and go nine against whatever them Romans had in mind.

He nodded briskly at us as if this wasn't the weirdest day of our entire lives and said, "Good. Let's go."

"Go?" said Davey.

"Go where?" I said with some suspicion.

The Professor shot me a look and said, "Outside, of course. To practice for real. As long as you boys promise to stop trying to fight everyone we see, that is."

We packed up and filed out. Playing a little pepper had lulled the fellas into some kind of normality in this crazy situation, and they all went meekly, trusting the Professor, but as we filed out of that pen he sidled up to me and, *sotto voce* as you might say, whispered, "Help me make this look good. We're playing for our lives here."

8
The Professor

"All right, fellows," I told them, once we were out on the dirt and in the sunshine. "The Romans just want to see what baseball's all about, so I told them they could watch us work out."

It wasn't quite as simple as that, but I thought I'd better ease into it, so I was holding a ball in my right hand, tossing it up in the air and catching it while I talked. "These guys here are athletes, fellows, and they tell me they have a kid's game like baseball. They call it "small ball." So I told 'em we all started playing this game when we were kids too; but where we're from, adults play it, and it's pretty damn entertaining."

I tossed the ball toward Enos Slaughter, our center fielder and the fastest guy on the team. He'd steal second from his own mother if she looked the wrong way for a second or two, and he had a great glove and a strong arm out in center, as well. He and I usually warmed up together, and today was no different. He caught it, grinned, and threw it back to me.

And the guys knew what to do from there. Everybody broke into pairs and started playing catch, loosening up the arms and stretching out the muscles.

Then, just like a bunch of kids marking off a field when we were ten-year-olds, we put down some caps to mark the bases. We had a rubber home plate with us, and we set that down for starters, and then used caps for first, second and third. Then I went over and found a couple of the rakes the Romans used to smooth out the dirt, and while the guys were loosening up I gave one of them to Bobby Gamin, and the two of us gave the infield the once-over. No grass and it wasn't pretty, but there weren't any rocks out there before and the dirt wasn't too bad. It was playable.

Normally we'd take batting practice then, and I always threw BP; but I was thinking maybe we'd dazzle those Romans a little bit first with some snazzy infield work, and let them see what outfield play is like too. So I had Quentin walk down the first base line with the fungo bat to hit some fly balls to the outfielders, and I used the other fungo to hit some grounders to the infielders.

Taking infield was always one of my favorite things to do, mainly because in some other life I'm a slick-fielding shortstop, backhanding that sharp grounder while I go toward third, and then pivoting on my right leg to bring my body around enough that I can sidearm the ball to first and beat the runner. So lots of times I'd get out there and trade off with Walter or Duke or Bobby and have some fun taking grounders.

But not here, not now. We needed to be at our entertaining best and that meant I was hitting the grounders and the guys were fielding them and looking sharp while they did it. I moved them around, hitting balls to their right or to their left, and hitting rollers or one-hoppers, and then a few infield pop flies. All so the guys could show off their skills. We did three rounds of throws to first, and then three more of turning two at second, and a few more turning two the hard way at first, and then a final round keeping Duke busy at third. Then I called in Quentin from hitting those fly balls and did my job as catcher while he dropped some bunts and then hit the ball to the outfield, and we made some plays at the plate. Our outfield arms were good, and the guys really showed that off. Quentin hit them fly balls they had to run to catch, but made sure they were playable. Then the guys set up the cut-offs and the Warriors were perfect as they threw to second and then to third and then to home. If you knew the game, it was a joy to see it played that well.

If you didn't know the game, I was sure hoping you'd appreciate what you were watching. Especially Domna. For all our sakes, I hoped to hell that she was up there in that room, looking out the window and liking what she was seeing.

After a half hour of that, I brought the infield in and told the guys it was time for batting practice. Then I grabbed the ball bag and walked out about sixty feet from our home plate and used the heel of the spikes to draw a line in the sand. That was my pitching rubber, and with Quentin wearing the tools of ignorance since we needed a backstop, I started throwing good fastballs right down the middle as the guys came up to take ten swings each. There was a guy at the plate, a guy on deck and another in the hole, and everyone else was shagging flies and grounders and tossing them back into me. As the hitters switched after their ten swings, I'd walk around and put all the balls that had rolled in back into the bag and we'd do the whole thing over again.

The right-handed hitters were having a field day. The way we had it set up, there was a short left field, no more than two hundred fifty feet, I'd guess. Then a good three-eighty or even four hundred to center, and forever, it seemed, off to right. The right-handed hitters were popping the ball over the fence with some regularity, and some of the legionaries and gladiators-in-training who were standing beyond the fence watching us got a chance to shag those balls and throw them back to us. That turned out to be a lot of fun, so much so that they started competing with each other to see who could make a nice bare-handed catch and then who had the best arm to throw it back onto the field. They were all a lot better at that than I'd thought they'd be.

Eventually all good things come to an end, and BP was over. Everybody'd had ten swings twice and most of the boys, even the lefties, had a homer or two to celebrate. I hit three of them out and laughed to think I'd probably ruined my nice level swing by trying for fly balls to left and batting-practice homers. But what the hell, we might not be alive long anyway, I might as well go out with some long balls. It felt good, even if it was a short left field.

I was the last to hit, so I was standing there with Quentin. He was still wearing the tools. The guys were trotting in from around the field. Looked like the workout was over. I wondered what was next? The only thing I was sure of was that it wouldn't be an afternoon game in Decatur, Illinois.

"Huh," said Quentin. "New player?"

I looked where he was looking, and there she was. Gone was the sumptuous dress; now she wore a plain grey tunic just like the rest of the Romans. Gone was the heavy waft of classical cosmetics, and her face was clean and shining and free of all makeup. A simple linen headband held her hair out of her eyes.

But more than her clothing had changed; it was her entire demeanor. For a woman—an empress of mighty Rome, for goodness sake—Julia Domna moved a lot like a ballplayer. Now that I knew she was mother to Caracalla and Geta, that meant she had to be mid to late thirties, but she sure as heck didn't look it.

She walked right up to us and said to me, in Latin. "I like your game. I played something very much like it when I was young. I was happy then."

Her words were flippant, even through that last part, but I saw a shadow move behind her eyes.

"Yes, Domna," I said to her. "Many of us play for similar reasons. Joy. Happiness. Childhood."

"Come then," she said, "and let us play." And she walked to her right, picked up Quentin's glove from where he'd dropped it, slid it onto her left hand, and said, "Give me a fastball, Professor, right down the middle."

Well, she'd picked that up by listening to us in batting practice, when the guys let me know what they wanted to hit. So I walked toward where we'd left our stuff and picked up my fielder's mitt and we got started playing some catch, me and the widow of the Emperor of all Rome, the mother of two sons contesting power, the focal point of a power struggle that would decide the fate of an empire and, maybe, the future of Western culture as well. Septimius Severus had managed to hold things together pretty good, but in the history I knew it was all downhill for Rome and the West from this point on. And here I was playing nice with Domna. I wondered, what the hell did she have in mind? Why were we here?

To play some ball, apparently. It turned out that Domna wasn't too bad. We played some catch and she loosened up, and then she trotted out to shortstop. Me and the guys all looked at one another and they shrugged. Hey, it was her home field. Walter and Bobby and Jake all trotted out to join her and then I hit her a soft grounder. Damned if she didn't charge the ball, gather it up pretty nicely, and then peg one over to Jake at first. Her arm motion was wrong, the sort of short-arm you see a lot in folks who learned the game late. She didn't bring the hand and wrist back far enough before firing it over to first.

But then I got a little more daring and hit one into the hole. She sprinted to her right, fielded it cleanly, and threw it sidearm to first. A rocket! "Good Christ Almighty," I heard Quentin say. He was next to me, catching up the balls as they came in from my odd new infield. "Did I just see what I just saw?"

I shook my head and laughed. "I saw it too, Quentin. She can play some ball."

"I'll be damned if she ain't a pretty good shortstop, Professor," he said, and then we watched as she went and proved that for another dozen or so ground balls. Sure, she was rough around the edges, throwing to the wrong side of the bag at second when she was trying to turn two. And she had trouble with pop-ups behind her. But, hell, who doesn't?

Most important, she was smiling, and having fun, and so were the guys. Sure, it was just one more strange thing in a long day of absurdities; but thank goodness she was as good as she was, since we were all still alive, even laughing and joking around, when she was done.

The guys had no idea who she was, which I figured was all to the good. If they thought she was just some rich wife of a Roman senator or something, that was fine with me.

I was about to try her out at bat when a bald man in a white tunic showed up in the entryway we'd all come in through and called out to her. I didn't catch what he said; by now I was so used to hearing Latin that by the time I realized he was speaking Greek, his words were scattered to the winds. Domna stopped where she was and turned, and a ball bounced past her into the infield.

Her expression had turned ominous. A quick nod to the messenger, another to me, and she was striding off the field with us all regretfully watching her go. Her body language had changed back again on a dime: imperious and commanding, she walked like a lady once more, not a ballplayer, for all that she was still wearing a tunic. At the edge of the field she remembered she was wearing Quentin's glove and dropped it into the dirt. Without even looking back she raised her hand in a curt signal to the stands, and then she was gone.

And as we all stood there, dumbfounded, the legionaries and gladiators who'd been our audience swarmed over the fence and came for us.

With cries of alarm the boys backed up, came together. Guys without bats snatched them from the ground. I heard Quentin saying, "Hey now, hey now," trying to calm them and Danny

Felton saying, "Not that jail cell again, no way," and my other boys saying viler things in their fear as those brutes marched towards us.

I took a deep breath, smiled, and stepped forward.

That night, I dined with an empress.

If I lived in Rome for a hundred years, I don't think I'd ever get used to eating lying down. I managed it for the first course of oysters, eggs, and turtle dove, but when they brought in the roast boar and poached lamprey, I begged and bowed and scraped and with a thousand pardons to my hostess, swung my legs off the couch and sat upright like a barbarian, stifling a belch. Wasn't sure I could eat a whole lot more of that rich food, anyway. I don't know how Domna could stay so slim on such a diet, and I felt bad for my boys, who were still back in the Ludus Magnus eating whatever the gladiators ate.

At least they wouldn't be herded back into the pen later. Tonight, my Warriors would be sleeping in the cells the most favored gladiators got, two men to a room, with a straw mattress each and a window for light and air. It wasn't luxury, but it wasn't a whole lot worse than some of the motels we stayed at on the road and was even a step up from sleeping on the bus. And they wouldn't be locked in. They couldn't leave the Ludus Magnus, but they were free to wander the halls, go to the latrines, or visit with one another.

Not that they'd be socializing a whole lot. They were dog tired. Turned out that those tough-as-nails legionaries and the even more terrifying gladiators, with all their brawn and scars and deadly swagger, all they wanted was to try their hand with a bat and ball. We'd had ourselves a four-hour pickup game, splitting into groups and trying to train the Romans up, show them what was what on a ballfield.

Not a one had Domna's skills, or anywhere close to that, but they had strong arms and dexterity and a ton of stamina. They were relentless, in fact. Either baseball had really stirred something within the savage breast, or they wanted to excel to curry favor with Domna. Either way, by the end we had to beg for mercy and it was only dusk that saved us.

I'd already known that the Romans played something like baseball, using a stitched-leather ball just a little bigger than a baseball, smaller than those used in their other ball sports. Roman women played it too, but their version had a lot fewer collisions and relied on finesse where the men relied on contact. But in both cases the players threw the ball, caught it, and even hit it, with sticks not that far different from baseball bats.

And as I was learning from Domna at dinner, her sons Antoninus—whom history would remember as Caracalla—and Geta also played the game and loved it.

Domna's late husband had been off fighting a war in Caledonia with both his sons when he had taken ill and died. The history I remembered said that it might have been poison. The boys had wrapped up the military campaign in short order, and were now marching their armies back to the Eternal City.

"And so, they come," she said. "Quarrelling all the way. Sometimes coming to blows, held apart only by their legates and tribunes. They are talking of splitting the body in two."

I shook my head, aghast. "Not...forgive me, Domna...you speak of the Emperor's body? Surely you do not."

Like the Brits and the Americans back home, Julia Domna and I were divided by a common language. I understood her words well enough but her idiom could be impenetrable, and to make it worse she was speaking Greek now. Turns out that Latin was her fourth language, after Punic, Aramaic, and Greek, which at least explained her accent.

Mercifully, she looked amused at my error of understanding. Domna raised a finger, and a slave hurried to spoon more fish onto her plate and fill up her beaker of wine and water. She switched to Latin. "I speak of the Imperium, Magister. They would divide my husband's empire, and rule half of it each. But that cannot stand."

I wasn't sure I liked "*magister*," but there were worse things she could have called me. "And so, small ball."

She was staring beyond me now, into the shadows behind the oil lamps that lined the walls, or perhaps even further back into the past. "My boys. When young, they played all the time. Competing, always, but laughing all the while. And then they grew up." She sighed. "These past years, it was only Severus who stopped them from killing each other."

Best to check, even though I thought I understood. "But now...?"

"But now, during the great Games that will begin as soon as

my sons return, Rome will play ball. And perhaps my boys will relax and be calm once more, and even laugh, and there will be peace between them."

Maybe I could take advantage of her reverie. I sat forward. "And so you chose us. But how on earth did you bring us here?"

Her gaze swiveled back to me, and she smiled enigmatically. "By the grace of the True God."

I considered that. "Which God?"

No God I knew, as it turned out. She spoke of Elagabal, the god of her homeland. Julia Domna was descended from a ruling dynasty of Priest-Kings in Syria, and her father was the High Priest of the Temple of the Sun God there, and so Domna had herself some serious favor with Elagabal. The True God spoke to her. She heard him, and she talked right back at him. Elagabal had told Julia Domna how to summon some entertaining warriors for the Games in the Colosseum marking Geta's and Caracalla's return, and even told her where to send the centurion and his guards to find us.

I frankly didn't know what to think about this ancient-world scripturizing and magicking, but Julia seemed sane enough to me, and we were all here now, and that was indisputable.

And perhaps the real story didn't matter. Somebody—or something, somewhere—had done an amazing thing, and that was probably about all I was ever going to find out about the mechanism of it.

I nodded diffidently, and with my heart in my mouth but as much confidence as I could muster, I said: "And when I and my Wandering Warriors have entertained you and Rome, and once your sons are reconciled? By the grace of the True God and yourself, we may return home?"

Again, that beautiful but Sphinx-like grin. "If Elagabal wills it," she said. And that was all I got out of her on that subject.

Using a traveling ball team from the future to heal a horrendous broken family and hold an empire together seemed like a tall order. I raised my own cup to my lips, and then put it down again. No more wine for me tonight. I needed to think.

"If your . . . boys play anywhere near as well as you do, it will be a great game," I said. With Caracalla's fearsome reputation, it was hard for me to keep calling him a mere boy, like a mother would.

Julia Domna shrugged. "They are not bad. They move quickly, think on their feet. Catch and throw the small ball well."

I nodded. "And today, while we were playing, your slave came to tell you... what?"

She brought those beautiful eyes to bear on me again, and studied me intently. I very nearly blushed. Maybe I even did. All I know is that I tried my best to withstand that gaze while she decided whether to tell me.

Eventually she said, "That 'slave' is a freedman. And word travels slowly on the road, and armies ride fast when they are angry."

"Yes, indeed," I said expectantly, but she had lapsed back into brooding, so I had to figure it out for myself. "Domna, when do Caracalla and Geta arrive back in the City? Perhaps sooner than you expected?"

"I had thought we had two months to train," she said. "Yet we have only one. Perhaps even less than that."

I whistled. "Then I hope your legionaries and gladiators learn fast."

Domna inclined her head. "With such a magister to teach them, I'm sure they will. But I grow tired of your many questions. Tell me more of... where you come from. Of your time, and the game, and where you play it? There is much that I would know of you and your home year, Magister."

I hesitated for a long moment, even beckoning for yet another plate of food to give me time to think. But I couldn't cotton to a single reason to stay silent. Would telling Julia Domna about the twentieth century alter the future? Surely nowhere near as much as having my boys and me sliding back in time.

And if nothing else, I needed the grace and favor of Julia Domna, the absolute ruler of the Roman Empire... at least, until her dangerous, violent sons came home.

And perhaps it wouldn't hurt to take my own mind off the seriousness of our situation, and brag just a little to a beautiful woman.

So, sure. I started telling her some baseball stories. About how Wally Pipp played through pain to become one of the Yankees' greatest first basemen, and how Babe Ruth won three hundred career games pitching for the Red Sox, and how Ted Williams was one of the greatest hitters of all time until he got shot down over China when MacArthur crossed the Yalu River in the China War. I told her how baseball was so much a part of life where we came from that we used its terminology all the time, hitting a homer with a new proposal at the office, or striking out if the boss said no. Or touching base with someone if you just wanted to check in with them on something. Or surprising someone during a meeting by throwing them a curve. Or stepping up to the plate if you were going to take responsibility for something.

She laughed, and I hadn't seen her do that before. "But that's what you and I are doing here, Magister. We are stepping up to the plate, yes?"

"Yes," I said. "That's about it." And, I thought but didn't say, this might work out, even though the whole crazy thing was definitely out of left field.

Two weeks later, I crouched behind the plate while Lucius Aurelius, the centurion who'd been sent to fetch us from the banks of the Tiber, delivered a pretty good curveball to me. Sure, he liked the high, hard fastball the best and I couldn't blame him. He was a soldier and in line for the Praetorian Guard. He didn't like to nibble at the corners. Straight heat, that was him, and I was having a hard time convincing him otherwise. But his curveball curved, so I was proud of him. And he had the knack of good control. Control is mostly a matter of belief on the part of a pitcher. You can't aim the ball when you let go, you have to just know that the motion you're using and the release point that feels natural will result in the ball going where you want it to. It takes a lot of confidence, and Lucius had that in spades.

We had four full teams now, all told: the Wandering Warriors, plus three squads of Romans. Eventually there would be seven Roman teams, one named for each of the hills of Rome, but for the time being, we just had the Palatines, the Aventines, and the Caelians. Today we were practicing all mixed up with the Palatines, who were Praetorians and other favored soldiers. They were okay; strong, disciplined, probably the most skilled, but taking time to gel as a team. The Caelians were a bunch of cheerful duffers, citizens of Rome who had started coming to the public practices out of curiosity and signed up to try the game for themselves. They worked great as a team, but most had no real ball skills. The Aventines were terrifying: gladiators all, they played with brute force and a lack of subtlety and would occasionally thump us or start fights when we got them out.

For the time being, we were playing here and there in the minor arenas around the city and even outside, building up support and interest. We would play our full-up showcase games in front of the co-emperors Caracalla and Geta, maybe a week or two from now. Perhaps even with them playing on the teams, if they wanted to step up to the plate. Domna would be playing with the Warriors and we were glad to have her. That meant moving Walter out of short and putting him in right field, or using him to pinch-hit and pinch-run, but he was okay with that.

She seemed to get better every day on defense. Good glove, soft hands, strong arm, turned the corner great in a double play. She had a flat swing and not much power at the plate, but as a singles hitter, she could spray the ball around and move the runners, and we needed that. Plus, we had to be careful with her, but it was fun to listen to her from the bench yelling at us to just get the bat on the ball, or hit it outa here.

Those showcase games would be played in the Colosseum, in between gladiatorial bouts. It would take some work to get the field ready for baseball after the gladiators had at it and there was blood on the dirt and sand; but the Romans could work miracles with that place, I'm telling you. They showed me how they could stage a sea battle in there, water and all, when they wanted to. I believed them.

I was enjoying the neighborhood games. Not too many spectators, but those who showed up seemed to be sticking around, figuring out how the game worked, enjoying the sportsmanship, applauding some nice work with the glove or a line drive in the gap, and then cheering with gusto for home runs. But the thought of playing in front of a bloodthirsty Colosseum crowd chilled me to the bone.

Nothing I could do about that, of course. Domna's city, Domna's rules.

Every day, the armies of the two brothers got closer. And every day I could feel the tensions rising on the streets of Rome.

I talked with Julia Domna most every day now. She was fascinated by us and keenly interested in the land we came from, far away in time: Land of the Free, Home of the Brave, a country of cars and airplanes and other marvels, of education for all, of sports stadiums where massive death wasn't part of the program. Every day she had new questions, and some of them were really *good* questions that I couldn't answer.

But if I had to eat much more peacock and lamprey and

dormouse, my innards were going to revolt. So whenever I saw Domna's freedman standing in the archway to the Ludus Magnus arena, my heart sank a bit. Julia, she was good company, but frankly I'd rather have eaten the gruel and plain boiled meat my boys got.

And I'd rather have stayed with the boys for other reasons too. I saw the looks as I walked away from home plate, unclipping my shin guards and chest protector and handing my catcher's mask and mitt to Quentin. I'd rather be with them, building the team, than have them jealous and muttering behind my back.

But Julia Domna was the boss around here, and if we were ever going home, I'd be doing whatever she said.

I didn't like going to the Palatine Hill after dark to dine with Domna. I'd be ushered through stinking streets by lantern light, grateful for the escort of the soldiers. The only other men abroad by night slunk in the shadows, mean and vicious-looking, or were carried by in sedan chairs with their own toughs to guard them. On my own and unprotected, I'd not have lasted five minutes.

Today, though, it was still late afternoon, and the streets were bustling with men and women, citizens and slaves alike, all hurrying back to wherever they were going to spend the night, or grabbing a bite in the tiny bars and taverns that seemed to line every street. It wasn't all Latin I heard on those streets, either; Romans mixed with folks speaking Germanic, Gallic, Greek, Hebrew, and several African tongues. Rome of this era was truly cosmopolitan, and as best I could see no one was being turned away from the pie shops and wine stalls because of creed or color. It looked like Jake and I and the "Cubans" might actually be treated more decently here than at home, which gave me pause, I have to say.

But much as I'd have longed to linger and explore, my soldiers hurried me through the streets and into a tunnel and up some stairs, and before I knew it I was in the palace of Julia Domna once again.

I thought I'd been dreading dinner, but I'd been using that word all wrong. Because Domna's freedman led me into a room I'd never been in before, and all of a sudden four tough-looking legionaries I didn't recognize appeared from nowhere.

They kicked my legs out from under me so I fell onto my knees, further pushing my head forward into a kowtow while roughly holding my hands behind my back.

With good old American oaths on my lips due to the pain in my legs, I looked up.

He was a bulldog of a man, his face square and flat and pugnacious, his hair cropped brutally short and his beard barely more than stubble. He walked toward me with his head forward, seeming to lead with his brow. He looked like a man afraid of nothing. No, that's not right: he looked like a man much more used to inspiring fear than feeling it himself.

Caracalla. And Julia Domna was nowhere in sight.

Okay, so *this* was what dread really felt like.

"Good evening, Imperial Majesty," I began in Latin, in the politest and most deferential tone I could manage. "My name is—"

Caracalla leaped forward and kicked me in the guts, hard. Knocked the wind right out of me. The soldiers dropped me to the floor, and so I did about the only thing I could think of, which was to curl up into a ball and protect my head when they started kicking me some more.

9
Quentin

Well, it was a shame that the Professor was called away, because the Wandering Warriors found ourselves visited by royalty, or whatever they call it when it's emperors and not kings.

We'd finished up our practice and were getting some chow, the usual gruel, more like breakfast porridge or grits than what a man would like for dinner; but tonight they brought us some salted ham and some olives and wine to go along with it. This cheered the boys up some, but not a lot, because they never liked it when we were separated from the Professor. We ate in the same long, low hall as the gladiators, but they mostly sat on their own benches to eat and didn't mix with us, which was fine. Those brutes scared the tar out of us.

So the fellas were grousing, but not too loud, while stuffing their faces, and then a tall and aristocratic young man walked in with an even taller Praetorian Guard on either side of him, and all the gladiators jumped and fell right down onto the floor and pressed their foreheads into the floorboards, and that was how we met the Co-Emperor, Geta.

Of course, without the Professor, conversation was all but

impossible. None of us spoke Geta's languages—he tried several—and we tried what few we knew: a little Spanish, a little Italian, and some Yiddish. But he smiled and clasped every one of us by the arm and studied us and mimed throwing and catching a ball, and gave us to believe by signs that he would be coming back to see us in daytime and actually play a bit. Walter and Davey were all for getting a ball now and trying to get some catch going once they realized he was an Emperor and all—even they could understand we needed to impress the powers-that-be, whenever possible—but Geta obviously had somewhere else to be, and after smiling a bit more, he left.

Wow. An Emperor. That bucked up the boys and no mistake, and made those gladiators look at us with a bit more respect as well, given that he'd spent twenty minutes trying to talk to us and had ignored them completely. So after Geta left the guys all went back for more food, even though the ham was all gone and it was just gruel again now, and another cup of wine, and the mood in the room got about as downright cheerful and neighborly as it had gotten since we had arrived in this time and place.

And I sat back and thought, well now, maybe everything's going to be all right after all.

10
The Professor

They dragged me along the corridor by my arms. Apparently walking under my own steam wasn't allowed, and I frankly didn't have my breath back anyway.

My ribs still ached, but I didn't think these goons had broken any.

Now a familiar voice, shouting. Julia Domna was marching down the corridor in her full makeup and hair, jewels dripping over a dress of white and purple, her expression livid. She walked right up to her son and got in his face, and he shouted back and pushed at her shoulder, and she shoved back. Caracalla was bellowing now, almost spitting, his face red and apoplectic. I couldn't understand a single word; they must have been speaking one of their other languages, Punic or Aramaic or whatever.

For all that Caracalla was a young guy—barely into his twenties, my guess—I found myself harboring the unworthy hope he'd just have a heart attack and die right there.

His soldiers had dropped back and were watching, hands on their gladius hilts, which scared me. Would Caracalla order them to draw steel on his own mother?

Almost as bad. She raised her arms above her head, almost as if she was going to pitch a spell on him, and at that Caracalla stepped up and punched her full in the face. Domna went over backwards.

I howled and tried to struggle up but Caracalla's legionary put his foot on my shoulder and trod me back down to the floor, and there I lay until Caracalla and his bully boys swept out, leaving me and the Empress Julia Domna sprawled on the marble floor, gasping like fishes. We weren't in great shape, either of us; but at least they'd left us alive. I had Domna to thank for that.

11
Quentin

The warm glow had worn off by bedtime, because the Professor hadn't come back. Most of the boys took it okay, heading off to their cells without mentioning it. But Danny Felton had a face on him like thunder, and he kept checking his wristwatch; and Enos, always impatient, was pacing.

Eventually I made 'em go to bed, trying to sound as calm and confident as I could, and I toddled off to my own cell too, where I lay on my back and stared at the ceiling for a long while.

I mean, I knew the Professor was having dinner with a pretty woman and all, but somehow, I just didn't see him abandoning us to stay out for a night on the tiles with Julia Domna. I didn't see that at all.

12
The Professor

We sat there, side by side in the corridor on the hard marble floor, our backs against a sumptuous fresco of the procession of Dionysus. Julia hugged her knees and rocked, lost in her thoughts, and I gave her a moment. She didn't suggest going anywhere else, and so I didn't either. Perhaps moving would have made it more likely we'd run into her psychopathic son again.

"He is much worse," she said, almost to herself. "Maybe it

was all the war, all the fighting. Maybe the death of his father. Some demon has him."

Or maybe, I thought, Caracalla just thought this was how you had to behave to be an emperor. If I remembered my history right, Septimius Severus had been no angel either, especially when he was young. But I said nothing.

Julia peered at me. "Understand, I have not seen him for three years, since he and my husband left to campaign in Caledonia. I had thought he would learn from his father, gain a cool head, grow out of his...rages. But..." She shook her head. "Whatever happens, do not address him unless you absolutely must. Never argue. Never answer back. He will find any excuse to throw you to the lions, or just slit your throat and be done with it."

I shivered. "All right. But what did he say to you?"

Domna blew out a breath, exercised her jaw back and forth. She was going to have a lovely bruise. "He is the Emperor, and he is very angry with me. And I am nothing. He made it very clear that he can have me killed whenever he likes. He wanted to remind me of that." She looked at me again with those piercing eyes. "And if he does kill me, you must do whatever you can to get away, because you will be next."

I nodded. No surprises yet. "But what's he got to be so mad about? I mean today, specifically?"

Domna looked desolate. "I was not expecting my sons for another week or more. But they galloped ahead of their armies with just a few centuries of men to protect them, because they had heard rumors from Rome. About you. Together, they burst in on me, at noon."

She checked the corridor. No one else about, so she reached out a pretty, long-fingered hand and wrapped it around mine. I squeezed her hand, and she looked down in surprise and then up at me again. "It is really my fault. I made a promise. The deep magics of Elagabal, I swore I'd only use by the grace of Septimius. And I have not, not until he died. But Caracalla says that now that I should only use them by *his* grace, when he gives his blessing. And he did not bless..." She gestured. "This. You."

"He's afraid of you."

She looked dark. "Maybe he should be."

I thought about it some more. "How about Geta? They're co-emperors, right?"

"Geta is a much nicer man. Calmer. A better son. And no match for his brother."

"So where is Geta now?"

"Probably barricaded into his own wing of the palace, behind his guards, so that Caracalla won't slay him in the night."

This was terrible. My mouth was dry, but I had to know. "Are we dead, Julia? Me and my boys? Is this over?"

"Not yet. Because the streets are buzzing about you and the Wanderers. Caracalla cannot just make you disappear before the Games." She grinned wryly, still wincing at the pain in her jaw. "There was method in my madness. Robbing the people of their bread and circuses would be an unpopular move. And above all else, my son craves the popularity of the plebs. So he will have to find another excuse."

"We can't..." I shook my head, thinking of Quentin and Davey, Danny and Walter and Enos and Jake and all, waiting patiently over in the Ludus Magnus like lambs before the slaughter.

And so I turned to her properly, and seized her arms and looked into her eyes. "Send us back, Julia. You magicked us here, you and the god Elagabal. Magic us away again. They don't deserve to be embroiled in all this, my boys; they're young and they're good kids and they just want to play ball. Damn it, you've been on the team for weeks, you know them, and not a one of them has a savage bone in his body. We're not just your toys, to perform and get slaughtered if it doesn't work out. Send us back home. Please."

Julia was already shaking her head. Gently, she pulled her arms away but rested her hand against my cheek. "I wish I could, Magister. But for that, you would all have to be out of the city. Rome is protected against the spells of foreign gods. We would need to get you far away. And that is not possible now."

I pushed her hand away. "Well, then, I should get home. Back to the Ludus Magnus, I mean, to tell my boys what's up."

Again, Julia shook her head. "The Palace is locked down for the night, and now that Caracalla is back, the Praetorians answer to him. I cannot order them out to guard you. You will need to stay here until morning."

My eyes swiveled to look into hers, incredulous. Surely she didn't mean...?

No, she didn't. She poked my arm and grinned, a little ruefully.

"No. Not that. But it will be a long night. Because we need to make a plan, you and I. Perhaps several plans."

You might at least say you're sorry, I thought, but now wasn't the time. And this wasn't even all about us; the Dowager Empress Julia Domna was in some pretty terrific danger herself.

If she wanted my help to plan and scheme our way out of this mess, then sure, I'd take her up on that. "All right. But are there any of those couches nearby?"

I pushed myself off the cold hard floor and up onto my feet, and reached a hand down to pull her up with me.

13
Quentin

"Where's the Professor? *Ubi est Magister?*"

The master of the Ludus—*lanista*, in Latin—stood with his arms folded and three toughs behind him covered in oil and muscle. I tried again. "We don't go out there and practice, we don't do anything, till we see the Professor again." I mimed it. Pointed outside, then crossed it out in the air with two decisive sweeps of my finger and folded my own arms. "Professor. Magister. Bring him back."

Behind me I heard Jimmy mutter a prayer and felt, rather than saw, Johnny Holman elbow him to make him shut up.

Morning light streamed through the high windows. We all could hear the gladiators already at work outside, whacking at one another with swords and tridents. The hard work of the day was beginning in the Ludus Magnus, and still we had no Professor.

We were all terrified; me too, but we had to make a stand.

The lanista pointed outside, mimed a bat swing and a catch. He was getting mad at us, and he was a man used to putting down trouble. I could see his toughs glaring at us, bouncing on the balls of their feet, ready to beat the living heck out of us.

There was a knock on the big doors, down the corridor, and everyone looked that way. The door-boys cranked the doors, the guards snapped to attention.

In walked the Emperor Geta, in a simple tunic, dressed for ball, with a few soldiers behind him.

Everyone's face fell, because we'd been hoping for the Professor. I stepped up to Geta. "Professor? Magister?" I even used his real name, and then raised my hands. "Where? *Ubi est Magister?*"

He obviously didn't know. And, equally obviously, had come to practice with us.

I hesitated.

"I don't care who he is, we still don't go out there till we get the Professor back." Danny Felton said. Of course it'd be Danny, the only Warrior who would actually start a bar fight.

But the others were stepping away, lowering their bats. "C'mon, he's the Emperor," said Walter. "We cross the Emperor, we're toast. There's dumb, and then there's *stupid*."

"*Co*-Emperor," Danny muttered, but Walter was right. We weren't about to go on strike with royalty standing there.

So we got changed, and we went out to play some ball.

14
The Professor

The next morning, I stood in the Roman Forum and did a long slow scan around it, still scarcely believing what I was seeing. Marble buildings surrounded me. Right next to me stood a huge triumphal arch. To my immediate left was the Curia, the Roman Senate House. Extending in front of me to my left was the civil Basilica of Aemilius and facing it to my right was another glorious-looking public building, the Basilica of Julius, all marble pillars and statues and spires. Arrayed behind me were temples to Vespasian and Saturn; across the Forum in front of me were temples to the deified Julius Caesar, and to Castor and Pollux, and between and beyond them I could glimpse the one that out-templed them all, the grand Temple of the Vestal Virgins.

And all around us a throng of people, hustle and bustle, the highborn and low, plus a few in legionary gear. Occasionally a sedan chair would nose through, held up by six brawny slaves; or patricians in togas would hurry by with their bodyguards, who could easily have been ex-gladiators by their bulk and scars. But by and large these were ordinary townsfolk in their plain tunics or rags, milling through and around the great Forum Romanorum and giving not a second glance to the opulence that surrounded them.

So this was Ancient Rome...except that it wasn't ancient yet. The Arch of Septimius Severus at my shoulder was less than ten years old, built in 203 A.D. Some of the other buildings and monuments around me must have been a hundred years old, or even two, but they were built stout and firm of good rock and marble and looked like they'd survive, well, a couple thousand years easily.

This was a living, breathing city of a million people. The greatest city in the world. I could have touristed it for a month, but I had only hours. I had work to do. And the Games to prepare for. Because over and above the temples I could see the line of the Colosseum, brooding over the city like a curse.

The Wandering Warriors would be in there very soon, in the arena, playing to a crowd that was more used to blood than ball games, our lives at the disposal of a capricious and psychopathic Emperor.

But still... Rome was damned beautiful. Just standing here was a dream come true.

I cleared my throat to try to shift the lump in it, shook my head, and turned to Lucius Aurelius and the two squaddies who stood behind him. My own bodyguards, courtesy of Julia Domna, to make sure I didn't get myself killed in the streets or try to do a runner. Not that I had anywhere I could go, and not that I would ever have left my team behind.

"All right," I said. "Next I need to see the Sacra Via and then whatever the road is that leads to the east of the Palatine, and then we can take a look in at the Colosseum."

Lucius damn near saluted before he remembered he was in a plain tunic today, all of us incognito. He just nodded, and I grinned at him, and off we went.

15
Quentin

We were missing two good players, Domna and the Professor, but when an emperor wants to practice, you practice. So we worked out Geta pretty hard.

He was a banjo hitter, but like his mother he had good, soft hands, so when we took infield, we tried him out at third, short, and second. It turned out he didn't have his mother's strong arm, so without making any kind of fuss over it—the last thing we wanted to do was cause a ruckus with a co-emperor—we left him at second once he got there.

It was hard to figure where he got the necessary skills to get those short hops, but get 'em he did. And he moved side-to-side real smooth, so on routine grounders anywhere near him, he was fine. When he had to go deep up the middle and backhand the ball, he was okay getting his glove on it, but he just didn't have the arm to get the ball to first. It was all he could do to spin on that right foot and try to sling it in the right direction.

We worked him hard, sure, but he seemed to be having a good time. A great time, in fact. When he booted a grounder, he laughed about it and waved at me to hit him another one. When he took batting practice, he slapped at it, but darned if he didn't hit enough bloopers that you'd think he'd get some base hits, and he really sprayed the ball around.

Really, the guys were impressed, and so was I. And working him out gave us a chance to work out ourselves one more time before the Games, so we took it seriously. There was a lot riding on how we did on the field against these Romans.

Working him out also gave us a chance to focus on something other than the missing Professor. But as soon as I picked up the fungo to hit infield, I was reminded that the heart and soul of the Wandering Warriors wasn't here. He'd normally be hitting infield while I hit fly balls to the outfielders, but we couldn't do it that way and it worried the hell out of me. Where was he? Would he get back to us in time for the first game? It was mid-morning now and the first game was set for noon, the Warriors against the Caelians. It should be a laugher, but it was one we couldn't afford to lose. Without the Professor or Domna, we didn't want to take the Caelians too lightly.

All too soon, and before I was really ready, it was time to go. The lanista blew a whistle to get us all to line up, and some of the gladiators came over to punch our shoulders and grasp our forearms in that Roman way of shaking hands. Others looked sour at us, maybe because they'd be fighting to the death today and we'd just be batting a ball around.

At least, I sure *hoped* we weren't about to be in any kind of real combat. But who the heck really knew? We were in *Rome*. I had the feeling anything could turn into a blood sport here, at the drop of a hat.

Even without us, the Games were already heating up. We'd heard the noise of the crowds in the plaza outside the Ludus

Magnus since early morning, and now that was being drowned out by a steadily growing din from inside the Colosseum itself, just beyond. Excitement was building. Excitement for the Games.

I had a dull ache in my belly, the acid taste of fear. I didn't want to do this. Wanted to be far away. In distance, and especially in years. I played baseball for fun, you know? I'd had plenty of fear during the war and I didn't want any more of it. But hell, we had no choice. It was time to go play ball.

16
The Professor

After I'd scoped out the city, I went with Lucius to watch the Wandering Warriors play the Caelians in the first game. This was one I was sure the guys could win without me, so I wasn't worried about not being with them. Yet.

It was amazing just being there. The Amphitheatrum Flavium, on the first day of the Games in Memory of the Emperor Septimius Severus, and in Commemoration of His Great Victories in Caledonia.

The Emperor is dead, long live the Emperors. Hmm.

I came in just like any other paying customer, past the hundred-foot-high gilded statue of the long-dead Nero in the plaza outside and in through one of the sixty-six vaulted entranceways that ringed the place. I liked to get the feel of a ballpark before a game, to absorb the atmosphere of the place through my skin, and today was no different. But the ballparks I knew weren't this solid. The Colosseum was mostly limestone, with lateral walls inside of brick, concrete, volcanic tufa, and pumice. With Lucius by my side, I climbed up stone stairs surrounded by excited crowds and the reeks of sweat and cooked meat and spice and stale beer.

I came back out into daylight in the third tier of seats, over a hundred feet above the level of the arena, and looked around me.

At once, I took in the arrangement; the Emperor's box at the north end, where Caracalla and Domna now sat, the Vestal Virgins' box across at the south end facing it. All around the arena at the same level were the expensive seats for the senatorial class. The next tier up was for nobles, and above them, where I stood, was the area reserved for the ordinary people of Rome.

Stretching above and behind me were the seats for the women and the poor. There, the seats were of wood rather than the stone of the lower levels. It looked steep, rickety, and dangerous, a death trap waiting to happen. At every level the tiers were divided into sections, and most of those sections were already packed with citizens of the Empire. There must have been fifty thousand people here already, with more still pouring in above, below, and beside me.

But all of this I took in in moments, because my eyes were drawn to the scene of death and devastation below me.

Men and women fighting animals, dying in droves.

The Colosseum may have had more than five dozen entrances and exits for spectators, but the arena had only two: the Gate of Life, on the eastern side, connected to the Ludus Magnus, and the Gate of Death to the west, which led to the place where they stripped off the dead gladiators' armor and piled their bodies, and the grim cart eventually carried them away to a pauper's grave.

Still standing, looking out over the massacre, I felt my legs begin to shake. This was brutal, inhuman. How could my guys play a kid's game here? How could we play *baseball* in front of a crowd baying for human blood?

I felt Lucius place his hand on my elbow. I allowed him to guide us to our seats, trying to take my mind off the savagery before my eyes. When we reached our seats, I looked out to the arena floor just as a gladiator wearing a helmet with a visor but armed with nothing but a spear was attacked by a leopard. The animal rushed toward him and leaped toward his chest. The man had one chance with the spear and thrust it, but missed, and the leopard knocked him onto his back in the sand and was at his throat in a second.

I looked away, not wanting to see the end of that confrontation. There was a hand on my shoulder. I looked and it was Lucius. He smiled and shrugged. Business as usual. And my Wandering Warriors would be out there soon playing baseball. I didn't see how they—or I—could survive the day.

Under the arena floor was a maze of gladiatorial cells, wild animal pens, armories, and changing areas, along with shafts and pulleys and surprisingly sophisticated hydraulic mechanisms to raise scenery and wild animal cages and the like up into the arena. I'd spent several hours down there already, but the Wanderers would be seeing it for the first time today. I wondered what they were making of it.

And now they had to play some ball, my Wandering Warriors, in front of this huge crowd that, mostly, was lusting for blood. How would the crowd react? Had the Warriors built up enough goodwill over the past couple of weeks of exhibitions that some of the rowdy crowd would cheer for them? Or would my Wandering Warriors be designated as the bad guys and be reviled by the crowd?

I wondered how they were feeling right now, Quentin and the rest of my boys.

17
Quentin

Normally the Wandering Warriors would take the field by just running onto it. But this was ancient Rome, and this was the Colosseum, so of course it had to be very different here.

They'd marched us through the underground tunnel from the Ludus Magnus and lined us up along a corridor. I could tell we were under the arena by the pounding from above, and the dull roar of the crowd heard through several feet of sand, stone, and wood. The walls behind us dripped with moisture. It was like a weird cross between a dungeon and an underground bazaar, because people were running everywhere. Gladiators clanked by in full or partial armor, or naked with a net and trident. We could see and hear wild beasts snarling in their cages, lions and tigers and, for all I knew, bears, and we could smell them too. We could also smell blood and latrines and oil. And our own fear.

The Professor would have known what to say to calm us all down. Me, I had no clue. So I just stood there.

Fortunately, it didn't last long. One thing I'll say for Rome, it was a well-oiled machine when it came to running the Games. Everyone knew where to be and what to do, slaves and gladiators and lanistas and beastmasters, oh my Lord. So we only had five or ten minutes to stare at the floor, quivering and trying not to let fear overwhelm us, before someone gestured us onto a large platform which looked like it belonged in a factory, with gears and hydraulics and stuff I hadn't known the Romans even had.

The boys looked uncertain. I strode onto it without hesitating, just like the Professor would've. Then the rest of 'em followed.

The ceiling above us opened to reveal sky and admit a giant roar from a crowd that we still couldn't see. And up we went, the Wandering Warriors, to face our first game in the Flavian Amphitheater of Rome in front of a capacity crowd.

I damned near had a heart attack when the hydraulics lifted us up into place in the arena. Damned near. Because the place was *huge*, and the baying of the crowd was ugly. This wasn't a good-natured bunch of folks from the Midwest but an urban mob from one of the world's most degenerate cities of the age, bloodthirsty fans of gore and death. And now about to... watch us play ball.

We'd need to make it good.

Right across the arena from us I saw another platform raising up into place. The Caelians, our opposition. I was gratified to see that they didn't look any less anxious than us. Upper-class Romans all, they'd never been in a full-up gladiatorial arena before, any more than we had.

"Okay, boys," I said, as our platform locked into place with a small rattle and shake. "Don't you mind that nasty crowd. We got us a job to do here. And we can do it. You all know we can."

I was pretty proud of myself, that my voice didn't wobble. I sounded confident. I didn't feel it. I tried to ignore the crowd, and instead looked around the oval arena.

"Bases already in place. Even a mound for the pitcher. Field's a little smaller than we're used to. But we knew that."

Suddenly I caught sight of patches of blood in the outfield, where men had died just moments before. I swallowed, cleared my throat. "So, looks like we're all set. Everyone okay?"

Everyone allowed that they were, though their eyes were big as saucers.

"Then let's get out there and warm up."

As soon as we started playing, our Colosseum nerves all drained away. And, just like I'd said, it turned out we had no cause to worry, at least not yet. I went behind the plate, Walter came in from short to do the pitching, Duke moved from second to short, and our very own Co-Emperor, Geta, played second. The Caelian pitcher was a guy named Petronius Valens, who was an important Senator and used to having things his way, but his fastball wasn't much and his curveball was a joke, so we batted around in the first inning and then took it easy after that, trying to hold the score down out of pity. Geta had a couple of hits and did fine at second, and Walter just threw strikes and let the Caelians, a bunch of upper-class Roman men—and three women, two of them pretty darn good—hit the ball when they could get wood on it. Our defense cleaned that up nicely and Walter got himself a complete-game win, 10–0.

Walter tried hard to get them a couple of runs in the bottom of the ninth, getting one strike out and then walking three of them to load the bases. I made a big show of walking out to have a chat with him, and the infield all came in too. I gestured to Geta, trying to get across the notion that maybe we should let the Caelians walk in a run or two, let them get on the scoreboard. Geta shook his head no, pointed to the other team, mimed swinging a bat, shrugged, nodded. I understood, better to let them hit it, and play it straight. Which we did. Their batter got ahold of one and sent a sharp grounder to second. It looked like it had a chance to get through for a single, but darned if Geta didn't make a nice play on it, moving to his left to field it, then turning to peg it to Duke who'd come over to second for the double play. Duke gloved it while stepping on the bag and then smoked one over to first and that was that. A really nice double play to end the game.

That was the good news, but there had been bad news too. I was getting worried about Danny Felton on third, who was getting into it with the Caelians' third base-coach; a stout, old guy named Tatius who actually learned a few words of English just to poke fun at us. He'd been at some of our practices and now was yelling out, "Rag arm! Rag arm!" at Walter, who just looked at him and laughed a few times. But Danny, playing third, was getting annoyed, and he was the one guy on the Warriors, I thought, who might blow his stack.

In the bottom of the fourth, he did. A routine grounder came his way and he muffed it, the ball trickling away to his left. He took two steps to pick it up and then threw way wide over to first. That put the runner on second, the first time the Caelians had a guy in scoring position.

"Rag arm! Rag arm!" the Tatius fellow yelled at Danny, and

that was just one taunt too many. Danny threw his glove down into the dirt and started walking toward Tatius with blood in his eye. Tatius squawked, he was no fighter, that was for sure; but the Roman bench cleared and they all came out to defend Tatius. I thought I better handle it myself, but by the time I ran down to third, clanking along in the tools of ignorance, both teams had converged and a fight was about to break out. The crowd was yelling in excitement; they thought it was great fun. But I was worried, thinking of that blood we'd seen in the outfield dirt.

I threw up my arms and yelled as loud as I could. "Back off! Back off!" and I think it was my size and that loud voice that gave everyone pause.

I walked up to Danny, who was still fuming, and I gave him the hook. "You're outa here," I yelled at him, all angry-like, and pointed toward the bench. Danny, bless his heart, settled down some, then said, "Okay, Quent," and walked away.

As he did, I wondered why we'd got off so easy. I thought that was turning into a brawl for sure, and the Warriors always gave as good as they got in such things. Instead, one word from me and the Romans had gone all quiet.

Then I looked around and figured it out. Geta was standing right on the bag, elevating himself a little, and three of his Praetorians were right there with him, swords drawn. I caught his eye and nodded, and he smiled and nodded back, and we went on with the game. But Danny, I knew, was a marked man for the next game, the big finale.

But right at that moment, after that game-ending double play, Geta was happy like a kid at his birthday party as we all came in from the field and shook his hand and patted him on the back. I wondered about the protocol of that, since Geta's Praetorians were right there watching, but I noticed he waved them off when they started to pull those swords and, instead, took the pats and the handshakes and allowed himself to be happy.

We were happy too, but we knew we didn't have long to enjoy it. The Palatines and the Aventines were already being lifted up onto the field on those fancy hydraulic platforms, and we'd play their winner for the championship of the world, I guess. Nobody else anywhere in this time was playing baseball. Oh, and we were also maybe playing for our lives. At least we had an emperor on our side.

Anyway, we didn't need to watch. We'd seen all of them play plenty for the past couple of weeks as we'd played exhibitions all over the city of Rome and even beyond it, in Ostia.

Still, I wanted to make sure we didn't come up against any surprises, so I told Walter, who was probably done for the day after pitching that shutout against the Caelians, to stick around and watch the game and see if there was anything we had to worry about. And then they took the rest of us back down into the bowels of the Colosseum, and this time showed us into a room with benches where we could sit and take it easy for a while. Geta, of course, had disappeared off on his own, which was okay because although we liked him, he made the guys a little nervous.

It was a big room, and without Geta around we could relax there for a couple of hours, drink some water, even play a little pepper if we wanted, and then it would be time to get back out there and win the game that really mattered. Maybe we wouldn't have the Professor or Domna, but we'd seen all these Romans play and we didn't think there was any question about who'd win the game. That'd be us, the Wandering Warriors. I'd be pitching, and I'd pitch the game of my life. Which, come to think of it, it probably would be.

The question was: where was the Professor? And Domna? And could we get ourselves back home to our own time and place, after the game? I didn't have any answers to any of that. So I played some pepper with the guys.

18
The Professor

I was relieved that the first thing I noticed was some cheering as the Warriors entered and trotted over to their bench. We'd made some friends, and I didn't hear anything too darkly negative from the crowd.

And then the second thing I noticed was that Geta was in a Warriors uniform! How the heck had that happened? And then as he took off his cap and walked around the infield waving to the crowd, everyone realized who he was and there was a huge clamor of approval and loud chants of "Ave Geta! Ave Geta! Ave, Geta!"

I peered more closely at the Emperor's box and noticed that Caracalla was pointedly ignoring what was happening on the field. He was busy chatting to the people around him, turning away to fill his cup with wine, glancing up to wave at the senators and other dignitaries behind him. Only when the tumult over Geta's appearance subsided did he turn back and make himself more comfortable on his wooden throne.

On the next throne over sat his mother, the same mother he'd punched the daylights out of last night right in front of my eyes. Domna was applauding as her other son walked around the infield waving at the crowd. Caracalla paid that no mind. But once she stopped clapping, he turned to her and said something, and Domna smiled and laughed and said something back, just as if nothing bad had ever happened between them. I'd have given a boatload of money to hear that conversation.

And then the game started, and it was the romp I'd figured it would be. Walter was pitching, and just trying to throw strikes. The guys played solid defense and hit the ball hard off that poor Caelians pitcher. But he stuck it out, to his credit, and went five innings before they brought in a reliever, the score already six to nothing and bound to get worse. The final was ten to nothing and could have been twenty-zip, but the Warriors took it easy on them.

The game was calm except for a little fourth-inning dustup when Danny lost his temper at third and Geta had to calm everyone down. And then it ended on an interesting note when Geta made a very nice play at second to start a game-ending double play. The crowd had lost interest in the game except for those moments when Geta came to the plate or when the ball went his way. That grounder was not an easy hop, and Geta had to glove it, move his feet and turn right, and then peg it hard to Duke, the shortstop covering the bag. Duke turned it nicely and got it over to first in plenty of time and the game was over, but not for the crowd. There was a mighty cheer from all fifty thousand of the men and women in attendance, sounded like to me, which was good news for Geta and probably for Domna too, if she could avoid getting killed by Caracalla right there in the stands.

I looked down there and Caracalla was fuming. He sat there, stone-faced, as his brother preened before the plebs, and then, after the Warriors left the field, he rose, took Domna's hand to bring her to her feet, and tugged her away as they left the stands.

I wondered if Lucius was seeing all this and looked over at him. He was, and "We go," he said, in English and so we went.

19
Quentin

They fed and watered us, down in our big comfy dungeon, just like we were cattle or horses or something, but no one gave us any info on how the other game was going, so all we could do was guess and wait until Walter came down to bring us up to date.

Which team would we rather play? The Aventines were gladiators, skilled and deadly fighters but not really baseball players. They came from all over the empire; captured in battle, mostly, and then sent into slavery where their one option for any kind of better life was gladiator school. The ones in the arena above us now were the best of the best; they'd survived months or even years of combat. And now they were playing baseball. No surprise, they played it to the death. Even during the exhibition games that led up to today they'd been dangerous. They'd happily run right over you at second, and I'd seen two plays at the plate that left the other team's catchers lying bleeding in the dirt. There would have been a third one, in one of their games against us, but Enos, out in center, had purposefully thrown the ball up the line so the Professor, doing the catching, had to dart away from the plate to go grab it.

Enos was one tough son-of-a-gun himself. He didn't mind making contact on the field or getting right up in your grill with his teammates; but he knew he held the Professor's life in his hands after catching that fly ball in center and he did the right thing.

Despite our name, the Wandering Warriors weren't much interested in dying over a baseball game. Most of us had seen action in the Pacific or England or both, so we'd seen plenty of death and violence; stuff we didn't really talk about, ever, as we drove around the Midwest playing a kid's game. We didn't want to see any more of that here.

Of course, what we wanted didn't matter.

I was thinking of that when I decided to check on the other game. I left our big room under the Colosseum and did a hand sign to the guards that I wanted to see the game. One of 'em might even have smiled at that as he nodded and led the way through the rabbit warren of tunnels and finally up some narrow concrete steps into the bright sunshine of the Colosseum floor. Walter was there, watching the game, and I joined him.

We were behind a wooden barricade within twenty feet of first base, so I had a good view of the Praetorian Palatines, who were in the field wearing snappy uniforms that reminded me of the women's professional league back home with those kilty things that looked like short skirts. I looked up at the simple scoreboard they had in right field and it said, IV for the Palatines and II for the Aventines. I looked at the guard and he held up four fingers. I nodded. Close game.

And then I saw who was pitching for the Palatines, going into his windup while we watched: Caracalla.

Well, I'll be, I thought. He'd seen Geta playing for us, and had realized he had to get himself into the game too. And you know what? Old Caracalla looked all right out there. His windup was all wrong but he was throwing strikes and there was no one on the Aventines who would dare to hit it too hard, so Caracalla was looking good. Two pitches later, one of 'em turned sideways to bunt and pushed the ball right toward Caracalla. He charged it, picked it up with the bare hand, and pegged it to first.

I thought I saw him smile for just a second after he did that. The first baseman threw him back the ball and he raised it high in the glove and waited for his subjects to roar out their approval. When the crowd's response was tepid, more a murmur than a roar, he held the glove up again, with the ball in it, and turned slowly around to make his point. This time the crowd responded with the adulation he was looking for.

Well, it didn't surprise me none that he was a showboat, and I grunted. I heard Walter beside me do the same, and I said, "Let's go, Walter," and we turned around to walk back down to the room where the Wanderers were waiting. When Caracalla's Palatines won then it would our emperor versus theirs in the final. Now wouldn't *that* be fun?

I sure wished we had the Professor with us to help me sort this through. And having Domna there would help too. She'd know what to do about a battle between her two sons. Wouldn't she?

20
The Professor

As we walked alone into the narrow tunnel, I suddenly realized I didn't know for sure where Lucius's allegiance lay. He'd obviously been taking orders from Domna when she'd sent him out to round us up at the river, but Caracalla was home now, and maybe he was calling the shots. I was unarmed. What if old Lucius had secret orders to kill me or usher me out into the arena with those gladiators grunting and hacking in mortal combat? I could just imagine how my pathetic attempts to defend myself would bring laughter to the masses. I'd never even held a gladius or a trident, a net or a spear.

But I survived the walk without a dagger in my back. We rounded a corner and there was Julia Domna. She nodded to me, but spoke to Lucius: "Your Emperor has decided to take part in the baseball game. And I am to take your prisoner with me."

"Julia Domna," he said, looking at her strangely, "I have no commands from your son about this."

I felt a shiver up my back.

"Now you do," Domna said. She reached out to take me by the hand. "Also, the Emperor wishes us both to play for this man's team against the Emperor's own team."

Lucius's brow furrowed. "But what if the Palatines lose the game they play now?"

"That will not happen. Even gladiators are smarter than that, Lucius. Caracalla will play for the Palatines, and they will triumph as your emperor hits the ball with the bat to end the contest in glory."

"Just so," Lucius said politely, and stepped aside. That all made perfect sense to him. As to who would win the finale, co-emperor versus co-emperor with their mother having chosen a side? Well, Lucius needed to keep his options open. He even wished me good fortune in the contest to come, as I walked by him. Sure, we were pals now.

And that was how it happened. Caracalla decided he was the pitcher and hitting fourth. All he could throw was a batting-practice fastball but he could mostly get it over. It should have been fat city for the gladiators, who'd been hitting the ball a ton in their previous games. But suddenly they were whiffing right and left or just laying down bunts. He walked in a couple of runs but that was it.

At bat, he went four-for-four as three fly balls fell uncaught into the dirt of the outfield and one grounder right at the second baseman mysteriously found a hole and trickled into right. So: three doubles and a single on the day. The only thing missing was the need for a home run at the end of the 8–2 game, but when he threw the final patty-cake of the game over the plate and the gladiator—a guy for whom death was a constant threat— swung mightily and missed, Caracalla took the ball back from the catcher and paraded all the way around the arena holding it high. And the stands erupted with thunderous cheering. I suspect a lot of the fans had no idea how contrived the whole game had been. Then Caracalla threw the ball high up into the crowd, and some lucky Roman treasured that ball for the rest of his life, I'll guess, sitting in a place of honor in the shrine to his household gods in his hallway. I wondered if it would turn up in some archaeological dig in a couple of thousand years.

21
Quentin

Well, it wasn't fun getting ready for our final championship game against the Palatines without having the Professor with us, but I figured we had to do what we had to do.

I told the fellas this as we sat on the benches in our big holding room and started putting on our spikes. "Boys," I said, "the reason we here are a team is because of the Professor. You know and I know that he'd be with us if he could." I looked all around, trying to see every one of them guys, eyeball to eyeball. There wasn't a bad one among 'em. "We know the Professor loves the game, and we know he loves his Wandering Warriors."

I took a breath and kept on going. "Look, boys, the Professor was pretty darn good at this game before the war, and he might still be playing in the big leagues if there hadn't been all that trouble. And I know about half of us went through that same thing. Some of us, and that includes the Professor—and me as well—saw some stuff we don't talk about. Awful things that we seen one human being do to another. Stuff so terrible it don't bear mention of any particulars."

Most of the guys were nodding their heads, looking down at their feet now, thinking about it. "Well, these here Romans," I said, "they don't know that about us. They think we're play- ing a kid's game." I paused for a second. "And you know what, they're right. We're playing baseball 'cause it's a lot more fun than shooting at people and getting shot at back.

"We lost friends in that war, and if things didn't make much sense to us, we still knew it was our job and we did it. Then we came home and decided to play some ball and look ahead of us, not behind. Now we're here and just like that war it don't make much sense. So let's just look ahead and not behind, fellas. Go out there and don't worry about things we got no control over. All we can do is play our best, right?"

There was a little murmur of agreement, so "Right?" I asked again, louder, and they all murmured again.

Just then, Geta and a couple of his guards came into the room. He held up his hand, saying hello to his teammates, and then he put his palm out toward us and raised it so we knew it was time to stand. Then the Co-Emperor of the Roman Empire led the Wanderers back out and up into the arena. And there, to our great relief, were Domna and the Professor! They were standing in the sunshine waiting for us as we trooped onto the dirt and sand.

You never seen such a happy reunion! Lots of handshakes with the Professor and cautious nods of the head to Domna. And then a hug between Domna and Geta. The co-emperor and his mother seemed very happy to see each other.

We walked onto the field, holding our bats and gloves up high, and then we walked completely around the arena to a great din from the crowd. Then, while we waited for the Palatines to do the same, the Professor and Domna and Geta disappeared. I was about to get nervous about that when they returned in uniform. The Professor wore his usual beat-up road grays like the rest of us. But Domna and Geta both came back without those Roman skirts on. Instead, they both wore long pants with stockings and the pants rolled up mid-calf and tucked into the stockings. It was great to see; just a little thing but it meant a lot to us. They wanted to be part of the team, they wanted to look like us. Like the Wandering Warriors.

22
The Professor

Well, it was certainly the most important baseball game I'd ever play in, and I knew it as I came back out onto the arena dirt and saw that huge crowd cheering in anticipation.

The Palatines had already taken their walk around, holding up their bats and gloves, with Caracalla leading the way. And then, while we played catch and a little pepper to get loose again, the Palatines took some infield.

To tell the truth, I'd been laughing inside every time I watched any of the Roman teams take infield over the past few weeks. There's an art to it that requires someone who knows how to use a fungo bat, and not a one of them could do it right. Really, it was kind of painful to watch as their coach used a regular bat that looked about thirty-six inch and thirty-ounce. Hard to do much with that.

This was baseball, and in front of a big crowd where most of them were seeing it played today for the first time. I wanted them to like it, to get the full flavor of the game, to feel the joy of baseball, just like we all did. I was standing there, leaning on my fungo, shaking my head, when Quentin looked at me and smiled. "Maybe we oughta show 'em how it's done, Professor?"

I nodded. "Let's do that."

I walked over to the coach, a Praetorian that I hadn't met before. He hit a grounder, a clumsy one that went foul of third, out of reach of the third baseman, and then he turned to look at me.

"Can I show you how to use this special bat?" I asked him, and held up the fungo.

His eyes narrowed. I guess constant suspicion was the only way to a long life if you were a Praetorian caught up in the intrigue of the Roman court. But then he looked over to Caracalla, who was warming up nearby, and Caracalla gave him the nod.

So I caught the ball as he tossed it to me, and I gave those Palatines the sort of pre-game infield they deserved. They were out there, they were learning, they were playing, and so I gave them ground balls right at them, and grounders to their right and to their left, and then worked them through some double plays, including making their first baseman do it the hard way. Next, I gave them two quick final rounds, one of them some blistering balls that were meant to short-hop them, and then some easy pop-ups and some hard ones where they had to backpedal or turn and run for them. Then a finale of easy grounders they could field and throw to first and look good.

The Colosseum had gone quiet during this little display, but when those Palatines trotted off the field, they got an immense round of applause.

Then I did the same infield for the Warriors, and it was night and day. My guys were slick, including our second baseman and our shortstop, the emperors' mother who wore pants, and the whole fifteen minutes of infield was a joy to watch. I was proud of my Warriors, watching them work, and I even took the risk of a deep pop-up into shallow left that Domna had to get on her horse to catch, but she did it, over the shoulder, and the whole arena cheered.

And then it was time to play the game.

Umpiring had been a problem from the start. At the demonstration games, me and Quentin had volunteered to ump when we weren't playing, and that had worked out all right. At least we knew the rules and the strike zone.

When the Warriors were playing, what we'd done was get two Praetorians—one each from Caracalla and Geta's guards—to ump. We explained the rules to them and vowed that we'd help them fairly if they needed it, and we had them switch off each inning on who was umping the bases and who was calling balls and strikes. It worked out all right, though they stumbled a lot on calls at first. But they got more confident as the games went on, and by the big game I felt like they'd get the job done.

The question was, would we? Or better, what was the job that we were supposed to do? There was no question that we could hit Caracalla's pitching, his fastball was in the seventies and flat: batting practice stuff. And his curveball barely existed. We could, I'm sure, score all day long on him.

And on the other side of the coin, not more than two or three of the Palatines could actually get wood on the ball if Quentin pitched like he normally would. They were all right on straight-ahead fastballs, but Quentin threw a lot of junk, sinkers and curveballs and screwgies and changes and even a nice knuckler. They really couldn't hit any of those. No shame on them for that: they were hard workers, but they hadn't been playing it all their lives like my guys had.

So the question was, should Quentin pitch like that? What would happen if we won, say, fifteen to nothing?

I decided to talk it over with Domna and Geta, who were

standing by themselves with a little coterie of guards around them, behind the bench. I walked their way and the guards crossed spears in front of me, but then together, mother and son, they barked a command and the spears opened wide.

"So here we are," I said, in Latin.

They both smiled. Geta asked, "Will we win?"

"We certainly will, Co-Emperor. It isn't as obvious to those up there watching, but these Palatines cannot match us in any respect. Also, we have the best double play combination in the league." And I grinned.

Neither one of them got the joke, though Geta was on second and Domna at short. I clarified, "We have you two on defense, and you both are very good." For beginners, I thought but didn't say. "And you both can hit their pitching." I looked at each of them in turn. "My question is, how would you like the game to go? We can control it. We can win easily. We can humiliate them. But we can keep it close if you like, let them score a few runs."

"We have seen battles like this in this arena many, many times, Professor," said Domna. "It is cruel, no matter how we handle it."

"But less cruel if my brother is allowed to play well," Geta pointed out. "If he hits a home run or strikes us out, mother and I, that would please him greatly, no matter the score."

Domna shook her head. I could hear her thinking. Geta, being nice again. Here, the empire was at stake, really. The two brothers had been away from Rome for years, and now they were back again, so first impressions really counted. Whichever one of them came out of this looking best would have an advantage with the plebs and nobles of Rome. If Geta got himself humiliated, it would be a disastrous and quite possibly fatal setback. For him, and maybe for us too.

Domna voiced her feelings. "You need to worry about yourself, Geta, not about your brother. Worry about your honor. Your future."

He looked at her. Geta and Caracalla had both been cruel when it was necessary. Probably, many had already died because of their decisions. And yet this young man, Geta, would make for a far better emperor than his brother. He held compassion and held Rome herself in as high a regard as cruel necessity.

"Veni, vidi, vici," said Geta, mimicking another great emperor. "But," he added with a smile, "let Caracalla have his personal successes even as his team loses the game. That will temper his anger."

In the history I knew, Caracalla wound up ruling Rome, and he wasn't much good at it. In fact, he was arguably the Emperor who started the long slide down to the collapse of the Western Roman Empire. If Geta could come out on top? I was pretty sure it would go differently.

And if it did go differently, what would that mean for us? When me and the boys got back to our time, would it be the same? Would there still be a United States that stretched from California to the Carolinas? Would there still be an armistice with Germany and would we still have used that superbomb to defeat the Japanese?

Would there still be baseball, or would there be some other sport to fill that bill as the National Pastime? Boxing, maybe? Basketball? They had a lot of fans, both those sports.

Or maybe there'd be gladiatorial arenas, with men fighting for their lives.

I had to shrug it off. I didn't know. Nobody did. All that was far beyond us. We just had to do what we thought was right, in the here and now. Live to the best of our abilities. Make good choices. Be our best. It's all anyone can ever do.

"All right then, I'll tell the boys," I said. "We'll control it and win it, but we'll make sure we give Caracalla some moments to shine. Agreed?" And they both gave me a slight smile and nodded.

I bowed to each of them and backed away to go tell the Wandering Warriors how we were going to play it. I didn't think I'd hear too many gripes. We all wanted to get through this last game and then get on home.

23
Quentin

It's been my experience that when things don't turn out the way you'd like, the best thing is take what you got and move on down the road. And that's pretty much what happened to us that afternoon in the Colosseum for the big final championship game between us Wandering Warriors and Emperor Caracalla's Palatines.

It started off just great. The Professor had talked to us all about how for our own sakes we needed to not make these Romans look too bad. And then he and I walked away for a minute to talk in private about it and he said, "Quentin, I know you'd like to mow these guys down, especially in front of this big crowd."

"That's the truth, Professor," I said. "You know there's not a one of them I'm worried about at the plate. I could dazzle 'em with all my junk and they'd just look silly up there."

He cocked an eye at me. "But you know we can't do that?"

"Of course," I said. "And I won't mind that, with most of 'em. But that Caracalla, I don't like him, and I got to admit it'd be fun to throw him a few curves."

"I bet," said the Professor. "And the crowd would love you for it, Quentin. Hell, you're already the most popular player out there. They love you here."

"Yeah, they do," I had to admit.

"But Caracalla is the most dangerous one of the three. He's murderous, Quentin. He'd just as soon kill us as look at us. Hell, he's ready, right now, to kill his own brother and his mother. He'll do it in a second, if he thinks he can get away with it. So it won't be easy, but we got to get the boys out of here in one piece despite Caracalla wanting us all dead. And that means we have to tone it down. I'm sorry."

"I know that, Professor," I said, and then it was game time, so I turned away from him and walked out to the mound with the ball in my hand while he went to the bench to put on his gear. A couple minutes later I was throwing a final few warm-ups to him, and he was pegging one down to second, and we got things underway.

We'd won the coin toss and so the Warriors were the "home team"—ha!—and that's why I was on the hill to get things a-rolling. And that was fine with me. I figured I could dazzle them the first time through the lineup, and then I'd ease up for the second time around.

So the first three batters came up to the plate, and I sat them right back down with strikeouts. Nothing but curveballs, which they didn't know what to do with, so the first two went down swinging. The third, a smaller man I knew pretty well from watching him in practice and other games, liked to bunt and he did manage to foul two of them before I threw him inside with a hard curve and he backed away and then it broke over the plate. The Professor helped convince the ump it was a strike by catching and rising to toss the ball back out to the mound while trotting toward home before the call was even made.

Our guys took it easy in the bottom of the inning, the first two slapping out groundball singles and the third one, Enos, rapping out a double in the gap in right to bring them. Then we went down easy with groundballs to second and to third and a long fly to left that left Enos stranded at third but gave us a nice little 2–0 lead.

In the top of the second I had to deal with Caracalla first thing, since he was hitting cleanup. I gave him straight balls—I wouldn't call them fast—and he hit a sharp grounder to second that his brother fielded cleanly and threw him out at first. Everybody was happy with that. Then I struck out the next two.

And that's how it went for the next five innings, us putting up another couple of runs when Enos rattled a triple off the wooden wall in right field to drive in two, and me letting some of them hit the ball and throwing batting-practice pitches to Caracalla, who turned one of them into a double in the gap and the other into a lazy fly that dropped in for a single in left. The crowd was loving it—two Emperors and an Empress on the field, and some pretty snazzy ball skills that even a rookie audience could appreciate, so the plebs were going bananas and that Colosseum was *loud*.

Maybe we should have known it was going a bit *too* well. Yeah. Frankly, we should.

It was 4–0 in the top of the seventh when things got *really* interesting.

24
The Professor

I thought everything had gone about as good as it could go. Caracalla's team was down on the scoreboard, but the big man himself was doing fine. And Geta and Domna were playing solid defense and each of them had a single, so they'd been productive and seemed happy. We were ahead four-nothing: respectable, but not embarrassing for the Palatines. Just the way we'd planned it.

But then, in the top of the seventh, Caracalla blew the whole thing up.

It started out simple enough. Quentin got the first guy up to foul out to me, a little pop-up behind the plate that was easy to make. And then the next guy took a mighty swing on an 0–2 count curveball and missed the pitch by a *mille passum*, which is Latin for one thousand paces. Quentin walked the third hitter, just to give the guy a chance to get on base, and then Caracalla came to the plate.

Quentin had been playing patty-cake with him all afternoon, throwing medium fastballs right down the middle so the co-emperor could get his bat on the ball. He'd grounded out to his brother the first time up, but had whacked that ball hard. Then he'd had a good hit the next time up, a double in the gap. Then Bobby in left had done a nice job of not getting to a routine fly, and that dropped for a single.

Now he was up with two out and a man on first, so it was a good time for Quentin to put another one right down the middle and let Caracalla move a runner around. Which he did, swinging away on that first pitch and, to his credit, stinging it, getting the meat of the bat on it and sending a sharp line drive deep to left center.

Everybody started moving, Bobby in left heading toward the ball but making sure he wouldn't get there in time to catch it, Enos in center doing the same, Domna heading out to serve as the cutoff when the runner rounded second and headed for third, and Geta heading toward second base to haul in what was likely to be a routine throw from Enos, holding Caracalla at first.

Pretty standard baseball, unless you're a co-emperor and used to having things your way. As the runner rounded second and Enos reached the ball on the first hop, Caracalla didn't hesitate at first, but rounded the bag going full tilt toward second. Enos caught the ball and came up throwing, knowing he had plenty of time to nail Caracalla at second and end the inning.

Geta was in the right spot at second when the ball came in on one good hop and he gloved it cleanly and started to put the glove down to tag Caracalla, who'd be sliding in. But instead of a nice exciting play at second it turned into chaos. Caracalla didn't bother to slide but instead came in on the right side of the bag, full tilt, shoulders down, and bowled Geta over so hard that he sailed backward a few feet and landed flat on his back. But the ball was still in the glove and Caracalla had been tagged as he hit his brother. So, even as Caracalla stood up, the umpire, who'd been calling balls and strikes from behind the pitcher and so was right there to make the call, called him out.

Calling out a psychopath, and one of the masters of the known world? That took a whole lot of nerve on the part of the ump, but he made the right call. Even as he did, though, Domna and Enos were running in to see if Geta was OK. He wasn't moving and he'd hit his head pretty hard when he'd hit the ground.

You'd expect a brawl to erupt, and in fact a few of the Warriors had already started running toward second, expecting trouble from the Palatines and all set to defend their second baseman. But even as they ran, just playing ball, everyone else in the Colosseum realized what had just happened before their eyes. One co-emperor had purposefully attacked and hurt the other.

I expected the bloodthirsty Roman fans to be in full voice over this, but instead there was an eerie silence. It was so quiet that from behind the plate where I was standing, I could hear Domna talking to Geta as she leaned over her son to see if he was all right.

He was. Caracalla hadn't argued the call, since the ball was right there in his brother's glove, but he glared at the ump and then trotted to the bench, ignoring what he'd done to Geta, who slowly came to and sat up, eventually standing with the help of Domna and Enos.

As Geta got to his feet the crowd finally erupted into applause. Geta stood there, then held high the glove with the ball still in it and the crowd got the message even if they maybe still didn't fully understand the rules, and then the game went on.

25
Quentin

After all the hubbub at second base, things were surprisingly calm when we all got to the bench for the bottom of the seventh. I was sitting on the bench next to Enos.

Now, Enos was from Carolina and so he and I had a difference of opinion about skin color and baseball. But he'd fought on some of the same islands I had against the Japanese and we both respected that in the other. Enos had been an army captain and earned himself a bronze star by blowing the treads off a Japanese flamethrower tank in Okinawa and saved a lot of lives in doing it, so I wanted to like the guy, despite his attitude. And when it came to me and Walter—the team's two "Cubans"—Enos had come a long way over the course of the season. He saw us now as teammates, and I gave him credit for that.

But he had a hot head and he held a grudge, and for the last three innings Caracalla, who'd pitched in the first game and started at first in our game, had been behind the plate, catching for the Palatines. He wasn't too bad at it, but then he didn't have to deal with a lot of foul tips or even swinging strikes. When the Wandering Warriors swung the bat, we usually made contact.

I didn't like what I was hearing from Enos on the bench. "Ain't right," he was saying, and "dirty player," and "cheap shot." And Danny Felton, of course, our team firebrand, was agreeing with him and playing it up.

Well, that was certainly true enough about that vicious play at second, but I leaned over to warn him, quiet-like: "Now, Enos, these guys, their emperor and ours, between them they're gonna run this whole Roman Empire. So we can't do one damn thing about that play except let those brothers decide it on their own. You know what I'm saying? Enos? You hearin' me?"

He nodded, looked at me, gave me a curious little smile and said, "Sure, Quentin. I hear ya," and then he went out to stand in the on-deck circle and swing a couple of bats.

I was hoping he wouldn't get into it with Caracalla behind the plate, and small favors, he didn't say anything to him. It'd be best, I thought, if Enos would just get himself another base hit and that would keep him happy and then we'd finish this game and get ourselves on home.

That almost worked out. Enos was up with Jake on second and one out and he went with the first pitch, ripping a sharp single into left. Jake scored easy on that but Enos had to pull up at first, where he stood there, a blank expression on his face.

He was taking a big lead at first, so the pitcher threw over there once to hold him, and that went OK. Then Bobby, at the plate, took a strike, then watched a couple of balls go wide, and then, as Enos went for the steal, Bobby smacked one hard into deep left center. And the Roman crowd, who were learning to like this strange game they were watching even if nobody ever drew blood, raised one hell of a cheer.

Enos was on his horse, like they say, and he never paused at second. The Palatines shortstop was out into shallow left center waiting for the relay from the centerfielder. It should have been a routine play, so he caught it, turned around slowly, and lo and behold, Enos was still motoring, not stopping at third like he should, but making a mad dash for home and—oh my Lord, I could see this coming—a collision with Caracalla.

The shortstop fired it toward home, where Enos was headed with a full head of steam, and where Caracalla had come out to guard the plate. The ball got there first and Caracalla made a nice play catching it on a tough hop. And then here came Enos, not bothering to slide any more than Caracalla had at second.

Instead, Enos just put his shoulder down and rammed into the emperor, and sent him flying.

But Caracalla held onto the ball, and stood up slowly and, just like his brother, raised the ball up high for the crowd and the ump, to see. And the umpire—to his great relief, I bet—thumbed Enos out, and that was that.

Enos walked on over to our bench, looking smug, and I asked him if he felt better now, and grinned at him. He looked at me, smiled, and said, "Now that's baseball, ain't it, Quent?"

And I agreed that it was, but I was thinking, at the same time, that that wouldn't be the end of it. Caracalla was taking his applause from the crowd, but his face looked like thunder, and some of those spectators right above us were beginning to shout stuff that sounded pretty ugly.

26
The Professor

So now we were at the beginning of the eighth and my guys were loose and happy—Quentin and Enos were sharing a joke on the bench, and Danny and Walter were grinning and punching each other's arms like schoolkids. Even Jake was smiling as he walked out to the plate, swinging his bat back and forth to warm his arm like he always did. Most of the crowd was happy too—the upper tiers, where the plebs were; they were Domna's crowd first and foremost, what with her sons being out of the country for so long, and Domna being on our team.

The senators and nobles, though, and the rest of the Palatines? That was a different story entirely. They were still seething about that play at the plate. Caracalla was obviously unhurt, and after all, he'd gotten the out and the applause for it. But I was sure it smacked of treason to the senators and the nobles.

I could see those worthy politicians bellowing and bawling up a storm, even as the lower classes raised a cheerful racket. I could see the fists waving and the red faces. And I could see them gesturing to the surly Palatines on the field, none too subtly.

Because those politicians knew how their bread was buttered. They were either Caracalla's men already, or knew that their best hope of advancement—maybe even survival—in the coming months was to hitch their wagons to Caracalla as closely as possible, because he was highly likely to be the new power in Rome.

Caracalla was still pacing to and fro. I looked over to Geta and Domna. They were standing several feet apart, Geta with Duke and young Davey, and Domna out by herself, and they were both looking all over the place, eyes moving here and there, picking up all the cues from the crowd and the players that my boys were missing. Something was going on.

And then Domna starting shouting too, gesturing and waving orders. But it was too late, because the very next moment any semblance of this being a baseball game ceased, and everything happened at once.

The Palatines sprinted to form a group around Caracalla, on some signal that I hadn't seen. From their clothing they were pulling daggers, small clubs, metal knuckledusters. They lined up alongside him as he advanced towards us. I had the feeling he wanted to do a lot more than just get even with Enos.

Then, from the wooden barricade behind first base, a dozen legionaries came crashing out with Lucius Aurelius at their head, swords drawn, and made straight for Domna. They would reach her first. No way I could get to her, and no way I'd be able to fight them all anyway.

And even while all that was happening, and worse than any of it: over on the eastern side of the arena, the Gate of Life crashed open, and gladiators poured through it in full fighting gear.

Above and all around us, that crowd of more than fifty thousand lost their minds. All on their feet, all howling, they became a mob. Fights were breaking out all over, those down in the nobles' tier just as vicious as those of the street toughs up in the nosebleed seats. Within moments the match had been lit and the tinderbox that was the Flavian Amphitheater, doubtless filled with the coarser elements of Roman society to begin with, had flared up into a full-blown riot.

I wanted to run to Domna, but that was madness; it was my boys who needed me, and it was to the bench that I ran, beckoning them to close up around me too.

Not that it would do us any good. We might be able to kick the Palatines' asses at baseball, but they were elite soldiers, trained killers; in any kind of a fair fight they'd destroy us and leave us bleeding and dead in the sand. And behind the Palatines were what must have been a hundred gladiators, with even more streaming out onto the sand behind those.

Over yonder, Lucius and his men rapidly encircled Domna and Geta to form a protective cordon, practically lifting them off their feet in their haste to carry them to safety. Well, good for them, because this was no place for an empress, and I was glad she was safe and that Lucius had picked the right team after all. But that meant our last protectors had left the field.

So it was all down to me.

Sure, the Empress Julia Domna and I, we'd hatched ourselves a fine old plan up there in the palace on the hill, after we'd gotten all bruised and beaten by Caracalla and his thugs. We'd talked big while Rome slept, and thought we were pretty cunning for a while. But that plan had no hope of success now, not with the Colosseum a riot zone from the arena to the top of the stands, and a mess of legionaries and gladiators coming at us.

Sometimes, things just don't pan out the way you planned 'em.

But if we had to die, at least we'd all die together.

I shouted over the hubbub, loud as I could, "Warriors! To me!"

27
Quentin

I was gathering up the boys as best I could. Half of them froze in terror, half of them ready to run in any direction and get themselves spitted on a Roman sword. The Professor was bellowing at the top of his voice. Couldn't hear him worth a damn but he was trying to get the guys to come to him, and they finally got it and started grouping up around him, even though God alone knew what good that would do.

But now the gladiators split up. Those vicious fighters weren't all Caracalla's goons after all. Yep, half of them had come to flank the Palatines and add to their numbers, but the rest were running between Caracalla's line and ours, and turning to show us their backs. They'd flocked in to protect us. To hold off the Emperor's men. Among them I saw members of the Aventines team and some other fellas we'd eaten chow with in the mess hall of the Ludus Magnus. Even without language, we'd tried to be companionable as possible, when they'd let us. We'd trained together. Kind of. And now that was paying off. They'd chosen a side, and it was ours.

The two lines crashed together, two ranks of gladiators just twenty feet away from us, all fighting in a big old brawl rather than dueling one on one like normal. It was a crush of steel and blades, and some among them were already going down, gutted. Blood spattered. Heads were literally rolling. If I'd had time, I might have thrown up.

The Professor grabbed up a sword where it had fallen. Danny Felton had seized a trident from one of the dead. Duke was holding a shield, but he was so clumsy with it that I doubted it'd do him much good if one of those muscular, oiled gladiators ran at him.

We kept moving, sideways across the arena, all in a bunch.

It looked like the Professor was trying to move us west, towards the Gate of Death, and *that* made no sense, because that was the exit farthest from us and it was guarded by a stoic rank of legionaries who were declining to join the fray in the main arena.

And *they* wouldn't be letting us pass. We were going to die out here.

All kinds of stuff rained down on us now. Rocks and stones. Half-eaten chicken legs. Seat cushions. Those good old Roman boys in the stands above us were having themselves quite the time, pelting us while they weren't pummeling one another. With gladiators fighting and dying around us and the crowd rioting in the stands I had to wonder just how many folks were going to die here today. Aside from us, I mean.

The Professor halted, looking carefully down at his feet. What in hell was he doing?

Then the ground fell away just in front of us in a big rectangle, and my heart leaped. Of course! We'd go down on one of those nifty platforms, back under the arena, and then we'd . . .

But no. That's not what happened at all. I leaned forward and looked down into that rectangular hole as the hydraulics clanked and rumbled away below me, and couldn't believe my eyes. I literally thought that perhaps I'd gone mad.

Or that the Professor had.

28
The Professor

Two of Caracalla's gladiators broke through and made a run at us. They'd killed the men they were fighting, split that line of gladiators who were doing their utmost to protect us, and were now pounding toward us. One was a lumbering secutor-type covered in plate armor with a heavy helm, his sword bloody, his shield raised. The other, ridiculously naked, was a retarius, armed with net and trident. In the brief moment I had to register it, I saw that he was also ridiculously good looking, despite the scars on his arms and legs. We were being attacked simultaneously by a tank and a Greek god, and behind them came four of Caracalla's soldiers, charging at us with swords raised, and a couple of the Thracian-type gladiators for good measure.

My boys stepped forward, all in a mess but bold as hell. Three of them were carrying shields they'd scavenged somewhere along the line. Three more had swords, though all of them were holding them two-handed like they were bats. The rest of the guys, well, they still clutched their baseball bats in their hands. A fine weapon for the gladiatorial arena...

The Wandering Warriors had stepped up to protect *me*, I realized. Me, and one another. Because whatever the hell this was, we were still a team, and we were all in it together.

I was never more proud of them than I was in that terrible moment, with death charging down on us.

I risked a glance behind me.

Up from the bowels of the arena came our dilapidated old Ford Transit bus, large as life. I hadn't seen it for weeks, and it looked odd to me now, out of place. Raised up out of the Hades below, to bring us life.

Well. Maybe.

29
Quentin

We clashed with the gladiators. I was swinging my bat like a club and trying to whack that armor-plated guy's helmet, and Enos was thumping him in the chest with his own bat, while Duke tried to protect us both with the shield. But that secutor, he was actually *laughing* at us, and then his sword sliced into Bobby's arm and Bobby set up a wail and fell to his knees, bleeding bad. Danny Felton, he had stepped up to that naked retarius and was swinging his trident like a bat. Having no shield, the retarius had to parry that with his own trident, which made it look like they were somehow sword fighting with big long fork-shaped spears.

Danny was good in a bar brawl and he certainly wasn't lacking for any courage, but he wasn't fast enough. The retarius swung him a good one and knocked Danny clean off his feet. I thought he might just kill Danny dead with that trident, stab three prongs right into his chest, but instead he backed up and whirled his weighted net around his head.

The very next second, the net flew through the air and spread out, snaring Enos and Johnny both. They'd been about to take on a legionary or two, but now they were flailing like fish under that heavy net. Which, of course, was the whole idea.

Then the secutor jumped back away from us, startled, and from behind me there came a very familiar wet cracking-sparking din as the Ford Transit backfired. It cracked a second time, and this time the engine roared into life.

All the soldiers were backing away now, and Caracalla with them, big brutish Caracalla with a sword in his hand and a mean look on his face, but even he was wide-eyed. It wasn't the bus's noise that caused it this time—the furor was so loud in the Colosseum that they might not even have heard that backfire from where they stood—it was that the bus existed at all.

What does a Ford Transit look like to a man who's only seen carts and, I don't know, chariots? What goes through his mind on first glimpsing something so massive and blocky, twenty-six feet long and nine feet high, and shiny? How does he know if it's a threat to him?

The Professor was sitting in the driver's seat, of course. He'd jumped down onto the platform while it was still rising. Even now the hydraulics had a foot or so to go before they brought it level with the arena's sandy floor. But our next move was obvious, and we did it. We grabbed bleeding Bobby and stunned Danny, and between us we dragged Enos and Johnny and the net and all back toward the bus, and somehow we all swarmed aboard it.

And so there we were...in the bus. In the arena. In the Colosseum. Unless we'd mounted a roof cannon on the Transit or something—which we obviously hadn't—or were relying on the Romans staying spellbound by the Wonder of Ford forever—which they obviously wouldn't—I had no idea what was going to happen next. "Professor?"

"Everyone sit down and grab something," he said tersely.

And he gunned it, and off we went.

The bus did not exactly leap forward. It sprayed sand and skidded rightward.

"Want me to drive?" I said. Couldn't help myself.

The Professor gave me the very briefest of irritated looks and tried again, more gently. The bus moved forward, wallowed rather, like it was wading. I wondered when the last time was we'd checked the pressure in those tires.

Out of the windows I saw the soldiers and gladiators continuing to retreat away. I was glad the bus's size gave them pause. Also, that they apparently didn't realize all this clear glass between us would shatter with a quick swing of any of their weapons. They could've mobbed the bus, clambered in, killed us all dead. But they didn't realize it and so they just stood there.

The Professor laboriously coaxed the bus around, double-clutched it up into second gear and then third, but it was still like driving in molasses. We lumbered in slow motion, toward the Gate of the Dead. Even so, the legionaries—no fools they—buckled and broke; they practically scampered aside to avoid us. Beyond them I saw a low tunnel that ended abruptly at what looked very much like a wall. "Professor..."

"Quentin, sit *down!*"

As we broke free of the sand, the bus lurched forward. That tunnel was only a foot higher than the bus with barely a foot clearance on either side. We skidded into the chute and it suddenly went dark, and the whole left side of the bus screeched and scraped against stone before the Professor, swearing, turned on the headlights.

We were still gaining speed as we thundered on through the Gate of the Dead. And I started saying my prayers while I still had time.

30
The Professor

I had to trust her. She'd had this bus carried all the way here from the Tiber on a huge cart. She'd had it installed on the elevator, just like she'd said. Sworn all her people to secrecy, telling them it was all part of a grand finale for after the big championship playoff, a spectacle they wouldn't forget. And so it was, I reckon.

So if Julia Domna had also told me rather blithely that once we were out of the arena, we should just keep going and stop for nothing at all, that's exactly what I had to do.

Even though I was driving toward a solid wall.

A few seconds before we'd have crashed up into it and crunched the bus like a pretzel, the wall swung away in front of us, men tugging on ropes that hung from one side to open it wide as I downshifted from second to first gear but kept us moving. I'd known it was a gate—the Gate of the Dead, where they hauled out the bodies of the gladiators after their fatal bouts—but those bleeding corpses were hauled down the narrow sloping corridor that had just peeled off to my left and right.

But I guess they had to get their big carts into the arena somehow, that contained all the sand and supplies and such. The Gate led to the outside, sure. And outside we popped, like a cork from a bottle, courtesy of some very last-minute action by some flunky of Julia's. Bless her.

Bright sunshine burst into the bus again. All of a sudden, we were outside the Colosseum, on its western side. Above me and to the right loomed the statue of Nero a hundred feet high, now converted into a more generic sun god, naked and gilded and with sunshine spraying out of his head. Dead ahead of us was the great marbled Temple of Venus and Roma. And beyond that was the Roman Forum, which was always packed with people. No joy for us that way, I knew.

I hauled the steering wheel left in a sharp leaning turn and heard various of my boys thumping up against the windows behind me and shouting out.

I didn't look back. I'd *told* 'em to sit down.

Besides, I had to concentrate. Out in front of me, Roman citizens were flinging themselves left and right away from the bus. It was now the full heat of mid-afternoon, and anyone who was going to the Colosseum today was already inside, so the crowds right here were pretty light, but still I had to slow down. These were ordinary people, families, workers; no one here deserved to be mown down by a giant five-ton vehicle from a distant future they couldn't possibly have imagined.

We lumbered on. I looked at the gas tank. Quarter full. Hoped that would be enough.

I skidded precariously around an arch, barely avoided a set of steps—in a city that relies on carts there's always a ramp somewhere, and I'd scoped all this out on foot—and we careered south down a broad boulevard. The Palatine Hill rose steeply to my right, crowned with palaces, in one of which I'd dined with an Empress. Somewhere off to my left would be the Domus Vectiliana, where the Emperor Commodus had died, what? Just twenty years ago? Yes...

A donkey cart was lumbering to get out of our way, but the road wasn't *that* wide. I managed to miss the donkey but clipped the cart good. It spun in the air, splintering in flight and scattering grain and wine amphorae everywhere. Whoops.

Well, carts weren't legally allowed within city limits during daylight hours anyway. Right? Really, that was all that was saving us from right now being stranded in the traffic jam from hell.

I barely glimpsed the Temple to the Divine Claudius as we rumbled by it, but here came the tall wall of the Circus Maximus, ahead and to our right as the road widened out into a triangular plaza. Just as I remembered. I honked the horn, sent pedestrians leaping and fleeing, and took a half-left out of that plaza into a much narrower street.

We were heading toward the city wall now. But we'd never get there unless Julia Domna had managed to pull off a little more of her secular magic on our behalf.

The road we were on led straight onto the Appian Way at the wall, but here it was a thin thoroughfare with high curbs on either side of the bus. The cobblestones were hardly made for twentieth century vehicular traffic, and even at twenty miles an hour we were getting bumped around and thrown all over the place.

But that was the least of my worries. In ancient Rome, streets like this flowed with open sewage. Even now, we were splashing through some vile stuff I preferred not to think about. And because of that there were high stepping-stones across the street every so often, so the more high-falutin' Romans could keep their pretty sandaled feet out of the mire.

Those stepping-stones were over a foot tall. Roman wagons had a high enough wheelbase to clear them easily, but they were way higher than the clearance of the Ford Transit. Hitting the stones would rip the bottom out of the bus and bring our getaway to a very abrupt and messy halt. But I kept my foot on the gas. Had to.

Ahead of me I saw more legionaries. Who now scattered as the Transit bore down on them.

"Ramps!" I shouted it aloud in my relief.

Up we bumped, up a very solid wooden ramp Domna had had made for just this purpose, and bumpety-bump we went down a similar wooden ramp on the other side of the stepping-stones. And in just two hundred feet it happened again: another bunch of soldiers, another pair of ramps. And once more, beyond that.

The third time, the bus grounded on the cobbles as it came back down to street level. We were killing the shocks.

I could hear swearing behind me.

I wondered how long it would be before we blew a tire.

We didn't. And now the Porta Appia, the Appian Gate, hove into view dead ahead.

And it was closed against us.

I was so focused on the street and on not hitting any of the pedestrians who were still jumping out of my way, even in the filth, that I didn't immediately see.

Within the gate was a door, just an ordinary people-sized door to let pedestrians in and out. We weren't about to fit through that. The gatehouse was guarded by soldiers, a full complement of legionaries who stood flabbergasted at the weird vehicle approaching them, even as we stared back at them in frustration.

I slowed the Transit, looked in the rearview mirror. We'd outrun pursuit, but if I was any judge of Caracalla's character, it wouldn't be long in coming.

"What now, Professor?" Quentin, of course. Good old Quentin. I didn't have the heart to break it to him that, after all this, it looked like we were sunk.

I braked to a halt, leaped up, threw the door open, bellowed at the soldiers. "Open up at once! By order of the Empress Julia Domna!"

The soldiers did absolutely nothing but stare at me.

Julia might have fixed the roads for us, but she hadn't been able to fix the gate. Or maybe she hadn't known that Caracalla would invoke some new law she hadn't known about. Those big old gates had sure been thrown wide when we'd first entered the Eternal City, and also when I'd been hoofing around it doing my reconnaissance for all this, just a few short hours ago.

"Here comes trouble!" Duke called out. Sure enough, out of the chaos we'd left in our wake came a swanky looking wagon pulled by two cantering horses, both frothing at the mouth. On the cart, soldiers. More ran behind, trying their level best to keep up.

We couldn't fight them. I was fresh out of fight. And if we abandoned the bus we'd never outrun them on foot down the Appian Way, even if the soldier-boys guarding it let us pass. It would be like a Chaplin farce. Until they caught us and gutted us, and it became a tragedy.

I shook my head, suddenly very weary.

"Professor?"

"What?"

"It's your girlfriend," Quentin said.

I looked again. Sure enough, sitting in the cart between two soldiers was the Empress Julia Domna.

She leaped down before the cart even came to a halt, running forward to shout to the soldiers at the gate. Even still dressed in her ball-playing garb the legionaries knew her, and you'd better bet they jumped to it quick as a flash. But the Appian Gate itself was pretty cumbersome and creaked open slowly, so slowly.

Yet again, I peered back up that road into the City, and here came more soldiers, a steady sea of them jogging after us with swords drawn, throwing pedestrians out of their way or just slashing them down where they stood. Yeah, those'd be Caracalla's thugs, all right.

Julia gingerly stepped into the bus, as if unsure whether it would allow her to enter. She looked at the shiny chrome, the twenty-seven identical cloth seats, two on each side and the three across the back, the rubber mats on the floor, all those glass windows. My big wide steering wheel, and the dials and glowing lights and gearshift. Only then did she look up at me and hold my gaze. "This," she said. "This is the real magic."

"Hell," I said, "it's just a crappy old bus."

She tugged at the door experimentally, but then I grabbed the lever on the dash in front of me to close it myself. I looked at the mass of Caracalla's soldiers pouring down the street toward us, and so did she.

At last the gate was open, and Domna—Julia—grinned. "Well then, Magister. Drive the crappy bus." She looked ahead at the Appian Way, cemented cobbles, wide and cambered, with its ditches and retaining walls, and her mouth twitched again. "Straight down the middle."

I looked at her, into her eyes, and said in Latin. "You're quite sure about this, Julia? Really?"

Her face turned somber. "I have done all I can. They are now their own men and must make their own way."

She meant Caracalla and Geta, of course. I nodded.

"And I do not want to give my life for Rome," she added, a little ruefully.

I didn't want that either. "Fair enough," I said.

The Appian Gate had a slight lip to it, so I had to ease the Transit over it. Just outside the city walls, a dozen street urchins stopped the game they'd been playing and stared at us.

Sticks and balls. Bases marked with rocks. A runner on first and the pitcher in the stretch, looking over there. It wasn't small-ball, nothing like. Me and my guys, we'd brought true baseball to Rome.

I waved at the kids, and rather tentatively they waved back.

"Wait, Professor."

Quentin pulled down a window and tossed out two bats, two balls, three gloves. The kids gaped even wider, if that were possible. Looked at one another, then stepped forward to accept their treasure from the future.

Julia looked back at the approaching soldiers and tapped her foot. "Magister..."

"Yes sirree, ma'am," I said in English, and winked at her.

Then I gunned the engine and it gave out a nice little back-fire and off we went, the Wandering Warriors and Julia Domna, bumping down the Appian Way toward freedom.

31
The Professor

It was the bottom of the seventh in Cairo, Illinois, and the Warriors were clinging to a one-run lead over the Egyptians in the second game of a doubleheader. We were playing two seven-inning games because that's how it was done for doubleheaders.

That part of Southern Illinois is called Little Egypt because of the two great rivers that meet in Cairo, the Mississippi and the Ohio, and because it's so far south, and so damn hot, that they used to grow cotton here. Cairo is pronounced "kay-ro," because that's how they pronounce it, but there's a Thebes too, and a Karnak. And the university's sports teams are the Salukis. You get the idea.

And those Little Egyptians can play some baseball. They'd been chasing us all afternoon. We were getting our hits: Julia Domna had two good singles and drove in a run both times, and everyone else was contributing too, so you'd think seven runs in seven innings would give you a nice lead. But not today. I think they'd seen Quentin once too often over the years because they were sitting on that curveball of his and knocking it around. He didn't have his good fastball. He said he was fine, but the pop just wasn't there. And we didn't have a good reliever, so he was just letting them hit it and counting on his defense, which carried us along okay for the first few innings and then we stumbled in the fifth and sixth. Julia muffed an easy grounder to let in a run, and then an inning later Enos out in center dived for a sinking liner that came his way and missed it, so the ball rolled all the way to the fence and turned an out into a triple, scoring three more runs for them. And now, in the seventh, Quentin had just given up a two-run homer, hanging one of those curves up waist high and that Egyptian crushed it.

So with no one on and no one out, I called time and walked out to the mound to talk to Quentin, mostly trying to buy him a little time to catch his breath in the damp heat of Cairo.

The infield all came in too, slapping Quentin on the butt with their gloves and offering encouragement. Julia, whose English was coming along good in the month since we'd been back, said, "Go get 'em, Quentin," and added, "Let 'em hit it, we'll make the plays."

Quentin looked at her and laughed. "Thanks, um, Julia," he said. We were all still trying to adjust to an ex-Empress being our shortstop and wanting to be called "Julia." But we were getting there.

And so was she. There were a half dozen other women players in our league. During the war, the league had opened up to women players; but there just weren't many of them playing the game. Watching Julia sweep things up at short, I figured that would change. A lot of young girls would see that they could play the game as good as anyone.

In fact, that had already started, since that day we all woke up back on the bus on the banks of the Sangamon River, back in our right time and place. No time had passed in the world as we knew it, so we yelled for the ferry and a guy brought it over and we crossed the river and drove a few miles of dirt road to where we picked up Illinois Route 48, which we drove like hell on to get Bobby to the hospital in Decatur, Illinois. There were a few of us vets on the team who'd seen wounds that bad plenty of times and we'd patched him up pretty good. The docs in Decatur did the rest, and Bobby pulled through OK. We sent him home to Hannibal and we'd pick him up there on our way north if he was healing all right.

After we left the hospital, we tried to get back into the right frame of mind by having breakfast at Emily's Diner on the outskirts of town, where they always served our two "Cubans" with a smile. After that, we all walked around town a bit to stretch our legs, and by 10 am, we were at Fans Field, taking some batting practice and getting ready for our noon game against the Dukes.

Truth be told, I'd been a mite worried about Julia. She'd been staring around in a daze all morning, trying to absorb the shock of the new, even while the rest of my team rejoiced at being back in the world they understood. I'd left 'em all window shopping on Main Street for a few minutes while I ducked into the Decatur Public Library and headed for their meager history stacks. There I learned—to my sorrow—that Caracalla had still prevailed over Geta, who'd been sent into exile in Caledonia. That wasn't the way I remembered it from school, so we'd changed a thing or two back there, given Geta a while longer to live. But the end result had been the same.

By my boys' accounts, Geta had been a good guy. Maybe we should have tried to bring him back with us too, but I suppose he wouldn't have come.

As for Julia, I needn't have worried about her. Once she got to the ballfield, she'd shaken off her funk and played a solid game, with a single and two double plays, starting one of them on a tough ground ball that she gloved despite a bad bounce; and making the put-out on the other one, stepping on second and jumping to avoid the sliding runner while she fired it to first. It was great to watch. At the end of the game, there were a dozen people wanting her autograph, three of them young girls. We played the Dukes the next day too, and word had spread: the place was packed and there was a line of thirty people—daughters, mostly, with their parents—looking to meet Julia and get her autograph.

At the next stop, in Carbondale, there were twenty or more of those girls for each of three games, and now, here in Cairo, Julia had at least fifty of them in line after the first game and I could see them all yelling and screaming her name as we played the second. That was great news for all concerned, I figured. What I didn't know was that the local paper, the *Cairo Evening Citizen*, had heard about her too, and there was a reporter at the game. And that wound up changing things.

We won the game. After Quentin caught his breath for a minute or two he got the next guy to swing a curveball down low for a strike out, and then walked the next guy in four pitches. I stood up and was going to walk out to him again but he waved me off, pointed at me with his glove to get back into my catcher's crouch and play some ball. Okay, I did that, and he threw three straight fastballs, all three of them low strikes and with good stuff on them. The hitter watched the first one, swung and missed on the second, and then hit a sharp ground ball into the hole, where Julia, seeing it all the way from the moment it left the bat, ran hard, backhanded the ball and flipped to second, where Duke caught it, sidestepped the sliding runner, and pegged it to first in plenty of time. Game over, and on a splendid double play.

The girls in the stands went crazy, which was great fun, and then they all came down for more autographs and maybe just to be near their hero. Julia Domna trotted in from the infield, heading toward the dugout and maybe hoping to avoid the whole thing by going straight to the clubhouse, but I wasn't about to let that happen.

"These girls are your fans," I told her in Latin. "They admire you. Stay out there and wave at them!"

She did that, and then the reporter from the *Evening Citizen* came up to me and said, "You're the manager, right? I'd like to interview your shortstop, if that's okay."

Well, I'd known this moment would come one day. Julia's English wasn't really good enough for an interview, but by acting as translator I could hopefully keep things under control.

I introduced Julia to Paige Bly, the reporter, in Latin, and she agreed to the interview. They'd had news of a sort in Rome in her day, the Acta Diurna posted on pillars and walls, bringing the citizens of Rome who read up to date. She understood the concept.

The first thing that Bly wanted to know was where Julia was from, and when she replied to me—tongue in cheek—that she hailed from the Palatine Hill in Rome, I translated that as "I'm from Italy, where many girls play baseball as children." Which was now true, in my time, though I wasn't sure it had been before we made our little journey back to ancient Rome.

And that's how it went for the rest of the interview, with Julia subtly tweaking me and me cleaning it up to sound reasonable to Bly. This would work in town after town, I figured, until we bumped up against some reporter who spoke Italian, or knew Latin. And we'd cross that stream when we came to it. Lord knows we were good at crossing streams, right?

It went on this way for the next few days: another doubleheader down in Paducah, then a day off for travel before we got to Hannibal, Missouri, where we visited with Bobby Gamin, who was recovering nicely. The town's name was a lot of fun to talk about with Julia: a place named after a great African leader who'd damn near defeated the Roman Empire. There were bigger and bigger crowds all the way, in Cedar Rapids and Davenport, and good stories in every paper, and then we finally got back to Rockford, only maybe a hundred miles from Chicago, and so suddenly we were talking to the *Chicago Tribune* and the *Democrat*, and the *Sun-Times*.

Through all this Julia was playing better and better all the time and the Warriors were on a tear, winning five in a row and losing one, then winning five more. The guys were hitting with

confidence, Enos was becoming a star out in center, and Julia's
English was coming along too. I really didn't need to translate
too much anymore, but now that I'd built up the story as far
as I had, I was enjoying the craziness. But I knew all along it
couldn't last. And after the end of a three-game stand against
the Rockford Blue Sox, this is how it ended:

Julia Domna was now leading off, and slapping the ball around,
single after single, at a good .375 pace. Her glove work was good
and getting better all the time, and her arm strength was improving. She couldn't make the throw to first from deep in the hole at
short, but pretty much nothing else got by her. The crowds were
overflowing the bandbox ballparks we played in and the papers
were having a field day. And then, as we all walked off the field
in Rockford and Julia stopped to sign autographs for the girls and
their mothers, a woman I recognized instantly came up to me.

It was Grace Comiskey, owner of the Chicago White Sox. I
stuck out my hand to shake hers, saying "Hello, Mrs. Comiskey,"
but she'd have none of that. She gave me a hug and said, "How
are you doing, Professor? Knees holding up? You looked pretty
good out there today."

I'd had a double, and done my job behind the plate, so I was
able to smile at that. When I'd left the White Sox a few years
before, the parting hadn't been all that harmonious. I'd had some
knee troubles, and even for the backup catcher that's a bad thing.
But I'd thought I had a couple more seasons in those knees,
even with the years I'd lost to the war. Mrs. Comiskey and her
general manager disagreed, and I was released. It all worked out
fine, of course, what with my starting up the Wandering Warriors and getting serious about my teaching career and all, but
it'd still left a sour taste.

"The knees are fine, Mrs. Comiskey, thanks for asking," I said.
"But I'm betting you're not here to talk with me. Am I right?"

She smiled. "Professor, I'm sorry about how it went at the
end. But it's never easy for anyone when their career winds
down, you know."

Well, sure enough. "I know, I know," I said, and then I saw
Julia Domna looking at us and I sighed and waved her over.
Baseball in wartime had made for a lot of changes in the game,
including everyone looking the other way at the black players
who claimed to be Cuban. In the minors, black ballplayers were

playing openly, and in a year or two, I knew, they'd be playing the big leagues. But credit Branch Rickey for that, not Grace Comiskey, at least not yet. But a talented woman shortstop? I was certain that Comiskey was here to talk business.

Julia came over, and I told her in Latin that I was introducing her to the owner of a much better baseball team, a team that would pay her good money to play and make her famous. She didn't say anything. She already knew what fame was like and the good and the bad that came with it.

Comiskey reached over to shake Julia's hand and then put her left hand over their clasped right hands and shook them once, hard. She looked into Julia's eyes. "You're a little older than I thought. But you play like you're twenty. Great range, strong arm. Courage at the bag."

Julia looked at me. I said, in Latin: "She says you look immensely old. But she likes your defense. She says you have great courage."

"You will need great courage, Magister," Julia replied, straight-faced but with a dark twinkle in her eye, "once we are away from this woman."

Grinning, I turned back to Comiskey. "Julia humbly thanks you. She's from across the pond. Good old Europe. We're still working on her English."

"You tell her, Professor, that I'd like to see her at our spring training camp in Sarasota next March first. We're going to give her a good tryout. And I think she'll make the team, and that would make her the first woman in the big leagues. She and I and you: we could all be proud of that. Please tell her that, Professor."

So I did, and Julia smiled. If this strange woman wanted her to play, well, she was certainly interested. She told me in Latin to say that last part to Comiskey direct.

Grace Comiskey nodded, gave that quick grin of hers I remembered so well. "All right, then. Professor, I'll get the paperwork to you within the week, and you'll help her get it straightened out, right? Oh, and I like that Slaughter kid too, so he'll get an invite as well. He's a mean son of a gun, and we need players like that."

"Right," I said. Enos would be pleased. He had ambitions.

About to turn away, Comiskey paused. "And, Professor? We're losing Billie Northworth at the end of the season. He's retiring. Might you be interested in that job? Third-base coach? Help out our catchers too? If you want it, it's yours."

Well, there it was. A way to return to the big leagues and good pay for not doing all that much. Coaching third is about the easiest job in baseball: stop the runners, or wave them on home.

"I'll think about it, Mrs. Comiskey," I said warmly, but I was just being polite. I already knew what I was going to do. I'd help Julia get established here, let her finish up with the Warriors over the next month. Then I'd teach my classes in those long-dead languages, Latin and Greek, and do my research at Washington U. in St. Louis. Julia could stay with me and polish up her English over the winter months before she took the train south to Sarasota. We'd get along just fine, I was sure, me and the widow.

Then, with the spring semester ended and Julia Domna playing for the White Sox—the first woman in the big leagues, something me and the guys could indeed be proud of—I'd tune up our old Ford Transit, get the timing right with that distributor cap. Me and the guys would get in a good week of practice, and work a couple of new players into the lineup. Then we'd pack it up and head down to Kankakee, and Decatur, and Carbondale, and Cairo, and Paducah, and back up to Hannibal and Cedar Rapids and Rockford. Playing ball, making a little money, winning some and losing some.

Staying on the road, like we always did in the summer. Me and the Wandering Warriors.

◇◇◇◇◇

Authors' Note

As with so many writing collaborations, "The Wandering Warriors" had its origins in a casual, almost joking conversation between friends. At the time, Alan Smale and Rick Wilber were participating at the annual invitation-only Rio Hondo Writers' Workshop, hosted by Walter Jon Williams in a high mountain valley near Taos, NM. The dozen pro writers stay busy at Rio Hondo, critiquing and discussing one another's stories during the exacting morning sessions. But with determination and efficient time management, there's still plenty of opportunity for mountain hikes in the afternoons, and for long conversations over dinner and into the night.

Alan and Rick had admired each other's stories during the workshop sessions. And so, during one of those afternoon hikes, they—frivolously at first—wondered if there might be a way to combine their passions: Rick's for baseball fantasy and science fiction, and Alan's for all things Ancient Roman. They'd both won the Sidewise Award for Best Alternate History—Short Form for their work in those areas, so the idea of combining them didn't seem as odd to them as you might expect. In fact, they quickly became fascinated by the challenge.

A little research revealed that the Romans had indeed played ball games, in one case using a ball not much larger than a baseball. This historical tidbit provided vital grist for their story-telling mill, and by the time they'd clambered about halfway up one of those mountains they'd already mapped out the bones of a possible plot and pointed each other toward some key historical figures in both the classical and ball-playing worlds. Maybe it was the thin air at 10,000 feet, but the idea seemed to work, and they left Rio Hondo vowing to continue the effort. Their book contracts required them to focus on other work for extended periods—Alan's *Clash of Eagles* trilogy, which features a Roman invasion of ancient North America, and Rick's *Alien Morning* trilogy—but they still managed to maintain a steady back-and-forth on the story they originally codenamed "Amor Autem Basis Pila," based on rather bad Latin punnery.

And so, in the fullness of time, "The Wandering Warriors" emerged in its final form, telling the story of a barnstorming 1940s baseball team whose members awaken one morning to find themselves in Ancient Rome at the end of the rule of Septimius Severus, one of the Empire's last great rulers before its long, slow decline. Severus's wife, the Empress Julia Domna, is well known in our timeline, as are her sons, who inherited a split empire from their father following his death, leading to an inevitable and bloody conflict. The Professor of the tale, a Latin scholar and veteran of some secret actions during the Second World War, is also a real historical figure. The story of how he led his ragtag team of baseball barnstormers into the brutal heart of Imperial Rome to help Julia Domna find a solution to her problems, however, has not been so carefully documented...until now.

—Alan Smale and Rick Wilber, July 2020

AUTHORS' BIOGRAPHIES

David Brin (b. 1950) is a Hugo, Nebula, and *Locus* award-winning author known for his hard science fiction, including his notable Uplift series, but not limited to that subcategory, as seen in his novel, *The Postman*, which became a movie, and in his short story included in this book. Brin has a PhD in astronomy from the University of California, San Diego. He was a postdoctoral research fellow at the California Space Institute, of the University of California, at the San Diego campus in La Jolla. He serves on the advisory board of NASA's Innovative and Advanced Concepts group and frequently does futurist consulting for corporations and government agencies. He lives in San Diego with his wife and children.

◇◇◇◇◇

David Drake (1945–2023) was best known as a writer of military science fiction, notably in his Hammer's Slammers series, which tells of the battles waged by the future group of tank-driving mercenaries, but he was a versatile author of much more, ranging from space opera to fantasy to supernatural horror. His RCN series of space opera novels were influenced by the popular Aubrey–Maturin series by Patrick O'Brian.

He graduated with honors from the University of Iowa, Phi Beta Kappa, with a degree in history and Latin, then entered Duke University law school, but was drafted into the U.S. Army, ending up in Vietnam and Cambodia with the 11th Armored Cavalry, known as the Black Horse Regiment. The experience later allowed him to give authenticity to both his portrayals of future combat and the strong characterizations of the fighting men and women in his stories. Upon his return, he finished law school, then worked as assistant town attorney in Chapel Hill for eight years before becoming a full-time writer, selling stories to magazines, and novels and story collections to Ace, Tor, and Baen publishers until deteriorating health forced him to retire from writing in 2021. He lived in Pittsboro, North Carolina, with his wife, Joanne, until his death in 2023.

◇◇◇◇◇

Eric Flint (1947–2022) was the coauthor of three *New York Times* bestsellers in his Ring of Fire alternate history series, and he appeared on the *Wall Street Journal, Washington Post,* and *Locus* bestseller lists as well. His first novel for Baen, *Mother of Demons,* was picked by *Science Fiction Chronicle* as a best novel of the year. His *1632,* which launched the Ring of Fire series, won widespread critical praise, as from *Publishers Weekly,* which called him an SF author of particular note, one who can entertain and edify in equal, and major, measure. A longtime labor union activist with a master's degree in history, he resided in northwest Indiana with his wife Lucille until his death in 2022.

◇◇◇◇◇

Randall Garrett (1927–1987), was an ebullient and frequently hilarious writer (in person and on paper) who often wrote as Randall Garrett, but also under a multitude of pseudonyms, sometimes using his father's names—David and Phillip—in constructing them. Mark Cole has a nifty biographical and bibliographical sketch of Garrett and his diverse works online, in which he laments a number of forgotten writers of yesteryear: "...how many still remember the marvelous stories written by such authors as David Gordon, Ivar Jorgensen, Jonathan Blake MacKenzie, Leonard G. Spencer, Gordon Aghill, Richard Green and Darrell T. Langart? Mind you, they might be a little easier to remember if we knew that they all happened to be one man, one brilliant if nearly forgotten writer named Randall Garrett."

Well played, Mr. Cole, even if I have to quibble that "Ivar Jorgensen" (sometimes "Jorgenson") was a house name, used by more writers than Mr. Garrett. That list of pseudonyms above, incidentally, does not include "Robert Randall," used for his many collaborations with Robert Silverberg in the 1950s. Thanks to all those pseudonyms, a full accounting of his work is probably not possible, though Cole mentions 22 novels and 130 short stories.

His first published story, "The Absence of Heat," appeared in *Astounding*'s "Probability Zero" department (which specialized in in short-short joke stories) in 1944 when he was only sixteen. Other bibliographies list "The Waiting Game," in 1951, as his first published story. Garrett is probably best remembered for his Lord Darcy series about a detective in a parallel world where magic works and is used in criminology as our world uses forensic science. Of his collaborations, I am inordinately fond of the three hilarious novels he did with Laurence M. Janifer (as by "Mark Phillips") about a hapless FBI agent named Kenneth J. Malone, who has to deal with crimes committed by telepaths, teleporters, and other psi-powered miscreants, the first of which ("That Sweet Little Old Lady" in *Astounding*, later in paperback as *Brain Twister*) was nominated for the Hugo Award. His last work was also a collaboration, this time with his wife, Vicki Ann Heydron: seven novels of sword-and-sorcery mystery, known collectively as The Gandalara Cycle.

Unfortunately (to put it far too mildly), Garrett contracted a brain infection that ended his writing and, later, his life. But he left us a substantial body of work, some of which is online as books, e-books, and audiobooks, and which is highly recommended. Also recommended is Mark Cole's splendid essay about Garrett, "The Clown Prince of Science Fiction," which can be found at http://www.irosf.com/q/zine/article/10578.

◇◇◇◇◇

Sandra Miesel (b. 1941) started reading science fiction at age eleven. She intended to be a biochemist when she grew up but turned into a medievalist instead, a skill set useful for working in the SF field. Since her first professional sale in 1974, she's written, analyzed, edited, and even stitched SF. (The last ability won her a place on the official NASA Artist team for the Apollo-Soyuz launch in 1975.) Sandra's approach to fiction is to insert a fantastic element into a precisely accurate historical setting. In addition to her SF novel *Dreamrider*, expanded as *Shaman*, and a handful of short stories, Sandra's scores of critical essays often focused on Poul Anderson and Gordon R. Dickson. She is the premier expert on their work and has edited collections of their stories. She also coedited a set of academic papers, *Light Beyond All Shadow: Religious Experience in Tolkien's Work* with Paul E. Kerry. Outside the SF field, Sandra coauthored *The Da Vinci Hoax* with Carl E. Olson and has published 500 nonfiction articles, mostly on history, hagiography, and art.

◇◇◇◇◇

Robert Silverberg (b. 1935), prolific author not just of SF but of authoritative nonfiction books, columnist for *Asimov's SF Magazine*, winner of a constellation of awards, and renowned bon vivant surely needs no introduction—but that's never stopped me before. Robert Silverberg sold his first SF story, "Gorgon Planet," before he was out of his teens, to the British magazine *Nebula*. Two years later, his first SF novel, a juvenile titled *Revolt on Alpha C*, followed. Decades later, his total SF titles, according to his semi-official website, stands at 82 SF novels and 457 short stories (though this may be an undercount). Early on, he won a Hugo Award for most promising new writer—rarely have the Hugo voters been so perceptive.

Toward the end of the 1960s and continuing into the 1970s, he wrote a string of novels much darker in tone and deeper in characterization than his work of the 1950s, such as the novels *Nightwings*, *Dying Inside*, *The Book of Skulls*, and many others. He took occasional sabbaticals from writing, to later return with new works, such as the Majipoor series. His most recent novels include *The Alien Years*, *The Longest Way Home*, and a new trilogy of Majipoor novels. In addition, The Science Fiction and Fantasy Hall of Fame inducted him in 1999. In 2004, the Science Fiction Writers of America presented him with the Damon Knight Memorial Grand Master Award. For more information see his "quasi-official" website at www.majipoor.com heroically maintained by Jon Davis (no relation).

◇◇◇◇◇

Alan Smale writes alternate and twisted history, historical fantasy, and occasional pure SF. His novella of a Roman invasion of ancient America, "A Clash of Eagles," won the Sidewise Award for Alternate History, and his series of novels set in the same universe, *Clash of Eagles* (2015), *Eagle in Exile* (2016), and *Eagle and Empire* (2017), is available from Penguin Random House/Del Rey. Alan has also sold more than forty pieces of shorter fiction to *Asimov's*, *Realms of Fantasy*, *Abyss & Apex*, and numerous other magazines and original anthologies, and his nonfiction science pieces about terraforming and killer asteroids have appeared in *Lightspeed*.

Alan grew up in Yorkshire, England; acquired degrees in physics and astrophysics from St. Edmund Hall, Oxford University; and then moved to the U.S. in his late twenties. He currently performs astronomical research into neutron stars and black holes at NASA's Goddard Space Flight Center in Greenbelt, Maryland, with more than a hundred published academic papers, and serves as director of a data archive that contains the complete datasets from dozens of astronomical satellites and experiments. Check out his website at AlanSmale.com, or follow him on Facebook/ AlanSmale or Twitter/@AlanSmale.

◇◇◇◇◇

Harry Turtledove (b. 1949) is an escaped Byzantine historian because he read L. Sprague de Camp's *Lest Darkness Fall* at an impressionable age, started trying to find out how much de Camp was making up and how much was real, and got hooked on the research. Since this left him unfit for any honest work, he has been a technical writer and freelancer since leaving academia in 1979. He writes alternate history, other SF, fantasy (much of it historically based), and when he can get away with it, straight historical fiction. He has also been known to make unfortunate puns. His wife is fellow writer and Broadway maven Laura Frankos. They have three daughters, two granddaughters, and three cats who are convinced they're only hired help.

◇◇◇◇◇

David Weber (b. 1952) is the author of multiple *New York Times* bestsellers and the recipient of four Dragon Awards. His most popular works are probably the Honor Harrington series—influenced by C.S. Forester, creator of Captain Horatio Hornblower—which details the exploits of a formidable woman starship captain, but his Starfire series (with Steve White), War God series, and others have also been very popular. He has a strong interest in history, which led to a master's degree in the subject from Appalachian State University, and he frequently employs his knowledge of the past in vividly creating future societies and their conflicts. He lives in Greenville, North Carolina, with his wife, Sharon, their three children, and a "passel of dogs."

◇◇◇◇◇

Rick Wilber (b. 1948) is an award-winning author with a penchant for stories that merge baseball and the fantastic. The son of a major league baseball player and coach, and a three-sport college scholarship athlete himself, Rick often incorporates sports into his fiction. His stories are published regularly in *Asimov's Science Fiction* magazine and other magazines and anthologies, with some two dozen of his baseball-influenced stories in print.

His stories often feature Rick's alternate history version of the famously intelligent baseball player and spy Morris "Moe" Berg, sometimes called "The Professor" for his Ivy-league degrees and ability to speak a dozen languages. In our reality, Berg was a catcher who became a spy for the OSS—the Office of Strategic Services—in World War II and helped thwart the Nazis' plans for an atomic bomb. In Rick's imagination, Berg and his friends travel through multiple realities to fight fascism. Or, in the case of "The Wandering Warriors," to have some fun teaching the ancient Romans the game of baseball. One of Rick's Moe Berg stories, "Something Real," won the Sidewise Award for Best Alternate History–Short Form in 2013, and another, "The Secret City," was runner-up for the award in 2019.

Rick has published a half dozen novels and short story collections, including the recent *Rambunctious* from WordFire Press. Other books include several college textbooks on writing and the mass media, a memoir about his father's life in baseball, and more than fifty short stories in major markets. He is a Visiting Professor in the low-residency MFA in Creative Writing at Western Colorado University. He lives in St. Petersburg, Florida.

His website is rickwilber.net.